THE TRYST

LAUREN BLAKELY

COPYRIGHT

Copyright © 2023 by Lauren Blakely
LaurenBlakely.com
Cover Design by © TE Black
Photo: Wander Aguiar

All rights reserved. No part of this book may be reproduced or transmitted in any form or by any means whatsoever without express written permission from the author, except in the case of brief quotations embodied in critical articles and reviews. Names, characters, places, brands, media, and incidents are either the product of the author's imagination or are used fictitiously. The author acknowledges the trademarked status and trademark owners of various products referenced in this work of fiction, which have been used without permission. The publication/use of these trademarks is not authorized, associated with, or sponsored by the trademark owners. This is a work of fiction. Names, characters, business, events and incidents are the products of the author's imagination. Any resemblance to actual persons, living or dead, or actual events is purely coincidental.

ABOUT THE TRYST

Some men are just off-limits. Like your ex-boyfriend's father.

But when I met the sexy, powerful older man shortly after my business school graduation, he was simply the seductive stranger I wanted to notice me, and he sure did.

Fast forward a few months later, when my college ex – now a good friend – introduces me to the person he looks up to most...his father.

The man I spent that one hot night with.

I should stay far away from the commanding business mogul. But my ex and I are planning a charity fundraiser that involves late nights at his dad's penthouse in Manhattan.

Nights where he can't stop looking at me with desire in his eyes that matches my own.

I try to resist him, playing the good girl in the city...mostly.

He's the perfect gentleman...until he comes

knocking on my door and tells me exactly what he wants to do to me.

And I say yes.

Stealing nights with him like this is supposed to be wrong, but it feels so right. And when he saves the day to protect his son at the fundraiser, my heart wants him as much as my body does.

Can we ever be more than just a tryst?

THE TRYST

By Lauren Blakely

DID YOU KNOW?

To be the first to find out when all of my upcoming books go live click here!

PRO TIP: Add lauren@laurenblakely.com to your contacts before signing up to make sure the emails go to your inbox!

Did you know this book is also available in audio and paperback on all major retailers? Go to my website for links!

For content warnings for this title, go to my site.

1

JUST SO YOU KNOW

Layla

I only have to last thirty more minutes. Half an hour is a good faith effort, right? I'm trying, really. It's not like I'm sitting in this bar across from Bryce Fancypants the Third for my health.

"So, yeah, when Topher came to me about a top-shelf, members-only distillery in Manhattan, I said, *I am so in and here's the check*," Bryce says, while rotating his tumbler in quarter circles every thirty seconds. I recognize the tactic from a post last week on *The Gentleman's Guide To Dating*—do this if you want to communicate power on a date.

Because, of course, that's exactly how a man should communicate power—by reading articles about how to do so.

"What a great friend," I say, like I'm reading from a script.

"Topher has been planning this since we went to Princeton together a few years ago," Bryce adds, no doubt in case I didn't hear the other three times when he told me he went to the Ivy.

"How fascinating," I say with a smile. You never know who Bryce might report back to. Like his mother at the tennis club, who'll tell my mother at the tennis club. Since this date, like all my dates, was her idea.

But dating is like makeup. I know how to put on a good face to make it through the day. I sit nice and straight and say all the right things to whatever Bryce blathers on about for the next thirty minutes, from the money he and Topher invested in the liquor, to the money they're making hand over fist, to the way they cater to old money, since old money's the only thing you can trust, right?

When the clock behind the bar strikes eight-thirty, I can taste my freedom. Bryce is paying the tab, and fine, I'll give him points for that. But after he signs the bill, he slides his credit card back in his billfold ostentatiously, giving me a chance to see that it's black.

"Soooo," he begins, running his fingers over his slicked-back blond hair, his gaze lasered in on my breasts. "This was great, Layla. I'd love to see you again. But just so you know, I'm really busy at work."

He's *just so you know*ing me? Does he think I don't know that's code for he only wants to fuck me?

I purse my lips to hold back a flurry of put-him-in-his-place zingers. Instead, I keep the stakes in mind and fasten on my best Park Avenue smile. "I love my job, too, and I'm super busy, as well. Text me."

"Sa-weet," he says, and he can't mask the *I'm going to score next time* smile.

He can think what he wants, but I have a get-out-of-a-second-date-free card, and I'm ready to play it.

We leave the whiskey bar, and when we reach the curb, Bryce clears his throat. "So, I'll text you, and we can do this again?"

"Sure!" I say brightly. "I'm just going to take off now and head home."

This is the real test. I have a feeling this barely twenty-six-year-old banker will fail to do the one thing my mother values more than any other—*protect her daughter*.

Holding my breath, I turn toward Park Avenue. Will he follow or go on his merry way?

"I'll text you, Layla," he calls out as he heads off.

Virtual fist pump.

Bryce doesn't offer to call me a cab, walk me home, or wait till my Lyft arrives. When my mother finds out, she won't hassle me to see him again.

His fail is my win.

Once I turn the corner, I order the fastest Lyft possible and wait at the curb. My fingers fly as I text my friends to confirm they're still at Gin Joint. They immediately answer.

> Harlow: Get your ass here and give us a report on Chad. Or Thad. Or was it Brad?

> Ethan: We're placing bets.

Of course they are.

My ride pulls up a minute later, I hop into the black SUV, headed to our favorite speakeasy in Chelsea. There, I find my true loves waiting faithfully for me on a velvet chaise longue.

Harlow looks elegant and artsy with her brown hair clipped back in a silver barrette. Ethan's the ever-cool hipster rocker in his skinny jeans and a thrift store button-down, his hair a wild mess.

I flop down between them, then blow out a long, heavy breath.

"Was it that bad?" Harlow asks, voicing the sympathy on both their faces.

"Nine out of ten," I say, wrung out by the hour with Mister Moneybags.

Ethan lifts both arms skyward. "Yes! Free mojito for me."

I look from one to the other. "That was your stakes? Like either of you couldn't afford your own mojito."

"Not the point," Ethan says. "Now, give us the full report."

"He paid for the drinks," I begin. "So there's that. But otherwise, he waved his big, rich dick around the whole time, and then he *just so you know*ed me."

"Aww, how sweet that he's *down to bone you*," Harlow says.

With an apologetic shrug, Ethan reaches for his yummy-looking mojito. "Yeah, sorry about...*men*."

"Nothing a drink can't cure." I bat my lashes at him, then the cocktail.

Ethan waves down a pretty redheaded server

named Martina and orders a mojito for me, too, as Harlow asks, "So, did he pass the Mayweather test?"

I can't hide my glee. "Nope. Said *see you later* on the sidewalk. Didn't even offer to call me a cab."

Ethan gasps. "Left Mama Mayweather's precious darling to travel the perilous city alone? How helpful of him to eliminate himself from consideration. I mean, douchebag behavior, but you're off the hook."

I smile like I got away with a theft. "I do love it when they make it easy."

I'll text my mom later with an update. She usually needs time to research the next *nice, well-educated, family-centric* candidate. Translation: she wants me to settle down with a rich boy from Park Avenue who's got a family she trusts, and to take over her makeup empire before I'm twenty-five. I've got two years, but the clock is ticking loudly.

When the server returns with my drink, I take a sip of the mojito, my skull rings glinting under the chandelier. The cocktail does the final job in erasing my mood from the bad date. When I set it down, I say, "But it's all for the best it didn't work out. I have a lot on my plate, so it's fine."

"Or maybe you just need a change of scenery," Harlow suggests. "A different vibe. What if you go out with someone tomorrow when you're in Miami? You could get on the apps and see who's there."

How would I even have time for that? "At the Innovation conference? I'm going there to learn and network."

Ethan whispers under his breath, "Fuck a hot dude at night."

I slug his shoulder. "It's supposed to be an amazing event. So many great speakers and business visionaries. Mikka Halla is the closing keynote. He wrote an amazing book about harnessing creativity in technology. I devoured it, and I've wanted to hear him speak for a long time."

"Is he hot?" Ethan asks, wiggling his brows.

"He's fifty-three," I point out.

"And...is he hot?"

"Shut up. Even you don't go for guys that old. And I am not going after Mikka Halla. He's not my type."

"Does he not like *good girls*?" Ethan teases.

"And are you *sure* you're going to be such a good girl in Miami?" Harlow goads. "The sun, the heat, the beach. You know how it goes."

"Of course you've plotted my deflowering already," I say to Harlow. She's the ultimate planner. That's how she got her own happy ending.

Ethan stirs his drink with the metal straw, giving me *that* look. "Babe, the conference is full of your type."

"Oh, you *must* mean other app nerds who are hoping to go big and desperately want to succeed without their mother's success," I say dryly.

"Yes, Layla. That's exactly what I meant." He clears his throat, then says, "But maybe Miami will be just what you need."

"You'll be away from New York," Harlow chimes in.

"No interference from Mama," Ethan adds.

"Lots of men who tick all your boxes," Harlow says, then grins. "Like, the *older* box."

In case I didn't know my type. Still, I manage a protest of sorts. "That's not always true. I liked David Bancroft in college."

"You liked him as a friend," she corrects.

"But I dated him for a couple months."

"It was practically platonic," Ethan adds.

To be fair, my relationship with David wasn't platonic, but it ended amicably and I'm still good friends with him.

But even so, I don't want to mix business and pleasure. I only have a few years to make my app go big. "I should focus while I'm there, guys." But I can feel my resolve weakening as I picture...*men in suits*.

"You can focus by day," Ethan whispers in one ear.

"Have fun at night," Harlow seconds in the other. "Just imagine men who don't tell you how much money they make."

"Because they're confident in who they are," Ethan adds.

"Since they're self-made," Harlow adds.

A whoosh travels down my belly. They make such good points. "You're making this hard," I grumble.

"And there's one more thing, *Lola Jones*..." Ethan emphasizes the name I use professionally for my app and my brand of online makeup tutorials. I registered for the conference under Lola Jones, as well. I don't like to traffic in the cachet of the Mayweather last name, especially when it comes to my burgeoning makeup dreams.

Ethan pauses dramatically, takes a drink of his mojito, and sets down the glass with panache. "Imagine a man your mother doesn't set you up with."

That does sound like my type.

But I'm not traveling to Miami to find a man. I don't need a man. I don't want to rely on someone. I never want to experience again the pain of losing someone I love. Felt it. Some days, I still do.

Only, I sure wouldn't mind going on a date where I didn't have to report back to anyone except my friends.

Just in case, when I'm packing for the conference later that night, I include a red, cap-sleeve dress with white polka dots.

Well, it does make me look like a good girl.

* * *

I spend the first day of the Miami conference in sessions from morning to night, as focused as a high-end Nikon. The next day, I meet with platform partners and marketers, showing them the growth I've achieved on my own with the makeup app I started a year ago. With "The Makeover," you upload a photo of your bare face, and it offers color and style suggestions paired with how-to tutorials from yours truly—AKA Lola Jones. I've been creating those videos and building a solid following online for more than five years. My little app has been chugging along all on its own, but we want to go big. After those meetings, I send a report to my partner, Geeta, back in Brooklyn.

When the sessions end for the day, I stop in my

room for a quick change into beach gear so I can join some business school friends for volleyball. Once I put on a red bikini, I hit the sand, playing against MBA-ers from another school as the sun dips lower in the sky. I'm poised at the back of the net, waiting for our opponents to serve, when I spot a tall, broad, well-built man walking through the sand.

Hello.

Light blue swim trunks hug his hips, showing off his golden skin and his V cut. My eyes travel up his strong body. Just the right amount of chest hair covers firm pecs. He's maybe in his late thirties, and he's heading toward the surf with purpose. I only catch a glimpse of his chiseled profile. A trim beard lines his square jaw, and crinkles form at the corner of his eyes. He looks just my type.

"Heads up!"

I jerk my gaze away just in time to dodge a volleyball to the face. That would have served me right for gawking.

* * *

Volleyball victory still burns in my thighs the next morning as I stroll across the hotel mezzanine, on my way to my next session. I'm checking the conference app on my phone when my skin tingles. I look up and glimpse another echo of yesterday—that same, strong, sturdy man from the beach.

He crosses my path, talking to a small group of attendees as he walks.

There's an intensity in his powerful stride as he makes his way toward double French doors that lead into a VIP room at the end of the hallway.

I stop in the doorway of my next session, stealing a few more seconds to shamelessly stare at him from this angle.

When he reaches the destination, he holds one of the French doors open for the attendees with him. Like a gentleman should. Once the last of the group disappears in the room, his gaze strays back down the hall, checking out his surroundings like a bodyguard checking for threats.

His dark eyes find me, and he doesn't look away for several tingly seconds. He just stares at me, unflinching, unashamedly. A tiger checking out his prey.

His eyes travel down my body, lingering briefly on the tattoo on my shoulder.

Then, he turns and goes inside.

I spin around, drawing a steadying breath as I smooth a hand over my sleeveless black dress with the cherry print.

You're here for work, Lola Jones.

I touch my conference badge; the skull-shaped rings on my fingers are a reminder too. I started the Lola brand when I was a senior in high school and desperately needed to become another version of me. Someone without news stories of family tragedy trailing her. Someone not bound by a promise.

Lola is carefree, independent, and happy-go-lucky. Lola earned my going-out money during college.

Lola can create a hell of a seductive smoky eye and design a terrific user interface for an app.

Most of all, Lola is just Lola. Here, I'm not the daughter of Anna Mayweather, the woman who founded a global billion-dollar makeup empire. Or *that girl* whose family was torn apart one dark evening in Manhattan.

With that, I march inside and settle down in a chair. I cross my legs. Open my tablet. Listen attentively.

Only, near the end of the session, my mind briefly wanders to the other room. Who is that guy dressed up in the smart, tailored clothes by day and dressed down in a sexy swimsuit by night? What is he doing here at the conference? And...will he go to the ocean again this evening?

Too bad I won't be playing volleyball then, since I've got a networking dinner to attend.

But really, it's not like I'm going to stalk him on the beach. I'm not even going to look up who's speaking in the VIP room right now to see if I can figure out who he is.

I'm here for my business. I'm not here for a man.

No matter how fast my pulse continues to race.

2

I DON'T ALWAYS FOLLOW THE RULES

Nick

This is a perfect morning for a swim outdoors under the bright, blue sky, the sun's rays warming my shoulders.

I freestyle my way down the pool for another glorious lap, shuddering at the thought of the gray skies waiting for me in London tomorrow when I return. I'm going to suck the juice out of every second here in the South Florida sun.

I should probably wear sunscreen. But I don't always follow the rules.

I finish the final lap, running a hand over my hair as I climb out of the infinity pool at my older brother's Miami Beach home. I grab a towel, and after I dry off my face, I tip my chin toward my brother. He's stretched out on a lounge chair under an umbrella, shades on, holding the last of a delicious-smelling espresso beverage. "Man, what kind of service is this if there's no Café Cubano waiting for me?"

Finn scoffs, the sun glinting off the few silver streaks in his dark hair. That's new, but I don't give him a hard time about it. My turn is coming.

"You get a free place to stay, Nick." He sweeps out a hand, indicating the pool here at his second home. "You get a free pool to use. Now you need free fucking coffee?"

I stand over him and shake my wet hair, flinging droplets like a Saint Bernard. Okay, less than a Saint Bernard would, but still satisfying.

"You asshole!" He sits up, wipes his face, and holds up his cup. "If you got chlorine in my cup..."

"Aww, did I ruin your coffee?" I ask, faking remorse.

After he takes the final drink like a stoic bastard, he sets it down on the table next to him with a loud clink. He lies back on the lounge chair, parking his hands behind his head. "My morning was more peaceful when you were in the pool doing laps."

"Ah, it must be good to live the unexamined life." I toss the towel on my chair and sit down at the end of it, lifting my face briefly to the gorgeous orb in the sky.

"Maybe I've been examining your phone," Finn counters.

That reminds me. Enough lounging. Stretching my arm, I grab the silver device from the table next to him. "Doubtful. It's only got a twenty-five-character password."

"Tech geek," he mutters.

"That's me," I say dryly. More like finance geek. But

I invest in tech so I can't entirely dispute his accusation. As I tap in the twenty-five characters—memorized, since it's not that hard to commit twenty-five characters to memory—I ask, "Did anyone call while I was swimming?"

"Am I your secretary?"

"I hope so."

"Were you expecting your conference hookup to call?"

An image from yesterday flashes past me. Blonde hair. Red lips. A fearless gaze. Temptation personified. And a helluva test.

I shove that image away. "I don't mess around at conferences. It's distracting," I toss back as I type.

"It might loosen you up a little bit," he suggests, the jackass.

"I am not tightly wound," I reply.

"Did you or did you not ask if anyone called the second you got out of the water?"

"That's the normal time to ask," I say. A lot can happen during a forty-five minute swim. I can't afford to miss a deal, a chance, an opportunity.

"That's tightly wound. That's obsessed with business," he says, like he's offering a character assessment in a court of law, when the fucker's exactly the same way. Hell, he runs in the same business circles I do.

But rather than fire off a *takes one to know one* reply, I simply shrug, owning my one true love—this company I built from the ground up over the last few years, thanks to my blood, sweat and tears. "Guilty as charged," I say, sliding open the missed calls and hoping one of them is the one I want. "Anyway, I'm pretty sure hookups text instead of call. But that's irrelevant, since the call I *am* expecting is from Vault saying yes to the term sheet we offered yesterday."

I feel pretty damn good about that offer. It's the kind that says we want to be your investor, we believe in your tech, and we will all get motherfucking rich off this deal if we play it right. If a term sheet could swagger, this one would.

I check the string of missed calls, and hallelujah. The first one's local, from the hotshot twenty-five-year-old CEO of the encryption technology firm I met with yesterday.

Quickly, I read the voicemail transcript.

This is Jared Song calling to say we accept your venture firm's offer.

"Hell yes," I say, pumping a fist.

Finn sits up again, eyes sparking. He mouths an appreciative "*nice"* then offers a high-five.

I smack back as I read the next voicemail transcript.
This is Valeria from the Innovation and Technology Leadership Summit. We spoke yesterday when you were part of our VIP one-on-one sessions.

We've found we have a bit of a situation. Our closing keynote, Mikka Halla, came down with laryngitis this morning, and we are desperately in need of a dynamic, engaging speaker for our final session late this afternoon. You were so terrific yesterday. Is there any chance we could convince you to fill in last minute? We're happy to pay a speaker stipend.

I scratch my jaw.

This summit is full of up-and-coming tech stars, newly launched startups, and partners they need to do business with. Honestly, the organizers should have asked me in the first place. But I've learned that nothing is handed to you in life. Everything is earned.

And sometimes, you earn it by capitalizing on someone else's bad luck.

This is a golden chance to put the Alpha Ventures name in front of the industry.

I look up from the phone and tell my brother the good news. "And to think I was going to take off for London this afternoon."

He holds his arms out wide, showing off the city he loves. "Like it's a hardship to stay another night in Miami."

I look around, inhaling the ocean air, the salty breeze, and taking in the decadent sun here at Finn's gorgeous beachfront home—his second home since he's mostly in New York. "It's so terrible to be here."

"You can stay another night." He checks the time on his phone. "Marilyn is flying in this afternoon, but…"

I wave off the invitation. Shit's been rough with his wife. The last thing I want to do is get in the way. I squeeze his knee affectionately. "Focus on your woman. I'll get a room somewhere."

"I'm sure she won't mind if you're here," he says, like a hopeful fucker who can't see the writing on the wall.

Marilyn *will* mind. She minds pretty much everything. I don't say that to Finn though. He's got to figure it out on his own—whether to Hail Mary his marriage or to punt.

"You sure?" he asks.

"No problem," I reassure him. "I'll call my assistant and ask him to handle the changes."

Five minutes later, Kyle tells me he has me booked into a room at the art deco Luxe Hotel on South Beach where the conference is being held. It's where I swam the other day in the ocean. "I got you into a suite. Just the way you like it," he says, a hint of Queens still in his voice. "And I've got you on a flight tomorrow back to London."

"Thanks, Kyle. I really appreciate it. Say hi to your pops for me."

When I hang up, my brother's looking at me curiously. "Is that Kyle, as in, Dad's friend Jack's son? The one who was in rehab?"

"Yup. He's clean now. The kid needed a job, so I gave him one."

Finn nods thoughtfully. "Any good?"

I shrug. "He's not bad."

That cracks up my brother. "You never think anyone is good enough, Nick," he says through his laughter.

"That is *not* true," I protest, but only half-heartedly, since it mostly is. I wish more people were more motivated. I wish people worked fucking hard. But people don't. Which just means more opportunity for me.

"Let me amend it," Finn says. "You never think anyone works as hard as you. Or is as smart as you. Or as ambitious as you."

Do I think that? I'd kind of be a dick if I did. But no one knows you like family. Maybe Finn's assessment is a little true. "My kid would be good enough if he'd come work for me," I say, but I'm resigned to reality. He's not coming to London to set up shop with his dad.

Finn smiles sympathetically. "That probably won't happen."

"Truer words. And on that note, I should get ready for the conference," I say, then make my way inside, returning Valeria's call as I pad across the marble floor to the guest room. "I'd be happy to do the speech this afternoon, but a stipend is unnecessary. You can donate my speaker fee to a local homeless shelter."

"That's so wonderful, Mr. Adams. We're immensely grateful." After that, she gives me the details, mentioning that the conference has attracted a lot of business press and podcasters, and they'll be wanting to do interviews after.

Even better. "I'm game," I say then I tap the names of the pertinent ones into my notes app.

After I end the call, I hit the shower. As I wash off the chlorine, an intriguing thought occurs to me. Since I'm here another day, maybe I'll see the woman in the cherry dress again.

I close my eyes, dipping my head back under the hot stream, letting myself remember her.

I didn't want to think of her earlier out by the pool.

But now that I'm alone, steam enveloping me, it's hard not to remember the way she looked standing in the doorway yesterday afternoon.

Blonde hair curled over her shoulders. Her lush lips shined, red and glossy. She was wearing the hell out of that dress that hugged her curves—a dress that made my hands itch to touch her.

A bold, blue daisy tattoo on her left shoulder.

Most of all, I can *still* picture exactly how she'd turned her gaze toward me. I couldn't tell the color of her eyes from a distance, but they stayed locked on me. I didn't look away, just indulged in the view and everything I could tell about her beyond those pinup looks. Looks are great and all, but they aren't what ultimately draws me to a woman. In those five seconds, she felt fearless and curious all at once.

One glance, one long-held stare, and I'd wanted to break my hookup rules, march over to her, and ask her out that night. Probably would have if I wasn't a believer in punctuality. But I had a commitment to that VIP session.

Now, I have a commitment to a keynote.

But if I see her again, I just might break my rules.

3

A CONFIDENTIAL MATTER

Layla

After lunch I grab coffee with a friend from business school, excited to meet up with Raven so soon after our graduation. We snag a nook in the conference center where we can chat and watch the four-lane traffic in the hallway go by. She lives in my neighborhood in Manhattan, running the site for her fashion upcycling business, so we debate every New Yorker's favorite topic —the woes of real estate—when a flurry of conference organizers marches down the hall.

The pack moves in lockstep, led by a woman with a short dark bob. The name Valeria shines on her silver name tag.

"Make sure the deck is queued up with the right name. If the wrong deck plays and Mikka's name appears, I will eat my shoes," she informs the man by her side.

I turn back to the fair-skinned, freckle-faced Raven, amused. "I'd pay to see that."

"Shoe-eating at three," my friend says, but she sounds distracted as she grabs her phone, swipes a few times, then slumps her shoulders. "*This* is what she's talking about."

She shows me the conference app on her screen where Mikka Halla's name is gone from the keynote list. Someone I've never heard of is replacing him. Nick Adams of Alpha Ventures will talk about opportunity. "Bye-bye, Finnish visionary I wanted to hear," Raven says with a frown.

Are you kidding me? I sigh, equally annoyed. "He was one of the big reasons I bought a ticket."

"Want to cut out of here early?"

Tempting.

But the word *opportunity* lodges in my brain. What if this understudy is better than the lead?

"I think I'll stick around. You never know," I say, rolling the dice.

She waves goodbye, and when she's gone I'm about to google the new guy but my phone buzzes. It's Geeta, so I take the call.

"So, I had this idea for a fantastic upgrade," she says, and brainstorming with her keeps me busy for the next hour.

* * *

As I queue near the front of the line for the keynote session, I google Nick Adams at last. His picture pops up, and I stifle a gasp.

That's him.

The man from yesterday. With the dark hair, the trim beard, and the eyes with the crinkles at the corner, showing some age, some maturity. And a delicious sense of power in the way he gazes at the camera with a challenging stare.

When I glance up from my phone, *those eyes* are looking right at me.

Again.

He's walking in the direction of the stage door on the other side of the wide hallway. My breath catches as his gaze lingers on my face.

Our eyes lock. There's a moment when I feel… caught once more by the man.

Then, he swallows, like he's re-sorting his thoughts, like he knows he shouldn't stare this long before he's about to go onstage and give a talk to a packed crowd.

But with the way he luxuriates on my face, it's like it's nighttime and I'm at a sleek, low-lit bar, and he's the man about to stalk right over to me, curl a hand around the back of my head, and press a *she's mine* kiss to my cheek.

As he passes, he glances down, but seconds later his eyes are back on mine again, as if he simply had to look twice, so I send him a hint of a seductive smile.

He catches it. I can tell in the slight quirk of his full lips. Then, quickly, he looks away.

I'm in his rearview mirror.

But only for now.

Good thing I'm early. I'm going to find a seat in the front row where I can watch that powerful man fight not to look at me as he talks about innovation and opportunity to the thousand attendees here.

And since I've been such a good girl all week, dedicated to business the whole time, I'm going to allow myself a little indulgence for the rest of the day.

Since I'd really like Nick Adams to innovate me.

Good thing Valeria didn't eat her shoes since those are some cute leopard prints she's wearing as she enters the stage and introduces the new speaker.

I'm buzzing with anticipation.

"I'm thrilled that so many of you stayed for our closing keynote," Valeria says to the crowd. "We are fortunate enough to have a wonderful replacement speaker in Nick Adams from Alpha Ventures. He founded his technology venture firm three years ago, and since then, his sharp eye and entrepreneurial spirit have led him to invest in a number of outstanding tech startups."

She lists some of those companies, many in Europe and a handful in the United States. All are wildly successful. "Without further ado, your new keynote speaker...Nick Adams."

I'm so glad my conference crush is a venture capitalist because that means there's zero conflict of interest for The Makeover or for me. Our app doesn't need venture funding. We're on the hunt for marketing and growth, for partners in social media and review management, but not for an investment.

Which means I can have fun with him as he talks.

The man of the hour strides in from the wings, thanks Valeria, then heads to the front of the stage. A mic is clipped to his teal-blue tie to capture a deep, gravelly voice that makes me wiggle in my chair.

"When I was swimming in my brother's pool this morning, the last thing I expected was to be called on to pinch hit for someone as stellar as Mikka Halla. But it was an opportunity I couldn't pass up. And that's what I want to talk about today." He pauses briefly and scans the audience, his gaze settling to the left side of the front row.

Onto...*me*.

I flick a strand of my hair. Flirting 101, but it gets my point across. I take notes for the next several minutes. But I'm ready for another round when he says, "Wayne Gretzky famously said *I skate to where the puck is going to be, not where it has been*. That's the metric for innovation too."

He's looking at the front row, so I nibble on the corner of my lips. His gaze stays on me for a second, then he turns the other way.

There's more note-taking for me, more visionary thoughts from him, then a little later, when he heads in my direction once more, I uncross my legs.

"Innovation comes from habit. The relentless habit of constantly seeking..." When his gaze lands on me, I cross my legs just for him. "Opportunity," he says, with the slightest rumble in his voice.

A rumble just for me.

When he's done delivering a powerful speech about seizing your chance, I do just that. Sure, I'm here for work and only work. But why not have a little fun before my plane trip home?

I'm up and out of my chair in mere seconds, heading straight for the edge of the stage. You've got to hustle to get what you want in life, and I'm hustling.

But so are plenty of others.

Dammit. I'm not the only one swarming the man. I've got to be faster and I pick up the pace, but the conference organizers beat me. They're flanking him, unclipping his mic, handing him a glass of water.

He takes a drink as he heads down the steps of the stage, ten feet away from me.

Judging from the phones thrust out, and well, the red ribbons on name tags saying *press,* I'll have to fight dozens of eager reporters, podcasters, and journalists wanting a word with him.

And...Valeria.

She's right by his side, helpfully taking his water, then speaking to the gathered crowd. "We're so glad Mr. Adams has made time in his busy schedule to chat with the media for the next thirty minutes. There's a press room down the hall," she says.

No!

I am not about to be knocked out of line just because I don't have a press pass. I'm definitely not going to be pushed away when it comes to the first guy —no, *man*—in ages that I've picked.

He's *my* choice and mine alone.

"Mr. Adams," I say, my voice carrying above the dozens of people surrounding him. "I have a question."

He whips his head toward me, and recognition crosses those eyes—they're hazel. But the darkest hazel I've ever seen. Flecks of gold flicker in them, right along with his dirty thoughts.

My pulse spikes, but I don't stop. I push on. "You mentioned that seconds matter when it comes to taking a chance, but that you should also not be hasty," I say and his brow knits, his eyes determined, like I'm the target in his crosshairs. "How do you balance that?"

All I've planned is the question. I don't know what I'll do or say next. But I want him to notice me. Maybe to see my name tag. To find me. To follow me.

After a thoughtful nod, he says, "That's not a quick question to answer." Then, his eyes dip to the tag on my chest. "Lola."

The way he says my name, in that rough rasp, sends a flush of arousal down my body, straight to my core.

I try not to tremble in the middle of the crowd.

"But I was hoping you'd ask that to follow up on the conversation we had yesterday during the VIP session," he continues, and holy shit. He's smooth on his feet. He can improvise. Then he turns to Valeria. "This'll be a minute. It's a confidential business matter."

Confidential is officially the sexiest word in any language.

In no time, he shoulders past the reporters.

My pulse gallops as he parts the crowd with his presence, his strength, his...virility. He tips his head toward a quiet corner of the ballroom, then sets his hand on my elbow as we walk.

My elbow is turned on. What kind of sex sorcery is this?

After we're a safe distance from the crowd, he stops, then turns to me. "Your question is probably best answered over drinks in the hotel bar. My last meeting ends at seven."

My breath hitches. This man just asked me out. But I can't stand here stupidly. I recover quickly from the shock and say, "I'll buy you a drink."

A sly smile lingers on his lips. "No. I'll buy you one." He tilts his head, studying my face like he's committing me to memory again. Then he steps closer, mere inches from me, as he touches my elbow once again. "Lola."

He turns to join the others.

He doesn't look back.

But he doesn't have to.

We both know I'll be there. He probably knows, too, that my elbow is on fire.

4

LADIES CHOICE

Nick

There's a first time for everything.

Like watching makeup videos, evidently.

But I need to know why the hell this woman made me throw out my no-dating-on-work-trips rule. Maybe the answer lies in the videos she makes—videos with tons of views.

As I brush my teeth in my suite, I am transfixed by the woman on the screen, swiping a pink pencil thingy precisely across her eyebrow.

"This step is for creating depth," Lola says, and I don't give two fucks about how to fill in a brow but Lola commands my attention with her confident yet accessible style.

I watch till the end. I barely blink.

"And that's how you blend in your brow, my pets." When she's done, she picks up a lipstick, slicks on some red gloss, then blows a seductive kiss to the camera.

Fuck me. I'm aroused from a makeup video.

I spit out the toothpaste and gargle some water.

But that barely douses my semi. As I move around my suite getting ready to see her, I start the next video and I don't stop watching. This is binge-worthy content right here in my hand. From my suitcase, I grab a pair of charcoal slacks with my free hand, then a tailored, black short-sleeve shirt. Perfect for a sultry evening out.

Setting down the phone on the bureau, I get dressed as I watch. I button up my shirt and hit play on another video. I don't need to know how to put on eyeliner, but I need more of her.

The blonde beauty I'm taking out tonight wears a tank top that shows off that stunning flower tattoo, the color of sapphire. She brandishes a makeup brush and a pot of blue shiny something or other. "Once upon a time, blue eye shadow was a joke," she says, and okay, that pot is eyeshadow. Cool, cool. "Now it's a must-have. So let's enjoy the blues together, my pets."

I tuck in my shirt as I learn how to make a midnight shade work for you. Who knew what blue could do for an eye?

Once I'm dressed, I hit stop on Lola. *Reluctantly.*

This woman could make me a video addict.

There's something in her that's impossible to look away from, both in person and online. She's got charisma, shine, chutzpah. Hell, she approached me after the show, ready to ask me out.

That's why I'm breaking my rule.

At a quarter to seven, I pocket my phone and head downstairs. The L Bar is already filled with the young, the beautiful and the nearly naked. Guys doused in cologne and baring wolfish grins are out in full force on a Friday night.

They're hunting.

The joint is teaming with the fairer sex too, with svelte and curvy bodies alike poured into tight dresses or bikinis, sky-high heels all around. South Beach is such a fiesta of flesh.

I say hello to the hostess then grab two stools at the sleek, silver counter, scanning the room in case Lola's an early bird. I don't spot her, and I'm glad she's not here yet.

A man should wait for a woman, not the other way around.

I turn to the clean-shaven man behind the bar who looks like he'd be carded in any establishment. He's probably my son's age—twenty-one. "How's it going, Enrique?" I ask, quickly reading his name tag.

"It's going well. What can I get you, sir?"

Sir. I'm not even forty, but I'll always be a sir to guys like him. But I wouldn't trade a thing to be young again. Those years were hard as hell.

"Whiskey, neat," I say.

"Coming right up."

I take in the lay of the land as I wait, reviewing the entrances—one from inside the hotel, where I came in, and an open-air one from the pool. A warm evening breeze wafts in.

"Here you go," the bartender says. I thank him, then slap down a bill.

I knock back some of the drink. It's ten minutes till seven, but I don't screw around on my phone. It's a special moment to witness a woman arriving for a date with you.

I take another drink, then inhale the scent of the ocean.

When the clock hits seven, a vision in red steps through the doorway leading to the hotel.

My skin heats and a rumble threatens to escape my lips as I drink her in from a distance. A red dress with white polka dots hugs her curves. Flouncy material hits at her knees. Perfect. The fabric looks easy to push up. All that lush blonde hair is swept up in some kind of clip that invites me to undo it later tonight, to watch her tresses fall, rope my fingers through those strands and then kiss the fuck out of her as she begs me for more.

Her fingers are covered in skull rings, an interesting contrast to her perky dress.

Before she turns to the bar, the hostess asks her a question, drawing her attention. A table full of young guys all swivel their heads toward Lola, and one with too much gel in his hair not-so-subtly points to her and mouths, "I call dibs."

I burn inside.

I stand, weave through the tables in the bar and push past them, making sure they see me heading straight for the woman in red. When I reach her, she swings her gaze slowly toward me, excitement flaring in her gorgeous, bright blue eyes.

"Hi, Lola. You look incredible," I say. Then I set a hand on her arm—possessively and obviously. I dip my face closer to hers, brushing a kiss across her soft cheek, savoring the way her breath catches.

But it's not just a kiss I'm leaving—it's a claim, letting everyone here tonight know she's with me and only with me.

I inhale some kind of jasmine scent on her neck, or maybe in her hair, and it is intoxicating, like everything else about her.

When I pull back, she looks a little woozy.

"Hi, Nick." She's breathless and it's beautiful to see.

"I got us seats at the bar. Come with me."

"I'm there," she says.

Yeah, same here.

I set a hand on her back, my eyes only on her as we return to the silver counter, passing the table full of dudes who wanted the woman by my side. *You don't get to call dibs, fuckers. She already called them.*

Ladies choice, and all.

At the bar, I ask her, "What can I get for you?"

She's decisive as she holds my gaze and says, "Normally I'm a mojito gal, but I think I'll do a French 75...*with you.*"

Those last two words linger seductively—with you. She's making an exception and I want to ask more about that. But first, a drink. I turn to the bartender, lift a finger, catch his eye, and then say, "A French 75 for the lady."

"Will do," the baby-faced man says, then grabs the

bottle of champagne. As he pours, I return all my focus to Lola.

"A mojito's your favorite?"

"Most of the time."

"Then why not get it tonight?"

"That's what I get with my friends," she says, coy, like a cat.

I like where this is going, and I like to play too. "You don't feel friendly with me?"

"Not really, Nick."

The way she says Nick—I want her to say it in other ways. Late at night. "You weren't very friendly during my keynote either."

"I wasn't?" she asks in mock surprise, then she flicks the ends of her blonde hair, just like she did this afternoon when I was onstage.

That move is just one of many that made today's speech the toughest ever. I'd gritted my teeth, white knuckling my way through my outline, hoping I wouldn't sport wood onstage. "You were having a good time in the front row, weren't you?"

"Did I seem like I was having a good time?"

"The best time. Is there a reason you were trying to distract me?"

She doesn't answer me directly. Instead, she crosses her legs, drawing my attention to them. Then she nibbles on the corner of her lips, bringing my eyes right back to that gorgeous mouth of hers. "It worked, didn't it?" she asks.

"How do you know it worked earlier?" I counter.

She gives a coy shrug, then gestures to me, her

fingers dangerously, distractingly close to my chest before she sets them in her lap. "Well, you're here."

I growl and it turns into a sigh of longing and lust. The bartender returns with a distraction and our drinks—a fresh whiskey for me as well as her drink. I peel off a few more crisp bills, and tell him to keep the change.

"Thanks, sir," he says.

I wish he wouldn't call me that in front of her, but c'est la vie.

"You're welcome," I say, then add, "sir."

I can be a dick too.

He heads off to the other end of the bar, and Lola tilts her head, her eyes locked on me. "So, you really were distracted by me during your talk?"

The question comes out innocently. Because I pulled off the speech. I didn't reveal to the audience that I wanted to stride off the stage, march over to her, and ask her to spend the night with me. "You tell me," I ask, picking up my glass of whiskey.

"Honestly, you seemed...in charge, and on top of everything. Like you knew exactly what you were doing." Her words come out full of innuendo. Everything that falls from those lips has a double meaning.

I lean a little closer, catching a whiff of her heady scent. "I'm glad no one could tell how hard it was for me. Didn't want to let on to a single soul that I just couldn't stop thinking of this woman in the front row."

She sits higher, almost preening, and lifts her champagne flute. "We should toast then. To distractions."

I clink my tumbler against hers. "To very worthy distractions and the opportunities they bring."

Then she takes a sip and I watch as the glass hits her lips. I'm jealous of that glass, but I try to console myself. I'll be kissing that lipstick off her by the end of the night.

I lift my whiskey, take another drink, then set it down. "So, Lola, I took the liberty of making a dinner reservation."

"Oh? You did?"

Yeah, that definitely surprised her. Maybe she's not used to a man who knows how to plan a date.

"I did. I want to get to know you better. There's this great place on the beach called Catalina's. It's fusion cuisine, Miami meets Cuban, with vegetarian, meat, whatever works for you. Can I take you to dinner?"

Her smile is a little like the sunrise. It dawns slow and easy, then spreads all at once. "I love that you ask. But you should know—the answer has been yes all day long."

I want to make sure the answer will be yes all night long too.

When we leave, I set a hand on her back, marking her as mine, since she seems to like that.

And I want to grab this chance to give her everything she wants because tomorrow, I'll be an ocean away.

5

THE RIGHT THING

Layla

Is this what a good date feels like? This fizzy feeling spreading through every molecule of my body?

I've felt this way for the entire meal, here in the warm night air, surrounded by the scent of the ocean on the patio of this open-air café on South Beach. Throughout the meal we've chatted about what we love about Miami (almost everything), what I love about New York (my friends and the way the city challenges me every day), and what Nick loves about London (the speed and the energy, but never ever the weather, and he still misses California, where he lived for a few years after he grew up in New York).

Now, as the meal winds down, I take a final bite of the plantains and peppers dish. The flavors snap, crackle, and pop in my mouth, but then finish like a sugary kiss.

After I chew, I set down my fork. "It's a little sweet and a little spicy," I declare.

Nick lifts a brow playfully. "Are you talking about the dish or the night?"

This man is such a dirty flirt. I bob a shoulder and give it right back to him. "I guess you'll just have to find out."

A rumble comes from his throat, sexy and carnal, then he says, "I'd definitely like to find out."

Tingles shimmy down my spine. He's so forward, so different from the guys I've dated. There is no *"just so you know"* to Nick. He puts his cards on the table. Like the fact that he's leaving tomorrow morning, which he told me after we ordered. "Don't worry. I'm leaving then too," I'd said.

Translation: I don't want strings either.

Except…I suppose he hasn't technically put any sex cards on the table yet. He hasn't exactly said if he wants this date to end in his suite or mine. Or the third, and horrid option—here at the restaurant.

I don't want to presume. I don't want to ask either. Maybe because I don't want to be disappointed if he's *not* angling for a one-night stand, like I am. This is a role reversal for me, to be the one wanting it.

And I am *wanting* it badly with him. From his swagger, to his confidence, to his maturity, Nick's everything I've been waiting for.

But I'm not quite sure how to play this round of do-we-or-don't-we poker. Best to wait. I glance around Catalina's, savoring the sultry atmosphere of the bustling patio, the vibrant music, the clever dishes.

"This place is amazing. Thank you for dinner. Are you a restaurant scout? Because...wow."

Nick smiles but doesn't gloat. "I'm glad you like it."

He leans a little closer, then lifts a finger, gesturing toward the edge of my eye. "So is that a winged eyeliner?"

My chest flutters. No man has ever asked me about my makeup before. "Yes. I did it myself."

"I had a feeling."

My pulse flutters even harder. He must have googled me after seeing The Makeover on my conference name tag. "Did you watch my videos?"

He takes a moment to take me all in. "I did. Like your blue eyeshadow one. You are gorgeous in blue, especially with your ink," he says, his gaze drifting to my left shoulder. My daisy's covered right now, but the stem is visible, including the two leaves at the bottom—designed like music notes instead of leaves. I feel a little self-conscious when he looks at it so I'm glad he doesn't linger too long before he returns his gaze to my face, then says, "Especially with your stunning eyes. But I suspect you look gorgeous in...*anything*," he says.

But I hear what's unsaid.

You'd look gorgeous in nothing too.

Only, I want to hear from his lips that he's dying to see me wearing that. So I wait. I'll wait all night if I need to. "Thank you, Nick," I say.

"I watched several of your videos earlier," he says and it's not said as a confession, like he's embarrassed he looked me up, or like he thinks he engaged in some dirty little secret as a heterosexual man watching a woman's makeup videos. There's pride in his tone.

"I had a feeling," I say.

"I wouldn't know a damn thing about winged eyeliner if I hadn't been addicted to my phone while I was getting ready earlier. My phone got a pretty good workout."

"The image of you watching my makeup videos while you got ready to see me is going to be hard to get out of my head," I say, unable to suppress a smile or to stifle the zing in my belly.

In fact, I do the opposite of stifling it. I'm jazzed from his interest, so I kick my sandaled foot under the table back and forth, feeling good, feeling frisky. Then Nick surprises me, capturing my ankle in his big hand.

First my elbow, now my ankle. These unexpected touches light me up.

With an audible hum, he slides his hand up, wrapping his palm around my calf.

That feels so good. So decadent. His hand is strong and determined. He rubs, leaving tendrils of heat in his wake, sparks that spread all over me. "I liked watching your videos, Lola. I felt like I was getting to know you. To understand you."

"What did you understand?" I ask, fighting to stay in the conversation rather than melting into a puddle.

"You love teaching, sharing, talking. You're vibrant, and I enjoyed watching you work."

There's a subtext to his words—he finds it sexy that I like what I do. He wasn't just staring at my videos because he thinks I'm pretty. He likes that I like my job. Perhaps because he so clearly likes his.

"I liked watching you work earlier today too," I say, winging a smile his way.

"But turnaround is fair play," he says devilishly, traveling his fingers down my calf now. "Maybe I need to find a way to distract you."

This is my chance to kick the door open more. To push closer to what I want without being a Bryce. "You could, say, leave comments online about what you want to do to me," I offer suggestively.

Immediately he grips my calf harder, tighter. Then his hand ventures up my knee, reaching the fabric of my dress. He pushes the material up, covering my knee with his palm. His fingertips stroke my skin, higher, a little higher.

"But see, I'm not the kind of man who'd leave comments online for the woman he craves. I'd tell you face-to-face. So I can watch your reaction. Savor it," he says, then grazes his fingers up my thigh. Heat spreads to the ends of me. "I just haven't decided."

My breath catches, and I feel wobbly even though I'm in a chair. "You haven't decided what you want to do to me?" I ask, so I'm crystal clear.

There's a confident nod. An intensity in his eyes. "There are so many ideas flickering through my head. So many things I desperately want to do to you later," he says, like he's playing with ideas, weighing possibilities.

Arousal floods me like a warm river. I'm wrapped in

a cocoon of pleasure and lust thanks to his words, his voice, his heady intensity. His raw sex appeal. Then, he lets go of my thigh, leans back in his chair, and parks his arms behind his head, all cool and man in charge. "But not quite yet."

I want to scream for him to touch me again.

He picks up his glass, takes a final sip, then signals for the check when he spots the server.

I take a moment to catch my breath. To fan myself.

After he signs the check, Nick turns to me and says, "Thank you for letting me take you out to dinner."

"Thank you. I had an amazing time."

"Me too." He stands, offers his hand, and I take it. We leave the restaurant and stroll down the block, neither one of us wanting this night to end, it seems. With a hand on my lower back, he says in a low voice, "I need to spend more time with you to decide what to do to you first, Lola Jones."

It's not the first time he's said my name tonight, but for a few seconds, a smidge of guilt wedges into my chest over the use of it. If I'm going to sleep with him—if I'm going to finally have sex—should he know my legal name?

But then I kick that guilt away. There's no need to tell him my real name because there's no need to bring up my too-well-known family. Not my mother. And certainly not my father. My chest squeezes painfully but I don't want to poke around the hole in my heart.

I only want to feel good tonight.

When I hear a poppy tune drifting down from a

nearby club, I'm desperate to stay in the moment with us, not my dark thoughts, so I ask, "Do you like to dance?"

Nick seems to chew on the question, then he stops walking, dropping his hand from my back. A crease digs into his brow. "I keep meaning to ask. How old are you?"

Whoa. That's a mood killer.

This conversation was inevitable, despite how long he'd waited to ask the question, I'd wondered if it was a non-issue for a one-night stand. I could lie. I could tell him I'm twenty-five. That feels *old enough*. And how would he ever know the truth? I'm not going to see him again after tonight.

But I'm not going to lie to get him in bed. I'd be livid if a man did that to me. So I lift my chin, all tough girl now. Only, before I can answer, my phone trills. I grab it from my clutch purse to silence it. The word "Mom" flashes across the screen.

My stomach roils.

Are you kidding me?

She's the worst person in the world to call right now. I hit ignore. But Nick's already seen the name winking on the screen.

Mom, Mom, Mom.

Could I seem any younger?

His expression shifts instantly. Gone are the sparkling flirty eyes. In their place is an all-business gaze. "If you need to talk to her, it's fine."

Just ask when it's my bedtime, why don't you?

I try to smile it away—the kind of unknowable smile I learned to use when I was exhausted from everyone asking how I was doing once I finally returned to my junior year of high school after *that night*. "It's fine. She's just a worrier," I say, lightly.

But I understand her worries. Truly, I do.

"Do you need to call her?" There's distance in his voice, like this whole exchange bothers him. It bothers me too. But I see she sent me a text.

> Sweetheart, are we on for lunch and tennis Sunday at the club? I want to hear all about Miami. Also, lock the chain on your door.

She knows I do, but she always reminds me anyway...but I get it. Also, I always lock the chain.

"She wants to get together when I'm back in the city. I'll text her later," I say to Nick, but I don't mention the tennis club because that screams Richie Rich. Then, fuck it. If this date is going tits up because I'm young, so be it. Better now than later. "To answer your question, I'm twenty-three. I graduated from business school a few months ago. I started The Makeover app while I was getting my MBA." Maybe this whole short-lived tryst with Nick will be over before it begins. I've finally had a great date and it's spiraling down the drain. But so be it. "So if that's a problem, then I'll say goodnight. Thank you for dinner, and I had a lovely time."

I take a step to leave.

"Whoa," Nick says and grabs my wrist, stopping me.

He looks me in the eyes, intense, powerful. "I had a great time. I'm *still having* a great time. But if you're ready for this night to be over, I'll walk you back to the hotel. I'll say goodnight in the lobby like a gentleman after I make sure you get safely in the elevator. But if you want to dance, then I want to take you to that club," he says.

I'm thrilled and relieved at the same time. It's not the end—it's the start of the rest of the night. "I do want to go with you."

He takes my *yes*—rightly—as permission to hold my wrist tighter. "I asked your age because, one, I'm curious. Doesn't take a genius to work out that there's more than a decade between us. But I also asked because I'm thirty-eight, and I don't usually go to clubs. I will take you wherever you want to go, but I'm not going to thrust my arms in the air and toss back shots and jump up and down."

I laugh at those images. "I don't want you to dance like that."

"Good." He inches closer, crowding me here on the sidewalk, the beach to one side, the South Beach scene to the other. He drops my wrist, his hand snaking around my waist instead. With him this close, I catch a hint of his cologne—he smells like fresh-cut wood and snow. Intoxicating. "If we go dancing, I'm going to dance like a man who wants a woman. Close to you," he adds, letting those words linger in the air between us like sweet smoke. "My hands on your soft arms, my chest pressed to your lovely back, my nose in your beautiful fucking hair that I've been dying to inhale all night long." His fingers travel lower, curving over the fabric of my dress covering my ass. "Is that how you'd like to dance with me?"

I can't speak.

I have no words. I simply *ache*.

"Yes," I whisper.

"Good. Then let's go. But first..."

He reaches into his back pocket and takes out his phone. He slides open the screen, clicks on it, then shows it to me. It's a text message to him from his mother.

> I hope you're remembering to wear sunscreen, Nick.

I laugh, all the tension defused. My wariness vanished into the night. "Well, did you, Nick? Remember to wear sunscreen?"

With a twinkle in his eyes, the gorgeous man shakes his head as if he's relishing his naughtiness. "I don't always do the right thing."

"But you said you'd walk me back to the hotel. That seems like the right thing," I say, back to teasing.

"I'm not sure dancing with you like I want to fuck you is the right thing. But I'm going to do it anyway."

I blink.

This is true speechlessness.

Then he brushes his lips against the shell of my ear, whispering, "Be a good girl, Lola. Write back to her and tell her you'll see her Sunday. Because later, you're going to be very, *very* busy."

Desire swoops down my body, pulses hot between my thighs.

I can't wait to be *very* busy.

He steps back as I click open the message from my mother and tell her I can't wait for lunch.

Then I stuff my phone in my clutch, shut the purse with a decisive snap, and take his offered hand. He leads me into the club, paying the cover charge. Under the deafening beat, he guides me to the dance floor, weaving between hot, sweaty bodies as we go. We pick a spot, and he moves behind me. Yanks my body against his. My back to his chest. My ass to his erection.

As promised, he buries his face in my hair and draws a long, lingering scent.

Goose bumps flare all over my body from his possessive, carnal move.

He can't seem to stop playing with the loose strands of my hair falling from my clip, catching hits of me as his hands slide down my arms then wrap around my waist.

I lift mine above my head, dancing the way I like. Free and easy. Living in my body. Embracing the night, grooving to the music, letting go.

But I'm dancing a whole new way too.

Close to him. My body melting against his.

As we move and grind, I have so many answers about this man—answers I didn't know I was seeking. Nick Adams likes foreplay. Nick Adams likes to take his sweet time. Nick Adams likes...me.

Lola Jones, the woman without a history.

And as he runs his nose along my neck, I have another answer too. I don't want to wait any longer.

I can't hear a soul above the loud thumping of the music, but my words are unmistakable when a few songs in, I slink around in his arms, face him, and mouth *fuck me*.

We're out the door in seconds.

6

CHALLENGE ACCEPTED

Nick

We're back to the hotel in no time. Once the elevator door closes, I punch the button for the fourteenth floor, then I crowd her against the mirrored wall, run a hand down her bare arm, and savor—absolutely fucking savor—the sight in front of me.

This woman is on the edge.

Just the way I want her.

Finally, after teasing her all night long, I'm going to have her.

And I intend to have her *my way*. I cup her cheeks, hold her beautiful face, and then brush my lips to hers.

A whisper of a kiss.

She tastes like a dream. Sweet and spicy, with a hint of lipstick. I'm pretty sure she reapplied her color at the club, and I'm pretty sure, too, it's going to be gone very soon.

I don't intend to kiss her softly much longer.

Picking up the pace slowly, but purposefully, I sweep my lips across hers. She moans against my mouth. The sound revs all my desires. Screw soft.

I kiss her like we danced—hot, hungry, horny. She was worth the wait, especially with those murmurs falling from her lips as I punish her beautiful mouth with more kisses. I push against her, letting her feel what she does to me.

"Oh," she gasps, and it sounds like she's just discovered the heft of my cock, and she likes it.

Excellent.

When the elevator slows, I break the kiss, then run my finger along her bee-stung lips. "All day I've thought about this mouth."

She tilts her head. "Just kissing it?"

Holy fuck. Her dirty mind.

There isn't enough time tonight to do the things I want to do to her.

After the door opens, I grab her hand. "There are too many things I want to do to you first," I say, answering her. "Things I want to do with *my* mouth."

When we reach my room, I slide the key over the reader in no time. Once we're inside, she takes the card from me and slides it in the holder. The lights automatically turn on and she spins around, drops the card into my pocket, then grabs my face. Didn't see that coming, but I don't mind it one bit as she steals a kiss right here in the foyer. It's hard and hungry for long, feverish seconds, but then it shifts. She slows down, takes her sweet time, lingering on my lips.

Lola likes to mix it up.

She likes soft and slow, then hard and fast.

She's eager, too, tugging at my shirt and then my belt.

And nope, that won't do. She can only hold the reins for so long. I'm in charge.

I cover her hands, stopping her. "You come first. And often."

There's something I need to do though. I reach for the clip in her hair and undo it, letting all those gorgeous locks fall. "Mmm. Beautiful," I say, then hand her the clip.

I scoop her up, carry her to the bed, and set her on it, but she places a hand on my chest. "Wait," she says, then slides off all her rings and sets them on the nightstand, along with the clip.

I suppose jewelry can get in the way if she plans to slide those fingers through my hair. And if I'm doing things right, she will be.

She returns to the edge of the bed, fingers naked and smile irresistible.

I kneel in front of her on the carpeted floor, my hands covering her knees, my fingers playing with the hem of her short dress. "Want to know what I was thinking when I was onstage this afternoon, talking about seizing opportunities?"

"Yes," she says, trembling with palpable excitement.

She presses her palms flat against the bed, her spine lifting those glorious tits higher like she's welcoming me, inviting even more touch.

All the touching.

"This," I say, dragging out the word as I push up her dress to her waist. Her white lace panties are soaked. I groan. "You're so fucking wet."

"You did it to me."

"Then let me do something about it," I say, sliding my hands along the soft flesh of her thighs.

"So, you've decided what to do to me?"

"I did." My plan is to tease her. To tease her relentlessly. To tease her till she begs. But I don't tell her that.

I *show* her.

I drag the pad of my index finger along the wet cotton panel of her panties.

A gasp. A tremble.

"I lied to you, beautiful," I say, a dirty admission.

"You're so bad."

"I'm fucking terrible. I decided a long time ago what to do to you. I decided this afternoon," I say, drawing a line back up her center, just enough to make her arch her back and seek me out. "When I was speaking about my three-pronged strategy for evaluating risk and you were crossing your legs at me."

On a shudder, she asks faux innocently, "I was doing *that*?"

Another stroke down her panties, then I dip my face, blow a hot breath near her center. When I pull back to meet her gaze, her blue eyes glitter with desire.

"Oh, you know what you were doing. You were taunting me," I say, spreading her legs open.

"I suppose I was."

"And I decided then, too, that I was going to punish you for all that torture," I tell her and turn my face to her inner thigh, rubbing my beard along her tender skin.

She whimpers throatily, then manages a feathery, "How, Nick? How?"

As I whisk my stubble along her thigh, she lifts her hips up, inching toward me, offering me that gorgeous pussy.

This greedy, beautiful woman. "By teasing you. Making you beg for it. Making you demand I taste your sweetness." I press a kiss to her leg at last, then run my nose along the seam of her panties. Close, so close, but not quite.

She shudders, her hands grabbing at my hair. She's begging with her body.

Yes, fucking yes.

"Please, Nick," she says, but her voice is different now. The temptress seems to have slinked away. Now, she's almost shy, a little innocent.

Must be part of our game, so I keep going.

"Are you sure?" I move my face to her panties, dusting a tender little kiss against the wet fabric. I can taste her heat through the lace, and it winds me higher.

"Nick," she whimpers, curling her hands tighter around my head.

I'm dying to strip off these undies and devour her pussy. But first things first. "Ask for it, beautiful. Ask for my mouth."

But she's quieter than I'd expected when she whispers, "Please."

Hmm.

There's that shyness again. With some concern, I lift

my face, needing to make certain she wants this—these games, this play, this exchange. I set a finger under her chin, draw her gaze down to me. "Are you good with this?"

Her eyes widen. "So good. I just..." She swallows then tries again. "I don't know what to say anymore."

Ah, hell. I get it. She might like to flirt over dinner, but in the bedroom, I bet she just wants *my* words. "You don't need to beg for it tonight, beautiful. I'm dying to go down on you."

"Yes," she says desperately.

And yup. She likes to hear dirty talk rather than to give it.

Fine by me.

"I'm going to take these off you and please forgive me in advance, because I'm probably going to groan like a caveman."

She dips her face, smiling again, nibbling on the corner of her lips.

I peel off her panties and groan as promised at the sight. Pretty, pink, and indecently wet. "Look at you. Wanting me," I praise.

"So much."

I can smell her arousal. I'm so hungry for her. So ready to eat her up. I'm going to adore her with my mouth. Show her what a man can do.

I kiss the inside of her knee, the supple flesh of her thigh, then I press a whisper of a kiss to her pussy.

A gasp.

I feel like a king already. I look up at her. "I told you it was a hard fucking speech. I looked at you and thought how very much I wanted to walk off that stage, stride over to you, spread these legs," I say, "and devour you."

"I've never come like this before," she blurts out.

Well then.

I was dead wrong. She had another reason for her silence. She had a confession to deliver, and I take it like the gift it is.

I flash her a cocky smile. "Challenge accepted."

Then, I get to work on giving her a first.

7

TREASURE MAP

Layla

Part of me wants to tell Nick I've never had sex. It's like giving a treasure hunter a map. The intel will help him along the way.

But another part of me—the stubborn, independent, private me—wants to keep my virginity to myself.

I don't need a man's permission to lose it. Nick already wants to fuck me, so why do I need to tell him he'd be the first to do so? It's my choice.

I weigh the matter for a few seconds as he licks me, until my brain scrambles. And holy hell, my body feels so good I can't think straight.

Or at all.

Because Nick's face is buried between my thighs, and he's eating me like he's licking a decadent dessert off a spoon. I feel like his treat as he flicks his tongue down, then tantalizingly back up. Circling a hand around my ankle, he lifts my right leg, drapes it over his shoulder.

He does the same to my left leg, then presses a gentle but firm hand to my belly. "Lie back, beautiful," he says.

I do, but I stop at my elbows, since I'm a visual person, and this image will be scored into my brain forever—Nick, scooping his hands under my ass then tugging me closer to his mouth.

But before he returns to his feast, he rubs his jawline against my inner thigh. One side, then the other.

I moan, shamelessly loud, a sound I've never quite made from a vibrator. But I never knew I'd like the roughness of a beard. Never knew I'd want his scruff so much. Or maybe it's how Nick wields his beard like a secret weapon till I'm arching, gasping his name.

"I've got you," he reassures me, his voice a dirty caress, then his mouth is on me again, kissing and licking.

Tingles spread everywhere.

Soon, I'm parting my legs wider, rocking against his face, gripping his head harder. "Oh god, oh god," I chant with every stroke of his magic tongue.

I feel everything, everywhere, all at once, then the pleasure coils tight and hot in my belly. "I'm coming," I call out, and he kisses me voraciously through an orgasm that rattles my body and my mind.

That makes me feel like I'm flying.

I'm shaking, barely aware of what's happening, but soon, I'm looking up at him. He's above me, braced on his palms, his lips ludicrously wet, his hazel eyes dark with desire. "You are outrageously sexy, and I want to make you come a million times," he says in a rough, husky voice.

Who is this man who's already obsessed with my pleasure? I want to come all night long with him.

"I'm in," I say, and there's my answer to my dilemma.

Maybe it's the orgasm drug. Or maybe it's the way he stares at me with naked desire, but whatever it is, I'm unlocked. I don't need him to know I'm a virgin for his permission. I *want* him to know so he can make sex better...*for me*.

And *for us*.

So I play with him again, like I did earlier today. "How did you picture it?" I ask. When his eyes flicker with question marks, I keep going. "*Fucking me*. When you were onstage, how did you think about fucking me?"

He sits up, kneeling between my still-spread thighs. He reaches for the top button of his shirt, undoes it. "Many ways. But mostly I kept thinking how beautiful you'd look riding my cock."

Yes, please.

"I want that," I say, sitting up too, undoing another button for him, then nudging closer to opening the treasure map. "But can you go easy on me at first?"

He lifts a brow in question but nods emphatically. "Of course."

He'd better not run away, but if he does, he was never the right man. "I've never come through sex either," I say. Then, since he likes when I flirt, I whisper against his lips. "But I bet you can make me come for the first time." I pause for dramatic effect, letting the words take shape and weigh on my tongue before I add, "And for *my* first time."

The map is open before him.

He stills. For several long seconds that make me tense. Then he pulls back, regards me curiously. "Are you sure, Lola?"

What a relief. I'd half expected him to run for the hills. "Yes."

Nick gestures from me to him. "You know what this is?"

I roll my eyes. "Don't worry—I won't be hopping on a transatlantic flight to surprise you at your flat in Knightsbridge next week."

He laughs, like *touché*. "I just want to make sure you don't have any other expectations...since the ocean is really big."

He says it like the body of water is the only thing between us. Not our jobs, not our goals.

But I focus on the moment. "I have a few big expectations," I say, with a coquettish bob of my shoulder. "I expect an orgasm from you. Maybe work on giving me one with your dick?"

He growls. Then in a flash, he gets off the bed, lifts me up, and tosses me over his shoulder. "More than one, beautiful," he says, smacking my ass as he carries me across the suite to the living room area, then sets me down on the couch.

When he undoes another button on his shirt, I'm

giddy with excitement. I'm about to get a show. The sexiest man I've ever met is stripping naked for me.

He tosses a careless glance at my clothes. "Take off your dress. Want to see those beautiful tits."

His filthy mouth is fire.

I pull my dress over my head as he removes his shirt.

His pecs are covered in a smattering of golden-brown chest hair that trails down the ladder of his abs, a happy trail guiding me to his dick.

"Take off the bra, Lola," he demands next, and I comply.

He hisses when my breasts are revealed.

Then, I make a twirling gesture with my finger. "Your turn."

He just smiles, like he can't believe the briefly shy girl is now a hungry woman again. And I am ravenous. I can't wait to see all of him. To watch this powerful businessman who commanded the crowds today take a risk with me.

He reaches into his pocket, snags a condom from the wallet, then tosses it on the couch next to me.

He makes quick work of his pants.

The clip of my heart increases. He's so turned on there's a wet spot on his boxer briefs.

For me.

He strips out of his briefs, and my lips part. His cock is thick, hard, and pointing right at me.

He comes around to sit on the couch, beckons me closer. "On my lap. You're going to ride me like this. Up close, so I can have my hands all over you as we fuck."

With a get-on-me smack of my ass, he sets the mood once more. I climb over him, straddling his muscular thighs as I gaze down at the handsome man under me, cataloging his features. His sun-kissed skin, his strong arms, his carved muscles.

My hands visit him all over, traveling closer and closer to his cock.

He's patient, letting me explore his body as he moans and breathes out hard. But I'm done. I want to *feel*. I reach for the condom and give it to him as anticipation slides down my spine. He rolls on the protection, then offers me his dick.

I rise up, finding just the right position. For a brief second, the reality of what I'm doing hits me.

I'm going to have sex for the first time.

And I'm ready. I've never wanted anyone else like this. Never felt this ache between my thighs so intensely, this tingling in my nipples so acutely. "I want you," I say.

"Then have me," he urges, holding his dick for me. Like he's handed me a baton in a sex relay, I take over, thrilling at the feel of his shaft in my hand.

I rub him against my wetness. I find just the right position, and I guide him inside. A half inch maybe. Then another.

And wow. That's...a lot.

I tense at the intrusion.

He runs a hand gently down the outside of my thigh. "Breathe, beautiful," he says in a tender tone.

I breathe in, out.

Once I relax, I lower myself more.

The Tryst

Wriggling. Adjusting. *Breathing.*

"You good?" he asks.

Mostly. "I think so."

He's stretching me. I feel full and he's not even all the way in.

"Take all the time you want. We can stop anytime," he says, like he's a first times sex guide I ordered on the Internet—*I'll have one night with a sexy, caring, older man who can go all alpha on me in bed and then take care of me out of bed too. Ideally, he'll be dirty and tender.*

His big hands curl around my hips, but he doesn't grip tight. He just waits patiently.

I inhale, then I sink down all the way.

It's intense. I feel him everywhere. He's nothing like a vibrator. This is worlds better, especially since he seems so enrapt, gazing at me with hooded eyes and a tight jaw.

The way he stares washes the last remnants of discomfort away.

I let a smile take over my face as I rise up, then sink down.

"You're so fucking pretty like this," he grits out, and his hands glide up my back into my hair, his fingers roping through my strands possessively.

"Was this how you pictured me?" I ask, wrapping my hands around his neck, my breasts grazing his pecs.

"Yes," he says, his eyes traveling all over me, freely gazing at my face, my tits, my stomach, my legs.

And where we connect.

"Look at you. You look so perfect on my cock," he adds.

And I feel…perfect too.

Nick lets go of my hair, gripping my hips. Like that, he guides me along, helping me find just the right angle, just the right pace.

Soon, we hit a rhythm.

He pumps up into me, and I grind down on him. I'd expected it to hurt, but I'm so aroused, so ridiculously wet, that I just feel stretched in the best of ways. It's deep and delicious all at once as I ride this stranger's cock into the night. But Nick hardly feels like a stranger. He's my perfect lover.

He gets a hand between us, and he's stroking my clit now, rubbing me intently.

My toes tingle. My pulse surges. And I ache.

Then I gasp as an orgasm wrecks me, so powerfully that I spin out. Or maybe the world does. Or my orgasm is my world. I don't even know anymore. I just feel…wild.

And beautiful.

I fall into bliss on him, crying out as this release washes over me for several seconds, maybe minutes—I don't even know.

When I open my eyes again, still moaning from the aftershocks, he's thrusting up into me, punching his hips.

Till he tenses, then groans a long, dirty sound as he comes too.

I collapse against his big chest, wrapping my arms around him and basking in the glow. He runs a hand down my back, soothing and reassuring.

I want more of him tonight. I want to feel these arms, these hands, his strength.

I'm still bathing in endorphins, but through the fog, a worry digs into my brain. Is this it? Do I leave now? We said no expectations, so perhaps the night is over.

When his sweet murmurs cease, he says softly, "Let me get rid of this condom."

That's...it?

Of course that's it. You said no strings.

And really, what was he going to say? "You're amazing, Lola, and, please, do surprise me at my flat sometime."

Please.

I don't want to wear out my welcome, especially since I've been so adamant about my own boundaries. I ease off him, but I don't watch as he heads to the bathroom.

I shut down, turning off whatever temporary wishes I had to stay a little longer. Quickly, I gather my clothes, hooking on my bra then tugging on my dress.

A minute later, his footsteps sound, and he pads across the floor, then stops. "Lola."

It's so stern.

I turn around.

His eyes are narrowed. Then he shakes his head, tsking me as he closes the distance between us and cups my cheeks. "Take off your dress. Get in bed. I'm not at all done with you."

I throw a parade as I strip, then race to the bed.

8

SEXY MAD LIBS

Layla

Before the sun rises, I'm on the cusp of my fourth orgasm. Nick's lying on his side, fucking me with his fingers. I'm a panting, gasping, writhing woman, my leg flung over him. I'm spread wide open while he works me into a frenzy.

I arch my hips and explode into bliss.

I can't stop crying out, can't stop moaning.

It's like I'm on vacation and every meal is more sinful than the one before.

Four.

Four.

When I finally shake off the orgasm fairy dust, I gaze dopily at the handsome man. "Can I do something for you?"

"I like making you feel good," he says, then shifts me so we can spoon.

Dear god, his warm body. His big arms. His obsession with my pleasure. He's like a fairy-tale prince who can fuck like a porn star.

But then, do porn stars fuck like this? I don't watch much porn. I mostly just watch gifs of men and women getting themselves off. Solo. That always does it for me—a personal pursuit of pleasure, no matter the seeker.

So all this sex stuff is new. Sex talk is new.

And so is *this*—cuddling.

He sighs contentedly against me as a sliver of light peeks through the hotel blinds. "Your flight's in three hours," he says.

"I know," I say, pouting, wishing this stolen night wasn't ending. But the rising sun says otherwise.

"Mine's in three hours and thirty minutes." He sounds wistful and that surprises me, so I wait to see where he's going. "If I didn't live in London, I'd ask you to dinner tonight," he says.

I tense. Isn't this what we said we'd avoid last night? Why is he creating expectations then? Hypothetical ones, but still. "You would?" I ask cautiously.

"Yes. Does that bother you? What I just said?"

I pause to assess what I'm feeling. Is he suggesting closeness? Emotional intimacy? Not really. So I'm safe. "No, but you said no expectations," I point out.

"And yet I want to take you out to your favorite restaurant, order a decadent dessert, then dance with you again."

Code for fuck.

But code for fuck sends a burst of tingles down my

belly, headed straight for my core. I let out a murmur, unbidden.

He tugs me closer. "Kiss you again. Taste you again. Introduce you to so many other ways to fuck," he says.

Hello, teacher. I wriggle against him. "Color me intrigued."

"Would you like that, Lola?"

Is this a real offer, or fantasy pillow talk? I don't even know what game we're playing. But I'm a good enough actress. I've learned how to put on a face. "You could take me to my favorite club in Manhattan," I say, since what the hell? I'll go along with him.

"Pull you into a dark corner," he says, brushing my hair away from my neck. Making me shiver.

"Touch me there. In public," I say, playing sexy mad libs.

"Get you all worked up. Then bring you back to my hotel and bend you over the bed."

Yes, this is the fantasy pillow talk portion of our one-night stand. I can handle this, even though his mouth cruises across my shoulder, drifting closer to my ink.

I tense briefly when he leans in to dust a kiss across the flower on my shoulder. But he either doesn't notice my reaction or he reads me instantly, since he doesn't stay there or ask me about it. Not that I'd tell him. I don't feel a need to tell anyone what my tattoo means.

"And then I'd take you to breakfast in the morning," he says softly, continuing laying out his agenda for this make-believe date.

Is a morning-after breakfast too much? But it's a

fantasy date so it doesn't really matter. Besides, I like breakfast, and him so far. "Sounds nice."

He exhales again, like he's letting go of the tale just as he lets go of his hold on me.

Nick flops to his back, parking his hands behind his head. He's staring at the ceiling. Maybe lost in thought. "There's this great wine bar I've been wanting to try. It's on Seventy-Third and Amsterdam. Hugo's. It opened a year ago," he says.

And the fantasy isn't over. It's getting awfully specific.

The sun is rising higher now, and the early light of dawn illuminates his handsome face. "I've heard about Hugo's. My friend Ethan is always searching out new restaurants, and he's been talking up that one, and my—"

I cut myself off before I say my mom loves to have her lawyer snag me reservations at the hottest joints.

I don't want to mention her again. It makes me sound younger. *My mommy gets me good rezzies.*

I quickly course correct with, "My friend has great taste."

"Then we'd go there tonight," he says, and that has to be the end. We've played our fantasy date to its logical conclusion.

My suspicions are confirmed when he swings his legs out of bed. "I should get ready. International check-in and all." With a yawn, Nick drags a hand through his hair. The signals are crystal clear. It's time to go. The night is over.

Last night was the true fantasy.

I try to zoom in on reality. I need to head to my room, pack quickly, order a Lyft. I slide out of bed and hunt for my clothes while he grabs boxer briefs. As I find my dress by the couch, his phone rings.

My back is turned so I can't see him grab it, but after a beat, he says, "Just a sec. That's my—" But then he must hit ignore, since he says to me, "I'll call him back later."

My radar beeps. A horrible thought lodges in my brain, shame and anger chasing it. Quickly, I tug on my useless panties then my bra, covering myself up and grabbing my rings before I spit out: "Are you married?"

His jaw drops. He blinks. Shakes his head in obvious shock. "What the hell?"

But I have to know. "Was that your wife? The *he* you'll call back?"

With angry eyes, Nick advances toward me. "Are you kidding me? I'm *not* married," he says, frustration laced in his tone. "I'd never do a goddamn thing we did if I were married, involved or dating." He points to his phone on the bed, like he's stabbing the air. "That was my brother. *He's* married and going through some stuff. I stayed with him for a few nights. He's calling and I wanted to see what's going on, but I hit ignore because I'm with you."

A new shame washes through me for thinking the worst. But the worst happens.

His bio probably would have revealed if he was married, but you never know. Wincing, I tug on my dress. "I had to ask. Just in case."

He closes the distance between us and holds my

face. A little hard, but a little desperate too. "I'm divorced," he says, with resignation. "I was married young. It wasn't...a good marriage. We split several years ago."

"Oh," I say, swallowing roughly, feeling guiltier, since I can tell he's a touch embarrassed to admit all of that. "I'm sorry."

"I'm not a liar, Lola," he says, his tone vulnerable.

"I just didn't want to be a fool," I whisper. "Or a home-wrecker."

"You're neither. I promise. You can look me up online later." He presses a gentle kiss to my forehead. "Want to share a car to the airport? I have one coming in thirty minutes."

I should turn him down. I should stay away from men I don't truly know. I should avoid anything more in case it leads to feelings. But when he kisses my hair, all I feel is my wish for a little more. "Yes. I'll grab my things and meet you in the lobby."

"Perfect," he says, and we pick a time, but before I can leave, his eyes twinkle. "But are *you* married?"

I laugh. As if.

He holds my gaze intensely. "It's not an unreasonable question."

He's not wrong. I assumed he was more likely to be married and cheat given his age, but I could be a liar too.

Anyone can.

People go on the road, they fabricate, and they break hearts. People do that at home too. You never know who your secrets and truths are safe with.

"I'm very single," I say.

"Good. Then we'll have our second date on the way to the airport. How do you like your coffee?"

I tell him, then quickly get ready for an unexpected date.

Only this second date will be real, rather than a fantasy. But it will end soon so I'll be safe.

9

RISK ASSESSMENT

Nick

I lied.

That wasn't my brother on the phone.

But I don't want to tell Lola my son called. I don't want her to see me as someone old enough to have a grown kid. Mostly, I don't want to have the inevitable conversation about how young I was when he was born.

That conversation opens up too much pain, too much judgment. I endured enough judgment from my ex's family, thank you very much. Don't need another serving.

And I definitely don't want to sully our last few moments together with any uncomfortable conversations. She gave me her body last night, and I won't take a chance in case she'd think she gave the keys to the wrong man.

Call it risk assessment. There's no need for full disclosure since I won't see her again.

After I pack, I grab breakfast, then meet her at the town car I ordered that's waiting in front of the hotel.

Our second date entails coffee. I hand her the black coffee and keep my own Café Cubano in my left hand as I open the car door for her with my right.

She slides inside the car, and I join her, then pull the bag of baked goods from my jacket. "I hate pastries," I say as she takes the bag and opens it.

"They're pointless. Utterly pointless," she declares, brandishing the sesame bagel. "But bagels? Well, the New Yorker in me can't resist."

"The New Yorker in me can't either."

She smiles at that remark, but it's a little wistful. Perhaps I'm reading too much into a *post bite of a bagel* smile, but maybe she's wishing I were still a New Yorker.

No expectations, man. You have work to focus on. You have deals to ink. Employees to pay.

As we dine in the town car, I shove off thoughts of what it would be like to live in the same city as her. "What will you work on when you return to New York?" I ask as the sleek black vehicle motors toward the airport.

"Following up on some of the meetings from here. I'll see my business partner, Geeta, Monday, and we'll review everything together. You?"

"Finalizing a funding deal," I say.

"Sexy," she says with a wiggle of her brow.

There. That's better. I'd prefer that she sees me as a powerful venture capitalist rather than a dad.

When we arrive at the airport, the car drops us off at concourse H, which handles domestic and international flights. We're both on the same airline, just heading in different directions.

I carry her bag inside. Roll it through the security line. Lift it onto the conveyor belt. Then I walk her to her gate.

Her flight is boarding now, and I wish I could delay time. A pang of missing wedges into my chest unexpectedly.

This was a one-night stand. Nothing more.

I really need to say goodbye. For once and for all. "Looks like you're out of here."

"I am. Thanks for walking me to my gate," she says. "And carrying my bag." Then she kisses me, a quick, firm kiss. "And for my first, fourth, and everything in between."

"The pleasure was mine," I say.

"No. Pretty sure it was mine."

"Fine, it was ours."

"It sure was."

With her standing by the gate, the hustle and bustle of the airport around us, I slide a thumb along her jaw. "I'm going to sound like a dick, but I'm so glad Mikka had laryngitis."

"Me too."

I haul her in for one more shameless kiss.

An airport kiss, tasting of a goodbye that came far too soon.

A kiss I hope she'll carry with her to New York.

Where she'll remember me fondly, and filthily, as the man who took care of her in and out of bed.

When I break it, I stare a little too long at her blue eyes, then her red mouth. And...fuck one-night stand rules. I like to break rules, and I like to bend them. "I meant what I said this morning. And I'm in New York three to four times a year," I say, bending the rules with an offer of sorts.

Maybe there can be *some expectations.*

A smile tilts her lips. "Look me up, Mr. Adams."

She heads to the gate, scans her boarding pass at the kiosk. As she steps on the jetway, she turns around and blows me a kiss.

Then, she's gone.

And I leave too, calling my son back as I board, trying to convince him to work with me. Then as I fly away, I replay last night and this morning. I try to review the term sheet for Vault, but I'm thinking about that woman more than I want as I travel across the really big ocean that separates me from her.

10

AN ABSOLUTE BEAST

Layla

"Mojitos are on me, my pets!" I call out to my friends as I stride into The Lucky Spot that night. I'm feeling triumphant, because triumph is a better emotion to nurture than missing a man who's far, far away.

Harlow and Ethan wait for me at the bar in Chelsea. The place is bustling since it's seven, so I weave my way through the crowds. When I reach my besties, they immediately thrust their arms up in victory.

Then Ethan turns to Harlow, staring at her pointedly. "Pay up," he says, wiggling his fingers.

I slide between them and poke Harlow's shoulder. "You doubted me?"

Harlow just shrugs. "You're notoriously picky," she says. "I didn't think it was going to happen."

"O ye of little faith," I say. Then I turn my gaze to

Ethan, snarling over the top. "So that means you think I'll just spread 'em for anyone?"

He cracks up. "No. It means I bet on twenty-three years of pent-up horniness spilling over in one week in Miami for you. And I was right."

I narrow my brow at him, then faux growl. "Damn you."

Ethan turns to the curly-haired man behind the bar, who does a double take when he sees my guy friend. But just as quickly, the bartender slides into business, asking, "What can I get for you?"

"His number," I mutter to Harlow, who nods big and long.

"Two mojitos," Ethan says to the guy. "And an iced tea."

"Coming right up," the bartender says, then flashes an unnecessarily large and wholly clear smile at Ethan before he heads off to mix drinks.

I hum a naughty little tune then nudge my matinee idol friend with the ink on his arm. "And will mojitos be on you soon too?" I wiggle my brows at the bartender.

Ethan shakes his head, but I think he's redirecting rather than denying. "Don't distract us." He pats the stool between him and Harlow. "Sit your ass down. And tell us a story. Leave no item of clothing undone, no bed sheet unturned, no condom unused. I want the full Monty story."

"I second what he said," Harlow says. "And start now because we've got two hours until Ethan's set."

Ethan stabs the bar with his finger. "Story time. Now. Spare no details."

The details are everything.

The details will feed my fantasies for a long time.

"He's a venture capitalist. He's got this whole intense, dominant charm and he's also a great listener," I say, then pause to set up my final point. "And he walked me to my gate this morning. *At the airport.* He kissed me goodbye right before I boarded my plane."

Ethan whistles in appreciation. Harlow claps.

So I give them a little more. "He was dirty and dreamy and demanding and also, obsessed with my pleasure. And he told me if he lived in New York, he would've taken me out tonight. He even said he'll be here later this year."

Harlow's eyes widen with intrigue. "So you are going to see this guy again?"

My heart does a loop-the-loop. Stupid, hopeful organ. I shake my head, making light of it. "It's just something he said. I'm not going to think about whether he's coming here again. I'm not going to look him up. And I'm not going to fantasize about an uncertain future," I say, then I glimpse a familiar face by the door when a striking brunette walks in alongside a busty redhead.

"It's our cousins," I say brightly, using the nickname we gave Jules and Camden.

Harlow turns and waves at Jules Marley. The brunette works with Harlow's boyfriend, Bridger. She's become his right-hand woman helping him run his new TV production company, and she's sharp as an eagle. Next, Harlow waves to Camden, Jules's friend.

More than a year ago, the three of us ran into Jules and Camden at a dance club, and Harlow pulled them into our spot on the dance floor, where we grooved the night away to pulsing music in a big group of arms and limbs and drinks.

So we annexed them into our group. I also convinced Jules and Camden to take Krav Maga with me, so they join me occasionally at the gym.

While the three of us—Ethan, Harlow, and me—will probably always be like long-lost siblings, Jules and Camden feel like cousins we just discovered.

When Jules, decked out in jeans and a shiny black spaghetti-strap top that shows off her creamy skin, curves, and strong arms, joins us, she asks, "Did we miss all the good stuff? If so, will you recap the juiciest deets?"

Yeah, she's definitely become part of our family. "Layla had an excellent—wink, wink—time in Miami," Harlow offers.

I just shrug impishly, owning the fuck out of my time there.

Jules's eyes twinkle. Camden's green eyes brighten in obvious curiosity as she asks, "I'm gonna need more. *How* excellent, exactly?"

Ethan clears his throat. "A quartet of excellent."

"Damn, Layla," Jules says, impressed.

"Lucky bitch," Camden chimes in.

We all crack up, then I tell the story again, and I

don't mind sharing the details of a night I'll never regret.

Because that's what it was—one wonderful night under the sultry Miami sky.

Later, as my friends and I head to Rebel Beat to rock out to Ethan's music from the front row, I do my best to put those details in the past and move forward into my future here in New York.

* * *

My mother is sweating.

It's a rare sight, but the woman plays like an absolute beast on the tennis court.

On the other side of the net, I'm tempted to shout, "Go, Anna," but she'd deliver a withering smile and tell me to focus on the match.

But we've been playing for too many points, too many games, just far too long, so even though I was raised to be a tennis beast too, when she serves the next ball I maybe, possibly, deliberately stretch my arm too far and miss it.

Oops.

It rolls with a thud to the edge of the court.

"Damn," I mutter, dropping my shoulders. Like this is the worst fate ever.

She arches a doubtful brow. Yes, from several feet away and across the net, I can read her dubious stare. "Darling, did you let me win?"

"Please. I'd never do that. I'm so competitive."

In business. Not in sports. I couldn't wait to hang up

my tennis racket when I was in high school. Just like I can't wait to pack it into a bag today.

Mom grabs a towel from a bench and wipes her brow. "Up for a rematch this afternoon?"

Where does she get her energy from? She's been like this for the last few years. *Busy*. I don't know if it's real or a new survival strategy. A distraction from pain tactic.

"I would, but I have to prep for seeing Geeta tomorrow," I say.

"Where are you meeting her? In public?"

"At a tea shop, so yes," I say, trying to hide the exasperation from my tone.

"Do you trust her still?"

"Of course, Mom."

She arches a brow. "It's not an unreasonable question when it comes to a business partner."

"But I'll never be able to give you an answer that's satisfying."

She huffs, perhaps knowing I'm right, but saying nothing.

"It's all good with Geeta, Mom. It really is," I reassure her. "And we have a lot to catch up on."

"Right, of course. The Makeover app gets all your attention," Mom says, shifting gears, and you can't miss the dig in her voice.

Or the envy.

I ignore it as we stride off the members-only court on Randall's Island, where the elite of New York play one of the most elite games. The membership roll call looks like descendants of the Vanderbilts and Rockefellers.

"So how was Miami? I can't wait to hear all about it. I'm not *that* jealous of The Makeover," she says, even though we both know she is. At least she's being honest about it now.

But she wants what she wants—and that's for me to ditch The Makeover app and come work for her, then to take over the company.

"It was great," I say, then share all the safe-for-work details as we head inside. Once we turn into the ladies' locker room, Mom gasps in excitement then wags a finger at a regal blonde with silver streaks in her hair. "Rose! You sneak. You didn't tell me you were coming today."

The tall, elegant woman shuts her locker and comes in for a cheek kiss, dusting Mom with one of her own. "Oh, it was a last-minute thing. My appointment with my stylist was canceled," Rose says when she pulls back, pouting for emphasis.

"Whatever will you wear to the silent auction next weekend then?" my mother asks in concern because attire to charity functions is the height of concern in their world.

"I don't have any idea. But Bertrand tells me he'll see me first thing tomorrow morning so, crisis averted. He can still pick my emcee gown for the literacy gala."

My mother wipes her brow dramatically. "Thank god." Then, she squeezes my arm, inviting me into the conversation. "Layla and I are going to catch up over cobb salad on all our various charitable board endeavors," she says, pride in her tone. "It's our thing."

Rose smiles approvingly. "I love your generosity."

"Yours too," Mom says to her, and even though there's some typical one-upmanship between them, they both back it up with their pocketbooks. Mom taught me the value of charity a long time ago.

Rose turns to me. "And did your mother destroy you on the court like she does with everyone?"

"She always does."

"Anna, do save a match for me," Rose says. "Perhaps tomorrow?"

"Sounds lovely," my mother says, then the woman leaves.

Once she's out of earshot, Mom whispers, "I want her to be my doubles partner. She's been through a lot too."

I'm not sure how to respond, so I simply say, "That's great."

Even though it's probably not.

When we're done showering and changing for lunch, we leave the locker room and head to the restaurant. As we walk down the hallway lined with photos of club members, Mom cups the side of her mouth. "Rose's son David is still single. You two would be so good together. He's very interested in charitable endeavors too."

This is what it's come to? I can't believe she's started recycling. With a straight face, I say, "Mom, I dated David Bancroft in college."

She blinks. "You did?"

My throat burns with the threat of emotion. Those were the Xanax years for Mom. She spent a lot of my college years struggling with depression. Completely understandable. She's only recently started to emerge from the fog of grief. So gently, I say, "I did. We're still friends. I haven't seen him in a few months since he went to Canada on a wilderness expedition."

"And Rose says he's returning this week. We're both so grateful he's finally done with that...*Jersey bartender* he met on the trails," she says, her tongue sharp, rankling me.

"Do you have an issue with her being from New Jersey, or her being a bartender?" I ask, guard up. Sometimes the older generation is so...judgy.

My mother stares at me like I've gone mad. "Darling! Neither, of course. I was simply saying he's finished his wilderness dalliance with a girl from the other side of the bridge. He should date you...*again*," she says, delighted to play second-chance matchmaker. "A Bancroft and a Mayweather."

I can see the Fifth Avenue wedding in her eyes. "Like I said, we're *friends*, Mom," I emphasize, trying to put her straight. She's convinced I'll be safe if I marry a man from a family she knows. A family she's vetted.

"I was friends with your father," she says, and I want to point out that that's not entirely true—they became the best of friends while married, but they weren't friends first. But it's better to let her memory remain untarnished. "Let's set something up," Mom persists. "He'd be so good for you. He'd definitely walk you home. Unlike Bryce." She sighs. "Forgive me for

Bryce. Let me make it up to you by working my magic with this new one."

The woman is nothing if not relentless.

Truthfully, I was going to see David anyway. He texted me a few weeks ago to tell me he was returning to New York later this month. Would it be so terrible if I said yes to Mom's offer simply to get her off my dating back for a little while longer? What's the harm in Mom thinking it could be something even though it won't? Saying yes would make her happy. I've seen so little happiness from her in the last six years. Seems the least I can do for her. I made a promise, after all.

"Sure. I don't think anything will come of it since, again, we already dated, but you can go ahead," I say. There. At least I was honest.

"Lovely. I'll put you two in touch," Mom says, cheery again.

But I know her cheer will drain away any second since we're near the end of the hall.

As if on cue, she stops in front of a cherished photo. The picture makes my heart lurch every single time.

My parents. Onstage at a charity ball held here.

Dancing, smiling, gazing.

So in love.

My fingers itch to reach out and touch his bow tie. I tied it for him that night. He knew how, of course. But I'd taught myself on YouTube, so I tied it in our living room. "A perfect bow for my favorite dad," I'd said.

"A perfect bow from my favorite daughter," he'd echoed. It was one of our games—the favorite dad/favorite daughter one.

The Tryst

When he left that night to take my mom to the ball, he kissed her cheek at the door, told her she looked radiant.

"You always say that, John."

"You always look radiant," he'd said, then he'd kissed her again.

No wonder she was so happy in this photo. He doted on her, and she adored him.

No wonder, too, it always makes her cry.

It was taken one week before the end of my father's life.

My mother stares at it like it's an altar she prays to. She purses her lips. Blinks back tears, then swipes a hand under her eye.

My throat tightens, both from her reaction and from the hole in my heart too.

"Miss you, Daddy," I say to the handsome, magnetic, protective man in the picture.

Then, I turn away from the photo, but I feel like I'm carrying it with me the rest of the day.

I've been carrying all the memories of him with me since the night he was murdered six years ago.

11

DISTRACTIBLE GUY

Layla

On Monday, I make plans to see David at the end of the week, then I take a ferry across the river to meet Geeta at a tea shop in Hoboken. We mostly zoom and call, but we try to meet in person now and then, and I do my best to come out here since it's easier for her. As she sips chai, we review my reports from the conference.

"I especially like Farm to Phone, and it's not just because of the clever name," I say, showing her the proposal from a hot-shot digital marketing firm that wants to work with us. "They've helped some of the best new apps rise up and get noticed. A handful of their apps have gone on to become part of Omega Media."

One well-groomed brow rises at the mention of an app holding company with a sterling rep. Geeta sets down her cup. "Let's sell this baby to Omega."

The endgame for us has always been an exit. We want to sell The Makeover to a bigger company, one with a family of apps already. I have two years to make that happen with Mom's timeline breathing down my neck.

"Definitely. Or Marcus Media. Or Limitless," I say, naming some other app holding companies. "Which is why I think we should consider Farm to Phone. We need a marketing partner and, with our growth this spring, now's the time to get The Makeover ready."

As she reviews the proposal on screen, Geeta twirls a strand of magenta hair amongst her sheet of black locks, then shrugs her yes. "If you like their proposal, I like their proposal."

When we're done with the recap, I check the time. "I need to shoot some new videos today. I should take off."

She sighs heavily. "Me too. This is my first time out in days. But I gotta jet. Dad's PT is coming over."

"Of course. Tell Dad I say hi," I say, though I've never met her father. He has MS and she lives with him and takes care of him.

"I'll send him your lipstick love. But I better get home before he flirts too hard with his PT," she says.

Laughing, I scoop up my laptop and take off.

Once I'm back across the river and in my Manhattan neighborhood, I swing by Blush, one of my favorite makeup shops on Columbus Avenue, where I hunt for a few items. When I spot a new pink lipstick and liner from a company called Mia Jane, I'm too enthused to keep it to myself. "You have Mia Jane," I say to no one in particular.

This brand is a dream. Started by the fashionista and former model Mia Jane, it's all cruelty-free and made in the USA. She ruled the runway a couple decades ago, and since then she's dabbled in several hustles from perfume, to cropped sweatshirts, to vegan purses. She finally jumped into the makeup world last year with a pop-up shop in Los Angeles for her brand. Hard to say if she'll stick with this new project, but her taste is extraordinary, and her rep is strong, especially among young people, since she offers one of the largest lines of inclusive shades for a wide range of skin tones.

A stunningly pretty man at the counter looks up and flashes a grin. "We sure do. Have you tried Mia Jane yet?" he asks. He's wearing silver eyeshadow, which pops beautifully against his skin. His name tag reads Storm/Store Manager.

"Yes! It's my go-to brand whenever I can get it. I went to their pop-up shop in LA last time I was there, but I could only stow so much in my luggage."

He laughs. "We're birds of a feather. I stocked up on her ebony shades for myself. That color's not easy to find." Then he brings a finger to his lips. "But don't tell anyone I wear foundation."

I mime zipping my lips, then say breezily, "What foundation?"

He smiles. "I knew I liked you. Anyway, I hope her lines go big. We've started carrying all her stuff, and rumor has it she might be opening some Mia Jane shops soon."

We both squeal.

I shop a bit more, then, goodies in hand, I head to the counter, where I study his lids. "Love that silver color, and your blend is perf, Storm."

"Thank you, hun." Then he blinks, points, grins. "Wait. Wait! You're Lola!"

I smile, giddy from the recognition for *this* reason. "That's me."

"Girl! You taught me how to fill in a brow with your series," he says, then he strikes a pose and gestures to his perfectly groomed eyebrows.

"That's fantastic. You should be doing videos," I say, then head home, saying hello to Sylvester, the evening doorman, and Grady at the concierge desk before I head to the sixth floor, lock my apartment, then deadbolt it.

I turn on all the lights and look around.

Once I'm safely inside and alone, I take off my skull rings, I'll put one on before I go to bed, since it's always wise to have a weapon with you, and these are self-defense rings, with a tiny, serrated blade hidden under each skull. Next, I set up my lights and shoot several new videos. They'll go on social, then Geeta will integrate them into the app.

Finally, Friday rolls around, and I head out to meet David. I haven't seen him in months, and I'm ridiculously excited.

Seeing him feels like a reward. I've made it through the first week without looking up Nick Adams.

That handsome man will remain a dirty, delicious memory.

* * *

The sound of Ms. Pac-Man eating a ghost greets me as I head into Cosmo's, a retro arcade in the Village. I scan the joint for my sandy-haired friend, but I don't see him at the bar, or the games, or at a table.

When Ms. Pac-Man dies loudly, someone behind me says, "Oh man, that's the worst."

Someone I know. My former boyfriend fills the arcade doorway, looking nothing like his history major, clean-shaven self of yesteryear.

"Is David Bancroft under that beard?" I ask. "Beneath that wild hair?"

"Don't tell a soul," he whispers, then wraps me in a tight hug in the entryway.

But I'm still shocked when he lets go. He seems so different from when we met at Columbia. I was a senior and he was a junior. He'd needed a math tutor, and the school's tutoring program paired us. We hit it off, working on equations and, admittedly, flirting. We dated for four months or so, but eventually agreed we were better off as friends.

"C'mon, let's grab a bite then play some games," he says.

We order sandwiches and beer and find a seat, and I park my chin in my hand. "So, tell me all about Canada. Where were you? What did you do?"

He regales me with tales of his treks deep into the forest, his experience with nature, and the meaning he found in connecting with the earth.

"It just made me realize I want to do something that

really helps the planet, you know? I'm thinking maybe I can do something for animals and the climate. Like when animals get displaced from homes or shelters due to hurricanes, floods, or forest fires. Maybe I could raise money for that."

We discuss his ideas over our sandwiches until he finishes with, "I'm going to do it. I'm going to use some of my trust fund from my grandparents. Start a little non-profit and raise money to help animal shelters in the area. I'll start with my mom's friends."

"I'd love to help," I say. "I've planned a few charity fundraisers over the years."

"You're the best," he says and reaches across the table to ruffle my hair. When he sits back, he shakes his head in amusement. "So ridic that our moms think we're a thing."

I laugh too. "Proof: you just ruffled my hair." *And never gave me an orgasm.* But I keep that part to myself.

"I definitely don't ruffle Cynthia's hair."

"Yeah, what's the story with this girl you can't get over?"

"She's a bartender at a bowling alley in Newark. Her brother works as one of the guides for the wilderness trek, and Cynthia and I met when she came along to help out on the trip. But she loves camping and hiking too."

"So you have the whole outdoor thing in common."

"We do." He sounds like a fool in love. But then his smile disappears. "I think I freaked her out when I proposed to her."

"What???"

He just shrugs. "Yeah, she kind of told me to slow down." He scratches his jaw. "Or maybe she said *slow the fuck down*. I just hope I didn't scare her away."

"Can you? Slow down?" I ask, genuinely concerned. David was always a full-speed-ahead kind of guy. I'm the one who pressed the brakes on us, though he immediately agreed that friendship felt right.

"Sure," he says, maybe too quickly. But he adds in a resolute tone, "I can. I will. I mean, I'm not driving out to Jersey every day, am I?" He glances up at me like he's looking for approval.

"That's good." I pat his hand affectionately. "So, a bowling alley in Jersey? Do I even have to ask if your mother had a coronary?"

"No, you do not."

* * *

Alone in my apartment that night, I settle onto the couch, check on my social feed, and respond to comments on The Makeover. There's a DM from Storm, too, thanking me for the shoutout the other day. Then he adds, *Plus, there's a rumor a Mia Jane shop is coming to New York soon. Prayers, girl!*

I send him a praying hands emoji, then a note: *I better be the first to know!*

We chat some more then I return to my comments. I'm about to close out, but then I do a double take when I spot a post from **DistractibleGuy**. It's a question —*Does it hold up when you go dancing?*

A warm flush spreads across my cheeks and down

my chest. Giddy with hope, I click on the name. I'm tingly, too, as I check out the profile, created just today. There are no videos. No photos. The profile pic is just an icon of a glass of liquor. Looks like scotch.

Then the description says...*An American in London.*

My breath catches. Forget tingly. I'm hot all over as I reply: ***I hope I'll find out someday.***

My comments are quiet while I get ready for bed, but when I slide under the covers, there's a new one.

From him.

Dirty hope spins in me.

It's three in the morning in London. I don't even know if Nick's there right now, but if so, he doesn't sleep much.

And I'm not sure how I'll get to sleep, either, given his reply.

You will.

12

MY PROPOSAL

Nick

Some women are just irresistible.

On my way to a meeting in Kensington a few days after I make the profile on The Makeover, I indulge in another hit of Lola as I step onto the Tube. Once the doors close, I click on her latest social media post—a how-to video on fixing a makeup mistake like smeared eyeliner. I watch it, then I leave a heart.

But I swear that red emoticon mocks me.

As well it should.

I roll my eyes at myself. I'm not a teenager. I'm not a fucking twentysomething. Yet here I am, posting goddamn emoticons for a woman.

I don't even like social media. I only got an account to flirt with her. Since, well, I fucking love flirting with her.

Still, this heart shit has to stop.

Except, algorithms love engagement. I ought to know. I made the money to start my VC firm with an app I created—an app fueled by a sorting algorithm. I went on to sell it for many, many figures.

Engagement matters in this digital world, and Lola's vying not just for relevance, but dominance. With some reluctance that it's come to this, I add a smiley face to the heart.

But that's enough.

A pack of men in suits march onto the train at the next stop, while I click over to DM her. It's become our thing these last few days.

> DistractibleGuy: Hey, you...I'm on the tube surrounded by bankers. I know they're bankers because they're wearing navy.

She's a busy woman, so I don't expect her to reply right away. I toggle to my email and check some contracts Kyle just forwarded to me. But as the train rattles underground, a notification from her pops up.

> Lola: What are YOU wearing, though?

> DistractibleGuy: Is that your shameless attempt to get me to send a selfie?

> Lola: Is that an option?

> DistractibleGuy: Probably not, but points to you for effort.

> Lola: I want more than points.

> DistractibleGuy: I'll give you a visual instead.

I peer down at my get-up and tap out another message.

> DistractibleGuy: Charcoal slacks, a dark green shirt, a light blue tie.

> Lola: Mmm. I do like a sharp-dressed man.

> DistractibleGuy: Lola. There seem to be a few typos in your last DM.

> Lola: Well, I don't know if I'd like you sharp-dressed, Nick. I didn't see you in clothes very much.

She makes an excellent point. And I'm not sure I want to rectify that no-clothes situation with her.

* * *

A few weeks later, as I'm boarding a flight to Vienna to meet with a former colleague of mine who I often trade ideas with—a *scratch my back, I'll scratch yours* deal—my phone pings with a very welcome notification.

> Lola: I'm leaving Krav Maga, wearing pink workout pants and a sports bra.

Damn, that's sexy, taking a bad-ass self-defense class. And wearing pink while you land punches.

I focus on the pink, though, not the punches. The way the fabric hugs her curves...I'm already assembling an image. Savoring it. Planning to use it later.

Lola likes to play.

I do, too, and write back:

> DistractibleGuy: I don't believe you.
>
> Lola: Why would I lie?
>
> DistractibleGuy: Maybe you're home wearing nothing.
>
> Lola: I'm walking past construction workers. I'm definitely not wearing nothing.
>
> DistractibleGuy: Prove it.

The proof arrives one minute later. A photo lands of men in hard hats. I laugh, then I reply in kind.

> DistractibleGuy: I'm on the plane, sitting in first class, wearing a tailored suit.
>
> Lola: Pics or it didn't happen.

I give her a shot of the galley, then put the phone away, my smile a little wistful. Lola is addictive. Such a damn shame about the whole "Atlantic Ocean between us" thing.

* * *

We flirt across the ocean for the next month. In July I catch up with Finn while he's in town. We're having dinner at our favorite Indian restaurant when my phone pings with the chime I've assigned to Lola. My dick jumps like the fucker's been trained. Pavlov's dick.

I hit ignore so I can give my brother my entire focus. "Have you thought any more about my proposal?" he asks, just as I take a bite of the eggplant bharta.

He has to wait while I chew. Finally, I answer, "I have."

"And?"

Setting down the fork, I take a beat, exhale. "It's tempting."

He grins. It's a precursor-type smile, one that says he likes where this is going. "It's always been your goal, Nick."

"It has." His proposal aligns with my big plans. Not much holds me back, but I like to do my research.

"So? What do you think?" he prompts, picking up his fork to snag a bite of chana masala.

My phone pings again before I can answer.

Finn arches a brow, glancing at the device. "That's definitely a hookup."

I do my best to keep a straight face as I silence my alerts. "It's nothing."

He snorts. "Bullshit."

But I don't want to give him an opening into the topic of Lola. Not now. Not when the ammunition is too good—me unable to stop thinking about a woman I saw once.

Ha. You're doing more than thinking. You're texting with her. A LOT.

"It's nothing," I say crisply, shutting him down with the tone our dad used to end a conversation when we were kids. The one my brother and I both use in business now.

Finn acquiesces with a nod. "Fair enough. We'll stick to the proposal."

I focus on a particularly appealing aspect. "I think I could convince my son to work with us," I say. "I've been talking to him about doing some marketing for the firm."

Finn's green eyes spark with intrigue. "Oh yeah? What does he say?"

I scratch my jaw, hopeful but cautious. "He seems... open to it."

With a gregarious grin—that's Finn's go-to smile—he leans back in the chair and stretches out his arms wide as if embracing the idea. "Do it. Do it. Do it."

"Let me think about it tonight," I say, as if my answer wasn't always going to be yes.

"Asshole," he mutters.

I enjoy his frustration and finish my eggplant bharta.

We finish dinner and say goodnight. Back at my flat, I jump on my texts as soon as the door swings closed. We switched from DM to text recently, and I'm dying to know what Lola's double pings were about.

> Lola: I know you've been wanting to see my exercise clothes. Thought you'd enjoy.

There's a shot of her folded laundry stacked on her bed next to pillows in silver, gold, and sapphire blue. I'm dying for a shot of her, but I haven't asked. The delayed gratification game is too fun.

> Nick: Nice pillows.

> Lola: You like my pillows?

> Nick: I really do.

> Lola: The color?

I unknot my tie as I type with one thumb. It's hot in here now. Tropical levels.

> Nick: No, Lola. Not the color.

> Lola: Then what, Nick?

> Nick: I like imagining you lying on them tonight. How your hair would look spilled out across them. How your face would look blissed out.

> Lola: Is that something you want to see?

> Nick: Very much.

I set the phone on my bare coffee table, trading it for my laptop. I take the computer out to the balcony and park my ass at the little table overlooking the hustle and bustle of Knightsbridge six floors below.

There, I review Finn's proposal. I've got to focus on these terms and not let anything cloud my decision-making.

Not a photo of Lola that, god willing, might arrive soon.

Not on those convos.

Not on my own wild thoughts of that woman.

I spend thirty minutes reading the terms again, but when my son's ringtone trills from inside, I jump up and rush to answer.

"Hey there, kiddo. What's going on?"

"Hey, Dad. Not much. Just trying to unpack."

I return to the balcony, phone pressed to my ear. "You hate unpacking."

"With a passion," he says.

I smile, remembering how he'd live out of boxes for weeks whenever we moved. Which was a lot.

"So I'm your procrastination?"

"Lucky you," he deadpans.

"Lucky me, indeed."

I hear him shuffle around the apartment he's subletting for the month and picture him opening boxes. I want to ask if he's thought more about my offer, but he does best when he comes to me. I have to be strategic and wait for my pitch.

Instead, we chat about baseball, and whether the New York Comets can beat the San Francisco Cougars until, finally, he says, "I think I'm in. Like, on a trial basis, if that's okay?"

I punch the sky. "That's great."

Later—much later—as I'm reading a book on my phone in the dark, a text arrives with a picture attached.

I suck in a breath through my teeth as I slide open the message.

It's only the side of her face, barely even a profile shot. But it's clear what she's doing.

She understood the assignment perfectly, and I don't look away for a good, long, satisfying time.

A few weeks later—after a signature from me and a signature from my brother—I send a very direct text to Lola.

No flirting, no teasing, no pics. Just a request.

> Nick: Can I call you?

> Lola: Of course.

My wingtips echo in my nearly empty flat as I pace, waiting for her to pick up my call. I've got a meeting to attend in an hour, so I'm still dressed for business.

"Hey," she says, and her voice is like dopamine. I'm feeling good everywhere from that sensual, feminine sound.

"Hey, beautiful," I say.

"Hey, you," she says, then laughs, embarrassed. "I guess I said that already."

Ah, hell, she's so endearing when she's a bit awkward. "Yeah, but I like hearing your voice."

"You do?" She sounds delighted.

"I do," I say, then I don't fuck around. I go straight for the prize. "Can I take you out next week on that second date? I'm going to be in New York."

She's quiet for a few seconds, but I can hear her breathe, and if a breath could sound excited, hers does.

"But it's our *third* date, Nick," she says, all seductive and bold.

"I stand corrected."

"And on our third date, you better take me out and then take *me*."

I groan, a rumble that I feel all the way in my balls. This woman. "Count on it."

We make plans, then my phone pings. As we talk, I open the photo and groan my approval. She's in her apartment, stretched out on a red chaise longue, wearing a white tank top, biting the corner of her sexy lips.

"Look at you," I rasp. "You're a fucking goddess. I don't know how I'm going to last through dinner with you."

"You'll make it through dinner because you enjoy foreplay so much."

She knows me well already. "I really fucking do," I say, then I amend that statement. Personalize it. "With you, beautiful. *With you*."

"Same...Want to switch to FaceTime?"

I say yes so goddamn fast. Moments later, I'm lying on my bed while she asks me a crucial question: "What do you want to do to me when you see me?"

She likes it when I take my time, so I cock my head, gazing at her lush body. "Why don't you slide your hand down your stomach and play with those pretty panties? It'll help me think."

She complies, her fingers teasing at the silky fabric. "Is this giving you dirty thoughts about me?"

I groan, then answer, "Filthy ones. It's definitely

helping me along. But maybe take off that tank, beautiful."

Her white top flies off, then her bra. I hiss at the sight of her full breasts, those dusky-rose nipples already hard. "Thinking more, Nick?"

"I'd like to bite those perky nipples, then suck on them till you squirm."

She writhes, her hand sliding into her panties. Soon, she's putting on a show for me. Panting, moaning, begging. "More. What else, Nick?"

That's so fucking easy. I miss her sweetness badly. "I'd pull you on top of me and tell you to sit on my face." My cock thumps against my pants. He likes that idea.

Her carnal moan tells me she does too. "I want that," she says, with desperation that makes my dick even harder.

"You'd grind that sweet pussy against my mouth," I rasp as I undo my pants.

Her eyes flutter closed, and she rocks her hips faster, murmuring *yes, god yes*.

"I'd lick and kiss you. Devour you," I say, gripping my cock to get some goddamn relief. I stroke as I paint a dirty picture. "I'm dying to taste you again. To hold those hips and eat you while you fuck my face."

The pictures...Dear god, the erotic pictures flipping before me—her grinding on me in a week, and her fucking herself right now—are driving me wild. My fist is flying. "I want you to ride my face till I can't breathe."

"Nick," she moans, then arches her back, crying out as I give her a fifth orgasm.

It's breathtaking to watch.

Then, it's mind-numbing to feel as my own arousal takes over, a climax barreling mercilessly through me.

When we've caught our breath, I excuse myself and go wash my hands, then I return to our FaceTime, my pants still unzipped.

"That's one of my favorite things," she says in a sexy confession.

"Getting off? Yeah, me too."

With a naughty smile, she shakes her head. "My go-to is gifs of men or women touching themselves."

That's too hot. "Yeah?"

She nods. "I like to watch pleasure. When I watch women, I imagine it's me and you're doing dirty things that make me want to touch myself. When I watch men, I picture you, getting off to me."

My throat grows dry. "I swear you're going to make me ready to go again," I growl.

"Good," she says with a satisfied grin. "I've been thinking about you *a lot* lately."

"Every night. Every morning," I agree. I don't know that I can survive her sensuality, but I will try. Too soon, I have to say goodbye. "I'll see you Friday night. We'll go to Hugo's. I'll make a reservation, and I'll get a car and pick you up."

"I can't wait," she says.

When I see her, I'll tell her more about me. The things I haven't shared yet. Things about my family. Things about my plans.

Like the fact that I'm not only coming to New York for a weekend.

I'm relocating there, merging my VC firm with my brother's under the name Strong Ventures, and I just bought a new place in Gramercy Park—a penthouse apartment overlooking the city.

That's where I intend to take her after our dinner. There I'll fuck her to her sixth, seventh, eighth orgasm, and then some.

13

A HINT AND A HEADLINE

Layla

My mom doesn't spend much time on the Upper East Side if she can avoid it.

But sometimes she has to visit our former neighborhood for meetings, or, like today, for a quick lunch appointment with moi before she sees her stylist on Madison.

I brace myself for a new set-up. Surely, she's had enough time now to flick through her Rolodex of families she trusts—Lennoxes, Christies, or Bettencourts.

But I'm not agreeing to a date when I'm seeing Nick tomorrow night, so I'll tell her I'm too busy with work.

With that bulwark in mind, I head into Patricia's Hole in the Wall. The lowbrow name is ironic. The place is owned by one of Mom's sorority sisters, and with oak walls and deep green booths with backgammon boards, it's as old money as you can get.

The Tryst

At the hostess stand, a perky brunette smiles, showing off straight white teeth. She's new here. "How can I help you?"

"I'm meeting Anna Mayweather. Party of two."

"Mayweather," she says, repeating the name. A second later, recognition dawns in her eyes. Then, shock. "Oh. *Mayweather*. You're Layla Mayweather."

She's not recognized me as the heiress to a lipstick line. In this kind of bar, money is presumed, it doesn't surprise. This is something else.

Six years after my father's murder, you'd think I'd be used to the stares. I mostly am, but I still don't like it. Her thoughts might as well be plastered on her face.

You were the one who walked in on your father's murder. You saw his business partner holding the weapon.

Then the question everyone wants to ask but no one ever dares—*what was that like*?

Knowing what hell is like can't prepare you for the flames.

I paste on a Mona Lisa smile, revealing nothing. "Yes, I'm Layla. Is Anna here?"

"Not yet, but I'd be so happy to show you to her table," the brunette says. There's an apology in her tone and then on her tongue. "I didn't mean to make you..." she fumbles. "I just meant..."

But she can't even say *uncomfortable* as she escorts me to a table. She just exudes her own discomfort.

"No worries," I say brightly. It's easier than holding a grudge.

I take a minute to reset, trying to put the encounter behind me and focus on happy things—like my sexy date tomorrow night. It'll be sex, and fun, and fantastic company, and that's all.

A few minutes later, Mom arrives, click-clacking toward me on Louboutins. "Darling. So lovely to see you," she says, then hugs me when I rise to greet her.

Once we're seated again, she touches my arm, her expression hopeful. "I desperately need your help. I have to give a speech before the whole company next week. I want to look accessible to the young people we've hired recently. I brought some pics of potential outfits to show you. Do you mind?"

"I don't mind at all," I say, then I look at photos on her phone throughout most of the meal.

It's a welcome change from dating machination.

When lunch ends, she heads to see her stylist, then sends me a shot of a pink pantsuit. *I picked this one!*

It's not at all what I suggested for her. She'll never wear it again, either, and in a month, it'll be in a thrift shop.

Looks great, I say, since it's easier than asking why she didn't pick the one I recommended.

But the outfit's inevitable future also gives me an idea.

As I walk to my next appointment, skull rings on, poised if I need to use them, I text Harlow and Jules and ask them to meet me tonight at my favorite thrift shop.

* * *

That evening, T-minus twenty-four hours until date time, I'm checking out the new arrivals at Champagne Taste in the Village, hunting for something to wear tomorrow night when I see Nick.

Harlow flicks through satiny tops while Jules fastidiously dismisses sundress after sundress. I scour the blouses, stopping at a pale pink short-sleeved one with tiny black polka dots.

"Oh, that's perfect for your pinup style," Harlow says approvingly.

Jules seconds the assessment with a firm *yes*, then studies the garment with quizzical eyes. "And you know that has never been worn."

Harlow chimes in with, "And it's hardly going to be worn on Layla at all."

"I hate you," Jules mutters.

I laugh as I head for the dressing room like I'm floating on a cloud of pre-date fun. But I haven't seen Nick in three months. What if things are different with him here in Manhattan? What if we don't vibe like we did in Miami? That was a bubble of heat and sex and flirt. This is my life. I was born in Manhattan. Wherever I go, I run into people I know.

And people who know me.

I plan to tell Nick my real name tomorrow night, in any case. Let him know I'm *that* Layla Mayweather, the daughter of makeup empress Anna Mayweather, founder, creator, and CEO of the makeup giant Beautique.

But if I'm lucky, Nick won't have heard what happened to John Mayweather. My father was a defense attorney, not a celebrity, so his shocking murder is more of a salacious New York society thing. An *if you know, you know* tale.

I know it all.

And all at once, memories flash brutally in front of me.

That night.

My home.

The ride in the ambulance.

I shudder as the images slam into my mind like a tsunami wave, crashing brutally, battering me.

I gulp in air, hardly hearing the gentle knock on the dressing room door.

Then it comes again, more insistent.

It breaks my anti-daydream.

I don't remember unlatching the door, but Harlow's inside the cramped cubicle, setting a hand on my arm. "You okay?"

My throat squeezes. Too tight. A noose.

Breathe, Layla. Just breathe.

And I do. I breathe, and I breathe, and I breathe like Carla taught me in the countless therapy sessions I attended in high school, then in college too. Soon, the images recede.

"It's been a while," I whisper.

"I know," Harlow says gently. "Do you need anything? Water? Want to sit down? Listen to music?"

I tip my forehead to the door. "Does Jules think I'm a freak?"

Harlow shakes her head. "No. I told her I was going

to check on the shirt, and she said she had to answer an email anyway."

Jules's professional voice floats from somewhere outside the door. "Thank you so much for the information on the foreign rights. Full stop. We'll review this shortly. Full stop."

I smile at the normalcy, the sheer Jules normalcy. "She's dictating emails."

"She never stops working," Harlow says.

I take another breath then turn to my friend, worry digging into my bones once more. "What if it comes up tomorrow night? The hostess at Patricia's Hole in the Wall gave me the *OMG it's you* face today."

Harlow rubs my shoulder sympathetically. "You'll deal with it with grace or humor or pain. Whatever feeling you feel." A squeeze of my arm now. "And remember, you don't have to tell him. You don't have to talk about anything you don't want to talk about."

One more big inhale.

Jules's voice carries once again, the cool, modulated response to another note calming me. As she dictates, I'm struck by a realization. My new friend has never poked for details or prodded for insight. She hasn't asked about my dad, or my mom.

That's been one of the best parts of this blooming friendship. Maybe it can be that easy with Nick, too. He's in London. Surely, he doesn't know.

I take Harlow's hand and exit the dressing room, leaving the persistent worries behind.

It's time to get ready for my date.

I pose in front of my friends. "Yes or no?" I do a

spin, awaiting a verdict, letting myself enjoy this pre-date ritual. Dating is like Christmas. You don't just put up your tree the night before Santa comes down the chimney. You do it earlier, so you can enjoy the twinkling lights with anticipation.

Jules fixes me with a serious stare, studying the blouse like it's a script she's evaluating for Bridger's production company, maybe something that needs an edit or a revision. "What if you did this?" She undoes the top black button, then the next one. "What if you wear a black corset? Do you have one?"

I shake my head. I haven't ventured beyond pretty bra and panty sets.

Jules smiles authoritatively. "Go to You Look Pretty Today. You'll want the Valentina corset. I'll call the owner and tell her to put one aside in your size."

I blink. "Seriously?"

Jules brooks no argument. "Then pair it with a skirt, jeans, whatever you want. But a corset is a statement if you wear it under the pink and black polka dots. It's a hint and a headline at the same time. And you need a statement top when a hot older man who flies first class, dines at Hugo's, orders town cars, and eats you out like you're his main course comes to town."

Harlow's mouth parts in an O of disbelief that Jules said that. I kind of can't believe it, either, and I laugh in surprise.

"Jules," Harlow asks curiously, "where was *this* Jules when we worked together once upon a time?"

The stylish brunette just tosses a sly smile Harlow's

way, then she fingers the pearl button on her own white sweater. "She is right there underneath the twin set."

But before I seduce Nick, I'll at least tell him my real name. I'll tell him where I come from. The kind of home I was raised in. That's all I can plan for now, but it feels right to share that much.

He's earned it.

I buy the shirt, then toss the bag over my shoulder when we head out. Jules waggles her phone. "I called the You Look Pretty Today owner while you were buying the top. The Valentina corset is waiting for you. A gift from Harlow and me," she says.

I throw my arms around each of them, then I wave goodbye and head to the subway, shedding my fears about tomorrow, deciding I can handle any conversation or question that comes my way.

* * *

With the hint and the headline tucked into my bag, I make my way to Neon Diner.

Maybe the corset is already giving me superpowers, because I fire off a text to Nick as I walk up Madison.

> Lola: I shopped for tomorrow.
>
> Nick: I can't wait to see what's under your clothes.
>
> Lola: Did I say I was shopping for underthings?

> Nick: You didn't have to.

> Lola: Maybe I shopped for overthings.

> Nick: You didn't.

With a buzz under my skin, I pull open the door to Neon Diner. A voice behind me says, "Let me guess—you went shopping."

Tucking my phone away, I let go of the door and turn around in time to swat David's shoulder with my bag from Champagne Taste. "You say that like I'm a clothes horse."

"Well, you don't exactly wear garbage bags in your videos," David says, then holds open the door, like a gentleman.

Like someone else I'll be seeing soon.

I chide myself. *Focus on your friends right now. Tomorrow night is all about Nick. Tonight is David time.*

We breeze inside and tell the woman at the hostess stand that we're looking for a booth. She points us toward a spot in the back.

"Sidebar," I say as we head to the booth, "My friend Raven once made a super-hot dress from a garbage bag. She's a fashion designer. We went to business school together, and she's all about low-impact creation. You'd like her." Then an idea springs, fully-formed, into my mind. "I could ask her to make some threads for the auction. Like to donate to a winner."

He whistles in appreciation then bows dramatically.

"I'm not worthy of you," he says. His hair doesn't flop over this time. He cut it a few weeks ago. Trimmed the beard too. He's rocking the banker style.

"That is true. So I'll let you pay tonight," I say.

"Happily, because I have an expense account now." He shifts gears once we slide into the booth and points toward the bag by my side. "I see a black satiny thing peeking out of there. Does that mean you've got a hot date this weekend?"

Not that I'm trying to hide the corset, but I didn't mean to advertise my lingerie. I tuck it back into the canvas bag. But the date itself isn't a secret. That's one of the nice things about truly being friends with your ex. We don't need to hide what we're up to romantically. "Maybe I do."

"So, 'fess up. Who are you cheating on me with?"

The man in my texts. Is he even in town yet? I've no idea when he's due to arrive, and I like the mystery. "Just this sexy, powerful man I met a few months ago at a conference."

That felt good to say. Freeing even. I'm not seeing Bryce Fancypants the Third, or Carson Winters of the East Hamptons Winters. I'm seeing a man my mother would lose her mind over. "He's coming to town for work," I add. "He wanted to see me while he was here."

The twinkle in David's eye says he knows what I'll be up to in twenty-four hours. He gestures to my clothing bag, but then the waitress swings by with water. Once she takes our orders, David lifts his glass. "I'll drink to your lingerie being ripped off tomorrow night."

That seems likely, so I clink back. Then we get to work reviewing the auction plans. "I've got tennis lessons on the auction list now. Mama Rose corralled someone at the club to auction those off," he says.

"And Harlow used her pull at the gallery to convince her favorite artist to donate a sketch drawing. Zara Clementine is a huge animal lover, so it's great."

"And I asked my dad if he could help out. He's well-connected so he might be able to scrounge up some good donations."

"Ooh, Daddy Bancroft. Work it," I say, using the nickname David gave his father back in college.

David's phone buzzes, and he shifts his focus to his text app. "You should meet him. Daddy Bancroft," he says, but he sounds distracted as he reads his messages.

I don't know much about his father. I only know a bit about his mom because she's friends with mine. David's dad lived in California, last I heard, but we didn't talk about our parents that much during college, and, frankly, we don't now.

His phone buzzes again. After a quick glance, he waggles it at me. "It's Cynthia. She just got off work. Her boss is being a dick. Do you mind if I give her a quick call?"

"Go, go," I say, shooing him away.

He scurries out of the diner and onto the street. While he's gone, I open the thread with Nick, then tap out a reply to his cocky *you didn't note.*

> Lola: I guess you'll find out tomorrow night.

I hit send, and a few seconds later, the hair on the back of my neck stands on end. The skin on my arms tingles. I catch the scent of falling snow and freshly cut wood and the sound of wingtips on the linoleum floor of the diner coming closer.

Maybe my sense memory is conjuring up Nick because I'm texting him. Maybe I'm so caught up in waiting for tomorrow night that I'm imagining the way he smells, sounds, walks.

But when I look up, my breath catches, right along with my curiosity.

He's here.

And he's walking toward me with wild curiosity in his eyes, like he can't believe his luck either. He's wearing black slacks and a sky-blue shirt that hugs his pecs and his arms. His purple tie is loosened. His beard is just a touch thicker than it was when we first met. My mouth waters as I remember how that scruff feels against my thighs. Then, our gazes lock, and his hazel eyes are full of delicious thoughts.

I can't hide my flirty smile.

Nick Adams looks even better than he did three months ago, especially when his lips curve into the most knowing grin I've ever seen. "Hey, beautiful."

I nearly melt. Christmas has come early.

14

DADDY BANCROFT

Layla

Sure, I run into people I know in New York every day. But Nick is the last person I expected to see at this diner.

What are the chances I'd bump into him on…wait… is this his first day in town? I'm staring up at him next to me as I ask: "When did you land in New York?"

"Earlier today. I've been in meetings since I touched down. Maybe I should have…" He shakes his head like he's dismissing his remarks about being busy. He drags a thumb along his jawline but stares at me as he goes, like he's imagining touching me with that thumb. He eyes me up and down. "You look…"

He can't seem to finish the thought.

But I can. "So do you," I say, sounding as intoxicated as he does.

Yes, the vibe is still strong between us. Maybe even

stronger. I suppose that's what weeks of texting and FaceTiming will do for people. I embrace the corset superpowers even more. I stand, step close to him, give him a chaste hug.

Oops. I lied.

It's not so chaste at all, since the second my breasts brush against his chest, he growls. Low, carnal, just for me.

"Mmm. I like surprises, and you're a very good surprise," he murmurs, then slides a hand down my back, settling possessively at the base of my spine. He presses harder, as if declaring *mine*.

I feel like his. I didn't expect to want that, but now I do. Perhaps because I feel like his in a passionate way, a sensual way, even under the fluorescent lights in this retro diner, with "My Sharona" playing overhead.

With his hard body a magnet for mine, I have another answer to my earlier worries—things aren't different now that we're out of Miami. *They're better.* Stronger. We didn't just happen because of the heat, the scene, the decadence of South Beach.

It was the decadence of us.

But if he keeps holding me like he wants to strip me naked tonight, I might turn into a puddle on the linoleum floor tiles.

Or come.

On that sexy but sobering thought, I wrench away. He darts his gaze to the entrance then back to me as if weighing something, he asks in a dark whisper, "What are you doing later?"

Feeling bold and daring, I answer, "I believe the question is—*who* are you doing later?"

Another groan, then he says, "Come over. I'll text you. I want to see you tonight and tomorrow."

Forget silver and gold. I'm diamonds and platinum. I've never felt so wanted. I've never known how good it would feel to be wanted like this. I've never understood why people would climb proverbial mountains for a lover, but at this moment, I get it.

I want to clear my whole damn schedule for this man and his desire—a desire that's taken hold of me, too, and won't let go. "I'll be there," I say. "Just name the time."

Then he breathes out hard, rough. He jerks his gaze to the door again, assessing something. I'm not sure what though.

I peer outside, looking for David. He's still pacing, his back to us. He looks caught up in his call. I should say goodbye to Nick, though, so I can give David my attention when he's done with Cynthia.

But when I look back at Nick to tell him I'm busy with a friend right now, that sexy, sultry glimmer in his eyes is long gone. He looks like…a hard-ass negotiator.

Hmm. I gird myself for whatever's coming next.

"Lola," he says, then scratches the back of his neck. "I need to go. I'm meeting someone here."

My senses tingle but not in a good way. "Why would you need to go if you're meeting that person here?"

My heart gallops, powered by fear and worry. Did he lie, after all, about not being married?

He shakes his head, swallows, then runs a hand

through his hair like he's rearranging his thoughts. "I'm...meeting...my—"

But he stops when footsteps interrupt—the familiar clomp of Vans. Then, a warm, bright voice says, "Dad!"

What?

I freeze, thoroughly confused.

But David's not at all thrown off by the powerful older man standing next to me. He beams, and the hair on my arms stands on end.

"Oh, man," David groans, "I wanted to introduce the two of you." But he sounds less disappointed and more delighted, which makes zero sense. "But I see you've already met my friend Layla. Layla, this is my dad."

I can't breathe.

I can't catch air.

I can't even move.

I'm a horrible actress after all. Because my face is numb with the shock of this news.

Somehow, I swallow down the bitter taste in my throat and then point to the man next to me. The man I bought the corset for. The man David teased me about cheating on him with.

I gulp out the horrible truth: "He's...Daddy Bancroft?"

15

NO COINCIDENCES

Nick

Way back in high school statistics class, I learned that in a room of at least twenty-three people, there's a little more than a fifty percent chance that two of them will have the same birthday.

It's not entirely a coincidence. It's a mathematical law that says life is random, the world is unpredictable, and when shit happens, it's rarely fate. It's probability, statistics, even inevitability.

There's a certain sick logic to this latest twist. We orbit in the same circles—tech, money, risk, New York.

But even though I'm a goddamn fucking student of the likelihood of coincidences, I'm still standing here, scratching my head like this just can't be.

My Lola is *his* Layla?

The Layla my son's been building his charity with? Layla, the college girlfriend he's still tight with? Layla is the one my son texted me about a little while ago and wanted me to meet?

But I don't need to ask again to be sure. She is clearly his Layla, and I need to deal with reality, stat. I fucked my son's ex-girlfriend, who's now his pal. I fucked her several times, including on the phone last week. And I need to manage this situation like it's a sensitive business deal.

First, with due diligence.

Did he see us hug like lovers? Maybe. But if so, I can recover, starting now. "It's a pleasure to officially meet you, Layla," I say, trying to mask the what-the-fuckery in my voice.

Like, why the hell did she keep her real name from me?

She extends a hand, too, and everything about this moment is a terrible lie—one I'm telling in front of my son.

I am a bad, bad daddy.

"Good to meet you. I've heard so much about you," she says, the picture of Upper East Side charm.

I've never heard that tone from her before. It's not even a professional tone. It's more like a polished one.

Why the hell would you have heard it? You've never met her on her turf. You don't even know who Lola, or Layla, really is.

"And David has told me about you," I say, the falsehood strangling me.

The truth is I know very little. I was living in San Francisco when David went to college here in New York. He had attended prep school in San Francisco, since Rose had been working there when David was a teen. I stayed there when he went back east, and I was still working in San Francisco when he told me one night on the phone that he was dating his college tutor.

She's a great girl, super smart and pretty, and I've got a huge crush on her... Then a few months later he said, *Yeah, Layla and I decided we were better off as friends.*

That was it. Fast forward to a week ago, when he accepted my job offer on the condition he could still work on his charity, the one his pal had been helping him launch with the first fundraiser. *She's a badass, and she's helping me with* A Helping Paw.

So, yeah. I knew three things.

But when life hits you with the law of mathematics, you need to deal, not whine. With intros done, David flops down into the booth. "We just ordered. But take a look, and you can get some food too," he tells me.

Lola—I mean, Layla—takes her seat across from us, sitting primly straight, like she's posing for a family portrait.

It's showtime. I sit and peer around for a server to ask for a menu. David laughs, thrusting a Lucite frame at me. "Dad, it's on your phone."

Great. Fucking great. I look old and like a tech loser. But I know how QR codes work, thank you very much. I just...wasn't thinking.

"Right," I say, then take the frame so I can scan it. But screw it.

I know how menus work, too, and if you've been to one diner you've been to them all. When the server stops by seconds later, I ask for a house salad and a chicken sandwich.

"Perfect. I'll add that to the ticket," she says and then takes off.

It's the three of us again in the most awkward meeting of a kid's ex-girlfriend ever.

But David doesn't seem to notice. Maybe Layla and I are great actors, since my son says, "I kept thinking last week that you should meet Layla, since she has this baller makeup app."

I know. I watched her videos. I flirted with her on her app. "That so?" I ask, like this is the first I'm learning of her business.

David gestures to Layla, giving her the floor. "Tell him about The Makeover app. He's a VC. I can't believe I didn't think about introducing the two of you sooner, but Daddy Bancroft was in London, and he does tech, not content," David says, then stops short.

Maybe realizing what he just called me—by my ex-wife's last name. Like Layla did earlier. "So, this is a thing? You call me Daddy Bancroft?"

"It's tongue in cheek," David explains, like he was caught stealing from my wallet. "I only call you that in front of my friends."

We don't have the same last name, and that wasn't my choice. That was the Bancroft family choice when I knocked up Rose, the Park Avenue debutante, fresh out of high school.

"I take it your friends don't know where the *Adam* comes from then, David Adam Bancroft." I say his full name a little more sharply than I intended.

And...shit.

That won't do.

I've got to get a grip on my annoyance. This won't do me any good with my son. I want him to love working with me. I want his life to be so much easier than mine when I was his age—twenty-one. I never want him to worry about where his next meal is coming from.

I try again, not just tempering my reaction but kicking it to the curb. "But hey, nicknames are cool," I add, then smile at him before I flash a smile I absolutely don't feel at Layla.

The woman who lied about her name.

If she lied about that, what else would she lie about? That I was her first?

A dark cloud settles over me. My shoulders tense. I clench my fists.

Then, my son's phone buzzes again. He grabs it, checks the screen. "Cyn's having a rough night. I'll be right back."

"Of course." I scoot out, let him go, and sit back down across from...the woman I don't know at all.

She stares at me like I'm a snake.

I feel like one.

I tilt my head, curve my lips, and say, "Hi, *Lola*. Oh wait. I meant...*Layla*." Then I flash her an asshole grin.

She doesn't bite. She's cool. Cooler than me even. When she speaks, she's as poised as she was moments ago. "Hi, *Daddy*."

Ouch.

Fine, fine. I didn't tell her I had a kid. I grit my teeth,

annoyed she's right to fling that omission at me. Time to own it. "Yes, I have a kid," I say, shoulders square, chin up. I'm proud of my son. I can't make my relationship with him seem like a shameful secret.

Like Rose's parents did

Like…I did in Miami.

"I shouldn't have tried to hide it from you," I say.

The intensity in her expression tells me she's adding up details, like the phone call I covered up that morning. "I guess he's who called you in your room," she says, nailing me with my outright lie.

"That was David. Not my brother," I admit.

"Why didn't you just tell me then?"

Why? Because I didn't know her, and I wasn't in the mood. But she lied too, so I toss her fib right back at her. "Why didn't *you* tell me your real name?"

"Why didn't you tell me you had a son?" she says, pressing again.

"It didn't come up," I say, defensive. Because it's easier to be annoyed than to explain I planned to tell her tomorrow night at Hugo's. When I planned to tell her, too, that I've moved back to Manhattan. But I didn't want to overwhelm her or scare her off. I don't want to put my cards on the table—that I was worried I'd send her running. If I let on, she'll know how much I was looking forward to seeing her tomorrow and asking her out for another date, then another, then another. I focus on Miami instead. "Your name came up though. *A lot*," I say.

She folds her arms across her chest. "You're really

annoyed I didn't tell you my *legal* name? When I gave you my business name? At a business conference?"

I'm not in the mood for logic right now. Not when my pulse surges annoyingly fast around her. "Were you planning on never seeing me again? Is that why you didn't tell me your name? Because you didn't want to see me again?"

"No," she snaps.

I've got a million more questions, but out of the corner of my eye, I spot our server heading straight for us.

Seconds later, she arrives with a sad-looking salad. "Here's your salad, sir," she says.

Why am I always a sir? But I can't very well call the waitress ma'am or I'm the dick.

"Thanks," I say, reading her name tag. "*Taylor.*"

"You're welcome," she says, then turns on her heels.

Once she's out of earshot, Layla pounces. "And how can you say I didn't want to see you again when we've been texting non—"

But we're not alone. David's back, so there's no way we're finishing this conversation now. I let him into the booth as he says, "Cynthia had to park in the far corner in her lot, so I stayed on the phone with her while she walked into her apartment."

I pat him on the shoulder. "Good man," I say, then I pick up my fork and stab a piece of wilted lettuce. I take a bite. It sucks.

A minute later, the server is back with the rest of the food, and once we tuck in, David draws a deep breath, then says, "So, Layla, like I said earlier, I asked my dad to help with the auction, and I'm stoked he's up for it. We can all put our heads together on it for the next few weeks. Plus, I'm going to be working at his firm. Not doing money stuff though. I'll be doing the marketing, since that's more my speed, and it'll help with my side hustle." Then he backpedals. "Well, trying it out for a few months."

Layla's brow knits.

"Longer, I hope. I plan to convince you," I say to David, patting his shoulder again. *This* is the relationship I should focus on anyway—the one with my kid.

Layla lifts her fork to take a bite of her pasta. But she's staring at David as if he no longer adds up. "In London? You're going to London?"

David laughs. "Dude, no," he says to her. Then, it's as if his thoughts just snagged on her last comment. He tilts his head, like he's replaying what she just said. Maybe catching her slip. "Did I tell you he lived in London?"

C'mon, Layla. You've got this.

With a sweet smile, she says, "Yes. When you said he was going to help out, you mentioned he lived there," Layla says, breezily making it sound like no big deal that she knew that detail about where her friend's dad lived.

I hope her cover-up is only obvious to me.

David must buy it easily, since he just shrugs, like *cool*. Then, he corrects her with, "Nope. I'm not going to London. Daddy Bancroft relocated here."

Layla's fork wobbles in her hand, but she steadies it

before David catches on. "Sounds fun. No more really big ocean in the way."

Ouch.

She's pissed at me. It's not evident in her tone, but it's one hundred percent clear from her word choice —*really big ocean.*

I fucked up.

16

A VERY BAD IDEA

Layla

When the waitress clears the plates and Nick asks for the check, I'm dying to say thanks and leave.

I can't sit here anymore with the man and my friend and this...corset.

I need to beeline for Harlow's and flop face-first onto her couch. Or Ethan's. I don't know. I don't care. I just can't sit across from the man I was dying to see tomorrow night. The man who didn't tell me a thing, it turns out. I hardly know him.

Of course you don't know him. You had a one-night stand and then phone sexted, and he didn't even tell you he was moving here.

Ugh. I can't believe I thought there was more to this thing with him. I felt potential. Possibility. Things I never feel.

I should know better. But good thing I'm learning

now. I try to shove those foolish fantasies far, far away and focus on simple matters, like manners.

"Thank you so much, Mr.—" I stop myself from saying Adams. Nick said earlier it was David's middle name but neither one of them actually said out loud that Adams was Nick's last name. Or did they? My brain is spinning. I don't know what I'm supposed to know. But after the London snafu, I have to be more careful. I definitely don't want to let on at all that Nick was my *fuck date*. Even if David wasn't my ex, he's absolutely my friend, and sleeping with your good friend's father is a very bad idea. That's just too complicated. I play the part of a grateful friend thanking her friend's parent for dinner. "Thank you, Mr. Bancroft. I appreciate you buying dinner."

"It's Nick Adams," he corrects tightly, like I knew he would. But I had no choice.

David's never gone into the finer details of why he has his mom's name rather than his dad's. We've never dwelled on the past or family, mine or his. That was one of the things I liked most about him.

One of the things I still like about him. His focus on the present. But now I wish I had known more.

Like why the hell Nick didn't mention he was moving.

I gather my bag, stuffing the lingerie at the bottom of it, wishing I could return the damn thing. "Thank you, Mr. Adams," I say, using my best Layla Mayweather tone, the one my mother taught me to use in social situations.

"You're welcome, Layla," Nick says, ever the proper *adult*. But something flashes in his eyes.

Like a quick calculation as he opens his wallet. He shifts his attention to David. "Son, can you go pay this up front? To make it easier for them."

"Of course," David says. Nick's speaking his language—being thoughtful about waiters, servers, bartenders and the like.

Nick hands David the credit card. "And get yourself a sandwich for the morning. You only ever eat breakfast if someone orders it, but you need to start eating it before you come to the office. Consider this me ordering you to have breakfast," he says in a commanding, bossy tone, like the one he used on me in bed.

I shiver.

It's still hot.

But I hate how hot it is.

David beams, then grins at his dad, clearly proud, clearly pleased with his pop. *Pop*. This is so weird. "Told you he's the best," David says to me as he squeezes out.

Then he's off, and strategic, smart Nick Adams, who ferried me away from the press scrum at the conference three months ago to ask me out, has once again engineered a moment with me. He wastes no time. "I need to apologize for being a dick," he says.

Wait. What? He's apologizing? That's a thing men do? "What do you mean?"

"When I first arrived. When we first spoke, and I gave you the third degree. I was frazzled. I came here to meet David. He'd texted me and asked me to join, but when I walked in and you were here, I stopped thinking." He gazes at me with heat and fire. "You were so fucking stunning, and all I could think was how badly I wanted to see you tomorrow, to talk to you, to tell you a bunch of things, to get you alone. And then I was thinking how lucky I was to see you tonight."

His vulnerable admissions—both sexy and borderline emotional—chip away at my annoyance and at my hurt.

"And I didn't want to scare you off by telling you I was relocating here," he says as he keeps going, reading my mind. "I planned to tell you tomorrow. I couldn't wait to see you. And then I thought *I can tell her tonight. I can see her tonight too.* And then...all of a sudden, you were Layla. And I was a jerk."

My heart softens from all those lovely admissions. Every single one. "I get it. The whole thing was just...a shock. But you have to know I planned to tell you tomorrow too that Lola's my business name. I wanted you to know who I am and who my mother is."

Just her. That's all I want to reveal for now.

Nick lifts a brow in question. Since he just spilled his truths, I unspool some more of mine. "She runs Beautique, the makeup conglomerate. Well, she's the founder. Anna Mayweather," I say, and that's something at least about my family. Now he knows that much, and the look in his eyes says *holy shit, she founded a wildly successful Fortune 100 company*, rather than *you're that girl from that night*. "And when I started The Makeover, I didn't want to be connected to Anna Mayweather or Beautique. I just wanted to do my own thing. Be my own woman. I funded The Makeover on my own with my own money from my videos, and I brought on a partner in Geeta. She codes. I want this to be all mine, and ours, so when I was in Miami, I was there as Lola Jones. I registered as Lola Jones. I don't want special treatment as Anna's daughter."

There. That's what I wanted to tell him tomorrow. At least I can walk away tonight knowing I've said the most important thing to him, but still I add, "It didn't feel like a lie to me. I am Lola, and I am Layla, and that night with you I wanted to feel like I was just…a woman with a man for the first time."

He steals a glance at the front of the diner, then darts a hand under the table and squeezes my knee. "I'm glad I was your first, beautiful," he says, and there's resolution in his tone, like maybe for a little while earlier he struggled with what was a lie and what was the truth. I'm glad he figured out on his own that I didn't lie about my inexperience.

"Me too," I say, sliding a hand under the table, covering his. In no time, he links our fingers with a desperate grasp.

My insides flutter. I feel warm all over.

"And when I was with you, I didn't want to feel like" —he stops, like the words forming in his throat are uncomfortable. But he pushes through—"I didn't want to be a guy who had a kid. I didn't want to have the inevitable conversation of *yeah, my son's twenty-one, and you can do the math. He was born when I was seventeen, and the only way his mom and I could go to college was if my ex-wife's parents raised him for those four years.*" He winces, then adds, bitterly, "By their rules."

My throat tightens with emotions. I want to hug him. "Oh, Nick," I say, squeezing his fingers tighter under the table. There are details I'm dying to ask about. But I'd only be satisfying my own curiosity. He's told me how he feels—in words and tone. So I say sympathetically, "That's a lot too."

"When I was with you, I just wanted to be a man romancing a woman," he says, almost embarrassed, but then he shrugs, like he's all good with the man he was that night. With the choice he made.

And the thing is—I'm good with it too. I run my thumb along his finger, savoring this stolen, under-the-table touch. "You did. Romance me, that is," I say, my chest fluttering, my heart beating so fast. From the memory, still fresh and hot, and from the here and now.

This is an unfamiliar rush. Though it's dangerous, too, this fizzy feeling. But it can't last, right? So I'm safe. But as he touches me, I hardly feel safe from emotions, and I hardly want to.

I just want this moment to last a little longer. I want to live in this warm, buzzy land some more.

"I think about that night all the time, Layla," Nick says, and it's the first time tonight my name on his tongue has sounded inviting. Like the way he used to say my name. I savor the sound of it. "And I've been caught up in you for the last week too. I can't get you out of my head."

"Same for me," I say softly, but there's regret in my tone too.

There's regret in his as well.

We both know what happens next.

Someone has to say it though. "And now we'll be... working together on this fundraiser," I say, "with your son."

A terribly sad smile comes my way. "Yeah."

It's an admission. There is no date tomorrow night. And I can't ever let David know his dad *was* my tomorrow night, so I wince, but say the hard thing. "We'll just pretend Miami never happened."

He's quiet for several wistful seconds.

"What night in Miami?" he asks, playing along, but I can tell from his eyes that it hurts him too, this charade.

That night already feels like a distant memory.

When we leave, Nick offers me a ride home. I turn it down, but they both wait till my Lyft arrives, father and son. A former lover and a former boyfriend.

But only one of them will likely stay in my life. The one who's a friend.

When I reach my building a few minutes later, I say hi to Sylvester, then Grady, then head to my sixth-floor home and turn on all the lights and deadbolt my door. Then I text *that one*. Telling David it was fun to meet his father.

I don't text my friend's father.

He doesn't text me either.

17

YOU WERE RIGHT

Nick

The next day I'm too busy to think of Layla. At least, that's what I tell myself as I finish setting up my spacious new place in Gramercy Park, making sure everything meets my specs.

There's not much for me to do, though, since Finn's wife insisted I use a friend of hers who's an interior designer. I didn't want to argue with Marilyn and piss her off more, so I said yes to using Ginny, even though furniture is not my thing.

Things are not my thing.

But I had nothing to move since I'd rented all my furniture in London, and I do need something to sit on and a bed to crash in.

Ginny found me all that and sent photos to me, and I signed off. Now, she shows me around, telling me all the details about the open-plan kitchen, the couch in the expansive living room, and the minimal artwork on the walls. "I wanted to make sure all eyes were drawn to the natural art," she says, gesturing to the floor-to-ceiling windows in the living room that offer a commanding view of the lower half of Manhattan.

"It's a stunning view," I say, and I do my damnedest *not* to think of bending Layla over the back of the couch, curling her hair into my fist, and fucking her hard as she enjoys the hell out of the *natural art* view too.

Ginny moves around to the couch, patting the back of it, and I hope she's not reading my thoughts. "And this is made from organic material in a low-impact fashion," she says.

But can it handle high-impact nights?

"Thanks, Ginny. Appreciate you sourcing all these things," I say cordially to the poised designer. She's a handsome woman, in a news-anchor type of way, with a brunette bob that doesn't move.

"I'm so glad it's to your taste, Nick," she says, and my name sounds awfully personal.

But I try not to read into the way she lingers on one syllable. Maybe she's just being friendly. Or friendlier, since she's been a little touchy all along, with her hand on my arm a few times, lots of laughter, and an *oh, that's so funny*.

"Everything is great, Ginny," I say, walking her to the door.

She stands at the exit but doesn't reach for the

handle. She tilts her head, as if waiting for something. Then she laughs and rolls her eyes. "Fine, fine. I'll do it," she says.

Do what?

I smile, a little confused. "My apologies, Ginny. Did I miss something?"

"My number," she says. "Would you like it?"

"I have it," I say. I don't want to be a dick to Marilyn's friend, so I play dumb. "Since we were talking before I arrived."

With a laugh, she sets her hand on my arm again. "Feel free to use it, Nick. And it doesn't even have to be about furniture."

Then she waits for a response.

I keep everything as polite as can be as I say a simple, "Thanks."

Then I shut the door, glad to be alone.

Even if I were interested in Ginny and we had chemistry, I didn't come to New York to date.

Lies. Sweet little lies.

I would date Layla if she weren't my son's ex.

Great. Just great.

There I go again with another Layla fail. I'm failing at *not* thinking of her, so I remind myself why I'm truly back in the city where I grew up. To see my dad and my mom. To spend time with my son. To grow the company and make this newly merged VC firm bigger, better, stronger. To have something to leave my kid with when I leave this world.

I won't leave him with nothing.

I want him to have everything.

All that is *only* part of why I've resisted looking up Layla online since I learned her real name. The bigger issue is I know myself. Know the rabbit holes I can burrow down. The Internet pages I can get sucked into. I've spent enough time watching her videos. I really shouldn't spend any more time checking her out.

Best for me to move forward. I can get addicted to things that have slipped through my fingers. I've done it with companies I've lost out on investing in. I've done it with chances I've missed. I've got an obsessive streak ten miles wide. I sure as shit don't need an obsession with a woman in my life.

As I head to the bedroom suite, I focus on one of my *whys* for being in New York. I dial David, eager to catch up since we didn't have much time last night. "How was breakfast?" I ask as I hang up a few more shirts from suitcases.

"Better than an energy bar. Can you do that every day?"

I'm feeling good about my insistence last night at the diner. Then feeling shitty. It served my selfish purposes, not just my parental ones. To steal time with his friend.

Out of mind. Keep her out of your mind.

"I could also teach you to cook," I say, leaving the bedroom so I can putter around the gleaming new kitchen with its sexy-as-sin stove.

David audibly shudders. "Cooking? What's that?"

"C'mon. You must have cooked during your wilderness trip," I point out as I test the burners.

"Does jerky count as cooking?" Before I can answer, David shouts, "Oh fuck!!!"

"What's going on?" I ask, alarmed from the intensity of his reaction.

"There's a rat in my apartment. It's the size of a racoon."

I don't think twice. "Move out. I've got an extra bedroom."

He doesn't need time to think twice either. "I'll be there tonight."

The next morning, David's conked out on the guest room's bed when I hit the pool a few floors below. After a long workout in the gym, I return to the penthouse and he's still snoozing.

I shower and get dressed for the day then head to the kitchen to make an omelet. As I'm dropping in mushrooms, he saunters out of his room, holding his phone, stretching his arms, then lifting his nose to the sky. "Smells good."

"Want me to teach you how to cook an omelet? My dad taught me when I was seven."

"That's young."

"He made me his sous chef."

"What about Finn?"

"He had to take out the trash," I say.

"Bennies of being the youngest," David says, then leans against the kitchen counter as I cook. "You got better chores."

He returns to his screen. I swear he's obsessed with that thing. "I need to give Layla a hard time about her date," he says, offhand.

I tense at the stove. A sharp bolt of jealousy slams into me. But I try to keep my cool as I say, "Oh yeah?"

Inside I'm thinking, *who the fuck is she dating already?*

David laughs. "She had a date last night with some dude she was into. She was telling me about it at the diner. I have to see if it was as good as she was hoping."

Oh.

Oh, hell yes.

I bite the inside of my cheek. Even with my back to him, I don't want to smile or scowl. Don't want to reveal I was supposed to be the hot date—the man she bought the underthings for. "Cool," I mutter. I can't think of a single other word.

When we eat, I don't ask if she responded. I don't want to appear interested in her dating life. Because my son and my former lover are tight. If he knew she was supposed to go on a date with *some dude*, he'll probably know the next time she goes out with some other dude.

But that guy won't be me.

On that bitter note, I down some coffee then tell him that, tomorrow, I'm going to teach him to cook.

"If you insist," he says.

"I do."

It'll be fun, and it'll take my mind off Layla's dating life.

* * *

One more lap.

My lungs burn, my shoulders scream, but I power through another lap, freestyling to the end of the pool in my building, trying to let go of the night that didn't happen, the woman I can't have.

I finish my fifty-fifth lap, then smack the concrete edge.

I hoist myself out of the water, scanning for the towel I left on a chair beside my building's indoor pool. But it's nowhere to be seen.

I groan.

Fucking Finn.

My phone is missing too. I left it on the table, thinking it'd be safe since I'd reserved the pool area for a solo swim.

I peer around for my older brother, but—no surprise—he's not here. I should never have told him to meet me on the gym level of the building before our dinner. Rookie mistake, giving him the code.

I head for the locker room to grab another towel when the glass door to the pool swings open. Finn strolls in, looking polished and sharp, my missing towel draped over his arm.

"Dude, you're going to be late for our dinner," he calls out.

"I won't be," I say. We both know that would never happen. We're meeting our dad in a couple hours. But first, we'll catch up on work at my place.

"Cocky," he says, then tosses the towel into a bin of dirty towels.

He's such a dick.

I'm not going to grab for the towel and give him the satisfaction. So I stand there dripping wet in only my swimsuit, assessing Finn. His phone's in his hand. My phone too.

I wiggle my fingers. "I'll take the phone now."

He adopts a confused look. "What? These are both mine."

"They're not," I say.

"I have two phones."

"Why would you have two phones?"

He rolls his green eyes. "One is for testing new apps. Obviously."

I appreciate his commitment to the prank. Truly, I do. But a brother's got to do what a brother's got to do.

I grab my phone easily, even as he protests with a *hey now*. Then I take his as well.

"What the hell?"

I toss the phones on a table a few feet away. They clatter lightly, but the alternative is them going in the pool with my brother. I have no choice but to throw him in.

Splash!

He resurfaces, annoyed but laughing while soaked in his fancy duds. I grin too. It's not quite as satisfying as a night with a good woman, but this is definitely the most pleased I've been in days.

* * *

An hour later, we leave my place together, both dry and dressed. David's not here. He's out seeing a friend. I didn't ask who. On the elevator down, I eye Finn's new clothes—jeans and a black Henley. "I would have loaned you something," I deadpan.

He snorts. "As if I'd have taken it."

Instead, he called a nearby men's shop, ordered new threads, and had them delivered in thirty minutes.

I'd have done the same. I'd never give him the satisfaction of wearing his clothes, but it's still fun to offer him mine, even after the fact.

We climb into the black town car waiting at the curb. I tell the driver the address of Antonia's, Dad's favorite Italian spot in Queens.

As the car weaves into traffic, Finn deals me an intense look. "So, Marilyn wants to know why you don't like Ginny," he says, plastering on an irritated grin, but it's not me he's annoyed with.

It's his wife.

Things with Marilyn have been even more strained since Miami. Finn's still trying, going to couples therapy every week. But as far as I can tell, Marilyn's still Marilyn—unhappy with everything.

"I like Ginny fine. As an interior decorator. Which is what I hired her for," I say pointedly, but it's aimed at his nosy wife.

Finn holds up his hands in surrender. "She said you won't go out with Ginny since she's older than you."

"What the fuck?" I demand.

"Yeah, she thinks you only like younger women," Finn adds.

I bristle, even more annoyed. "Where does that come from? I don't have a track record of dating younger women. Rose was my age. Millie too," I say, mentioning my last girlfriend. "Fine, she was three measly years younger. Big deal."

"Exactly," he agrees, then he drops his head against the back of the seat. "Nick..."

He sounds so strained. So exhausted.

I shed all my annoyance. "What is it?"

He lifts his face, meeting my gaze. "She's convinced I'm going to leave her for someone half her age," he says. "What the hell am I supposed to say to *that*?"

"Are you? Is there someone else? Half her age, twice her age, any age?" I ask. If he needs to confess something, I'm glad he's coming to me. Vault and all.

Finn stares at me sharply. "C'mon. You know me," he says.

"I do. Just making sure," I say, then pat his knee.

"The other night, I met up with my friend Tate for dinner. His daughter was there. She's in her mid-twenties, I guess. Marilyn was there too."

His voice is heavy, and I know where this is going.

"Did she accuse you of staring at Tate's daughter the whole night?" I ask.

Finn taps his nose. "Bingo. And, I was not looking at her. I'm disgustingly faithful, and I just want my wife to be happy with me again. Is that so much to ask?"

Poor guy. He tries so hard. "I don't think it's too much," I say.

"I don't either. So I guess her being mad that you're not into Ginny is her way of punishing me," Finn says.

I'm glad he put two and two together himself. But I bite my tongue the rest of the car ride, so I don't say something like *Good luck making her happy*.

But Dad doesn't have my restraint. Over spaghetti and meatballs, he points his fork at Finn. "Is your wife still busting your balls on everything?" he asks. The man doesn't mince words.

Finn shakes his head. "It's fine, Pops. Nothing to worry about."

"You sure?" No wonder he picked tonight to meet us. Mom's busy with her book club. She'd never let him give Finn the third degree when it comes to romance.

"It's all good," Finn insists.

"You need a woman who understands you," he says, stabbing a meatball.

"Dad, you need to cut back on red meat," Finn says, shifting gears.

"I didn't cut back on smoke inhalation for forty years at the firehouse. I don't need to cut back on meat."

He takes another bite. Defiantly.

Hard to argue with the salty old bastard so I don't even try. Nor does Finn. Instead, I wrestle the conversation away from the thorny subject of romance. "Thanks again for connecting me with Jack's kid. Kyle's working out well," I tell my pops.

"Good to hear. Jack appreciates what you did and so do I," he says gratefully.

"Kyle's a solid employee, so the appreciation is all mine," I say.

That takes some of the heat off my brother as we catch up on Jack and Kyle, then the guys from the firehouse. Then Dad says Mom wants to know if we've remembered to get our flu shots.

"It's August," I point out with a laugh.

"Mom says the flu's coming early this year," Dad says, shrugging, acknowledging the request is a typical mom one.

"We'll get them soon," Finn says lightly.

On the way home, my brother huffs out a frustrated breath. "Dad's wrong, isn't he? About Marilyn?"

Ah, hell. Does he want me to lie? It's not my place to render a verdict on my brother's marriage, so I say, "No one truly knows a relationship except the people in it."

Finn turns to the window, staring for a while at the buildings streaking by, the lights, the road.

When he shifts his gaze back to me, he just nods, perhaps both resolute and resigned as he says, "Yeah, that's true."

The car drops him off first, and I give him a clap on the shoulder. "You're trying, Finn. That's all you can do. Just keep trying your best."

He'll beat himself up for the rest of time if he thinks for one second he didn't give something his all. Especially something as important as his marriage. "Thanks," he says, then pushes open the door and tosses me an evil look. "Don't think I forgot what happened at the pool."

"I'd never think that," I say, then he flips me the bird and leaves.

I smile, glad he's back to himself again.

Once I'm home, I say hi to David, who's camped out in the guest room watching a show on his laptop. With Cynthia, it seems, judging from the square icon on the corner of the screen that matches a framed photo of her on the nightstand.

"Bedroom looks good," I say, though he didn't do much with it. Ginny set it up, navy and white, guest-room style, and that seems to suit David's temporary needs.

"It's nice and rat-free," he remarks.

"One of my favorite perks of this place."

"Thanks again," he says, then to the screen, he tells Cynthia he'll be right back. He mutes himself and closes the laptop halfway. "I'll look for a sublet this week, Dad."

"No rush. Whatever works for you. Stay as long as you want," I offer. It's not his style, but damn, does it feel good to make the offer. To have the space and the means to make his life easier.

"I know," he says with an almost embarrassed grin. "But my dad taught me to stand on my own two feet."

Ah, hell. Way to make my heart thump with pride too. Like I have a choice but to cross to the bed and ruffle his hair. "You're doing great, kiddo. Let me know how I can help."

"I will," he says, then fidgets with the laptop, clearly eager to get back to his girl. I ignore the slight pang of envy I feel that he can FaceTime her, focusing instead on how relaxed and calm he seems with her. I hope this blooming relationship continues to make him feel good.

I head toward the door. "Good night."

"Night, Dad," he says. That's much better—Dad.

But just so there isn't any confusion...

"No more Daddy Bancroft," I say as I leave, voice stern.

"Yes, sir," he says, and I don't mind the *sir* one bit in this situation, because it's a fitting response to a parental order. He better not call me that nickname again.

I get that he thinks it's funny, and maybe it is to him. But not to me. Rose's parents barely let me see my own kid when I was in college, right after he was born. I didn't have much choice in the matter. I had more choices when I married her after college, but his name was his name then.

Now? I have choices. And David needs to know my choice is to be Dad, only Dad to him.

Alone in my bedroom suite, I take a shower then get ready for bed. As I'm brushing my teeth, my phone buzzes with a text. I set the toothbrush in the holder and check the screen.

My pulse surges the second I see the name.

Fucking annoying reaction.

I don't want to be stupidly excited over a text.

I should ignore it.

I flip the phone over without opening the message, then head to bed, pull down the covers and grab my eReader.

I click on a book I downloaded the other night—a digital economics professor's theories on how the elite will or won't survive the future. But one page into the admittedly riveting opening, and I'm powerless to resist the device in the bathroom.

Tossing the covers off, I trudge back to the bathroom counter, grab the phone, and shake my head, annoyed I gave in so easily.

Besides, the text is probably nothing. It's probably housekeeping stuff about the fundraiser planning this week. I shouldn't even care so much, want so much. I open it in case it's something I should deal with.

Her new name blinks up at me, with a double dose of irony. I changed her from Lola to **Friend** the night I met her at the diner.

It's both a reminder and a precaution.

> Friend: I meant to reach out yesterday, but I wasn't sure if I should. But since I'll see you this week for the fundraiser planning, I wanted to let you know that even though David asked how my date was, and even though he told me he mentioned it to you, he doesn't know the date was supposed to have been with you. In case you were wondering.

My gut was right. It's all housekeeping stuff. Housekeeping *us*. And the trouble is, *she's* cleaning up the mess. That's not fair or right, but I don't see another way around the problem. But I can offer her one thing to help ease the load: gratitude.

> Nick: I apologize that you had to deal with that. I wish I could have taken that one for the team.

>> Friend: Thank you for saying that, but it was fine. David and I are used to talking about dating. So it wasn't unexpected.

I *could* end the convo at that, but I can't quite let go. Yes, there's more I want to know, but I also crave this connection with her. Clutching the phone, I head back to bed, flop down, and ask a question I don't truly need the answer to.

> Nick: What did you tell him?

>> Friend: That the guy canceled.

> Nick: Ouch.

>> Friend: It was the easiest answer.

> Nick: That guy sounds like a dick.

>> Friend: He missed what would have been an excellent date.

I grip the phone more tightly.

Just shut it down, man.

I should end the exchange here. There's no need to keep it going. Truly, I should set the phone on the nightstand, return to the futurist's theories, and stay in a cerebral state till I fall asleep. But that date I missed would have been damn good. I had big plans to catch up with her, learn more about who she is, the friendships she values. I planned to tell her more about my life, and then I wanted to bring her here. *Right fucking here.*

I am not in a cerebral state whatsoever as I tap out a reply.

> Nick: He knows. Trust me, he knows.

I wait too long for a response that never comes, then I turn off my phone for the night. In bed, I lie awake, staring at the ceiling. In just a few days, she'll be here, visiting, finalizing plans for the fundraiser. How the hell am I going to survive being in my home with my son and his irresistible friend?

No idea.

* * *

In the morning, I find a reply. In the form of a photo. It's a shot of a black satin something. Then a note. Dear god. I groan for several seconds as I stare shamelessly at the image, then read the delicious words.

> Friend: You were right.

I love that I was right. And I hate that I was right.

18

THIS CORDIAL GAME

Layla

The DM from Storm delights me.

It's winking up at me as Jules, Camden, and I leave Krav Maga on Tuesday morning. *Girl, you need to come by the store! I haven't seen your face in two weeks. Plus, I have news!!!*

As I walk up Amsterdam, I tap out a reply to my new favorite makeup store manager. We've become fast friends over the last few months since I met him at the start of the summer. *Way to keep a girl waiting! Tell me now.*

Storm's quick on the draw with his reply: *My lips are zipped. Come by! It's good! The store isn't open yet, but your BFF Storm will take care of you.*

I show the message to my friends as we near a smoothie shop. "What do you think it is?"

"I don't speak makeup, but it sounds cool. You better tell us everything," Camden says. "And bring us some free swag."

Jules taps her chin, contemplative. "Or maybe he has a new hot thing for you." She knows what went down at the diner. I told the crew the whole sorry tale when I convened with the Virgin Society the morning after the diner shock.

"Yeah, that's what I need. A new man," I say dryly.

Jules arches a brow. "Did I say man? I meant makeup. Pretty sure makeup, chocolate, and face masks are excellent replacements for romance."

Camden snorts. "Yeah, but they don't have ten speeds like my favorite Just For Her vibe."

"You both make good points. And on that note, I'm off."

Ten minutes later, I'm standing outside Blush on Columbus, but it's no longer Blush. It's…Mia Jane, and it's gorgeous. With an all-peach storefront, and the name in a huge block font, the store screams "take a picture in front of me for social media."

Which is an excellent marketing strategy.

Storm's inside, working on a laptop at the counter. When I rap gently on the glass, he lifts his head, smiles brightly, then scurries to the door to unlock it and let me in.

Storm spreads his arms out wide. "Is this good news or what? It's all Mia now. I told you she was going to start opening shops, and yours truly is the new manager of the flagship New York store," he says, clearly proud of his little corner of the makeup world. Perhaps of his relationship with her too, since he's using just one name for her—Mia. They must be close, since Mia Jane is her public name.

I turn in a circle, effervescent as I'm surrounded by my darlings—gorgeous glosses, and fantastic liners, and terrific toners. I feel like I'm home. "I love it."

He sets a hand on my arm, squeezing. "And that's not all. I told Mia about you," he whispers, even though we're the only ones here.

"What did you tell her?" I ask, and I don't bother to hide my hopeful smile.

"Showed her your vids. She loves them. She wants you to come by the store and do a training sesh with customers on your fabulous smoky eyes and winged liners. She'll pay you, obvs, and promote it as an event with The Makeover," he says, grinning from ear to ear. He's suddenly stern. "You better say yes."

"I'm saying yes, Storm!" I'm saying yes so hard.

"Excellent. Mia will reach out, and we'll set it up. She'll be here too."

I need to catch my breath. "Pinch me."

Instead, he blows me an air kiss.

I might have lost the guy, but I have a new friend, and a new business opportunity. Once I leave, I text Geeta, and she replies with dollar signs, then words. ***Market the hell out of The Makeover. We will sell the bajangajang out of it!***

That's the plan. Creating content and organizing those classes keeps me busy until the evening, when it's time to see David, and his too-sexy-for words father.

Leaving my apartment, I draw a deep, cleansing breath, vowing to think clean thoughts about that dirty man.

* * *

I've seen a lot of swank buildings in Manhattan. But Nick Adams' glittery high-rise is something else. It kisses the blue skies of New York City.

And yet it doesn't need to be the tallest or the biggest building in the skyline. It's simply content to be the most beautiful with its art deco style.

Ethan and I turn onto Nick's block, and his Gramercy Park palace comes into view. My friend whistles as he stares. "Damn, girl."

I gaze at the gorgeous structure too; its beauty is a wonderful distraction from the looming dread of going inside, up to the top floor, and planning an event with my friend and his father. If awkward had a headshot, it'd be me.

"This won't be weird at all," I say.

"You'll be fine," Ethan reassures me, squeezing my arm.

We took a bus together—I don't like subways—since Ethan's meeting Martina for ping-pong tonight at a nearby bar. Of course he remained friends with the sexy redheaded bartender from Gin Joint after dating her and then breaking it off. Same for the guy at The Lucky Spot, the one who recognized him and came to his show then talked him up afterward. They went out a few times too, and still work out together, even though they don't date anymore.

Ethan just has this way about him with people. Which is why I asked him to walk me here. I didn't want to face this alone. "How am I even supposed to act with the two of them?"

We stop several feet from the building's entrance, and the look in his eyes says he's about to dole out some tough love. "Like you haven't seen both of them naked."

I groan from the depths of my embarrassed soul.

"I'm right though," he adds.

"I know," I say, stepping closer so I can drop my face against his sturdy chest. "Trust me, I know."

He strokes my hair. "I mean it, Layla. Just focus on the planning. The charity. The reason you wanted to do this with David. He's a cool dude. We all like him. Everyone likes him. He's like a good dog."

David's not quite a part of the crew, but we've gone out a few times as a group. He joined us for karaoke shortly after he graduated.

I raise my head and concur. "He's a Golden Retriever."

Ethan smiles slyly. "You do know a Golden Retriever boyfriend is a good thing."

I laugh. "And yet neither one of us has one," I say.

"Maybe I'm waiting for the same kind of man you are," he whispers as if he's sharing a tawdry secret. But he's telling me something we both know. We have similar taste in men. A little edgy, a little dirty. He gestures to the building. "Because obviously you fucked a sex prince."

I laugh. "Yes, a rich sex prince, with a fantastic dick, a to-die-for beard, a dirty mind, and oh, one more thing," I say, then lower my voice since you never know who's listening. "I can't ever see him again, since his son is my ex and my friend, and also his son is the sweetest Golden Retriever ever."

Ethan gazes skyward, shaking his head wistfully. "I really shouldn't say this, but I bet the sex in *that* penthouse with Hot Daddy would have been torrid."

"You're not helping. Do you want me to torture you with stories of forbidden affairs? Someday, you're going to meet a hottie and then you're going to discover they're your new bandmate."

"Don't curse me," he says.

"Maybe it's a blessing."

"Only if it ends in a blow job."

I bump my shoulder to his. "You pig. Is that all you care about?"

"Have you ever had a blow job?"

"Shockingly, no," I deadpan as we walk the remaining feet to the building.

"I rest my case," he says. We reach the entrance, where a doorman in a burgundy suit stands dignified. The place is so classy the doormen don't even need to dress in livery costumes. Tailored suits will do, thank you very much.

But now that I'm about to go into the Lair of Awkward, my stomach dips with nerves again. Setting a hand on my stomach, I strip away the banter, going straight for the bare truth. "Ethan, I feel like such a little..."

I hate the word *liar*.

The man who killed my father accused him of being a liar. My father wasn't. I knew he wasn't. My father knew he wasn't. We all knew that his business partner was the liar.

But I feel maybe I am. So I say the word, no matter how much it hurts. "I feel like a liar."

Ethan rubs my shoulder with a sympathetic hand. "What were you supposed to do though? You weren't going to 'fess up over fries that you already knew his dad. That you'd spent time with him in Miami. That you had a date with him. That would have been unnecessary. Just try to leave it all behind you," he says, and the thought of leaving Nick in the past makes my chest ache. But I know it's for the best.

I know, too, I'll have to do a better job than I did the other night when I texted Nick that photo of my corset in a moment of weakness. I can't keep teasing him with the possibility of an us. I can't keep toying.

He didn't even respond. Let that be my lesson to shut up.

"I'll try," I say, chin up, resolute.

Ethan wraps an inked arm around me and kisses my cheek. "Let me know how it goes, babe."

I smile, grateful for the pep talk. When we let go, I pat his strong chest. "Have fun with Martina and the crew. And I hope your next blow job is...well, a revelation."

"Let us pray."

Once he's off, I go inside, saying hello to the doorman, then I head to the concierge and give him my name.

"Excellent. Mr. Adams is expecting you, Layla," the man says politely in an Australian accent.

"Thank you," I say, then head to the elevator. Once inside, I hit the button for the thirty-second floor, just as a voice brushes down my spine like a lover's touch.

"Hold the door, please."

Please let him be alone.

I can't face Nick and David in an elevator.

I turn around, pressing the hold button. I get my wish—one terribly handsome man in a tailored charcoal suit strides across the polished hardwood floors of the lobby.

How is it possible to walk sexily?

I don't know, but Nick Adams has mastered it.

But the closer he comes, the more I can see his mask. His face is impassive. Unreadable. He's like any powerful man in any big, tall building in Manhattan as he enters the elevator.

There's no spark, no wink, no secret little exchange.

"Hi, Layla," he says, and his eyes don't linger on me as the doors shut.

He simply faces the front a few feet away from me, the gleaming brass reflecting us back—a man in a suit, and a woman in a red blouse and designer jeans, second-hand, thank you very much.

Well, that's clear.

The past is the past. This is the present, and we are definitely pretending Miami never happened.

My jaw tightens with annoyance as I look away from our uncomfortable reflection.

But what did I expect would happen? We agreed to move on.

I'm the one who sent that photo. Not him. *Of course* he didn't respond.

I'll have to do a better job pretending Miami never happened.

"Hi..." I begin, but what does he want me to call him in this post-Miami world? Nick feels too familiar. "Mr. Adams."

"How are you today, Layla?" He sounds so cool, so removed.

"Great. And you?"

"Excellent." He looks at his watch. "David's checking out a sublet after work. But he should be here in five minutes."

"Thanks for letting me know," I say.

"You're welcome," he says, just as stiffly.

I get why he's acting this way, but I don't intend to lose this battle. Wait till he sees how well I can play this cordial game. "How is everything going with your new firm in New York? Are you enjoying working with your brother?" I ask, both because it's a necessary diversion tactic, and because I'm legitimately interested.

"I am," he says as the lift rises. He sounds more energetic now, less distant. "We each have different areas of focus but they go well together. I think we can grow this into something strong and meaningful."

That last word catches my attention. "Meaningful? In what way?"

"I try to work with companies that don't just have innovative tech, but that truly support their employees, use sustainable business models, and give back," he says.

Oh.

Damn him.

I wish I didn't like that so much. I wish we didn't share the same values. It'd be easier.

"I'm glad to hear that," I say, but he doesn't seem to want to talk much about his work.

"How's everything going with The Makeover?" He seems legitimately interested. "I've been hoping you're enjoying working with Farm to Phone. Are you?"

When he was in London, I told him we'd inked a deal with the marketing firm I met at the conference. "It's going great," I say, sliding into business talk with ease, like we did in Miami. "We've landed some press coverage and grown our user base. And Mia Jane's just asked me to do an event at her new store in New York."

Ha. I'm a lady boss. Take that, world.

And maybe I like showing off for Nick. He's so successful, so Mister Midas Touch. I want him to know this gal can hold her own without any help from her mom, thank you very much.

"That's terrific," he says.

The elevator stops on the thirty-second floor. Our destination. The doors whoosh open, and we turn down the wide hallway, heading to Nick's penthouse. "It should be good marketing for The Makeover. It'll help with our goals," I say, staying as professional as can be.

"Absolutely. Especially since you've got a natural enthusiasm for her products. And your videos using them have been terrific," he says as we near his apartment.

"You've been watching still?" I'm not sure why this surprises me. Maybe because I thought he'd tune them out since we can't be a thing.

"You're passionate," he says, matter-of-factly. Then his mask disappears and in a heartbeat the Nick from Miami is back. There's fire in his eyes but also, honesty. This is how he talked to me when we met, how he talked to me while he was in London, how he spoke at the diner. "I've become a little addicted to them," he says as we reach the door. Then, as he turns his back to me to unlock it, he adds, quietly, "It's something I have to watch out for. A tendency." There's a pause. "Do you know what I mean?"

His tone is a warning, but his words are an admission.

He's given me a piece of himself, something I suspect he keeps close to the vest. "I do, Nick," I say softly. "I do."

When he looks back at me, our gazes lock for a few, heady seconds. I can sense the fight in him. The resistance. The war.

It excites me more than it should.

And I hope I don't become a little addicted to him.

Or more addicted than I already am.

* * *

David should be here any minute, so I use the time to admire the view out the floor-to-ceiling living room windows. "I never tire of the views of New York. This is stunning," I say as I drink in the vista of my favorite city. New York stretches as far as I can see.

I catch Nick's gaze and something dirty flashes in his eyes. A sexy gleam maybe. It sends a hot shiver down my spine. But then that after-dark look vanishes, replaced by a smile.

"Thanks," he says, with obvious gratitude and a touch of humility too. "It's a little different than what I grew up seeing."

That's an opening if I ever heard one, but before I can ask more, his phone buzzes from the living room table. After he grabs it, he says, "David's in the elevator now."

There's no time to linger on growing up questions so I zero in on a practical matter. "What do *you* want me to call you? When we're all here together?"

"Don't call me Mr. Adams," he says, bossy again.

Don't ask. Just say thank you for the info. "Why?" I blurt out, as he heads to the door.

"I'd rather be Nick," he says, his gaze lingering on me for another few seconds, before he says, "with you."

Tingles rush down my spine, but I have to ignore them since it's showtime.

Nick opens the door for David, who sputters in. His banker's hair is a mess. His messenger bag is sliding off his shoulder. "I'm so freaking stressed! I just realized we have less than three weeks to get this all done," he says, bug-eyed and frazzled.

David beelines for the couch, slumps down and blows out a long breath. It's like he can't even move.

With a practiced familiarity, Nick joins him and clasps a hand on his shoulder, a warm, reassuring parental move. "We'll get it done."

What would it be like to feel that from a father? I can't quite remember anymore, and that's part of the empty ache in my heart.

I look away. It hurts too much to witness.

I miss having that anchor in my life.

Fifteen minutes later, Nick has taken over with a kind of efficiency that I never knew was a turn-on till now.

Thanks, Nick, for being a sexy...doer. Damn you.

We're seated at the kitchen island, huddled around David's laptop. Nick types something into a spreadsheet. "There. Everything is set with the hotel," he says, and it turns out Nick was the one who arranged to rent the ballroom at a boutique hotel. Funny, how I knew the fundraiser was being held at the Fox Walk Inn but didn't know Nick had hooked up his son. But that's only the tip of the iceberg of the things I didn't know. "That should help, if we divide and conquer like this," Nick says, then he looks up. "I'll work on the guest list. And I'll make some calls to my contacts and make sure they show up too."

David relaxes. "Thank you. Mom has a few she's talking to. I marked them off."

"Of course," Nick says, clearly diplomatic, like he doesn't want to say something cutting about Rose.

He looks to me, running a hand along his stubbled jaw, as if the motion helps him sort through the freeways in his mind. "Layla, can you coordinate all the auction items?"

"Absolutely, Nick," I say.

His lips twitch almost imperceptibly, then he turns to David once more. "You should do the shelter outreach since that's your thing."

"Perfect," David says, then like a Golden Retriever who's found a tennis ball, he pops up. "I'm going to start now. Little Friends is nearby, and I can take pictures that we can show during the auction. The director's there in the evening. We'll meet back here later?"

Which means Nick and I will be alone.

"Sure," Nick says, tentative, perhaps caught off guard by David's disappearing act.

Same here, but I push back. "If I'm making calls and your dad is too, why do we need to meet? We can just group chat later."

Not that I don't want to be alone with Nick. I definitely do, which is why I need to get the hell out of here.

David ruffles my hair, laughing. "Duh. To make sure it all worked out. Plus, you two should work together. Some of the peeps on the guest list are also donating items, so it just makes sense the two of you coordinate," he says, then laughs. "Sheesh. Do I have to do everything?"

I laugh uncomfortably, even though I'm glad David's mood is better. He looks relieved as he takes off, the door snapping shut with a *be careful what you wish for* finality.

I'm alone with his father, once again.

19

THE FRIENDSHIP STRATEGY

Layla

I stay at the kitchen island the whole time, making calls and sending emails. Nick paces by the living room window, and it's hard not to watch him. I have a thing for the way he walks.

Not helpful, libido.

But in my libido's defense, have you seen him in those tailored pants? That snug shirt? That undone tie?

As he chats with college friends, tech gurus, colleagues, and the like, he progressively tugs on the maroon silk.

During the first call, he fidgeted with it.

During the third, he loosened it.

During the fifth, he unknotted it.

Now during his eighth or ninth call, as I'm texting with Raven about her designer donation, he's undoing the fabric.

I steal glances in between texts as his nimble fingers undo the silky material.

"It'll be great to see you there, Trav. And no, I will not go easy on you on the basketball court next week. I will never go easy on you," he says, then ends the call with an amused shake of his head.

"You play basketball?" I ask, setting my phone on the counter. I'm far too interested in this tidbit about Nick.

"Pickup basketball," he says.

"I figured as much."

"Why's that?"

"Well, I didn't think it was pro ball."

Dropping the tie on the back of the couch, he laughs. "I mean why did you figure I'd play pickup."

"You seem like the kind of guy who strides onto a court when he damn well pleases, trash talks his friends, and takes their money when he beats them."

Nick's eyebrows rise as he crosses the room. He likes that compliment. "Thank you."

I laugh. "What if it wasn't a compliment, Nick?"

"It was a compliment," he says, and I like this banter. I'd rather we get along for real.

"Cocky," I tease.

"And you like it," he says, then he shakes his head, muttering, "Shit."

"What's wrong?"

He stops at the end of the counter, dragging a hand through his hair, roughly. "I need to do better."

I wish I could play dumb, but I know what he means. "I think you're doing fine," I say.

I mean it. I like this Nick better than the cordial one in the elevator. At least he's being real. I feel less weird with Real Nick than Cordial Nick. Even though I'm still hot for him.

He deals me an intense stare. "It's hard," he says on a sigh, then gestures from him to me.

"It's hard for me too." Maybe this charity planning will be easier if we just acknowledge how tough it is to be together when we can't *be together.*

"Yeah?" His voice pitches up the slightest bit.

"It is. But we could try to be friends," I say brightly, offering that as a strategy. A damn good one if I do say so myself.

He snorts. Then the snort turns into a laugh.

"You're not friends with women?" I ask.

"Of course I am." His denial comes too quickly, and I must tease him about it.

"Are you though?"

"Yes," he says, adamant.

"Name one," I challenge.

He hedges too long, thinking too hard.

I point at him. "Ha. Called it."

"I'm friends with women," he says, trying again. "There's...Eunice at work. She's a VC."

"Fine. A work friend," I say, in a tone that makes it clear colleagues don't count.

"There's..." But he's struggling, even when he snaps his fingers and says, "Danielle. She's a cool bartender I was buds with when I last lived here. She and her wife are in a pickleball league."

I sit back in the stool, laughing. "So it's Eunice from work, and Danielle and her wife from a few years ago."

"Yes," he grumbles. "Do you have many guy friends?"

Ha. Who does he think he's dealing with? "Ethan. He walked me here. We've been friends since—"

"—Grade school," he says.

His recollection of the details I shared about my friend in Miami makes me feel a little warm and fuzzy for him. Which is also not entirely helpful. But I try to redirect those warm feelings toward friendship.

"David," I add. "Obviously he's a very good friend."

"Yeah, too bad you didn't mention him in Miami," he mutters.

Ouch. "Was it? Was it too bad?"

Nick jerks his gaze toward the window, staring too long, then looks back at me, quietly admitting, "You have to know I'm glad you didn't. Say you know it, Layla."

Now I'm warmer. Like equator levels. "I know," I say.

"Good. Because I have no regrets," he adds, and why does he have to be so damn sexy that I'm aroused again?

This is going to be the hardest charity event I've ever planned. Must focus on my new strategy. "So, do you want to be friends with me?"

Nick seems to consider it for a beat. But in the way you consider something that's your only choice. "We're kind of stuck doing this. We should try," he says, amenable.

I extend a hand. "Let's be friends."

He clasps my palm in a friendly gesture. But I don't think friends shake this long, since he doesn't let go immediately. He curls his fingers around my palm, then runs the pad of his finger along my skin, tracing me, touching me. Like he did early that morning in Miami.

He's a thief.

But I'm not going to turn him in as he stretches the definition of friendship and curls my toes with one risqué touch.

"Friends," he says, but I hear five words in that one. I hear *I want you so much*. More so, I *feel* it.

So I don't let go.

But then, I do, missing the sensual connection once it's broken.

"Friends," I echo, as I brush my palms along my slacks, like that'll erase the moment.

A few minutes later, David returns.

I still feel awkward as we recap our work on the auction, but I feel less awkward than I did when I arrived.

If I can be friends with the son, perhaps I can be friends with the father. Besides, it's safer that way.

* * *

A few days later, I'm putting the finishing touches on a smoky eye for the former fashionista in her new shop. The event came together quickly, courtesy of Storm.

I didn't even have enough time to be nervous. I met

the fashion icon moments ago, and she told me to call her Mia.

Now that I'm here, swiping mascara over her lashes, I don't feel anxious. I only feel confident and strong. I'm in my element as Lola Jones, creating a new look like I once created a new me.

"And after you put on powder, then finally, you apply the mascara. That way you don't get beige powder all over your beautiful black eyelashes," I tell the crowd as I finish Mia's face.

"And you know mascara is sacred," Mia says, in her warm, honeyed tone, a contrast to her jet-black hair, cascading in finger curls down her back. When I step away to show her off, the icon turns to the assembled crowd packed into her little shop. "Especially when you're a woman of a certain age," she stage-whispers, gesturing to her own face, with laugh lines and crinkles at the corners of her eyes. "We forty-something gals need our daily doses of mascara."

I laugh. "Don't you mean mascara is for everyone?"

Mia makes an oopsy face then points to me. "What Lola said. A mascara in every purse, makeup bag, medicine cabinet, and home in the world!"

Storm claps from the counter. "Our new rallying cry. Long live mascara."

Then I answer questions from customers and take turns showing them some of my techniques.

"Thanks, Lola," a dark-haired teen says, adding in a quiet voice, "Thanks to that video you did a while back, I learned how to cover up some red spots on my face."

"You are gorgeous," I tell her.

An older woman chimes in with, "Love your app, Lola. It helped me prep for a job interview. And I got it."

"I'm so happy for you," I say.

Lola, Lola, Lola.

It's so nice to only hear that name. To only hear questions about the present, not the past.

When the event winds down, it's just Storm, Mia, and me in the store. Mia's waggling her phone, cooing at the social posts as she rattles off comments, then she stares at me intensely. "This is everyone's new favorite thing in New York. Say you'll do more, Lola. Say it. Say it now."

Storm chuckles. "Give a girl a second to think, Mia."

Mia taps a watch she doesn't wear. "There. One second."

But she had me at hello. "Name the time and place."

We make plans for another event, then Mia walks with me down the block, dropping her big, bold persona for a beat. "Seriously though. I'd love to find more ways to work together. Maybe we can partner up in a bigger way? I have some ideas," she says, then shares a few.

"I'd love that. I'll talk to my business partner."

When we part, I call Geeta, whose only response is an enthused "hell fucking yes."

* * *

The time the Mia Jane collaboration will take will be worthwhile for another reason too. I'll have a legit excuse to turn down my mom's matchmaking efforts.

I'm simply too busy.

After I play tennis with her on Saturday morning, she asks me to join her and Rose for lunch. "We had an idea for you."

Forget her idea. I'm bristling at the mere mention of Rose. I've never bristled over Rose before.

But now I know my mom's friend is Nick's ex-wife. In Miami, Nick told me he'd married young, that it wasn't a good marriage, and that they divorced years ago. Why, then, does my chest feel like it's on fire? Am I actually jealous of someone Nick hasn't been with in probably a decade? What is wrong with me?

As I shower and get dressed, I try to put Nick out of my mind. I mentally prep ideas for Mia as I blow out my hair. When I grab my bag from my locker, a woman across the way whispers to a woman next to her. I swear I can hear the words *his business partner*, then *she walked in on it*.

I grit my teeth and try to ignore the way I'm a sideshow to the New York elite. I bet they whisper about my mother too, then put on false faces and eat cobb salad with her.

When I leave, I meet their eyes, then smile. They can't break me. I was broken years ago, and I had to put myself together again.

I did it thanks to Carla, and thanks to my friends. I touch my tattoo for strength as I exit, leaving them in my wake, like I'm a hurricane and they're the damaged homes.

I join my mom and Rose at the table. Rose takes a sip of Perrier then says, "I hear Kip Cranston's family is donating a set of golf clubs and golf lessons at their country club to the auction you're working on with David."

"And that gave me an idea. Since you and David insist on being *just friends,*" my mom chimes in, sketching air quotes, like our friendship is a personal repudiation of her matchmaking attempts.

Rose goes next, breezily suggesting, "Perhaps Kip could be your date to the auction."

Wow. This is a new tactic. The have-a-friend-make-the-case tactic.

But no. No on so many levels. I'm not attracted to the man. I don't like to discuss yachts, and country club memberships, and secret societies at Yale.

I've got an ace up my sleeve, and I play the hell out of it with a cheery smile. "Thank you for thinking of me, Rose," I say to the woman I strangely dislike.

"Of course, dear."

I turn my focus to my mom. "And I'd ordinarily love to, but I'm incredibly busy. I'm doing some collabs with Mia."

Mom lifts a brow and asks archly, "Oh?"

But I stand my ground. "I like her product and her business practices," I say, then tell her about my recent event and its potential. Like what it could do for Geeta and me. Especially Geeta and her responsibilities with her dad.

Mom brightens, but I can't tell if her shift is real or fake. "Lovely. All that work will help you when you come to Beautique," she says, and the answer is neither real nor fake—just selfish. "I suspect you'll be more than ready to start as a high-level marketing VP. And just think how proud your father would be if you were working with me."

I brace myself.

She'd better not say the next thing.

She'd really better not.

"You know your father would have wanted you to," she adds.

She went there.

The place I can't argue from. Did my father even say that to her? Was it his dying wish? Or is it hers? I don't know. I'm afraid she'd break down if I even ask, so I've never questioned her. I've never told her about the promise I made him either, so I have no choice but to believe her.

I'm about to say thanks but no thanks to the Kip date when she sets a hand on mine, squeezing. "I worry about you, Layla. I want you to be safe. I want you to be with someone who comes from a good family," she says.

The implication is clear—Dad's business partner did not come from a good family. Joe McBride was from a rough section of Boston. He was the first in his family to go to college. He had no pedigree.

"Would you do this for me? Meet Kip?" Mom asks in a low voice. Rose has the decency to look away, fidgeting with her pearls.

I want Mom to be happy. I've always wanted that. There were so many nights when I was sure she'd never survive the loss of her love, her best friend, her rock. No matter how complicated our relationship is, I want her to find peace and joy in life again. I've found it with my friends and with my work. I don't know if she truly has.

I relent though I don't give all the way in. "I don't want a date to the auction. But I'll have coffee with Kip when I return."

I haven't seen her eyes sparkle with so much happiness in years.

Maybe this is a pyrrhic victory, but I'll take it, especially since she says, "I wish I could be there at the auction, but I have to visit our offices in Los Angeles that week and I'll be staying for a spa weekend."

Oh, hello, empty home in the Hamptons. You are mine. "I'll miss you, but could I use the house that weekend?"

"I had the alarm company test the system last week after the upgrade. It's the most secure one out there. And you're always free to use the house," she says.

That's always a win in my book, even though I have a date in a few more weeks.

Too bad it's not with the only man I want to see.

20

THE HANDLE ON THE POT

Nick

So this is friendship with a woman. If so, I don't know that I want to sign up for another stint of it.

Being with Layla over the last week has been painful and wonderful at the same time.

On Thursday evening, David's off in Brooklyn with the shelters he coordinates with there, while Layla and I roll through our task list. This time we're on the couch. She's on one end. I'm on the other.

This space between us is good. Empirically good. It'll keep me from being obsessed. If I'm lucky, maybe it'll keep me from thinking of how sturdy this couch is.

Even though I'm distracted by her call.

"Yes, the golf lessons donation is fantastic, Kip," she says on the phone as I answer an email. "Can you take a picture of the set of clubs you're including? Yes, I know the clubs are PXG."

A pause, then she laughs sweetly. "I would, but I'm so busy."

I'm instantly jealous. Who the fuck is this guy who wants her to come over and take a picture of a couple pricey golf clubs?

"You're a good photog," she says, clearly flattering him. "Just take a well-lit wide shot and send it to me."

Another pause. "Yes. After the auction. See you then."

She hangs up, then dusts one palm against the other, like she's relieved to have that call done. "And the golf lessons and the clubs are in. You better bring rich people to bid on them."

But I'm too irritated to address her demand. "Who's Kip?"

Her brow knits, like she's unsure why I'd ask with such vitriol. "He's donating golf lessons at his family's country club, and a set of golf clubs. I thought that was clear."

"It was," I say, then bite out, "Who is he?"

She quirks her head to the side, puzzled but a little amused too. "Why are you asking it like that?"

"You sounded friendly with him. Is he a friend?"

"Like you and me?"

I growl. "Better not be like you and me."

She laughs, leaning back into the sofa. "Relax. He went to Carlisle Academy too. A few years ahead of me. His mother is friends with my mom and your..." There's a pause, like she's debating whether to say the next words, then she does. "Your ex-wife."

Which means Kip is close to her age.

Which means Kip can likely date her.

Which means he can...

I need to stop. This is not friendly terrain at all. I have to try to be friends with her. I have to get a handle on these reckless emotions.

Besides, falling harder for this woman would be a repeat of my past. I fell hard for the rich girl more than twenty years ago. Then I knocked her up, pissed off her family, and nearly derailed her life.

I should stay far away from the Park Avenue elite.

Sure, I can compete with all those rich fuckers now in the wallet department, but I'll always be the guy from the other side of the tracks. Guys who went to community college, then state school, aren't part of the Carlisle Academy crowd.

But I picture Layla—Lola then—working her ass off in Miami, making contacts, building her app on a new name.

Not a family name.

Goddammit, she's hardly part of that scene either. Why does she have to be so alluring?

I need a distraction. I glance over at the ticking clock by the kitchen. Cooking always calms me. The rhythm, the focus, the creativity. "Want dinner?"

"Sure," she says, perhaps as eager for a change of subject and scenery as I am. "I can order from someplace?"

"Or I can cook," I offer.

That gets her attention. "You can cook?"

I laugh, gesturing to the open-plan kitchen. "Why

do you think I have all those pots and pans in the kitchen?"

"For show?" she asks, serious.

I roll my eyes. "For real, beautiful. For real," I say, before I can catch my mistake. But fuck it, she is beautiful. Maybe I don't want to correct my error—not with the Kips of the world trying to get the woman I can't have. "Want a veggie stir-fry?"

Her smile is utterly charmed, and fuck Kip. I put that smile there. I bet Kip can't cook. "That sounds great," she says.

A few minutes later, I'm in the kitchen, chopping red and orange peppers on a cutting board while Layla grabs broccoli from the veggie drawer.

"Can you grab the tofu too?" I ask. "Wait. I didn't ask if you like tofu."

"I like tofu if it's cooked well."

"I can cook it well," I say, with a confident grin. "Second shelf."

She finds it and sets it next to me. "Have you always cooked?"

"Always. My dad taught me when I was seven," I tell her as I cut the orange pepper into thin slices. "He likes to go out once a week to a restaurant, but the rest of the time he makes dinner at home. Finn and I took him when I first came to town. He lives in Queens with my mom."

"You can see him regularly," she says, sounding a little wistful. Maybe even amazed. "Is he retired?"

"He was a firefighter for forty years. Retired at sixty-five."

"Did your mom work?"

"She was in dispatch. That's how they met. He cooked for their first date. He still likes to cook for her."

Layla purses her lips as she opens the tofu. "That sounds nice," she says, but then she stops opening the container, almost like she's flummoxed by it.

Trying to figure out why she seems off, I ask, "Are you not used to people cooking for you?"

She shakes her head. "My friends and I don't cook much. And my mom kind of stopped after—"

When she doesn't finish, I stop chopping, my spine tingling with concern. "Is your father...not around?"

I put the knife down. It feels wrong to hold it right now.

She draws a deep breath, like she needs fuel. "He," she begins, then she takes another fueling breath, staring at the tofu, only the tofu. "He was killed six years ago."

Oh, shit.

My sweet, hurting Layla. Instantly, I close the distance between us, wrap my arms around her. "I'm so sorry, Layla."

She sniffles against my chest but then just nods. "Thank you."

I don't know what she's thanking me for—the hug, the question, or something else. But I don't think now's the time to ask. Not when she wraps her arms around me too, circling them around my waist, squeezing. It's one of the first times we've touched that's not sexual. That's just comforting. I'm surprised by the tenderness and her clear need—a need that I can fill.

"Do you want to talk about it?" I ask gently.

I can feel her swallow against me. She shakes her head. "No. But thanks for asking."

She lets go. Backs away. Studies me like I'm a curio in a shop. "You didn't look me up?"

The question comes out with a touch of wonder.

I shake my head. "No. I didn't want to—" I stop myself before I say *become obsessed with you.* "Rely on what others say. I'd rather know you from you."

She gives a faint smile. It seems both sad and happy. Maybe like her thanks. "That means more than you can know, Nick."

My heart aches for her. Absolutely aches. I'm naturally curious. Anyone would be. And I want to ask what she means by killed—like by a car, a plane, or something more sinister. But I do the math. She takes Krav Maga. She wears all those rings, which could easily be self-defense rings. I don't think her father was killed in an accident.

But clearly, she values privacy. Now's not the time or place to ask for details she may not be ready to share, now or ever, especially since she grabs the conversation with her own question, making her needs clear. "Will you tell me more about your mom and dad? All my *friends* tell me about their parents," she says, and there she is again.

The Lola I first knew. Playful.

"I can," I say as I file away all the new details I've learned about the other side of Lola—the Layla side.

I can start to see how complex her relationship is with her mother. How much she values friendships.

How she uses humor and charm and smarts to dance away from the things she doesn't want to discuss.

How she's let me in a little bit more every time I've seen her.

And I want to know more of her.

As a friend?

No.

But it's all we can have.

"I'm just a guy from the other side of the bridge," I begin as I resume cooking then tell her more about my gruff dad, my no-nonsense mom, the rough-and-tumble public high school I went to, and the two-bedroom apartment we grew up in where I shared a room with my brother.

Soon I serve her dinner at the kitchen island, wishing I were spending the rest of the evening with her.

Especially since she tells me more about her favorite people. "And Ethan's in a band. Do you want to hear his newest song?"

"I do," I say.

"Good because I play it for all my *friends*," she says, a grin on her gorgeous face again. "But it's kind of alt. Can you handle it?"

I roll my eyes. "We are not that far off music wise."

"You like polka, right?" she teases.

I narrow my eyes. "I'd like to spank you for that."

Her eyes spark. Maybe she wants a spanking. Maybe I want to give her one. But now's the time for music rather than kink, and she hits play on the song.

It's sultry and sexy, full of longing.

I don't tell her I'm feeling unfriendly as I imagine the song playing in a club, pulling her close, kissing the back of her neck, and whispering sweet, dirty nothings in her ear, then taking her home and letting all those dirty nothings keep us up all night.

When David returns an hour later, I've given myself a medal for restraint. Look at me, world. I'm aces at resisting my son's friend.

Yeah, that's called basic decency.

The three of us catch up on the auction details, and when we're done, Layla gathers her canvas bag from the living room. "And I'm going to prep for tomorrow's video shoots. Winged eyeliners don't make themselves," she says.

I look away because some days, it's damn hard putting on a poker face.

Like when I think about the first time we talked about winged eyeliner...and other first times.

"Did I tell you Cyn loves your videos?" David says as he walks her to the door, while I head to the kitchen to finish cleaning up. "Maybe we can double date with Kip. My mom told me about the date."

Wait.

What in the ever-loving hell?

"I had no choice. I had to throw her a bone," Layla says, with a *what can you do* sigh in her voice.

But what the hell *did* she do?

"I can't believe they wanted you to go with him to the auction," David says as I pick up a pan to clean.

Oh, hell no. She'd better not bring a date there. I scrub the pan harder.

"You can't believe *that*? They tried to set us up again," Layla says with a laugh.

"Fair point. I shouldn't put anything past the matchmaker twins," he says.

Out of the corner of my eye, he hugs her, and a plume of jealousy rages in me. But this fire isn't over my son.

It's over this asshole Kip.

"Bye, Nick," she calls out as she leaves.

"Bye, Layla," I bite out, and I hope, I really fucking hope, my irritation doesn't show through.

When David strides into the kitchen, he gives me a look like he can smell my annoyance. "You okay?"

I need to get it together. "Just this damn pot. Needs so much scouring," I mutter as I attack the clean surface. Then, because I am obsessed, no matter how hard I try to fight it, I give in a little more. "So your mom tries to set up your friends?"

David laughs, like this is nothing to him. "Evidently. Layla's mom does it to her too. She's got a date with that guy after the auction."

I nearly rip the handle off the pot.

* * *

I can barely concentrate as I head into the office on Friday. When I reach the corner suite, Kyle springs up from his desk, says hello, and updates me on calls and research reports he's compiled for me, and I just grunt out a thanks then shut the door to my office. I'm heads-down most of the morning, buried in research, a pen in my hand as I take written notes, but I swear I have read the same sentence twelve million and ten fucking times.

Who the hell is this Kip Jackass?

I won't google her. I won't go down that dangerous minefield. I won't violate her privacy.

But fuck it.

I need to know who the hell she's dating.

Kip Cranston.

The second his photo appears, I hate him with the rage of a thousand black tar suns. I flip the pen in my hand back and forth as I study this asshole. He's a frat guy. A fifth generation Yale legacy. Just like Rose. He likes classic sports cars.

Oh, that's original.

I bet he expects women to bend over backwards for him.

I bet he thinks he's great in bed because he has family money.

I bet he doesn't listen to what women want.

I bet...

There's a cracking noise. What the fuck?

Ink leaks all over my hand. I just broke a pen.

I stare slack-jawed at the black splotch on my hand. "What is wrong with you, man?" I mutter.

I head to the restroom. At the sink, I scrub, and I scrub, and I scrub.

The ink is still there ten minutes later when Finn strides in and glances at my palm. "You broke a pen again."

"Yes," I mutter.

"You haven't broken a pen since Millie wanted to know if you'd join the country club with her. And she flipped a lid when you said no."

I seethe over the painful memory. "I hate country clubs," I grumble.

"I know that, buddy," Finn says, then meets my gaze in the mirror. "Is this about a woman?"

No point lying. He's been onto me from the start. "Yeah. Someone I can't have," I say, then I leave.

Early that evening, Layla arrives at my place right as David's leaving.

"Always taking off," she says playfully as he grabs his phone from the table by the door.

"Fingers crossed. I'm checking out a sublet. Then popping over to a shelter in the Bronx and picking up the golf clubs from Kip's. We can all meet back for food and maybe come up with a plan for picking up the rest of the items?"

"Sounds good," she says, then he waves goodbye to her and to me before he rushes off.

"He's less frazzled," she remarks as she sets down a canvas bag, then follows me to the kitchen.

I gesture to the fridge, trying to focus on something simple and mundane, so I don't spiral into Kip-fueled frustration. "Want something to drink? Water? Tea? LaCroix? Scotch? Moonshine?" I need a scotch, that's for sure.

She doesn't answer or take the bait of the moonshine joke. She points to my hand. "What happened?"

I won't give in. I can't give in. I refuse to give in. "Nothing."

"It's not nothing, Nick," she says, gentle but clear. She's refusing to give in too.

I wish her strength weren't so alluring. "It's just a pen that broke," I say as I poke around the fridge.

She sets a hand on my shoulder.

I tense, but it feels so good too.

"Hey. Are you okay?" she asks.

I get what she's doing. This is the friend routine. But we're not friends.

I shut the fridge door and turn to face the bold, brilliant blonde beauty I can't get out of my head.

Screw friendship.

Obsession wins. "I don't want you to date Kip," I say. As soon as I do, I want to take it back, but I want to imprint my inappropriate demand on the sky too.

"You don't?" Her blue eyes flicker with curiosity.

I clench my fists, hiding the stupid ink spot. "I don't, and I have no right to say that. No right to feel it. And yet I fucking do."

She inhales, watches me, then nods like she's gearing up for something. Then, she unfolds a story. "My mother likes to set me up. She has this fantasy that I'll meet some blue-blood Park Avenue guy from a good family, and then she can leave the company to me, and she won't have to worry, because she trusts no one because of my father."

There's too much to unpack there, and I feel like a jerk. Like a jealous, selfish jackass. She's got real stuff to worry about. I just carry a chip on my shoulder about where I'm from. I drag a hand through my hair. "I'm sorry, Layla," I say, heavily. "I shouldn't care."

She takes a step toward me. "But you do?"

I take a breath. Try to will away the dragon of jealousy inside me. But it's billowing great plumes of smoke. The only thing to calm it is the truth. I advance toward her and confess, "I don't want another man to date you. Or to touch you. Or to kiss you. I have no right to feel this way, and I'm doing a terrible job at being friends with you. Because I'm pretty sure you aren't supposed to feel this way about a friend."

Her lips part. Her tongue flicks across the corner of her mouth. "What way?"

I don't think. I cup her cheeks and bring my lips dangerously close to hers. "Obsessed."

She lifts her chin, like a dare. "Show me how much."

21

CORAL LIPS

Nick

Her coral lips are a tantalizing invitation.

She doesn't need to tell me twice to kiss her. Touching her is all I can think about. In an instant, I'm sweeping my lips to hers, tasting her sweet mouth once more.

I groan.

In relief, in desire, in need.

I've missed this so much. Wanted her so deeply.

I clasp her face, kiss her lips, craving even more of her. I'm intoxicated by the sight, the sound, the taste of Layla. The flavor of her lipstick is like peaches, and there's never been a more perfect taste for a woman.

She's a delicious sensory overload as the peach lipstick mingles with the heady scent from her neck, or her hair. Something fresh and floral, like jasmine. I don't know if it's her perfume or her shampoo, and I want to know, but I don't want to stop this chaotic kiss for anything.

It's wild and needy. The kind of kiss that you can't control. It's a kiss that controls you.

I hold her face tighter, kiss her more deeply, but it's still not enough. For her either, since her eager hands travel up and down my arms, grabbing at me as she goes.

She's trying to hold on tight too. Like we both know this is a flash of a kiss. It's lightning, and it won't last long.

But I want it to. God, how I want it to.

Her hands loop around my neck. She tugs on my hair. Pulls me closer.

My Layla is hungry, and I want to give her everything she needs. Curling my hands around her hips, I break the kiss then lift her up onto the counter.

In no time, she parts her legs.

"Yes, missed this so much," I say, approvingly as I slide right into the V of her thighs, pressing against her center.

"Me too," she gasps as I grind and rub, kiss and touch.

We're fully dressed, but clothes feel like a formality. Like they'll come off with a thought. This kiss feels like a prelude.

Shoving up her skirt to her waist, I yank her closer, jerk her against the ridge of my erection. She leans her head back, letting me lead the kiss entirely, urging me to claim her mouth, her neck, her whole body.

I want to claim her in every single forbidden way.

I kiss her ravenously, our tongues stroking, our lips consuming, and this feels dangerously close to fucking. I break the kiss, needing to get a handle on the situation.

Maybe.

Maybe.

I stroke her blonde hair, brushing some strands from her face, then gaze at her swollen lips. I did *that*. And this flush on her chest? Yeah, that belongs to me. "I want everyone to know you're taken," I tell her in a harsh whisper and a barren confession that surprises me.

I don't usually feel this way. This...possessive.

I can't have her, yet I want to keep her all to myself.

Her blue eyes flicker. "I'm not seeing anyone. Not for real. You have to know that," she says as she slides a hand up my shirt, grips the collar. "You're the only one I want."

I breathe out hard, trying to get a grip. "I want you so much it's driving me crazy," I say, then drop my face to her neck and lick a path up her throat, reveling in the heady, delicious taste of her. "I'm dying to go down on you. Want to make you come on my lips. I fucking missed you."

She shudders and parts her legs wider.

I'm helpless. She's irresistible.

I raise my face, a wicked grin forming on my lips. Nothing else matters right now but this sizzling connection. This wild spark between her and me.

The world can go to hell.

She's melting, and I'm running a hand down her

blouse, over the buttons, on a mad path to her sweet pussy.

All I want is another taste of her. And I've got to have it. *Now*.

My hand journeys up the soft flesh of her thighs. I can feel her heat before I touch her. Can sense how wet she is. And when I reach the apex of her thighs and run my finger down the soaked panel of her panties, my chest swells with pride.

I nuzzle her neck. "You're so wet," I say, praising her as I stroke.

"Touch me," she pleads, sounding like she's seconds away from coming, feeling like it, too, as I stroke her through her wet panties.

"I will," I say, then I hook a finger around the seam.

I'm so ready to please her. So ready to eat her, taste her, make her come ridiculously hard. But as I stroke her slickness, my phone buzzes.

Loud and insistent.

With my son's ringtone.

22

OLD STANDARDS

Nick

I'm definitely not winning any parent of the year awards. Good dads don't scramble to lift their son's friend off the counter, then wash their hands while talking to their kid.

"What's going on, kiddo?" Do I sound too chipper or what?

Layla doesn't even look my way as she flies through the living room, toward the bathroom, presumably. Meanwhile, David says, "I got the sublet! I'm moving out."

My first thought is embarrassing so I squash it. I won't go there. I will not think that his absence will make it easier for my sex life.

You don't have a sex life, man.

"That's great. I'll miss you, but I get that you want

your own place," I say, meaning it. I swear I mean it. I'm happy for my boy.

"I can move in tomorrow, but I don't think I can get everything done tonight and still meet you guys. Can you ask Layla to swing by Kip's home to get the golf clubs?"

Kip. Fucking Kip. Why does it always come back to the guy who *gets* to date her?

"Sure. Does she know where he lives? Wait. Just text it to her," I say, since I shouldn't ask, shouldn't care, shouldn't be involved in Layla's dating life.

What I should do is send her on her merry way and ask my son how I can help with his passion.

"I sent it to her," David says. "He's on Central Park West. Not too far from her place, so it should be easy. Maybe she can grab it and bring it over tomorrow?"

"Sure. We'll sort it out. And listen, I'm done with all those calls to guests. We've got lots of people coming. Why don't you let me know what else I can do while Layla's getting the golf stuff? What do you want me to pick up? I'm at your service," I say, like that exonerates me.

Like my willingness to play gopher will cover up my sins.

My lies.

My ferocious appetite for his friend.

I drop my head, shaking it in disgust.

David clucks his tongue. "Actually, I can't believe I didn't think of this sooner. But maybe just see if Layla wants help?" Then he lowers his voice, perhaps in case she's nearby. "She might not want to drag golf clubs around the city. She doesn't love to be alone at night."

Alarm bells sound. "I'll go with her."

We say goodbye just as Layla emerges from the bathroom. She's put together again, her skirt straightened perfectly, her hair smoothed neatly. Her lipstick reapplied.

The evidence of our brief tryst is mostly gone, but now she looks too poised, like she's trying to cover us up.

Another reminder I can't keep pursuing her. I can't make her lie through her presto-chango routine.

I have to focus on the task—helping my son's friend. I clear my throat. "David wants me to go with you to get the golf clubs. I can order a car service to make it easier to grab them. Then I can drop you off and bring them back here."

There. That was businesslike. Not rip-her-clothes-off-like.

She nods toward the door. "Kip texted me. He's at their Greenwich home tonight. And I have a car."

"You have a car?" No one in New York has cars—well, except for those who do.

As she picks up her bag, a fond smile tilts her lips. "It was my dad's. He got it when he won a big case. It was custom-made from a guy named Max Summers. It's electric. It's red, a dream to drive, and hot as sin."

Sounds like her.

"Let me drive," I say.

She shakes her head, amused, but we both know she's really saying yes.

* * *

We cruise along the highway as the sun dips lower in the late summer sky. Music blasts from the car stereo, a playlist Layla cued up. Alt music, she said. New and emerging bands her friend Ethan turned her onto.

I like...some of them.

"Are you a music person? Or are you more a podcast/NPR/news type of guy?" she asks. Then she shakes her head. "Don't tell me. Let me guess."

With one hand on the wheel, I toss her a glance like *try to get it right*. "Go for it," I say, since this is better than talking about Kip, and dating, and my insatiable need to touch her.

This is safer.

Driving her. Taking care of her. Helping her.

She taps her chin. "Podcasts, I bet. On economics, and theories of the universe, and how stuff is made, and why certain micro trends portend the future of business, and how the universe operates, and we're all connected."

Whoa. Can you say mind reader? I crack up, then answer, "Did you just potluck my podcast tastes? Turn them all into a big *business guy* stew?"

"I guess I did," she says, staring at me with anticipation in her eyes.

My lips twitch as I return my focus fully to the road. "You're right," I mutter. She nailed me.

She pumps a fist. "Knew it."

"I'm that easy to read?" I ask, a little annoyed, but only because I don't want to be predictable to her.

She shakes her head. "No. But I feel like *I* can read you."

My chest warms. Dangerously. "Why?"

"I saw you speak. You like theories of the world and business. You like understanding why people do and buy and think what they do. And also, it makes sense. If you're going to take chances on little companies, you need to understand the big picture."

"I guess you *can* read me," I say, then hold up a finger to make a point. "But I do like music too. I listen to a lot of tunes when I'm at the gym. Or when I'm cooking."

"What do you like?"

"Besides polka, swing music, and old standards?" I tease.

"Obviously."

With my gaze fixed ahead, I grumble out an answer. "Old standards."

She laughs, tossing her head back. "That is fantastic."

"Hey now," I tease.

She pats my arm, then lowers her voice to a stage whisper. "I like old standards too."

See? I can do this. I can just *be* with Layla without devolving into grunts or groans.

We can talk about likes and dislikes, and that's all good. But there's more I want to know about the woman by my side. I pat the dashboard briefly for emphasis as the GPS chirps, letting me know we're a mile from the Greenwich exit.

"So this was your dad's car?" I ask, careful as I broach a sensitive subject.

"I helped him pick it out," she says, and she doesn't sound sad, or distant like she was the other day. She sounds proud.

A sign to keep going. "Oh yeah?"

"He'd always wanted a sports car, and when he was researching makes and models, I suggested he try a custom-made electric. He liked the idea," she says. "I've tried to encourage my mom to change some of her business practices—to make them more clean. But she never really did. My dad was open to it though, and that meant a lot to me."

That's a passion point of hers. David's too. And honestly, it's become one of mine. But I don't want to pat myself on the back. I'd rather give credit where it's deserved. "It's nice to see your generation caring so much. Taking on a stewardship role."

"My generation?" she asks, with an arch of a brow. "We're fifteen years apart, Nick. I don't think that's a generation."

It's not the age though, really, that's keeping us apart. It's the person. And I can't keep playing these bedroom games behind my son's back. "Layla," I say, my voice heavy.

She draws a sharp breath. Holds up a hand. "I know."

I sigh again. "I can't do this to David. It's wrong."

She nods, looking straight ahead. "I know," she repeats, crisply.

"It's not fair to him," I add, flicking on the signal as I switch lanes to the exit.

"I know," she says in a three-peat. But she sounds more clipped with each answer.

I steal a glance at her. Her lips are pursed. Her jaw is clenched. And I've upset my beautiful woman.

My heart is stretched in too many directions.

I shut up as I drive the rest of the way to Kip's house.

I'm a good guy as Layla introduces me to the secret society Yale grad. I'm a great guy as I make small talk and thank the guy swimming in family money. I'm a fucking saint as I carry the golf clubs out to the circular driveway in front of said family's Greenwich mansion.

The polished blond in the mint-green polo and khaki shorts reaches for the bag as Layla pops the trunk. "I can put them in there," Kip says, reaching for the golf bag as dusk covers us.

Like that'll happen. With a jovial grin, I hoist it in. "No worries, kid. I've got this."

Kid. Ha. Take that, all you fuckers who've called me *sir*.

With the bag in place, I close the trunk, then offer a hand to shake. "Thanks again for the donation. The golf lessons will be in high demand. David and I truly appreciate it," I say with genuine gratitude. I might not like this guy, but he is helping my son, and that's something.

"So do I," Layla chimes in.

The Ken doll looks me in the eyes and says, a little smugly, "You're welcome, Mr. Bancroft."

Fuck. You.

"It's Adams. Nick Adams," I correct.

"Oops. My bad," he says, but he doesn't sound apologetic one bit. Bet he doesn't know how to apologize or why it's important.

Yup. He's an asshole. I was right.

When he lets go of my hand, he turns to Layla, holds out his arms wide. "It was so good to see you again, Mayweather."

As he hugs her goodbye, I roll my eyes. I want to laugh at him. Good luck, Kip. No woman wants a man who calls her by a buddy name—her last name.

"Good to see you too, Kip," she says, and I'm not truly irritated since I know Layla's heart and body and mind, but I do want to rip him off her, because he's touching her far too long.

If I can't touch her, he sure as shit shouldn't.

Finally, he lets go, flashing her a *smooth operator* smile. "I'll see you after the auction."

I glance down at the ink that I just couldn't scrub off my palm. And that feels like a goddamn metaphor right now.

Only, I don't know what to do with the figure of speech on my hand.

When we get back in the car, Layla's quiet again as we drive away. But she's the kind of quiet that says she's working through something. When I come to a stop at the end of Kip's road, she whips her gaze to me, sets a hand on my arm.

My skin burns with desire.

Just. Like. That.

"You're right, Nick," she says carefully, like she's been mulling something over. "It's not fair to David. Or right. But life's not fair. And there's a side road by the country club about a mile away. You're probably going to turn me down. You're probably going to say no. But what if we just—"

"I'm there."

I hit the gas and go.

23

THE WILL AND THE WAY

Layla

Backseats of expensive sports cars were meant for Hermes shopping bags and tennis rackets.

But where there's a will, there's a way. And I know exactly how to find the intersection of the two.

As Nick drives into twilight, I point right, giving directions with a determined efficiency. "Turn there." Then, right again. "There's an access road with a turnout."

"Got it," he says, all business as he drives. He doesn't ask how I know the layout of the Greenwich Country Club and its golf course.

Maybe he's connected enough dots.

Spend enough time visiting family friends in Greenwich and a girl and her pals will wander. My ride or dies and I found our way over here as kids, exploring the outskirts of the club and the course.

Finding all its hidden nooks and crannies.

Good thing I was a curious kid since it's paying off as an adult. Only, I'm curious about other things now. Namely, how long it'll take Nick to make me come.

"There," I say, pointing to the final turn onto a dog-leg road.

Once Nick reaches the dead end of that road, he cuts the engine then turns to me, heat in his eyes.

"Backseat's tiny," I say, in a coy breath.

He grabs my face. "Don't care."

"Me neither," I say.

I twist my body over the console, diving onto the black leather.

With an amused shake of his head, he follows me.

It's no small feat for a big, broad man. But he stretches alongside me. We are shoehorned into this space and I don't care one bit. We're side by side, and I hitch my leg over his and grab the neck of his shirt.

We pick up where we left off in his penthouse—making out like bandits.

His mouth is incredible. His lips are so possessive. His beard drives me wild. He kisses like I'm the only woman he's ever wanted to touch in his entire life.

Rationally, I know that's not true. But it feels true.

One hand of his travels to my hair, stroking. The other roams over my right breast, squeezing. I moan into his mouth, then kiss him harder.

But a soft, firm laugh comes from him. "I've got this," he says, then he takes over the kiss, pushing me to my back, gliding his hand down my side, over my hip, to my thigh.

As he goes, he crushes my lips. Kisses me ferociously until his hand slides between my thighs, and he cups my sex.

I wrench away from his mouth so I can unleash a needy groan. "Yes, please yes," I pant out.

He teases at my wet panties. "You want me to fuck you with my fingers?"

A sharp burst of pleasure jolts me. I feel savage as I nod. "Yes, and don't stop this time. I want one last orgasm from you."

There. I've acknowledged the reality. We can't be a thing. We can't keep doing this. And really, that's fine. At least, it has to be fine. I have no other choice but to be okay with the reality of us. But the reality is also that I've been aching for him for months. And that ache is at an eleven now. He has to ease it.

"I'll finish what I started. I'll always finish you," he rasps, but that's a promise he just can't keep.

Only, I don't care about promises this second. I care about pleasure. And I want mine.

When he slides his hand under my panties, he shudders from head to toe. "Fucking yes," he groans approvingly as his fingers glide across my wetness.

I moan my approval too.

"Mmm. You're soaked," he praises as he runs his fingers down my center, exploring me.

Already, I feel like I'm floating. "You do this to me," I tell him, feeling bolder than I did in Miami. More daring with my words.

He rubs a delicious circle against the rise of my clit. I try to spread my legs, to invite him in deeper, but there's hardly any room. We're bumping elbows, knocking knees. We're this close to falling off the seat but none of that matters because Nick's relentlessly pursuing my pleasure.

His confident fingers stroke me just so. I move with him, rocking into his touch as best I can in this confined space.

"You were going to leave me hanging," I say breathlessly, rebuking him. "That would have been so mean."

"Forgive me," he says, husky and low.

"Only if you make me come."

He covers my mouth with his, giving me a bruising kiss before he pulls back. "Your mouth. Your sexy, dirty mouth is so hot."

I smile. I didn't try to work on dirty talk. I just feel it with him. And Miami unlocked something in me, I'm learning. This side of me. The side that wants shameless sex and words. Unfettered passion.

"Like yours," I whisper.

He gives me another commanding kiss, pulling away to whisk his beard across my face as he whispers, "I'll get you there. I'll always get you there."

He strokes and teases, fingers and thrusts, following my cues.

The faster he goes, the more pleasure cascades down my spine, radiates through my legs.

Soon, the march of impending bliss begins. In my thighs, in my belly, in my center. Everything tightens. Ecstasy curls, twists inside me in a spark.

"Yes, give it to me," he urges, grunting in my ear, his

fingers filling me, rubbing me, his possession enveloping me.

I grab his arm tightly, dig my nails into his flesh, desperate to hold on to him.

I shatter, breaking apart into forbidden bliss in the back of my sports car on a deserted road outside a country club in Greenwich, Connecticut.

With a man I can't have again.

A man who sees me for Lola and for Layla. But who sees my present, not my past.

He sees me as I want to be seen, and I don't think that's because I've held back pieces of me.

I think it's because of him. How he is. Who he is.

And I like who he is so much it hurts.

24

MAYBE IN CONNECTICUT

Nick

Sure, I did say this was wrong.

But I guess I bent the rules again.

You broke them, dickhead.

But dammit, breaking the rules feels so good as Layla's skin flushes, her cheeks red in a post-orgasm glow.

We're sardines here in the backseat of her sports car, parked outside a country club Rose's parents belonged to way back when.

The place I worked at in high school, waiting tables. I traveled here from Queens, since the tips were better in Greenwich, so I know all the nooks and crannies, but I don't want to tell her my stories of the club right now.

Nope.

This is the place where I was looked down on.

Where the members tossed their greenbacks at me with barely a second thought.

I feel a little defiant tonight, wrapped up with Layla outside the country club that I could now buy a million memberships for. But I never will. I won't buy one. Anywhere.

I like it better on the outside.

And on the outside, I get to have *this*. A woman who doesn't judge.

This fantastic woman, basking by my side.

And I think I'll take a little more of her, thank you very much.

As she breathes out hard once again, I lift my fingers to my mouth and suck off the taste of her.

I groan salaciously.

She turns her head, watching me with avid eyes. "How do I taste?"

"Like salt and sex and sweetness," I tell her.

Her gaze drifts down me to the ridge in my slacks. Hard, insistent.

I'm not asking for a hand job. I'm not asking for anything. I didn't make her come so I could come too. But when she palms me, I groan.

"Let me," she whispers.

I shake my head, but it feels futile already. "You don't have to. I just wanted to take care of you. I always want to take care of you."

"And I want to touch you," she says, insisting, gripping me tighter.

"There's hardly any room here. Don't want to make a mess of this car," I say, to give her an out.

With a roll of her eyes, she tsks me. "I'm not going to use my hand."

Oh, fuck. Oh, hell. Oh, yes.

That's a horse of a different color—the blow job color.

"Suck me off, beautiful," I tell her.

"I thought so." She's speedy, maneuvering between my legs, undoing the button on my pants. I help her along, eagerly pushing down my slacks, my boxer briefs, then offering her my throbbing cock.

She nibbles on the corner of her lips, then curls her fist around the base. Lust rattles through my whole body. I'm a raging forest fire already.

"Lick it," I command.

She obeys, her lush blonde hair spilling across my lap as she flicks her tongue over the head.

"Yessss," I gasp.

I'm in dirty heaven as she draws me into her warm mouth. It's a fiesta of my favorite things—her hair fanned out on my lap, her lips around my dick, her scent filling the car.

Her.

Just her.

She's diligent, a blow-job worker bee as she sucks with speed and purpose. Fine by me. No woman should have to finesse a blow job in the back of a car.

"Won't take long," I mutter as she swallows more of me.

I swear she smiles against my dick.

"Gonna watch you the whole fucking time," I say.

She lifts her face briefly, her eyes flashing with wickedness. Then, she's back to work.

Pushing those gorgeous strands away from her face, I savor the filthy view. My dick filling her mouth, pushing on her cheek. Her swollen lips stretched around my shaft. Her eyes watering just a bit.

What a sight.

My thighs shake.

She sucks harder.

I'm not far off. "Do that again," I urge as my chest heats up.

She complies, sucking harder, taking me deeper.

My balls tighten. "Gonna come," I warn.

I lose it, coming down her throat in seconds as I enjoy the fantastic sight of this beautiful woman hell-bent on owning my dick.

Well, she does own it.

But she's owning a hell of a lot more of me too.

That's the problem. And I'm not sure I'm going to find a solution to it tonight, so I stop trying.

It's only an hour to Manhattan. But a few minutes into the return drive, her stomach growls.

I grab the opportunity her belly is offering. "Let me feed you before we get back," I say.

Once we reach the city, I'll have to snap back to my proper role. Father, businessman, friend to Layla.

Here in Connecticut, we're still in no-man's land. The tryst zone.

"If you insist," she says.

"I do."

Ten minutes later, we're walking into a roadside diner at a rest stop. Layla tosses me a smile. "I love diners," she says.

"How unusual."

"Don't mock me for liking something," she says, a little hurt.

No way do I ever want to hurt her. "Sorry. That was a dick move. I'm glad you like diners," I say, to ease my callous remark. "Especially since not everyone admits they do."

"But I've never been to a rest-stop diner," she adds, quick to forgive.

I wrap an arm around her waist. "Good. I get another first."

She shivers against me, then eyes my arm. "I thought this was wrong," she says, like she's catching me on a technicality but one she wants to find too.

Let's take this loophole we're making up on the fly, Layla.

"Maybe in Connecticut, it's not," I offer as we reach the door to the diner. "Want me to stop?"

She meets my gaze, her eyes wide, vulnerable. "I don't. That's the issue."

I squeeze tighter, a little sad, but glad, too, for this stolen moment. "Same here," I say, then brush a kiss to her soft cheek.

A hostess ushers us to a booth for two, and we order quickly, Layla opting for a salad and fries while I pick an omelet.

When we shut the menus, she looks at me with a particular intensity in her eyes. "So, what did you mean with the whole *not everyone admits they do* comment?"

Ah, I figured I wouldn't get away with mic dropping that. But it's for the best. "I just like that you're…real. You don't seem to have these judgments about school, or jobs, or where people come from."

She smiles, shakes her head. "I hope I don't." But then she winces, like the question pains her. "But others have?"

I heave a sigh, drag a hand across my beard. Do I want to dive this deep into my past? We're not supposed to get close.

Or…closer.

But one look at Layla and the patience in her eyes, and my plan to keep my younger years to myself crumbles. I want to get closer to her, even just for tonight, so I serve up my past on a plate. "My ex's family hated me. Maybe that's understandable. I'm the asshole who got their princess pregnant. *Their words*. But they didn't like where I was from," I say.

"What do you mean?"

"I waited tables at that country club where they were members. That's how I met Rose. I was the guy from the other side of the tracks because my family didn't have money."

"That's terrible," she says, quick to defend me. "That's a shitty way to treat someone."

She sounds so tough, so independent, and so damn certain of what's right and wrong. A welcome sign perhaps that twenty-somethings are less judgmental than their grandparents. I sure hope so.

"I'm over it," I say with a shrug that I hope comes off as careless.

"But it still stings?" she asks gently, seeing through my act immediately.

I don't say anything at first. This kind of vulnerability with a woman is new to me. Hell, it's new with friends, with family, with anyone but Finn. Vulnerability is not an emotion I like to traffic in too much.

But I invited her into this conversation. I ought to let her in all the way. "I suppose," I mutter.

Her expression is warm as she says, "I know that was hard for you to say. But thank you. I want to know *you*," she adds, then bobs a hopeful shoulder. "Since, maybe in Connecticut we can get to know each other."

My heart lurches. "I want to know you too," I say, then clasp our fingers together and return to the tale. "Anyway, my parents lived paycheck to paycheck. I had to earn my own dough and find scholarship money to go to college. I was here *a lot* working. All day. I'd have swim team practice all week, meets on Saturday morning, then I worked the rest of the weekend," I say.

She listens attentively. "That's a lot to balance, Nick."

"It was, but my friends and I—the waiters, the caddies, the club attendants—we had fun after work. Hung out in that spot where you took me tonight."

"You knew that spot," she says, a smile breaking through over this shared history.

"I did, beautiful. Bet you came here with your dad,

bet he took his lovely family out to lunch, bet you and your friends sneaked off to explore the grounds," I say.

The smile widens. "We did. But I never took a boy *there*."

I return her smile, feeling a little like I have an ace up my sleeve. "And I never took a girl there," I say, playing my card.

"Really?"

"I swear," I say.

"So I get a first of yours?" She sounds too delighted, and I want to stay here in this happy, flirty place with her all night.

"You sure did," I say, reaching for her hand and running my thumb along her index finger. She shivers.

But that's my cue to stop. I can't get caught up in her and me, in our sweet nothings. I clear my expression so I can focus on the serious story I need to tell her. "Anyway, like I was saying, I met Rose here. Waited on her family. And then later, when Rose found out she was pregnant, her parents kind of took over all my choices." A flash of self-loathing hits me square in the chest. Those hard days return to me in sharp relief. I'd fucked up. Big time. "Which made sense. They were rich. They had means. They had nannies. I was heading to a community college, hoping to land a swimming scholarship to a state school, which I did. But Rose had already been admitted to Yale. And her parents pulled me aside after the lunch service one afternoon. I was in my waiter's uniform, and her dad said to me in a quiet hallway behind the clubhouse, *Rose is done slumming it with you. And you will not ruin our daughter's chances at Yale.*"

My face is red hot, all over again.

Layla reaches for my hand across the table. It feels good—her touch as I tell this story.

"He said *she will finish college like all Bancrofts do. And if you want to go to school too, we will raise* her *child while she's at Yale. He'll have our name. He'll be a Bancroft.*"

"Oh, Nick. That's what you meant by their rules," she says, frowning.

"Yeah," I say hollowly, scrubbing my free hand across my jaw, like that'll erase the shame I felt then. But time has healed that wound, since that's what time does. "They barely let me see my own kid when I was in college, right after he was born. I didn't have much choice in the matter. The only way either one of us could go to school was if the Bancrofts raised David in those early years. Rose and I were lucky, I suppose, to have that option."

"I understand what you mean," she says.

"I wouldn't quite call it a Faustian bargain, but I had to go along with their wishes if I was going to carve out a life someday for myself, for my son, for the mother of my child."

"That's hard. You made the only choice you could make," she says.

I'm glad she sees it that way. That's how it felt to me. I had no other options. "I just wanted to pay the bills, make my own way. Take care of my family," I say. I don't share this story with just anyone. Hell, I don't think I even told Millie. But I want Layla to understand me. To know why I said *this is wrong*. "So that's why David and I don't have the same last name. When Rose and I graduated from college and finally got married, there was still no relenting. A name was a little thing. I didn't push. I just said thank you, then moved into a small apartment with my wife and my kid. Until Rose and I both finally admitted we were a terrible match."

Layla links her fingers through mine. "That's a lot to go through," she says.

But she's been through a lot too. "We all have stuff to deal with. I'm just glad he's a good kid. I'm glad I have a good relationship with him. We're in the same city again. We work together and see each other a lot. I don't want to mess it up, Layla," I say, and I sound desperate.

Desperate to have it all.

But I can't.

Even when she squeezes back. Even when it feels so right to share pieces of myself with her.

But it's not right, and we're going to leave Connecticut very, very soon.

25

LITTLE RICH GIRL

Layla

After Nick parks the car in my nearby garage, he walks me to my home on Seventy-Third. We stop by the stoop of the brownstone next door. He looks up at my building with obvious admiration in his eyes.

It is, by all measure, a gorgeous building. One that most twenty-three-year-olds wouldn't live in on their own.

And, really, I don't.

After what he told me in the diner, I might as well slap a sandwich board on my chest—*I'm a little rich girl*.

It's borderline embarrassing that I don't pay for my beautiful, sunlit, sixth-floor one-bedroom by myself. I don't pay for it *at all*. In Miami, I held back pieces of myself. I've still clutched tight the stories I don't want to share.

But he opened the drawer to his past tonight,

offering the unvarnished truth. And the more he gives of himself, the more I want to give him the real me.

All of me.

The desire to open up is almost rabid, like I have to exorcize words, and stories, and truths. This impulse is so new. I certainly didn't look for this kind of connection with a person. I didn't expect it. I even tried to avoid it.

And yet every time I'm with Nick, all I want is to get closer to him. I can't physically. We have to stand a few feet apart, and I hate the distance. It's the opposite of what I want as I succumb to this animal instinct clawing at me to share with him.

Even if we can't be a thing, I want him to know the me without makeup. "I have a trust fund. My mother is disgustingly rich. My father was very successful. I've never struggled like that," I say, the truth tasting saccharine-sweet for the first time. "I'm sorry."

His eyes are soft, caring. "Don't say that. Don't apologize."

"But I feel bad. I'm everything you don't like."

"Stop," he says sternly as he wraps a hand around the railing behind him, like he needs it to hold him back from touching me. "You are everything I like."

I don't deserve that kindness. I didn't earn it. "You must think of me as the poor little rich girl," I say, as I wave a hand at the beautiful brick building I didn't earn, the residence most New Yorkers would trade an organ for. This building is straight out of a silver-screen romance. "I didn't even have to use my trust fund money for this. My father owned several apartments in this building. He was a defense attorney. The best in the city. The apartments were a real estate investment he made after a particularly good year at his law firm," I say in another confession that feels almost shameful. Like, *look how one percent of one percent I am.* "Well, my mom owns the apartments now. Everything of *his* went to her. Including what was left of his law firm, Mayweather and McBride."

There. I've inched closer to that awful truth too. I've breathed *his* name out loud to Nick.

His eyes fill with sorrow. "You don't have to justify yourself to me. And you absolutely don't have to justify your family to me."

"But I feel like I do," I say, and my voice is pitchy and it's irritating me. It must irritate him. "I don't want you to see me that way," I say, desperation twisting up inside me like a coiled snake. I point at all these *things*. "I have this car, and this free home, and a house in the Hamptons, and even though I pay my own way with my app and my videos, I don't really because I don't pay rent. And you must think I sound like all the people who looked down on you when you worked at the country club."

"I don't think that," he says, insistent. "How could I?"

"How could you not?" I ask, backing up against the railing on the first step, because I just can't tempt myself with closeness.

But he lets go of the railing, moves closer to me, sets a gentle hand on my cheek. "I don't hate money. I don't hate people who have money. I *only* hate the way it changes people," he says, and his warm voice is so kind, I want to wrap myself in it all night long.

All week.

All month.

But that's pointless.

I don't even know why I'm trying to prove myself to him. We can't be together. We can't be a thing. We are just two people who can't stand next to each other on the street because we're too forbidden. But the prospect of him walking away tonight and thinking for even a second that I'd have said those things to him that others did, that I'd have treated him like he wasn't good enough, rips me apart. "Just because my mom wants certain things for me," I begin, the words catching in my throat, stirring up emotions I don't want to fully face—her wants, her wishes, her future dreams. "That doesn't mean I'm like that," I add. "I'm not looking for a rich guy. I'm not looking for a name, or a pedigree, or an Ivy diploma. I'm not looking for anyone."

At least, I wasn't.

Then I got to know him. And the desire to touch him turned into the desire to know him. And for him to know me.

So I stop before I reveal too much. But then, screw it. Tonight is for revelation. "I've already met the only man who interests me, but I can't be with him," I say, laying out my heart. "You, Nick."

His expression darkens with dashed hope. "Same here," he says, regretfully.

"So I don't want you to think of me like those jerks in your past. Okay? I just don't. I'm not like that."

With surprising tenderness, he leans in and presses his forehead to mine, in spite of the risks. "I know, beautiful. I know who you are," he adds softly, and I'm dying to rope my hands around his neck and kiss him passionately right here.

Instead, I grab the railing behind me, like he did before.

He must sense the tension in me, and how hard this is, since he backs away, resignation in those haunting hazel eyes. "If I stay here any longer, I won't leave. I'll toss you over my shoulder and kick down the door, then spend the night showing you exactly what I think of you," he says with both heat and affection.

I manage a smile, a small thanks for that sexy and warm sentiment. "I wish you could."

"I wish I could too," he says, in a sad whisper. Then he shakes his head, huffs out a breath. "I should get going." He drags a hand through his hair. "I'll see you...around."

I swipe a hand across my cheek, then nod as resolute as I can. "See you—"

But I swallow the word when I hear a familiar voice call out: "Layla!"

I snap to attention at the sound of Raven. Her voice is coming from behind me but crawling up my spine.

This is not how I should feel about a friend.

Putting on a false face, I turn around to see my business school colleague staring curiously at me, then at Nick.

Did she see Nick's forehead touching mine?

Did she hear his sweet nothings?

Or my confessions?

My stomach twists. "Hi, Raven," I say brightly, way more cheerfully than I normally would. "What are you up to?"

She swings a purple boho purse over her shoulder. "Just finished a date. It wasn't too bad. And you?"

She looks at Nick, and my neck goes hot.

The implication. Dear god, the implication.

But I'll have to squash it with a lie.

"We were just picking some things up for the auction," I say, trying but likely failing to mask how uncomfortable I feel.

I'm a liar.

I can hear my father's murderer saying those words to him the week before his death. The accusation so loud, so vitriolic, it seeped through the phone call in my father's home office. Then, I recall the worry I felt when I asked Dad after he hung up, "Is everything okay with Joe?"

"Just a disagreement," my father had said. "It happens in business."

I try to shake off the terrible memory of a week later when I opened the door to my home.

Clearing away the past, I gesture awkwardly to the handsome man by my side. "This is," I begin, pausing to collect my thoughts better.

But Raven's eyes shine with recognition. "You're the guy from the conference!"

Great. Nick must think I blabbed to Raven about banging him. "Nick Adams," he says, with a professional grin as he extends a hand. "Strong Ventures now. Nice to meet you."

He's a pro at navigating weirdness. He's dealt with uncomfortable social situations since he was seventeen. But I can't let him manage this one solo. "The guy who keynoted in Miami," I jump in to clarify as she lets go of his hand. Raven has no idea Nick and I were a thing that night.

"Right. I heard you were great," she adds, and it's not her fault, but she still makes it sound like I kissed and told.

"His speech was great," I add, and why am I not better at this? I know how to fake it when my mom sends me on dates. Why can't I be more smooth right now when I need it most? When my insides are jumpy and my heart is too tender?

"That's the word on the street. Anyway..." Raven's gaze flickers from Nick to me. And I know, I just know I'll be getting a text from her later asking what's up.

"Nick and I are doing some work on planning David's fundraiser. Picking up auction items," I say, finally explaining myself. "For A Helping Paw. The one you're donating to."

"Yes, thank you. We appreciate that," Nick adds.

"Oh, right. You're David's dad," Raven says, then she shakes her head, like she's admonishing herself some more. "I really should have gone to your keynote. But you know what? I'm going to download it from the conference app tonight and listen to it on my morning run."

"I hope you enjoy it," Nick says smoothly.

"I know I will." Raven comes in to give me a quick hug. "Details," she whispers in my ear, then waves a hand and saunters down the street.

When I return my self-conscious gaze to Nick, I feel foolish. I feel young. I feel...like a little liar.

"I should go," I say so I don't do another risky thing tonight.

"Me too."

I turn to head into the lobby, then stop. "I never said a thing to her. About us," I whisper. "I need you to know that."

"I know that," he says, then sighs heavily, and drags a hand over the back of his neck, like whatever's coming next pains him to say. "But Layla?"

He doesn't even have to say the next thing. *We can't do this again.*

Forget tender. My heart feels bruised. "I know we can't do this again, Nick. Good night."

Then I run past the doorman and into my building, up the elevator, into my apartment. I shut and deadbolt the door quickly, turning on the lights, refusing to look back.

I have to move forward.

When Raven texts me a few minutes later, I vow to take the first step in moving on. From my bureau, I grab a tank to wear to bed, then I click open her text. But I already know what it's going to say. And I'm right.

> Raven: Did I pick up on a vibe with the hot daddy? Because I'm pretty sure I picked up on a vibe.

I curse under my breath as I sit on the edge of my red chaise longue. Then, I ignore the kernel of guilt wedging itself into my chest as I tap out a reply.

> Layla: Ha! Would it be terrible if I said I wish? I mean, the man's hot and all, but he's more like a mentor.

There. It's true enough.

> Raven: Ah, got it. Well, maybe in another life. Let's catch up soon! You owe me some clubbing time.

> Layla: I do! And you can cash in. Can't wait to see you in the Hamptons.

I toss my phone on my bed, far, far away where I won't have to tap out any more lies. A true enough lie is still a lie.

26

WHATEVER IT WAS, WHATEVER IT WASN'T

Layla

On Sunday night, Jules reclines on my purple sofa, staring daggers at the bottle of pinot gris, like it's the cause of my romantic woes. "Fuck white wine. You need whiskey after that sad story," she declares when I finish giving them chapter and verse on my sorry situation.

It's a girls' night in at my place, and Harlow, Jules, and Camden are gathered around the olive and cheese tray on the coffee table. A deck of cards sits next to it, along with poker chips.

But we paused our game of poker once I told them about the Friday night run-in with Raven. "So yeah, that was super fun," I say, flipping a poker chip absently. "Telling a big fat lie to a colleague."

"You win. That's definitely the suckiest romantic situation I've heard in a while," Camden says, then points to the wine. "And you don't need wine or whiskey. You need a massage, a pedicure, and a blowout from the best in the city."

I laugh, skeptical but interested. "Blowouts cure the man blues?"

Camden flips her red strands. "Fact: a good hair day is the only true fix for a dating conundrum."

"Conundrum," Jules deadpans, staring at her bestie. "More like a dating dead end."

I whimper, then lift my glass and glug the rest of my wine.

Harlow leans her head against my shoulder. "My poor pet."

I set the glass down on the coffee table with a thunk, then sigh. "I mean, whatever. I can't be that sad. It's not like we were even dating," I say, trying to keep the whole thing—whatever it is, whatever it was, whatever it wasn't—in perspective.

Camden scoffs. "Oh, I'd be sad if I couldn't have hot sex with my friend's dad."

Jules swats Camden's shoulder. "Girl, do not even think about my dad that way."

"Not your dad, babe. But some dads are hot," she says with a *you know it* shrug.

"Fact," I chime in, smiling for the first time in several minutes. "Like David's dad."

Jules doesn't break her stony expression, still directed at Camden. "But not *my* dad. Not Tate Marley."

Jules huffs but then draws a circle in the air around us. "No one here is banging any of our dads." She crosses her legs, kicking her Mary Jane heel back and forth, looking like some kind of *come at me* siren. But that's Evening Jules. With her short plaid skirts, and button-up white blouses, she's got a whole naughty-but-tough schoolgirl look going. Makes me wonder how many costumes she has.

Harlow pats my shoulder. "Exactly. Layla's banging her *ex's* dad," Harlow chimes in.

I gasp. "You're evil, Harlow."

"I mean, you *are* banging him," Harlow adds, then lifts her iced tea, smirking above the rim before she takes a sip.

"We did not bang the other night," I point out, squaring my shoulders.

Camden clears her throat. "Wasn't his dick in your mouth?"

"In the backseat of your sports car?" Jules adds.

I grab a pillow and throw it at Jules.

She catches it. "I'm just saying. You were pretty much banging."

I hold up a stop-sign hand. "And there is no more banging. It's a bad idea. A very bad idea."

"Banging an ex-boyfriend's dad does seem complicated..." Jules adds, going thoughtful, letting go of the tease as she meets my eyes. "But it also sounds like it was more than banging. It sounds like you like him."

That's the million-dollar issue. I sink back into my couch. "I do." I swallow roughly, past the knot of emotions tightening my throat. "I didn't want to. I didn't want to feel a thing. But now I feel so much it scares me."

The mood shifts in my living room. The easy vibe

slinks under the door. "Is there a way at all?" Jules asks, carefully.

I've played out scenarios. But they're all so complicated. "I don't see how there could be. He's such a good dad. He cares so much about David, and he's focused on his son. Which only makes him more attractive."

With a sad smile, Camden reaches for the wine bottle. "Maybe you two just needed to get it out of your system, and when you see each other again, everything will be fine."

But will he be out of my system? *I wish.* Though it hardly feels possible. I pick up the deck to deal.

"Who knows?" I say as I shuffle. "I'll see him at the auction next weekend. And probably this week, too, to finish up some prep, but I don't know if I'll ever see him alone again."

Though, I do know. I probably won't see him by himself. That's what we agreed to on Friday night. I haven't heard from him all weekend. He hasn't called or texted, and I haven't either. Nor has DistractibleGuy left any comments on my videos.

I know why he hasn't. Truly, I do. But I wish he had.

I hold up my glass. Camden refills it. "Maybe that's for the best," she says, sympathetically.

There's a collective nod.

"Maybe it is," I say reluctantly. Only, I'm not certain anymore. I've let Nick in more than anyone except my friends, and I can't help but think he's worth it.

But we're just not in the cards.

I deal the next hand and go on to lose the game. I try not to view it as a metaphor.

* * *

Two days later, I meet with Mia and Storm at a pool hall. The fashionista loves to play, and she's been teaching Storm, she tells me.

Storm taps her shoulder with the pool cue. "She's the pool mentor I never knew I needed. Do you know how hot guys think it is when you can play pool?" He brandishes the stick with a wicked smile.

"Gee, I wonder why," Mia deadpans, staring pointedly at the stick.

"You said it, hun," he says in playful accusation. He has pet names for everyone. It's delightful.

"Hmm. What about pool hall makeup," she muses, changing topics on a dime. She looks to me, her gray eyes twinkling.

"We need a how-to on that," we say in unison.

"Yes! And we need events, and sessions, and so many things," she declares.

As the three of us play, we brainstorm our next collaborations. At the end of the game, Mia sets her palms on the edge of the table, her loose curls flowing around her like she's an ethereal dark angel. "I want to integrate your app into my brand, Lola," she says, going starkly serious again. "With you running it still. With your vids. I think it could take us both to new levels."

I'm a little giddy with hope. Especially since it sounds too good to be true. Still, when we leave, I say, "By the way, my real name is Layla, as you may know. You can call me Layla if you want."

"What would you like me to call you?" she asks.

"I'm good with both," I say.

"Then Lola works for me."

"You're my Lola girl," Storm chimes in.

I smile, then I take a mental picture of the three of us. I imagine we look as hopeful as I feel.

Then, Mia's phone trills. She emits a squeak when she sees who's calling. "Oh! That's my honey in California. Ciao!"

In a heartbeat, she's off, turning the other way, tra-la-la-ing down the block like the fashionista the media has made her out to be. Flighty and whimsical.

I like her. A lot. I want to believe she's not simply Mia Jane, that she's also the Mia I've come to know in these brief interactions—a smart businesswoman. Someone who makes things happen, opening up flagship stores in a heartbeat. Someone trustworthy. But what if she's not?

After all, hopes can be dashed in the blink of an eye, so I try to temper mine.

* * *

When I leave, I meet David at a coffee shop in Chelsea, and I feel like a liar once again just by breathing.

He wraps his arms around me in a hug. "Dude, I have good news!"

"Tell me," I say, eager to keep the spotlight on him.

"Cynthia is going to come with me to the auction. She wants to help out backstage."

I squeeze him harder, sharing his excitement. "I

guess things with her are definitely going well then?" I ask when I let go.

"They are. But you'll forgive me for cheating on you, right?"

I laugh to cover up my feelings. "Of course. But she better not emcee it with you," I say, wagging a finger, keeping the mood playful.

"You're my auction emcee. She's my date," he says, sounding proud.

"You're not going to propose again at the auction, are you?"

He laughs. "Probably not. But I do think the whole slower-speed approach worked. Work has been tough for her since her boss at the bowling alley is a hard-ass. Plus, she's saving to go back to college. She's balancing a lot. She admitted that's what freaked her out when I proposed."

"I'm glad she told you that."

"Me too. It helped," he says, and then his smile brightens more, so it's nearly contagious. "Oh, and my dad's going to meet her tomorrow night."

That's...wow. I *should* say a simple *that's terrific*. But I'm feeling too many things at once—surprise at this news, a little disappointment that Nick didn't tell me, then foolishness for thinking he would. We're not having *that* kind of relationship. We're not having any kind of relationship.

His relationship is rightfully with his son. "That's great," I say, meaning it. These two men care so deeply for each other. I should not get in the way.

David beams, nodding a few times. His enthusiasm

makes him look even younger than his twenty-one years. "Yeah, I'm stoked. Especially since my mom has no interest in meeting her. But no surprise." He's trying to sound blasé, but I'm not buying it.

"She'll come around," I reassure him, even though I truly have no idea. With Rose, it seems like, well, like the apple didn't fall far from the tree.

David shrugs lightly, as if he's taking it all in stride. "It is what it is. Even though she's a bartender, she's kind of shy when she's out of her element. And my mom is a little, how shall we say, intense. My dad's good with people though. But you know that already," he says, and wham.

One mention of his dad and me, and tension slams into my bones. Does David know something? Is he onto us? Did Raven say something to David? They aren't that close, but you never know. I'm on alert as David adds, "And thanks again for getting those golf clubs from Kip."

"It was my pleasure," I say, then wish I could take it back because of the double entendre.

"Maybe you and Dad could grab some of the final items later this week?"

Yes, god yes.

But no, just no. Nick and I agreed to stop. "Why don't you send me the list? I'll grab them in my car," I say.

"But then you'd have to park at, like, five different places in the city."

Solving a Rubik's Cube in under a minute would be easier, but still, I say, "I really don't mind doing it. I could even ask Harlow or Ethan. Or Jules. Or Camden."

I might as well list everyone I'm friends with.

But David waves a dismissive hand. "You know what? I'll go with you. It'll be fun."

David Adam Bancroft is the happiest person I've ever known. My heart warms up just being near him, and I'm aching to tell Nick that he did right with this kid. That no matter how complicated the situation was when David was born, somehow, his dad—maybe his mom too—managed to give their son what he needed to become this good, upbeat, kind young man.

But truthfully, I know David's heart comes from one person—his father. David is the man he is because of Nick.

And that makes me happy. But a little sad too.

Central Park is fifty-one blocks long and three blocks wide, and every time I walk through this centerpiece of the city, I feel like it contains so many secrets in plain sight. Secrets that its forty-two million visitors a year walk past day in and day out.

I almost feel like I could disappear in there, and sometimes that's what I need. That evening, with the sun still high in the summer sky, I head into the park on my way home, walking along the lake, past joggers and cyclists and after-work exercise warriors till I reach the edge of the water. A little bit beyond, I find an empty green bench under a tree. I beeline for it before anyone else can claim it.

I do some of my best thinking here, and, admittedly, my worst thinking too.

Alone, I replay the last several days, the last several weeks, all the conversations, with my friends, with David, with Nick. I wish there were an easy answer. I wish I could ask someone for the right answer.

Would I ask my dad if he were here?

I don't honestly know. It's not as if we talked about romance or boys when I was seventeen. He was a typical dad like that, and I was a typical girl.

Would I ask him now that I'm twenty-three?

I don't know the answer to that either.

Instead, I ask myself the questions.

But I don't like the answers I'm giving me, so I stand, run my thumb along the glistening metal plaque on the top slat of the bench, and then go.

27

FOUR DAYS AND FOURTEEN HOURS

Nick

It's Wednesday, and I'm stepping into the elevator in my office building, checking the time on my watch.

It's one-thirty, which means it's been four days and fourteen hours since I left Layla.

I've been non-stop since eleven-thirty on Friday night. Like I had any other choice. You have to fight fire with fire. Obsession with obsession. So I poured myself into work all weekend, coffee and me powering through my days and into the night, stopping for little except dinner with my parents and Finn on Sunday evening. Dad gave Finn more tough love about Marilyn. Finn grumbled more, then Mom told Dad to let Finn figure it out in his own time. Finn asked me later if that meant Mom thought Marilyn was bad for him.

We all do, I'd wanted to say. Instead, I'd said, *Everyone just wants you to be happy and you haven't been.*

Since then, my week has been wall to wall, and that's both good for business and for sanity. I just finished a lunch meeting with the founder of an encryption app that has my brain buzzing. I'm itching to crack open my wallet and fund the startup now. But due diligence matters.

And due diligence damn well better keep me busy for the rest of the day.

When I get off the elevator on my floor, I'm in the zone, ready to power through my afternoon. First, though, I head down the hall and pop into David's cube to say hello. I try not to visit him too much at work. Don't want to look like I'm giving him special treatment, but I do want to make sure he's fitting in and learning. His small cube looks like his already. There's a framed picture of Cynthia and him on the desk, from the hiking expedition over the summer. Then a stress ball to squeeze, and a wall calendar from an animal shelter.

"How's everything going, David?"

He looks up from his laptop with a droll expression. "Well, considering your social media was white bread until I arrived, it's better."

Whoa. "Someone is cocky," I say, jerking my gaze back. Then I furrow my brow. "Also, what's white bread?"

"Boring, Dad. Boring," he says.

"Then make it...un-boring."

"That's my goal," he says, then shoos me away. "Don't want anyone to see the boss hanging around too long."

"Message received," I say, then rap my knuckles on the padded half wall in a goodbye. "See you tonight at Dragonfly."

A smile tilts his lips as he says, "See you then."

There. I'll be busy tonight too. My schedule is so damn full.

I leave, heading toward my office where Kyle greets me from his desk just outside. "Hello, Mr. Adams," he says. "Did you have a good lunch meeting?"

"Fantastic, Kyle," I say, since I'm staying in the work zone. "And now I need to bury myself in research."

Bring it on, research. Rain down from the sky in a deluge.

"Great. Don't forget we have the HR session though at three."

That slipped my mind. Maybe I've been too focused. "Remind me?"

A shock of sandy-brown hair falls on his forehead, and he pushes it back. "The HR consultant you and your brother hired as part of the merger is hosting a series of sessions on creating a culture of respect in the workplace. The first session is today."

I snap my fingers, remembering. That's important, even though I'll have to leave my cave for it. "Right. Right. I'll be there."

"Oh, and I confirmed your reservation for three at Dragonfly tonight. The address is in your calendar."

"Excellent," I say, and I thank him and head into my office.

But before I can dive into work, Finn raps on the door, then strides in. "Find any good tech to invest in, or can I plan on beating you with the firm's next big funding?"

"Like I'd tell you before I reeled them in." This competition with my brother is half the fun of being in business together.

Finn scoffs. "Like I'd tell you about any good content plays before I snagged them."

There's a freedom and a shorthand in working with Finn at last. *You don't play in my sandbox. I don't play in yours.* But together we make it rain. And it rains on our terms—the terms of two brothers from the wrong side of the tracks who made it big.

All on our own.

He glances at my palm which I've wiped clean of evidence of my Layla obsession. "Guess the woman isn't driving you wild anymore," he observes.

I wish.

"I'm all good," I say. It's the furthest thing from accurate. But I'll have to make it true, or I might go crazy. Especially when I head to the session at three. This discussion of inappropriate workplace language is making me think of other inappropriate things.

David warned me that Cynthia might be a little shy, and she was at first, but an hour into dinner, she seems to be holding her own.

We finish our dishes debating how to bowl your best game. "Look," I say. "Here's my official take: it's all about the swing..." I pause, lift my bottle of beer, then add, "But honestly, it's down to the beer."

Cynthia laughs. "Beer does make you bowl better."

"Fact," David chimes, then sets down his chopsticks. "We should all go bowling sometime. There's an alley in Brooklyn near my new place."

"I'd like that," I tell him. "But I have to warn you—I'd beat you all. Get ready for a phenomenal level of destruction." I am smug but honest.

David whistles, then claps Cynthia's shoulder. "Dude. Are you taking on my girl? She's the queen of bowling."

"You *and* her," I say. "*Dude.*"

"Hey, everyone's dude to me."

"I've noticed, and yes, I will take you both on." Then I turn to include David's date. "As long as that works for Cynthia."

"I'm game," the brunette says with a smile. "How are you so good at bowling, Mr. Adams?"

I've asked her to call me Nick, but she seems more comfortable with the formality, so I don't insist again. As for her question, I could tell her my dad played. That he taught Finn and me from an early age. That it was part of our world. But there's a simpler answer. "Because bowling's awesome," I say, then finish my beer.

When the meal ends, I call a cab to take the two of them to Brooklyn, since Cynthia is staying in the city tonight.

At the curb, she extends a hand. "Thanks again for

dinner, Mr. Adams. I'm so glad we could meet before the auction."

The reminder of the auction jolts my brain back to Layla.

I try not to think about seeing her there, dressed up in something stunning. Because she's always stunning. She'll be hosting the event with David. We'll be in the same room for hours, while I have to keep my cool.

I try, but I fail, since I'm thinking of her jasmine scent, her lush hair, her soft skin.

What is she doing tonight? Is she having a hard time *not* reaching out to me too? Is she forcing herself to make ten million makeup videos to stay busy?

Focus, man. Fucking focus.

I concentrate on David and Cynthia. "It was good to meet you too." I shake her offered hand, telling them goodnight as the cab idles.

David scoots inside the yellow car and snuggles up against his woman as they drive off into the New York night.

Lucky guy. But hey, that's the benefits of falling for a woman you can have.

And now I'm jealous of my son.

I head home and go straight to the gym to burn off my inappropriate feelings with exercise.

The next day, I'm up at dawn. I hit the pool for a swim then march into work before anyone else. I am nose to the grindstone all day long, and all these fantastic metrics, like ROI potential, and market share, and scalability, have my mind exactly where it should be.

At the end of the day, though, David knocks on my door, too fast, too frantic. His hair's a mess. He tugs on his tie. "I don't know how to get all this done before the weekend," he says, then as he heads straight for the couch, he rattles off a list of final details he needs to take care of—a shelter visit for more pics, a phone call with the hotel, ferrying some auction items out to the Hamptons tomorrow since he has the day off. "And I promised Layla I'd go with her tonight to pick up the final things around the city. And I don't want her to have to do it alone."

He flops onto the couch, flat on his back, like he's at a shrink's. "I don't know what to do."

My heart aches when he's like this—nearly immobile from the weight of it all. And I haven't seen him this stressed since the night we started planning the auction at my place. I take the wheel now like I did then. "I'll go with her."

He breathes a huge sigh of relief. "Really? You don't mind?"

It's amazing how much I don't mind. "It's no problem."

"Great. I'll text her," he says, then taps away on his phone. When he looks up, he says, "She'll pick you up at your place at six."

I don't want her to drive around the city alone either. A new count begins—sixty minutes till I see her.

There goes my six-day chip.

I head home quickly and shower.

28

FOR TONIGHT

Nick

Layla pulls up at six on the dot, the sight of her sports car kicking up my pulse.

Great. Just great.

I grab the handle of the passenger door and get in, feeling like I'm in a foreign country and I don't speak the language.

"Hey," I say.

"Hi. I mapped out the stops. Put them in my GPS to crunch the traffic times. We should be able to pick up everything and have it back to your place by eight-fifteen."

Well, Robot Layla is in the driver's seat.

"Let's get going then," I say, following her cool lead.

With a tight nod, she pulls into traffic, heading toward Lexington.

I watch her out of the corner of my eye, trying to

read her. Her jaw tightens. Her hands curl tightly around the steering wheel. She stares straight ahead. Sure, she's driving, but her body language doesn't require a translator.

This is how we're doing it.

Post country club.

Post rest-stop diner.

Post Raven run-in.

"How's your week been?" I ask, hoping meaningless conversation will make the next two hours and fifteen minutes less uncomfortable than stark silence.

"Great. Super busy. Yours?"

Ah, so we're at the peppy, short sentences stage. Got it. "Same. Non-stop. Can't complain," I say.

"Good. Good," she says as she weaves through traffic, artfully changing lanes to dodge a cab in rush hour.

Goddamn, that's hot, the way she maneuvers her car in the stop-and-start, honk-infested slog of New York City.

I clench my fists, wishing this were easier. But two minutes have passed, so there's that.

"And things should be good for the auction too," I say.

We talk about nothing but our tone reveals everything.

Too bad the scent of her hair and the sound of her voice make me want to spend more than the next two hours and thirteen minutes with her—I want to spend the night, and the next one too.

* * *

When she pulls over on Spring Street, she cuts the engine then says, "The Chopards are on the fourth floor. They have a vintage necklace, some other vintage jewelry too—"

I cut her off. "David told me. I know." Then I'm out of the car, heading to the lobby and meeting one of Rose's parents' friends.

A woman in her late sixties waits in the lobby. She wears a silk blouse and smells of Chanel No. 5.

"Thank you again for donating, Mrs. Chopard. David and I are so grateful," I say as she hands me a box.

"So happy to help," she says, then peers past my shoulder at the car waiting at the curb. "And how is that dear doing lately? Is Layla okay? I think of her so often."

I'm thrown for a second, but then I put two and two together. This *has* to be about her father. Layla wouldn't want me to reveal a damn thing, so I smile and say, "Layla is wonderful. Thank you again."

When I return to the car, I set the box in the backseat.

"Thanks," Layla says.

For doing my job? For helping my son? For not flirting with you? The only thanks I'd even want is for protecting her privacy, but I'm sure as shit not telling her about Mrs. Nosy Chopard.

"Sure," I mumble.

We're silent the rest of the way to the West Village, where I snag a couple of framed playbills from *Crash The Moon*. The director is donating a set of box seats and a backstage tour to his newest musical, a revival of *Ask Me Next Year*. I thank him for the playbills—those will go on the auction table to represent the big prize—then return to the car.

"Got 'em," I say.

"Wonderful," she says like she's interviewing for a sorority.

Next, we head in silence to Chelsea. The popular romance author Hazel Valentine is donating several sets of her signed bestsellers. Her boyfriend is, too, since he's also a writer. We swing by their place, where Layla double parks and then tells me to stay with the car. "I know Hazel. I want to say hi to her."

Well, la-dee-fucking-dah.

Like I've been admonished, I stay in my seat, stewing. But when I peer into the side mirror, there's a cop car trudging down the street.

Maybe he'll give her a parking ticket. Maybe I'll even let her get a ticket. Take that, Miss Silent Treatment.

I cross my arms.

The black and white inches closer.

Ah, hell. I can't. I climb over the console, adjust the seat, then pull out. By the time I've circled the block, Layla's waiting on the curb, her head tilted. I lean across and push open the door as she hops inside. "Cop?"

Are you kidding me? We're back to one-word sentences?

"Yes. And I'm driving now," I say as I hit the gas,

because I need something to do. "I'm not a good passenger."

She shuts the door. "Oh," she says, and now she sounds admonished.

Good.

When she clicks the seatbelt in, she must adjust her mood since she gives me a plastic smile that's straight out of a debutante handbook. "Thanks for doing that," she chirps. "Three down, two to go."

And now we're back to the fake portion of the night. Fine by me.

"Almost done," I bite out, and oops.

Did I sound like a dick?

Yes. Yes, I did.

"Yes, we are," she says, still peppy. Then, she stares out the window as the billboards flash by.

This errand is worse than I'd even imagined.

Over on Park and Thirty-Third, she snags a chess set—it's a Staunton, so that's the real la-dee-dah—then sets it in the backseat, before settling into the passenger seat again.

She smooths a hand over her black skirt. It's a flowy little number that makes me think bad things.

What a surprise.

But I've made it this far. I can last through one more pickup. "Hugo's, then we're done," I say. The wine expert and restaurant owner is donating a private dinner party at his restaurant, as well as a few vintages of his favorite wines. We're picking up the wine bottles, and then we'll be finished.

"Actually," Layla begins, and her voice signals *change of plans* before she says the next thing. "Why don't we drop all this stuff at your place since we're close to it? And then I can handle the Hugo's pickup solo since it's near me."

How fucking stubborn is she? Does she think she can go toe to toe with me in the bossy department?

Come at me.

"Yes to the drop-off. No to you picking up the stuff at Hugo's solo," I say, brooking no argument.

"It just makes sense, Nick. I live on Seventy-Third. It's a couple blocks from Hugo's. Then, I'll just bring the wine to the auction," she says, like logic matters right now.

When it definitely does not matter.

As I weave through traffic, I shake my head. "Nope."

"Why not?"

"Because you'd have to park your car in the garage, then go to Hugo's, then carry the wine to your apartment yourself," I explain crisply as I slow at the light.

"And?"

Once I stop, I turn to her, my brows narrowed. "One, I told David I'd do this with you. And two, I don't want you walking around the city at night, carrying a box of wine," I say.

"I think I can handle it."

"No doubt you can. But I'm still going with you, carrying the wine, and walking you home."

"I can get myself home. I do it, like, gosh, every night," she says, sarcastic.

And that pisses me off more. "But tonight, you're not alone."

"Guess what? Tomorrow I will be," she spits out.

I grit my teeth, holding in my irritation as I drive down the road. But a few minutes later, turning on my block, I'm still a pot, bubbling over.

Trouble is, that's not the kind of man I want to be. I can't let this anger win. When I reach my building, I cut the engine in front of it and turn to Layla. "Just let me," I say tightly.

Her eyes are icy. "You can't protect me. You can't save me from the city. You just can't."

"But I still want to," I say, a new head of steam building inside me. "Why won't you just let me? Why are you acting like this? Why are you so fucking..."

"What, Nick? Why am I so fucking what?" she challenges.

My god, this woman is older than her years. Tougher than her age. She's not afraid of anything.

"Cold," I spit out. "You're so cold and so...cordial. And so Upper East Side."

She rolls her eyes. "Is that the issue? That I'm Upper East Side tonight?"

"Yes," I answer, matchstick. Except, it's not. I shove a hand through my hair, trying to rewind the night, to sort out my feelings, to fix this mess. "No," I correct. "The issue is," I say, then take a breath to collect myself, and when I do, the frustration steps back, and the hurt

I'm feeling strides forward. "Why are you shutting me out?"

"You shut me out," she counters.

"I had to," I answer.

"I know!" she explodes, then immediately covers her face with her hands, shaking her head, muttering, "I'm sorry. I'm sorry. I'm sorry." Her voice stutters, filling with tears.

In no time, I reach for her, wrap my arms around her. "Baby, I'm sorry too," I whisper. "I don't want to fight with you."

"I don't want to fight with you either," she chokes out.

I gather her closer, stroke her hair. She ropes her arms around my neck, tucks her face against my chest. "I was a bitch," she whimpers.

"No, you weren't. I was angry," I admit.

"I was too," she says. "It's just so hard with you. Being with you. And *not* being with you."

My heart squeezes painfully like someone's grabbed it, twisted it in a fist. "Same for me."

"I was just trying to make it through tonight," she says.

"Me too," I admit, pulling her impossibly closer.

She snuggles up against me as if she's seeking the comfort I have to give, the shared apology in our touch.

"I just want..." She doesn't finish. She doesn't have to.

I feel the same. "I know. I want that too."

We stay like that for a few more seconds, letting the heated moment fade some more and turn into something softer, something tender. When I separate from her, she looks up at me, regret in her beautiful blue eyes. "If you still want to, you can walk me home."

I run the back of my knuckles against her soft cheek. "Yes. I do. At least for tonight." Then, since I don't always follow the rules, I offer her a smile and add, "Why don't we get a bite to eat at Hugo's while we're there?"

Her eyes flicker with secret happiness. "Let's do it."

29

I AM MY PAST

Layla

We're finally having our dinner at Hugo's.

When we walked in to pick up the wine, Nick noticed there was only one table left—a quiet one in the corner, accented with a red-brick wall.

He asked the owner if he could seat us there, and since a reservation had canceled, the table is ours.

It's perfect for us—friends who are lovers who don't want to be seen. The lights are low and candles flicker on the table.

It's a make up dinner in every sense of the word. Making up for the fight and making up for the date we never had when he arrived in the city.

This date won't end with the promise of another night. In fact, it'll end far too soon since we've just finished a sumptuous meal—a risotto for me and a seared salmon for him, but the best part was a fantastic conversation about trends in customer experiences with apps, the disruptive business models he hunts for, the collaborations I'm doing with Mia. Over a sauvignon blanc with tangerine notes, we didn't once discuss us or the big obstacle that makes another night like this an impossibility.

That we can't be a thing.

This is so much better than cold shouldering him. I can't believe the ice age lasted as long as it did in the car. That was a feat of sheer will on my part. A necessary one though at the time. I lift my glass, swirling the last of the wine. Old standards play softly overhead. Ella Fitzgerald is crooning right now, and the tune gives me a wistful, achy feeling in my heart, especially when she sings about lipstick's traces. "They're playing your songs," I say then take a sip, savoring the taste.

"And you like them too," he counters, never missing a beat.

I do have an affection for those tunes. "I grew up listening to them," I say, inviting him in more.

He arches an eyebrow. "Parents loved them?"

I smile at the sweet memories. "They did. Used to dance to them in the kitchen."

"Some songs are just good."

I'm quiet for a moment, content to zoom in on the lyrics about an airline ticket to romantic places, then feeling the possibilities of them, like a little zing. "Maybe I could even dance to it."

I smile. Nick smiles back.

"Bet you'd enjoy dancing to Ella with me," he says.

I picture that. It's a good image. "Are you a secret

ballroom dancer and you never told me?"

"Maybe."

"Shut up. Are you really?"

He laughs, then shakes his head. "No, but my mom made me take dancing lessons at Johnny Angel's School of Dance when I graduated from college. That was her graduation gift. She was convinced I was going to need to foxtrot or waltz with Rose at our wedding."

Funny, how I felt a flare of jealousy over Rose the other week. Now, I understand his story, so I feel curiosity rather than envy. "And did you?"

"Nope. After all that, we had a small civil ceremony. Just family. We didn't make a thing of it at all."

"Was your mom devastated that you didn't get to foxtrot?"

"I think so, but she's a stoic woman so she didn't let on much. Just gave a harrumph and said *Let me see if I can get a refund for the rest of the lessons.*"

"And did she?"

He holds up a finger. "One lesson. She snagged a refund on one lesson since I never got to the tango."

"She got the tango refund," I say, admiring her already from a distance. "But were you even going to tango at your wedding?"

"No, but she's all about preparation. Covering your bases. She didn't want to take a chance."

"What's your mom like? Besides, well, determined."

"That describes her well. She's no-nonsense. Direct. Very mom-like too. She worries about flu shots and sunscreen and whether I packed enough underwear for a trip."

I burst into laughter, covering my mouth. When the laughter subsides, I say, "Still? She still worries about your underwear?"

He nods, grinning. "She sure does. And yours? What's she like?"

That's a loaded question. It's one I've covered in therapy ceaselessly. But now's not the time to focus on the push and pull between us. I home in on the good. "She's always been driven and dedicated in everything she does. She works long hours, and is passionate about her work, and that probably rubbed off on me."

"I'd say so. You're intense and driven," he says, already knowing me well. Then, like he's seizing the chance of this conversation, he asks, "What drove you to start the videos?"

Instantly, I feel seen, and I'm not even sure why.

Maybe because he asked without an agenda? That must be it—his genuine interest in knowing *me* rather than the headlines. Nick never looked me up. He kept to his word. He wants to hear about me from me.

That impulse I felt to share a week ago awakens again. But it's not quite as feral now since I know where it's coming from—it's coming from my heart. I want to be close to Nick, even though intimacy has always been terrifying. But it's not scary with him. It's comforting. It's warm and hopeful.

With a gulp, I open the door. "I started doing the makeup videos after my dad's death. I also started wearing makeup after his death. A lot of it," I say, finally going there, to the place that marks my before and after.

With a somber nod, he says, "That makes sense."

"And I did come to love it. It's fun, it's artistic—it's like putting on a costume. But I think it was a mask at first. A necessary one."

"One you needed to make it through the day?" he asks, getting it. *Getting me.* Showing me yet another reason why I want to be close to him. His kind and patient acceptance. His understanding.

"Yes, I needed it. Desperately. Like my mom needed Beautique. She poured herself into the company after he was killed," I say, then almost apologetically I add, "She was crazy for him. His death was hard for her."

"Of course it was," he says, then takes my hand gently, encouraging me to say more if I want to. Or to stop. I can already read his touches. He's saying without words that he'll listen for as long as I want to talk.

Briefly I look away, staring at the other tables at Hugo's, full of couples, families, friends, colleagues. Are they talking about loss? Are they digging into their wounds? No, they're probably discussing stocks and social media.

I turn back to Nick, wanting to give him an out. "We don't have to talk about it."

Nick rubs a thumb along my hand. "We don't *have* to. But I want to...if you do." His voice is gentle, but his intention is clear. He's telling me he's a safe space.

And I feel that deep in my heart—he is the safest space for who I am and who I was. I'm not simply my present. I am my past. With my free hand, I rub the daisy on my shoulder, drawing courage from it.

"She tried everything to deal with the loss, Nick.

Yoga, meditation, therapy, Xanax, burying herself in work, obsessing over me. I think he was her obsession when he was alive. They went out every weekend on dates. Dinner, dancing, movies, just the two of them. They had this intense bond. He was so devoted to her. But he was still a great dad," I say, my voice full of the missing I still feel every day.

"What was he like?" His attention feels like a strong, sturdy hug.

I hardly ever have the chance to talk about the *before*. No one asks about my father as a person anymore. He's been an event rather than a man.

"He walked me to school every morning. When I was younger, we lived here, on the Upper West Side, but my school was across the park. So he'd walk me through Central Park every day to school. We'd walk past all these benches. You know the benches in Central Park?"

He nods. "Yes, you can give them as gifts. Or in memory of someone."

"We'd read the names and the sayings on the plaques along the way. Some were sort of public secrets —like *now it's your turn*, and others were direct, like *in loving memory*. Some were proposals. Anyway, he loved the park. He used to donate for its upkeep."

Nick smiles. "That's nice that he did that—enjoyed the park and looked out for it."

"I think so too," I say, then impulsively I blurt out, "I donated a bench for him."

"You did?" he asks, with new emotion in his eyes. A deeper affection perhaps.

"I did," I say, and I'm still a little surprised I've told Nick. "I've never told anyone that. I've always sort of felt like it's just mine, the bench. My little public secret."

"Do you go there a lot?"

"Not as much as I thought I would. I used to go a lot though. After therapy. Or before," I say.

"That's understandable. You'd want someplace to process or to prep."

"Exactly. Now I just go there when I need to...talk to myself," I admit.

"It's good that you have it." Everything Nick says is like a warm invitation to keep sharing.

Or maybe he's the invitation to share.

My mind rushes forward to teenage memories of my dad. "Anyway, later, when I was in high school, he was strict, and he set strict curfews and bedtimes, but he also encouraged me to pursue my dreams. We did this thing where I'd say he was my favorite dad, and he'd say I was his favorite daughter." I stop to take a breath, but emotions crawl up my chest, lodging themselves there. "I miss him so much."

"Of course you do, Layla," he says, tenderly, emotions leaking into his tone too. "Is that why you started The Makeover? To help you handle the loss?"

"Yes," I say, then I take the last swallow of my wine. But it's not for liquid courage. It's functional. I'm going to say something that will scrape my throat down to my soul. "But I also started it because of what happened to me." I meet his gaze, then face the past head-on. "The man who killed him tried to kill me too."

30

THAT NIGHT

Layla

After slapping down some bills on the table, then tucking the box of wine under his arm, Nick hustles me out of the restaurant.

With his jaw set and his gaze intensely serious, he walks me to my nearby building. He stays glued to my side the whole time, like he's my bodyguard and his goal is to steer me out of the public eye for the rest of the story, even though no one at the restaurant seemed to be listening.

But I'm grateful he sensed a restaurant was not the place for this conversation. I'm grateful, too, for the way he tries to shield me from the city. An impossible mission, but I appreciate it nonetheless and in a way I couldn't earlier tonight.

When we reach my building, Sylvester holds the brass door open. "Good evening, Layla."

"Hi, Sylvester. Thanks for the door."

"Thank you, sir," Nick echoes.

Soon, we're on the sixth floor at my apartment. I punch in the code, then we go inside. By muscle memory, I conduct my normal checks, taking off rings and deadbolting the lock. I flick on the light in the living room, then turn toward the kitchen and do the same there. "I, um, always turn on all the lights," I say stupidly, lest he question what I'm doing.

"Let me do it," he says, but it's more like a plea.

He doesn't know the layout of my place or where the switches are. But I say yes since he wants to help. Soon, my one-bedroom is lit up, and he returns to me in the living room, then holds my face, his big hands so warm, so safe.

"Sweetheart," he says, and that's new. I'm *sweetheart* now. It's like a romantic upgrade from beautiful. He's gone from a compliment to a term of endearment.

A terribly tender one that I love.

"What happened?" He bites out the question.

Nick's no longer patient. He's desperate.

"I'll tell you," I say, taking his hand from my cheek then guiding him to my purple couch.

We sit. My hands are clammy, and my heart is speeding uncomfortably fast.

There's only one way to tell the story. In medias res, like it happened to me.

"We lived on Park Avenue then. It was a Thursday evening. I was at home with my dad. We'd just finished dinner. My mother was away on a business trip. She was flying home at the time. We had delivery from a

Vietnamese restaurant I liked. My father said as we ate that it was because I was his favorite daughter," I say, then purse my lips to fight off the first lump forming in my throat. "And when we finished, I said I'd pick up a book he wanted at the bookstore since, well, since he was my favorite dad."

I shrug, offering a sad smile at the sweet part of the memory. The part no one can tarnish.

Nick smiles sadly too, his eyes shining as I keep going.

"So I got ready to leave to pick up a legal thriller. He loved those. Loved critiquing them. As I was grabbing my phone, his rang. It was Joe. His partner at the firm. When I was at the door, my dad told me Joe was coming by, but it wouldn't take long. He just needed to chat about a case, and he was in the neighborhood," I say. The short sentences help. The almost procedural-like recap is the only way to tell this. "I left to pick up the book. I saw him when he turned onto my block."

I close my eyes, picturing the man I'd said hello to at dinners, events, and charity functions for years. An ordinary face. Nothing special. I open my eyes. "He said hello to me, but his tone was distant. I said, hello, Mr. McBride."

I see his face. His worried eyes. His fidgety hands.

With a wince, I blink away the images. "I don't think he went there to kill my father. I think he was a frustrated guy heading to see his business partner. I was the daughter going to run an errand. That was all."

Nick shudders out a breath, perhaps bracing himself for what's coming.

"At the bookstore, there was a short line at the counter, and the clerk had to grab the book from the back, where it had been put on hold," I say, my voice hollow. "Then I went home. The whole trip took around thirty minutes. I went back inside, up the elevator, down the hall," I say, then my shoulders shake.

I exhale. Inhale. Count to three. Breathe again.

Nick runs a hand along my arm. "You can stop. You don't have to tell me. You don't, Layla. You don't. I swear."

With a sniff, I shake off the out he's giving me. "No, I want to," I say, my throat raw. I haven't shared this with anyone except the police that night and my mother, of course. Then, with Harlow, Ethan, and my therapist after. There's been no one else I've wanted to share this with.

Until now.

And now I'm stronger than I was when I had to tell it years ago. Stronger than when the police asked me questions. Stronger because I survived.

"Outside the door, I heard their voices. The commotion. They'd been arguing. They'd been arguing a week before too. I'd heard pieces of the conversation. Joe had lashed out at my father on the phone. Called him a liar because of what my father had learned."

"What did he learn?" Nick asks, hanging on my every word.

"Joe had been stealing money from the firm, from the clients' trust funds. We only know this because my father recorded their conversation on his phone that night."

"Smart man," Nick says, respect in his eyes.

"Yeah, he was," I say, taking a levity break to praise the deceased. "He was very smart. And my mother had the passcode, so she found the file. Joe had come over that night to plead with my dad. Told him he'd pay the money back. My father said he'd have to report it to the State Bar, because he was required to...but that meant Joe would lose his law license. And that's when everything escalated."

Nick swallows roughly, scrubs his free hand across his beard. "I'm listening," he says quietly, tightly.

I try to imagine I'm floating above the room, telling the story, but it's too hard a trick to execute. The only way through it is, well, through it. "When I opened the door, I walked in on it."

"Oh god," Nick whispers, shock thick in his voice.

The memory. The images. The scene. My heart shatters all over again but I push on. "They were fighting in the kitchen. My father was still standing but clearly losing. He was bleeding. Joe had taken a knife from the counter," I say, trying to tell the story in short bursts, in quick clinical details. "He'd stabbed my father multiple times. I screamed *stop*. Then I stopped thinking. I lunged, tried to grab the knife from him, but he spun around and attacked me."

Nick stutters out a breath. Red billows from his eyes—a new kind of rage I've never seen in anyone. He clenches his fist. "He hurt you," Nick hisses, reaching for my left shoulder instantly.

Nick obviously knows the outcome. I'm safe. I'm

fine. But I can hear retribution forming on his tongue —*where is he, I'll find him, I'll kill him.*

"He went for my heart, but he missed. Badly. He got my shoulder," I say, then I can't stop the tears. I just can't. They rain down as I choke out, "My father grabbed the knife from Joe as he lunged at me again. The knife fell to the floor, then Joe panicked. Ran from the apartment, down the hall to the stairs," I cry. "I called 911, but the EMTs were already there. The cops too. My neighbors had heard and called. Everything happened in a blur. My dad and I were in the ambulance being rushed to the hospital. I held him as he…"

I stop to refuel. Nick's clasping my hand, his gaze locked on mine.

And I will make it to the end of this story, dammit. No matter how hard the next part is. "He whispered something to me," I say, barely audible.

"What did he say, sweetheart?" Nick asks as a tear rolls down his cheek.

I don't know if I can speak through the rainfall. But I try. Dear god, I try, repeating his last words. "He said…*I love you. Take care of Mom.*"

"Oh, Layla," Nick says, clasping my hand tighter, holding me so I won't fall apart.

"And I promised I would," I go on. "But I didn't tell my mom he said that. It would have been too much for her to bear. Later, I told her that Dad said he loves us, and that's not a lie. He died a few minutes after we arrived at the hospital."

I'm near the end. I'm close, so close. The last part of

the story should provide some closure. But it's still awful in its own way.

Nick huffs out a breath. "What happened to Joe? Where is he?"

"After he left our building, he ran to the six line. He jumped in front of a subway train. He's dead."

"He's in hell, where he belongs," Nick says, full of righteous fury, then extraordinary gentleness when he adds, "And you're here. Thank god you're here. Thank god your father saved you."

For the second time that night, Nick wraps me in a hug. I don't let him go.

I don't think I can. I'm so wrung out. So tired.

Sometime later, he carries me to bed, lays me down, and slides under the covers with me, holding me close as I drift off to sleep in his arms.

31

THANK YOU

Layla

In the half-light of the dawn peeking through my window, I rustle, shifting in the bed, wearing only a tank top and panties. I brushed my teeth in the middle of the night. Nick did too. Then we fell back in bed, only with fewer clothes on.

Nick stirs then blinks his eyes open. "Hi," he whispers, voice rusty.

"Hi," I murmur.

He's behind me, spooning me, wearing his boxer briefs. He kisses my hair lightly then grazes his hand up my left arm, traveling higher, closer to the flower. "Can I touch you here?"

I didn't want him to touch my tattoo in Miami. Or to find the scar it covers. Now, I do.

"Yes," I say, granting permission I've never given anyone.

"Thank you," he says, then drops the gentlest kiss to my flesh, dusting—I think—the petal of the blue daisy tattoo. I shiver at the zing of pleasure.

He pulls back, tracing his finger along the jagged cut, then down the stem to the musical notes at the base. "Why a daisy to cover up the scar? And musical notes?"

"Gerbera daisies are Harlow's favorite flower. And the notes are for Ethan since he's a musician."

Nick hums softly, kissing the back of my neck with a new kind of reverence. "The ink is for them. Because they helped you through it," he says.

I smile from the comfort of his answer and the peace of his understanding. "Without my friends, I'd be lost."

He strokes my sleep-mussed hair, brushing it behind my ear, tucking it there. "I'm so glad you have them," he says, and his voice is trembling now, like he's on the verge of saying something else.

Something bigger.

I'm not sure I could handle anything bigger right now. Last night was intense. "I've never told that story to anyone but a therapist and those two friends. Even Jules and Camden don't know the details, and they go with me to Krav Maga."

"Thank you for trusting me," he says, kissing the tattoo again. Then again. Then once more, with an urgency now—an urgency that's both sexual and also emotional. He kisses my shoulder with a fresh passion, murmuring as he goes, like he's uttering an adoring thank you to my friends, to my father.

To me.

For being alive.

I feel alive in other ways, too, thanks to his kisses, to his hands.

Tingles race down my skin, skating over my flesh, sliding between my thighs. He journeys from petal to petal. I can't see him kiss me, but I can feel him moving around the art while he traces the musical notes with his finger.

By the time he's circled the flower, I'm a puddle of need and desire—but it's deeper than before. This is something more. "Nick," I moan.

He grabs my face, turns me toward him. "You," he utters, then he shifts me fully, tugging me against him. We're side by side, and he reaches for my thigh, hooking my leg over his hip.

He runs his forefinger over my top lip. Then the bottom one. He's memorizing me with his touch, and I don't ever want to be forgotten. I want to be more than remembered. I want to be his present.

I rope my arms around his neck and tug him close. "I want you. So much," I say, trembling everywhere, my voice, my body, my heart.

"Want you too," he answers.

The rest of our clothes vanish in a flurry, then I find a condom in the nightstand drawer. "Bought these for you. When you were coming to meet me at Hugo's," I tell him.

"I did the same. You're the only one I've been with in a long time," he says, then he takes a beat. "But first, let me fulfill a promise."

After he sets the condom on the sheets, he moves down the bed, settling between my legs.

I ache for him. But he doesn't make me wait this time. He doesn't tease. He French kisses me, his beard deliciously scraping my thigh.

"Oh god," I gasp, as he spreads me open, licking me, moaning obscenely.

In no time, it seems, I'm arching against him, gasping out, then coming.

I'm still panting when I open my eyes to find him kneeling, rolling on the protection. "I couldn't help myself," he says in a wholly unnecessary apology.

"You're forgiven," I say.

He notches the head of his cock against me.

For a second or two, I feel caught once again. Caught by his gaze, by his heart, by his big emotions.

They scare me, but I also don't want to deny them anymore. "This time is different," I whisper.

"I know, sweetheart. I know."

I shudder out a breath as he enters me.

I've missed him so much.

When he's all the way in, he lets out a long, sensual groan. "My brave, bold Layla," he says. Braced on his palms, he eases out then thrusts back in. "My Layla. My Lola."

I'm both to him now. He's telling me he sees all of me. Wants all of me.

As he rocks in and out with a new passion, the moment is almost too much. Almost too intense. But I stay in it. I loop my hands around his neck, wrap my legs tighter around him. "Deeper," I urge.

He nods savagely.

My heart beats harder. Louder. Our gazes lock for several seconds, the connection burning bright and powerfully.

Then, he complies, driving into me. "Yes," he mutters, swiveling his hips. I rise up, meeting him thrust for thrust, grabbing his ass.

He watches me as he fucks me. Watches me with an adoration that's rich with possession. That's brimming with emotion.

My heart gallops faster, my skin tingling everywhere from the sheer pleasure but also from the intimacy. True and real.

If something happened to him, I would hurt. But I want him anyway. Desperately, recklessly, and truly.

I try to tell him that with my body, moving to greet his mouth with a passionate kiss.

He takes my kiss and matches it with a heated one of his own, like he's telling me the same thing.

He wants this.

He wants *us*.

He wants more than these stolen moments.

We kiss and fuck and consume each other. Soon, my world narrows to the slap of sweat-slicked skin, to the grunts and groans of a race to the end, then to the cries of bliss coming from deep within me.

I surrender to an orgasm that's as lustful as it is emotional.

It crashes into my body, radiating through me to my fingers, my toes, my hair. Seconds later, he's falling under too, shuddering then stilling as he groans, a long, deep rumble.

Then, we're quiet, tangled together as we come down.

Soon, he'll have to go.

But after we straighten up, he tugs me back to bed and brings me close to him once again. Strong arms wrap around me. Warm breath tickles my neck. "I don't want to leave you," he rasps out.

It sounds like a confession.

"I don't want you to go," I say.

We stay like that, together and quiet, until he breaks the silence. "Layla," he says, importantly.

I tense, but then he soothes my worries with his words. "I want to stay. I do."

I take his hand, wrap his arm tightly around me.

But eventually, the sun rises, and he leaves.

32

THE SERIOUSNESS OF TIRAMISU

Nick

The first thing I do when I reach the Strong Ventures building is go straight to Finn's office.

I rap on the open door and stride in before he even looks up from his laptop.

When he does, he freezes, his coffee in hand. Then, he sets down the mug and points to the small brown box with the clear window on top in my hand. "Shit. It must be serious. You brought tiramisu."

My brother has a hell of a sweet tooth. "I hope you have room in your dessert drawer."

Finn pats his flat stomach. "Always," he says, but his tone is grim, matching mine. He tips his forehead to the door. "Better shut that."

But I'm already closing it, locking it too. I won't take any chances.

I stride to his desk, setting down the offering along

with the fork. "It's from Sunshine Bakery," I say. I don't tell him Layla lives near the bakery. That I picked this up when I left her home this morning since the bakery was open early today. That I'm a fucking mess. I don't have to tell him the last one.

"My favorite," he says, then takes the treat, opens the box, and sniffs like it's a fine wine. "This is going to hit the spot."

He closes the box, rises, and heads around the desk, patting a leather chair for me, then grabbing another one for himself. He sits across from me. "What's going on?"

There's only concern in his voice. No teasing, no needling.

I drop my head in my hand. "Where do I even start?" I mutter.

"Maybe at the ink spot you had on your palm the other day? I'm guessing that's a clue as to why you're here."

I raise my face, drag a hand down it. Then I just nod. I practiced the words to say during my swim when I got home, then in the shower, then on the walk to the office, espresso-soaked cake in hand.

But the dress rehearsal doesn't make this confession performance any easier. I lick my lips, trying to find a better way to start than *I fell for my son's ex-girlfriend.*

"So there's a woman," Finn says, taking the conversational reins. He stares pointedly at me, like he's saying he started it, now it's my turn.

I jump off the cliff. "Yes, there's a woman," I say, though that hardly covers the magnitude of my feelings for Layla Mayweather. But this ought to cover the problem. "And she's my son's ex."

Finn flinches. "Fuuuuuck."

I laugh mirthlessly. "I know."

"Fuckity fuck, Nick."

I laugh again, for real this time, and at Finn. "Yup. It's a whole lot of fuckity fuck."

"With a side of tiramisu." He blows out a long stream of air then cracks his knuckles. "All right, let's do this. How? When? And does David know?"

"Miami. A few times. And fuck no."

Another big breath. "And the payola," he says, gesturing to the treat on his desk, "is because you need my help breaking it off with her, telling him, or borrowing my Miami home to sneak off for another tryst with her?"

That's the thing—I don't want just a tryst with her. "I don't know what to do, Finn."

My older brother takes a beat, studying me with wise eyes. "You have feelings for her," he says, simply.

It's a statement of the obvious. But sometimes you need to know what you're dealing with. "Big ones," I say.

Last night was the tipping point. I was already crazy for her. Then, she opened her heart and her past, and all I want to do is take care of her, adore her, and treat her like the goddess she is to me. But how the hell *can* I do that? "She's his good friend now too. She's a huge part of his life. And I can't stop thinking about her. I can't stop seeing her. I can't stop wanting her," I say.

Finn clears his throat. "Actually, you *can* stop seeing her. Sounds like you're *choosing* not to."

Chastened, I lower my eyes. "Fine," I grumble.

"I'm just saying," Finn adds, pulling no punches.

But that's why I came here—for the unmitigated truth. I meet his eyes. "Are you saying I should stop?"

I'd rather eat metal.

He sighs heavily but doesn't give an answer. "She used to date David, right?"

"Yes, but in college," I say quickly, like that covers up my sin, the distance in years.

"You're trying to make a silk purse, man," he says.

Punch to the gut. Just what I need. I rake my hand through my hair in frustration. "Fine, okay? He went out with her in college, they stayed friends, and they're still friends. There you go."

"And she's helping him plan his charity fundraiser, right? He mentioned her to me when I was chatting with him the other day about our social media. She's hosting the auction with him tomorrow night, isn't she?" he says, refusing to let me get away with anything.

"Yes," I bite out, hating that he's making me sound like such a schmuck. But this is why I came here. For an icy dose of reality, and Finn sure as hell is dumping the freezing cold bucket of water on my head.

"And how long have you been sneaking around with her?"

"Jesus, Finn. Why the hell didn't you go to law school?"

He smiles evilly. "Because Wall Street made me more money," he says, giving an answer I can't argue with. He worked at a hedge fund before he started his own venture firm.

"If you need a second career, you should consider—"

"—How long, Nick? How long?"

As he cuts to the chase, I huff out a breath. "I met her in Miami. Didn't know who she was. She didn't know who I was. We spent the night together. Fast forward three months and several transatlantic texts and phone calls later, and we made plans to see each other when I moved here. Then, I ran into her at a diner with David. Turns out she's David's Layla, and we put on the brakes right away." I stop to stare out the window before I confess the rest of my lies or in case he calls me on another euphemism. "I thought it would end there. We'd be friends, we'd keep the past in the past, but then…"

He nods, his gaze gentler, along with his tone. "And then?"

"And then I kept spending time with her prepping for the fundraiser, and seeing her, and…when I thought she was going on a date with another guy, I broke the fucking pen."

"And did you tell her that?"

"I did, and then I told her a ton of other things. About Rose, and her parents, and the country club, and the things Rose's dad said to me."

Finn whistles. "Damn."

"Yeah, exactly. And I tried to stop seeing her. But then, last night…" I flash back to last night. It belittles everything she shared to refer to it as a night spent together. I won't reduce her vulnerability to that. "I fell for her."

"Yeah, I got that impression," he says heavily, then leans forward, pinning me with an intense look. "What are you going to do about it?"

I hold out my hands, helpless. "I should stop seeing her, right?"

"Will you though?"

"I should. Really, I should."

"Nick," he says, never looking away, clearly gearing up to give me some bad medicine. "You've been lying to your kid."

I'm a bad father. I'm setting a horrible example. "I have. And you're saying I should...?"

"I'm saying you should stop lying," he says.

He's absolutely right. And there are two ways to do that. I have to choose which one.

On that mic drop, he rises, claps my shoulder, and returns to his desk, sits in his power chair like the king of Manhattan.

With a satisfied sigh, he picks up his fork. "Did I earn my tiramisu or what?"

Can't argue with him there.

33

TWO GIRLS AGAIN

Layla

On Friday, I'm running around the city to meetings, seeing Farm to Phone, then popping into the Mia Jane shop to grab some fresh mascara for tomorrow night's fundraiser.

The busier I am, the less I have to think about how I'll feel hosting a charity auction with the son of the man I'm falling for.

Or the fact that I can't ignore these feelings much longer.

Storm's helping a customer, so I head to the counter with the tube and hand it to a woman with a nose piercing. "I'll take this little darling," I say.

"Perfect. And when is your next event?"

"Soon," I say, since I don't know if Mia's told her team that it's the end of next week. "I'm just figuring out details with Mia."

That must catch Storm's attention since he spins around, indicates to his customer he'll be right back, then heads to me. "You better not leave without saying hello and goodbye." He pouts.

"Of course not, but you look busy, and busy is good."

"So they say," he adds, then walks me to the door, lowering his voice. "Mia's going to make the integration of your app into her brand official, but you didn't hear that from me.

Then he mimes zipping his lips as he returns to his customer.

I zip back, but I can't zip up my smile, especially when he invites me to a meeting next week to talk more about the collab. I say yes, then leave, floating on a cloud of possibility.

As I head home so I can grab my bag then pick up my friends, I call Geeta, updating her on the Storm tidbit. "That makes us even more attractive to a company like Omega, or Marcus or Limitless!"

"Yes. Yes, it does," she says, and it sounds like she's dancing in her little Hoboken abode. "This could be huge, and it all started in Miami," she says, and I can't escape the reminders of Nick, and my selfish choice to keep falling back into bed with him. "Seriously, all the work you did finding us marketing partnerships at that conference. We could be making bank soon, baby. I am super grateful. And that means I can maybe get a full-time caretaker for my dad."

There. See? I didn't just help myself in Miami. I

helped our business, and in turn, her father. "That would be great," I say.

We chat more as I walk home, but when my phone buzzes with a text, I tell her I have to go. Mostly because I want to see if Nick's texted me.

Yep. I'm *that* girl who's hooked on a guy.

Great. Just great. I open it anyway, but it's not from Nick.

It's David, and I detest that I'm less excited to hear from a friend who's in my life than a man who may or may not be.

> David: Cynthia says no tie for tomorrow night. Do you agree? P.S. She says she can't wait to meet you.

As I walk, I stare at the text for too long till the words seem like they're levitating off the screen. My head swims, and my heart twists in on itself.

When I reach my building, I answer him at last.

> Layla: No tie and same here.

Then I head to the sixth floor with a lead weight in my chest.

I'm about to meet my two best friends, the people I'm closest to in the world. My friendships mean everything to me. But on the side, I'm having a secret affair with another friend's father.

Last night, and this morning with Nick, I finally felt like one whole person—like I wasn't broken, just bent.

Now, I'm two girls again.

Something I no longer want to be.

I type Nick a note on my phone, then in a flurry, I finish packing for the Hamptons, tossing a few more items into my overnight bag. After sliding on my rings, I take off for my car, then pick up Harlow at her place.

Bridger's waiting with her at the curb, an arm draped possessively around her waist, whispering something in her ear.

When I pull up, I call out, "Get a room!"

Bridger turns to me. "Thanks. I'll do that."

"Or maybe not," Harlow says, then presses a goodbye kiss to his lips. "Don't work too hard while I'm gone."

He scoffs. "Not possible."

She takes a step toward my car, but he grabs her wrist and hauls her in for one more kiss. When he finally lets her go, he says to me, "Good luck this weekend, Layla."

I thank him, then we head off to pick up Ethan.

The three of us cruise out to the Hamptons, and I try to stay in the moment behind the wheel, the wind in my hair, the sun on my shoulders. To savor the jokes and the laughter, the music and the chatter.

The honesty too.

It's enough to make everything clear.

Once we reach my mom's home on the beach, I'm feeling less guilty and more resolved. We make cocktails and mocktails, then gather by the pool, lounging on the outdoor couch as the sun sets. Harlow and I paint our toenails in between drinks. Ethan hunches over a notebook, scratching out lyrics—I think—to a new tune.

A bird squawks as it circles the house next door, perhaps hunting for bread from dinner. The waves crash in their steady rhythm. This place is so familiar, and the peace I feel here with my friends clears my head the rest of the way.

It's time. "I told Nick about this," I say, touching my tattoo.

Ethan stops writing.

Harlow stops painting.

"You did?" she asks.

"And I wrote him a note earlier. I haven't sent it. But I need to," I say, resolute as I pick up my phone. I have to be resolute. There is no other option.

Ethan and Harlow scurry next to me on the couch, looking over my shoulder at the screen.

> Layla: I care about your son too much to keep sneaking around. We need to talk when the fundraiser is over.

Ethan lets out a low whistle. "Damn. You don't fuck around."

Harlow leans in closer. "I'm proud of you. When are you going to send it?"

"Now? Can I send it now?" I might sound overeager, but I'm just ready. I can't keep doing this.

Ethan and Harlow meet each other's gazes, then nod. "Shoot your shot," Harlow instructs.

I hit send, then I make a show of turning the phone to do not disturb. "Now, my pets. Tell me all about your weeks. Your day. Anything. Spare no detail," I say. I've taken up enough of the spotlight.

We chat and catch up on work and life as Harlow tells me about a new exhibit she's curating, then about the success Bridger is having with his TV production company. "He's getting ready to launch Ellie Snow's new show," Harlow says, clearly proud of her guy. "The love letter theme is so...chef's kiss."

"Of course. Because you and your man inspired it," I say, with a knowing grin.

She just shrugs happily. "Maybe a little."

"I can't wait to see it," Ethan says.

Then I pat his thigh. "Your turn. Tell me stories."

Ethan shares the latest on Outrageous Record, finishing with how he's trying but failing to write a new song.

"What kind of song are you hearing in your head?" Harlow asks.

"Something you can make out to," he says, decisive.

"Duh," Harlow teases.

"Those are the best kinds of songs," I say, forcing my mind to stay right here with them rather than on the man I want to make out with.

"I want something sultry. The kind of song that hits you right in the heart, and in the panties," he says with a salacious grin. "But I could use a little inspiration."

"Like a burst of creativity?" I ask.

"I was thinking more like a hot hookup," he deadpans. "I mean, I do find blow jobs super inspiring."

Harlow slugs his shoulder. "You are obsessed with blow jobs."

"Truth. He was raving about them the other week."

Ethan rolls his eyes. "Like the two of you don't radically enjoy face jobs."

Harlow raises a hand. "I solemnly swear I love them."

"Me too," I say, lifting my palm as well.

Harlow sits up straighter, her eyes twinkling. "Wait. Maybe your song should be titled 'Blown Away.'"

Ethan jumps up, grabs his pen and notebook, and writes that down. Then, he paces around the pool deck for a while, busy with his muse as Harlow and I talk about everything and nothing.

When Ethan finally settles back in with us on the couch, he shares a few lines. Damn, my friend rocks. "Would it be a total blow job of a compliment if I said that's really fucking good?" I ask.

"No, it'd be a face job of one, Lay," Harlow says.

"Let's give it up for both BJs and FJs," Ethan puts in, then the original Virgin Society says a collective thanks for the great joys of oral.

I feel like I'm home again, like I'm all me again, and it's great. But when I go to bed that night and finally turn my phone back on, I'm still foolishly hoping for a response.

A message blinks up at me. My stomach swirls with nerves as I open it.

> Nick: We do. Let's talk Sunday night.

I'm dreading Sunday now, and I also want to speed up time.

34

MY UTTER OBSESSION

Nick

I've decided.

As I walk up the sand on Saturday after an early morning swim in the sea, I feel certain. Calm too. I'm at my friend Riggs' Southampton home—he's not here, but he's letting David, Cynthia, and me use it for the weekend. Rose made a big donation and said she'd drive in this afternoon to attend the event, so I'm grateful he'll have both his parents here.

David and I took the train here last night. He's running some errands in town right now in Riggs' car but should be back soon. Then, he'll pick up Cynthia at the train station a little later today. She had to work late last night.

As I near Riggs' home, I review the plan once more since there's only one solution to the Layla problem.

When I reach the deck steps, I stop and look to the left. Layla told me her mother has a home nearby and that she's staying there. I don't know the address, but it's not far away, as I recall her saying. Pretty sure she's maybe half a mile up the sand.

She feels worlds away right now.

That makes my chest ache. I can't give in though. I can't reach out anymore. I have to do the right thing.

I tear my gaze from the white and cream beachfront mansions and head inside to take a shower, but before I can strip off my bathing suit, my phone rings. I grab it from the kitchen counter. It's David. "Hey there, kiddo. What's going on?"

"Cynthia was in a car accident. Dad, I'm freaking out," he blurts out.

Fear slides down my spine but for his sake, I hide it as I ask, "Is she okay?"

"I think so. Her brother called me. She was driving to the train station when some asshole who was texting smashed into her. They think her leg is broken. She's at the hospital now, and she's asking for me. Shit, Dad. What do I do?"

I go into crisis-solving mode immediately. "You go be with her. I can handle the auction. If you want me to, that is."

He breathes out a grateful sigh. "Are you sure? I feel like a jerk for not being there."

"She needs you. She's where you should be. I can host it."

"Thank you," he says, grateful, like I've absolved him, but still terrified.

"She's going to be okay," I tell him, as calm as I can be. That's what he needs from me.

"You think so?" His voice pitches up.

"I do. Now, where are you? I'll help you figure out the fastest way to get to her."

He's at the grocery store a mile away, so I triage his travel, comparing train and bus traffic times. But in the end, I want him to get there as soon as he can and with some privacy to make calls if he needs it, so I order him a car service and then I tell him to go.

* * *

"Any news?"

Those are Layla's first words to me when she arrives early that evening at the Fox Walk Inn, the boutique hotel by the sea where the fundraiser's being held.

She wears a bold pink dress with black polka dots, her blonde locks pinned in some kind of French twist, and I can barely breathe. But I don't even have a moment to say "you look stunning" because she's not only all business here in an alcove off the lobby, but she's also with her posse. The brunette with her must be Harlow, and the guy has to be Ethan.

Once again, gratitude floods me, and I want to say thank you from the bottom of my fucked-up heart to the two of them, but Layla wants an answer from me.

"Cynthia broke her femur. She's going to have surgery tonight on the fractured leg," I tell her. "David just arrived, and he says she's lucky she didn't have any other injuries. Just some bumps and bruises."

Layla's shoulders relax. "Oh, thank god. I've been so worried since you told me," she says. I called her earlier to let her know about the accident, but I didn't learn anything more till David and I spoke again a little while ago. Quickly, Layla shifts gears, introducing her friends to me, then adding, "And during the auction, Harlow can introduce the Zara Clementine since she arranged the donation through her gallery." She says all this with the crisp efficiency of a businesswoman handling her task list.

"And Ethan, since your band is donating a performance, did you want to introduce that?" I ask the dark-haired guy next to her.

"Sure," he replies.

"That's amazing. Your songs are great," I say, but that sounds so sanitized. I wish I could say Layla played his tunes for me when I cooked her dinner last week, but I don't know what they know.

I swallow the rest of my compliments—*she's shared your music with me, she's so damn proud of you, and she's been telling me about the two of you since the very first time I met her.*

"Thanks, man," Ethan says with a grin that says he's young enough and new enough to savor every compliment.

The conversation falters after that because what else is there to say?

But Layla doesn't let it drag. Her boss-lady mode is activated. "So, here's the plan. We'll emcee the evening and the entertainment together. We'll introduce the cocktail hour, and after that, we'll have reps from various shelters, plus Harlow, and they'll share some of the details on our donations—the Zara, the golf clubs, the jewelry, Raven's designs, and so on," she says, all boom, boom, boom.

"Yep," I nod since I know all this. Have known it for weeks.

"Then everyone will have a chance to wander around the tables to check out the info on the items, and then the bidding begins," she adds, motoring through more details.

I wish I could get a minute alone with her, and honestly, I could. I could say *let's talk*, but that'd be a dick move given the situation. I have to set my misplaced emotions aside and focus on the bigger picture—making sure this fundraiser goes off without another hitch.

"And then at the end we'll announce who won each item," she says.

Does she think I've been zoning out the last few weeks? "I'm aware. I've been part of the planning," I say gently.

"Right. Of course," she says, then shakes her head, like she's a touch embarrassed. "I'm just worried about Cynthia."

Ah, hell. Here I thought she was giving me the cold shoulder again. But maybe she needs some strength, too, just like David did, so I try to give it to her. "She's going to be fine. David's going to be fine. We will know more after her surgery and figure out how we can help her and David. We're going to do this tonight for him, and it's going to be amazing," I say, reassuring her.

Harlow's green eyes widen.

Ethan grins.

Layla smiles warmly. "It is. Thanks. I needed that." She gestures to her friends. "They're going to help me set up. I'll see you when it starts."

She sounds a little wistful but also resigned. I'm desperate to grab her hand and steal a moment. But instead, as she heads off, I watch her go.

There's no time to linger on her retreating silhouette either since my phone buzzes in my pocket.

> David: She just went into surgery.

He adds a Band-Aid emoji.

The fact that he's still using emojis tells me he's managing well. Still, I want to make this situation with his girlfriend as easy for him as I can.

> Nick: Let me know when she's out. I looked up the name of the surgeon you gave me, and Cynthia's in good hands.

> David: THANK YOU.

I tuck my phone in my pocket, turn away from the entrance as a green sports car pulls up, and stay out of Layla's way for the next hour.

The closer I am to her, the riskier it is for me. I can't have all of the guests at my son's event knowing how I feel for his ex-girlfriend.

* * *

A little later, I've got my game face on and I'm mingling with a packed ballroom of guests nibbling on smoked salmon crostini and mushroom tarts and drinking champagne. Beyond the floor-to-ceiling windows, the sea gently laps the shore. Rose isn't here. David said she texted that she'd stay in the city instead once she learned he wouldn't be here. She made another donation, so that's...*nice.*

It's still odd being at events like this, where the well-to-do give away money. Before I made money, I was never invited to shindigs. Now that I make plenty, I can get in almost anywhere.

It's a little ironic, but I don't mind the schmooze. In fact, I'm a goddamn mayor at events like this. That's the only way to make it through this evening where I'm playing so many parts—managing my son's worries, hosting an event unexpectedly, and wishing it were Sunday so I can finally grab a moment with the woman in the pink and black dress.

I have to play another part. The good host.

I make small talk with the Steinbergs, who donated the chess set.

"This is so amazing, what David's done," Mrs. Steinberg says, eyeing the pretty crowd in their summer evening finery. "Such a shame he can't see it come together."

I waggle my phone. "I'm taking lots of pictures for him," I say, then I excuse myself to say hello to the Chopards, who contributed the vintage jewelry.

After I'm done thanking them, I spot Kip the Ken doll, but the jealous dragon in me remains asleep this time. I know Layla's only interested in one man, and it's not Kip.

I take a minute to send the latest pics to David, then make my way to the guy who's *supposed* to have a date with Layla next week. I lied...the dragon raises its snout as I remember the annoying fact that her mother thinks she's single, that everyone thinks she's single. That she, effectively, *is* single.

But I ignore those facts for now since I need to be a good host. "Good to see you again, Kip. I'm guessing that green Dodge Viper is yours?" I say, giving him a firm handshake as I lay an easy bet.

His smile both tells me he's impressed I made the connection between him and the car, *and* that he likes impressing people with his wheels. "Sure is. I snagged that beauty a year ago," he says, then goes on and on about horsepower and how she rides before he tilts his head. "And what did you say you do, sir?"

I didn't fucking say, but of course that's all you care about.

"I'm in VC," I tell him, downplaying my role as the head of one of the top firms in the world.

"Nice. I work on Wall Street. Would I know your firm?"

Yes, you asshole.

"Strong Ventures," I say.

His eyes pop. "Holy shit, man. You funded Vault when you led Alpha Ventures. Before the merger," he says, and a surge of well-earned pride rushes through me. Vault is killing it in its early days. Kip rattles off several more startups that I turned into gold. It never gets old, watching someone's attitude change. Suddenly, I'm *somebody* to him.

"Yes, we did," I say, then I spot my buddy Travis, holding a beer, checking out the crowd. "I need to say hello to a college friend. But it was good chatting with you, Kip."

"You too, Mr. Adams. We should talk shop sometime," he says, and I'm no longer *sir*. I'm not Mr. Bancroft either. He's finally calling me by my name.

Too bad I don't give a fuck about impressing the Kip Cranstons of the world.

Too bad the entire interaction was only momentarily satisfying.

I walk away, heading for Travis. But when I catch a glimpse of Layla across the room, chatting amiably with some younger guests, my pulse kicks. Briefly, I stop. Consider. I want to go over there so I can wrap an arm around her, join the convo.

But that's not in the cards, and so I resume my path to Travis, congratulating myself for having made it through the cocktail hour without obsessing too much over my...well, my obsession.

"Hoops. Next week. My gym," I say to the guy I've known since we shared a dorm sophomore year.

"A hundred says I destroy you one-on-one," Travis replies.

"I can't wait to collect," I tell him.

It's time to hit the stage, so I check my texts once more, corresponding with David for a minute. Tucking my phone away, I find Layla near a ballroom exit, chatting with her friend Raven, the one who ran into us outside her home. Raven takes off before I reach Layla, and that's for the best. Raven seemed too astute the night I met her, and I don't need someone trying to read me right now.

Not as my heart beats too fast just from looking at Layla.

But I shove all those overwhelming emotions down. "Ready?"

"I am." She's not cold like she was Thursday night in the car. She's businesslike and focused. That side attracts me too. Every side of her does it for me.

"The turnout is amazing," she says brightly as we head backstage.

"It is. I took pictures and sent them to David."

"Did he reply?" she asks, eager to hear how her friend is doing. Her genuine concern for my son does not help my resolve tonight. But I've got to stay strong.

"He wanted to know how the food is," I say dryly.

She chuckles. "That sounds like him. Did you tuck some mushroom tarts into a doggie bag for him?"

"I sent him dinner instead. A meatball sub from a place near the hospital," I tell her.

"That's sweet," she says with a smile I ache to kiss off, then she purses her lips and looks away, like this conversation is ripping away at her heart too. But she's always been strong, so she turns back and says, "It's great that you jumped in to help him. Seriously, Nick."

The way she says my name. The way she looks at me. The way she *is*.

She is killing me.

"It was nothing." I brush off her compliment. The praise makes me want to grab her, push her against the wall, and kiss her hard to punish her for making me fucking fall for her.

"It's not nothing. It's everything," she adds, a solemn note to her voice.

I'm not sure what to make of that sound though. If it's good or bad. Or what even is good or bad anymore.

But it's time to go on the stage. I put on a smile and stride to the podium with her, fighting the urge to take her hand in mine. I can't do that. I just can't.

"Welcome to the inaugural fundraiser for A Helping Paw," she says to the packed room. "I'm Layla Mayweather, and it's been an honor to help David plan this event, but the credit all goes to my friend."

"I'm Nick Adams, David's father, and I'll be pinch hitting tonight for my son," I say, adding a few more words about the animal shelters David's raising money for.

When it's time for the main event, Layla and I trade off, rolling through the auction items, talking up each one. I do my damnedest not to inhale her jasmine scent. Not to gaze into her eyes. Not to stand so close that my heart thumps loud enough for the room to hear.

I can't let the whole goddamn Southampton world know the hot mess I've made of my life.

I smile, and I chat, and I make jokes, even as my mind is pulled in too many directions.

The auction lineup ends with Raven, who cuts across the stage in a short red dress.

Layla introduces her. "And this is my friend Raven, who's so talented she can make a dress from a pillowcase. Tell them a little bit about what they're bidding on."

"Thanks, friend," the budding designer says, then chats about the personalized outfits she'll make for one winner. When she's done, she turns to me. "And, Mr. Adams, you are a great pinch hitter. From the Miami conference to here, you're the man to fill in."

Worry darts through me at the mention of the night I met Layla. Fine, we were both registered at the conference; that's no secret. But I don't want to gab about it before this crowd.

"Thanks, Raven," I say. "Some winner will be very lucky." Then I turn to the audience and prompt. "A round of applause for our contributors."

That takes the spotlight off Miami.

At least for now.

But when we head offstage, Raven turns to me again. "I did listen to your speech. It was stellar. No wonder Layla raved about it."

"Speaking of raving," Layla cuts in, setting a hand on Raven's arm. "I want to special order a dress just like this."

"Of course. You know where to find me," Raven says, and I exhale.

Layla helped deflect. Which was brilliant. Unfortunately, I want to thank her with my mouth on hers.

As we circulate once again, making small talk with guests and contributors, I fight off the desire to set a hand on her back, to look at her the way I want to. To be by her side.

As I smile, I'm just pretending.

By the end of the night, this inn has me feeling claustrophobic. I've said goodbye to the last of the guests, and I'm eager to leave and do... *something*. But it's my job to settle up with the event coordinator.

I barely have time for a cursory goodbye to Layla as she leaves with her friends. I catch snippets of plans to hit the town and wince at the idea of them hitting the dance clubs. I'm annoyed because she's going out. She's having fun. She's dancing without me. But I haven't earned the right to be invited.

By the time I'm done, it's late, but I call David to check in and ask about Cynthia.

"She did great," he says, clearly relieved. But tired too. "I'm glad I made it here. She asked for me after."

My heart expands for him, for all the emotions he's feeling right now. For the love, I think, that's blooming between them. "I'm glad you could be there too."

When we say goodbye, everything's clear. I'm not going to wait till tomorrow night to tell Layla how I feel and what I want. You never know what might happen.

I know, too, that Finn is dead wrong about one thing.

I *can't* stop seeing Layla, but it's because I don't want to. I want to be the one who's there for her.

After a quick Google search for the nearest club, I call a Lyft.

I'm tired of waiting for the right time.

Now is the only time.

35

ABSOLUTELY EVERYTHING

Nick

Twenty minutes later, the car drops me at The Wave, the nearest dance club to the inn, according to Google. It's on the beach with indoor/outdoor dancing.

I pay the entry fee, and go inside the dark club, with purple smoky lights sweeping across the dance floor and bass thumping in my bones. I scan the packed house for the woman.

She's not by the bar.

She's not on the dance floor.

She's not by the stage.

With nerves strung tight and unraveling, I march to the door leading outside to the beach. The late summer night air warms my face. Music blasts and bodies grind, and tequila flows. Ignoring the scene, I hunt for Layla, but I don't see the beautiful blonde who owns my heart.

I spot Harlow in the middle of the dance floor,

bumping hips with Ethan. I weave through bodies, stalking over to her right as the music downshifts at the end of the tune.

"Where's Layla? Is she here? I have to see her."

Fuck tomorrow.

I need tonight.

Harlow must sense I'm not in the mood for games. She rises on tiptoes and shouts in my ear. "She went home. She wasn't up for dancing. We offered to go with her, but she insisted we stay. But I should warn you, if you're going to break her heart, you need to tell me so I can be there for her."

Damn. She does have amazing friends.

"I don't ever want to break Layla's heart. I'll protect her. I promise," I say, then with an honest smile, I make the request of my heart. "Can I have the address, please?"

I could get it from Layla, but I have a different plan.

Harlow tells me, then I thank her and leave, and once I snag another ride, I have the driver take me to Layla's home. When I'm a mile away, I call her. I can't bang on the door at night uninvited.

She answers with a tentative, "Hi."

She sounds sad, and I'm sure it's my fault.

"You left something at the hotel," I say.

"I did?"

"I have it. I'll be there in three minutes," I say. It pains me to fib, but I also won't tell her the truth on the phone.

This is not a phone call conversation. This is a face-to-face conversation.

When the car arrives, I thank the driver, then race up the steps two at a time. I rap on the door, and in seconds, I hear movement. She's probably turning off the alarm, unbolting the lock.

She opens it, and I waste no time. "I was wrong. I was the one who left something at the hotel."

I've confused her even more. "What did you leave there?" she asks.

"*You*," I say emphatically, standing in the doorway. Then, because I have to earn her, because you should always earn all the good things in life, I stop saying things like *we can't do this again*, and I start saying *let's give this a chance*. "I want to be with you for real," I say without any finesse, just speaking the truth of my heart. "I don't want to stop. And I don't want to sneak around anymore. I don't want to slip out of your home before the sun rises. I don't want to walk around an event pretending I feel nothing for you, when I feel...*everything*."

Her smile can't seem to contain itself. It's instant, a star lighting up the whole night sky. "Everything? That's a lot, Nick."

There she goes. Teasing me, like she did the day I met her. It feels so right.

"I feel absolutely everything for you, Layla Mayweather and Lola Jones," I say, still completely serious. I have to be. I'm the one who has to make this choice and hope she'll go along with me.

"I need to tell David about us," I say. "I was going to ask your permission to tell him as soon as I could do it in person. I was going to say all this to you tomorrow, but I can't wait any longer. My heart hurts when I'm with you but not *with* you."

Some of the tension leaves me—the stress of holding the door closed on my emotions. In its place comes a new, hopeful tension as I pray she's willing to take the risk with me.

Layla doesn't make me wait. She reaches for my tie—the ruby red one I wore tonight—and tugs hard on it. "Get inside."

Leaving all the tension behind, I kick the door shut behind me. "I won't say a word unless it's okay with you. But I couldn't wait any longer to tell you. I would have told you this morning, but then—"

"Oh, shut up. You found what you left behind."

She kisses me, and it feels, at last, like the start of something.

It feels like the start of everything.

I'm in her bedroom, lying down on the king-size bed, my hands parked behind my head, desire filling every cell in my body. "Undress for me, beautiful," I tell her.

After a good long stretch of dizzying kisses, we finally made it to the bedroom, where she pushed me down on the mattress and stripped me. Fair's fair. Now I want to enjoy the show.

"If you insist." Layla nibbles on the corner of her lips, then lifts her hands behind her neck, untying the pink strap of her dress.

When it falls, freeing her beautiful tits, I growl.

I'm up and out of bed in a heartbeat. "I'll finish the job," I command, and I slide the dress off her lush body, kissing her as I go. Her neck, her throat, her nipples. Then I'm down on my knees, kissing her soft belly.

I savor the jasmine scent of her skin. The feel of her soft flesh. The way she shudders under my hands. I press a kiss to the top of her panties and then whisk those off her too.

She steps out of them, roaming her hands through my hair, gazing down at me as I look up at her. "Are we really doing this?" she asks with wonder.

I kiss her stomach reverently. "We are, sweetheart. You're mine. I need you," I tell her, desperate for her once again.

Her soft fingers tighten in my hair, and she forces me to look up at her. "I need you too. But you have to be here for me."

My brow knits, and I rise, sweep her hair from her face. We're both naked, and it's an odd moment. Standing in our birthday suits, pressing pause on the fucking. But her concerns are too important to ignore. "I will be," I tell her, meaning it completely.

"I want you all the way. I want you in my life," she adds, emphatic.

"That's what I want too," I say, then I lift a brow. "I thought that was clear?"

She swallows, maybe a little uncomfortably. "It is. But I just want to make sure. I've never felt this way. I don't want to feel like this and then have you walk away. *If...*"

I get her meaning. I haven't done the hard thing yet.

I haven't *declared* us. But she deserves this promise. She's giving me not just her body, but her big, beautiful heart. "I promise, Layla," I tell her, with all the conviction I feel. "I'm not backing down. You can trust me."

She cups my cheek, then runs her thumb along my jaw. "I do trust you. I always have."

"Good." I kiss her tenderly. When I break the kiss, I say, "We can wait. We can stop. We can see each other in New York after—"

She laughs then rolls her eyes, pushing me back to the bed again. "I believe you've been wanting *something* in particular for some time."

A rumble works its way up my chest as I settle onto a pillow, then pat my shoulders. "Fuck my face. And don't hold back."

In seconds, she's climbing over me, her knees on the pillow, her hands on the headboard, and her hot, sweet pussy on my mouth.

Grasping her hips, I pull her close then moan salaciously as I taste her. "It's only been a day or two, but it's been too long," I murmur against her.

"I think you're insatiable," she says.

"Ya think?"

"And I like it."

With a pointed flick of my tongue, I mutter, "Good."

But then I'm done talking. My lips and tongue are busy pleasing her.

Devouring her.

Savoring her moans, her cries, her *oh gods*.

She tastes so good and sounds so sexy that my dick is thumping, begging for attention. I don't deny myself

The Tryst

either. My Layla likes it when I'm horny for her. I let go of one hip, grab my cock, and stroke.

"Nick, that's so hot," she says on a breathless pant.

She's craning her neck, watching me jerk, all while she rocks faster, more urgently against my mouth.

I'm on fire.

My cock throbs and I give another tug while I flick my tongue faster over the hard nub of her clit.

"Yes, do that again," she urges.

I'm not sure if she means my tongue or my hand. But I'm sure both would do the trick for her. Good thing I can multitask. I lick and I jerk, giving her a show while I consume her pussy.

Until she's smothering me and losing her mind. I couldn't be happier, but I do need to focus on finishing her.

I let go of my dick and don't stop a goddamn thing till she's screaming in bliss. Then quaking above me.

When she comes down eventually, I lift her off, wipe a hand across my lips, and give her an order. "Get on your hands and knees. Need to fuck you hard." Then I add, "For the first time."

"You do," she says as she smiles, woozy and sex drunk. But then she complies, offering me her body as I grab the condom that I left on the nightstand and put it on.

I move behind her, but I don't sink into her right away. I slide my hands over her ass, up her back to her soft hair. I bend lower, kiss her earlobe. "There are so many ways I can fuck you, beautiful," I say, hearkening back to a fantasy promise I made in Miami. But this is a real promise, sealed with emotions. "And I'm going to start right now."

She trembles and meets my gaze. "Do it. Because I want to come again."

Well, a gentleman should give a lady what she wants.

But I'm not gentlemanly at all as I kneel, then sink into my woman.

A scorching zing of desire shoots down my body from the feel of her. She's hot and welcoming and mine.

I grab her hips, pulling her tighter on my dick, letting the insane pleasure ratchet through me. "Mmm. You feel so fucking good," I tell her.

She wiggles against me. "Everything does, Nick."

She's right. Everything *is* good tonight, now that we've decided. There is no more living in the in-between. There is only being together.

That's how I fuck her—like we belong to each other. I thrust deep inside her, savoring each sound she makes, each sway of her hips, each breath carrying the scent of our intimacy.

She rocks back, asking for more, asking for me, only me, to please her, to have her, to be hers.

I listen to her cues, picking up the speed, then I roam my hand down her back. She bends with me, dropping down to her elbows with a long, seductive moan.

When she's grabbing at the sheets, her fists curling tighter, I rope a hand around her, find her clit, and stroke her while I take her to the limits of pleasure.

Like that, she gasps, then moans before crying out as another orgasm wracks her body. It ignites one in me too. I shout a filthy *yes, fucking yes*, as my climax obliterates me with a soul-deep passion I don't want to lose.

And I don't intend to.

I will fight for her. Even if it hurts.

36

COFFEE AFTER YOUR BANGOVER

Layla

As I pad out of the bedroom, Harlow's waiting in the kitchen, tapping her foot. The morning sun streams through the windows as Ethan hums while brewing coffee at the counter.

Wearing a tank and sleep shorts—like I am—Harlow stares at me pointedly. "Finally. You're awake." It's said with an over-the-top exaggeration that makes me grin.

I stretch my arms above my head, yawning for effect.

Harlow peers behind me as I join them. "Well, where is he? He did come over last night, right?"

"I'd say someone *came* over and over, judging from that three a.m. wakeup call," Ethan says, coughing under his breath as he pours a cup.

I blush. But it's a proud blush, if such a thing exists.

And if it doesn't, maybe it should. I stretch my neck like I'm working out the kinks, then point at the coffee pot. "Fuel. Need. Now."

"I thought you might, *Miss Do It Again*," Ethan says, adopting a feminine tone on those last few words.

Now I blush harder. "Shut up. I did not say that." But I'm lying. I totally demanded a repeat when Nick smacked my ass in the middle of the night.

"Own it, girl," Ethan says with a smirk.

"And spill it, girl," Harlow adds, staring with wide eyes but still hunting around for Nick, like she can find him behind me, slinking around the hall, hiding in a cupboard. "Where the F is Mister Storm Into the Club for his Woman?"

The image of Nick hunting me down last night sends fresh tingles to my belly. He told me he went to find me at the club. "I sent him home a couple hours ago. Because of this," I say, making a circle around the post-mortem crew.

"Because of us? Your besties?" Harlow asks like that's absurd. But it's not them, per se. It's the situation, in all its fragility.

"I thought it would be weird if the four of us were hanging out in the kitchen on a Sunday morning drinking coffee," I admit.

Harlow scoffs. "That's the weird part? Coffee after your bangover? Not, say, the fact that it's already nine and you've told me nothing? That's the weird part, lady. You're in trouble."

I laugh, no longer feeling so weird. I take a drink of the fuel and when I set it down, I give them the Spark-

Notes, trying but failing to wipe a grin off my face as I tell the tale.

"That sounds both hot and emotional. And inspirational. So, I hate you," Ethan grumbles.

I pat his shoulder. "It was all three. And I can still feel it today."

"Fuck you too," he adds, then downs some more coffee.

"But I think Nick and I should return to New York sooner than planned. He wants to go see David. And I should see him too." I gulp, my stomach swooping with nerves. Nick has to be the one to tell him about us, but I can't imagine David will be thrilled with me either. "And with Cynthia in the hospital..." I add, and I feel terrible once again about the timing. Terrible too about how to tell my mother, since I'll need to do that soon too. But I can't wallow. It's time to woman up. I fell for someone forbidden. Now, I need to own it for the world to see. That's how we become un-forbidden. "Anyway, I can catch a train and you two can take my car back anytime. Or we can all leave together, the four of us, but I don't want to make you go sooner if you want to stay."

Ethan meets my gaze from across the counter. "Because that would be weird? The four of us in your car?"

"Or the four of us in your car after you begged for his cock last night?" Harlow asks innocently, fluttering her lashes.

Briefly, I'm tempted to cover my face with my hands.

Instead, I square my shoulders. Raise my chin. And own the fuck out of my desires.

I'm womaning up in every way. "It's a very nice cock."

* * *

They decide to take the train later. Harlow can't resist a day lounging by the pool, catching up on her art journals and research. Ethan says he has a song to write, and the sea has always been a muse for him.

I don't even have to *give* them the use of my home. In a lot of ways, it's been ours for a long time. They come and go with me, and we loll around like a family.

"Enjoy your Sunday," I say as I toss my bag into my car.

"We will. And good luck," Harlow says seriously. "It won't be easy, but you can do it."

Nick and I just have to get through today.

I've already texted David, letting him know I want to see him and Cynthia this week when she's up for visitors. David gave me her room number, so I sent flowers to the hospital. Nick did too. She loves dahlias, Nick had said. David told him that one night.

That's a start, I hope, of showing how much I value my friendship with David.

Ethan drapes an arm around my shoulder. "Try not to worry, babe. I'm sure David will understand. It's not like the two of you..."

He doesn't finish though. And there's no need to. It's best not to make comparisons about our omissions.

I smile faintly, then say goodbye and hop in the car. I swing by Nick's friend's home and pick him up so we can drive together

He holds my hand some of the time as I drive. But he lets go when David texts him as we arrive in Manhattan. When he's done writing to his son, we're near my garage. "He's going to come over this afternoon. For coffee. I'll talk to him then," Nick says, his voice calm and capable.

But I can't even imagine how that conversation will go. "And then you want me to talk to him tomorrow or whenever he can? I want him to know where I was coming from too."

"Of course," he says, and he seems so strong, so tough. But would he let on if he was worried? That's not his style, but I wonder if it will be? As we move forward, will he let me in when the world isn't going his way?

I go quiet as we grab our bags, and he walks me to my building then into my apartment. Once I shut the door and set down my luggage and phone, he tilts his head to the side, studying me with obvious concern.

"What's wrong, sweetheart?" he asks.

"Nothing," I say quickly.

"Layla, I can be patient on a lot of things, but on this I'm going to push. What's wrong? Let me help."

That's always his first instinct. Or maybe it's his love language—helping. He speaks it quite well, since I'm opening up. "I was just wondering. If you had a bad day, would you tell me? Would you turn to me?"

He takes a beat, as if he's mulling this over. "I think I would."

"You think?"

"Well, I don't know. I haven't had a bad day yet since I came to New York," he says wryly, then pulls me into his arms. "But I want all of you. I want your heart, mind, and body. And I hope you want all of me. Even if I'm a surly jackass."

I laugh, looping my arms around his waist. "I doubt you could be a surly jackass."

He arches a brow playfully, but then he's dead serious as he asks, "But would you want me if I were one?"

I press a kiss to his lips. A firm, declarative one. "I want to see all of you. Not just sexy, dominant, possessive, Nick."

"Don't forget obsessive," he adds.

"Obsessive, possessive Nick," I say, liking the sound of that on my tongue.

"You're my obsession," he says, in a low, smoky voice. His kiss on my throat tells me how much he likes this obsession.

His growl says he wants to act on it.

But he needs to focus on his son.

I set a hand on his chest. Gently push him away. "Go home. You need to get in the zone. Call me later, okay?"

"Invite me over," he instructs.

"So bossy."

"Yes. I want what I want. *You.* Invite me over tonight," he says, repeating his demand.

"Really?"

"Yes. I'm not going to tell my son I fell head over heels for his friend and then *not* see you," he says dryly.

Head over heels—that's how my insides feel right now. "Come over tonight."

Another kiss on my neck. One more on my earlobe. A final one on my lips, chased with a sexy murmur. "I will."

He leaves, and I lock the door, sighing happily.

But I'm not completely happy.

I won't be able to relax till we sort this out and make things right.

I fuss around my apartment unpacking but a few minutes later, my phone rings. Figuring it's Nick calling to say something sweet, I trot over to the living room table and grab my phone. I'm about to say *so, you missed me that much* when I bite my tongue.

It's David.

I feel sleazy as I answer with a too-bright, "Hey, you! How's Cynthia? How's everything? I can't wait to tell you all about last ni—the auction," I say, course-correcting mid-stream.

"Yeah, I want to hear," he says, sounding off, but maybe he's just exhausted. "And I have a thank you gift for you. Can I come up?"

He's here?

I didn't see that coming.

"Of course," I say, but my gut instinct tells me something is wrong.

37

I DIDN'T KNOW YOU WERE FRIENDS WITH MY DAD

Layla

Once inside my apartment, my sandy-haired friend hands me a blue box wrapped with a white ribbon. Lulu's Chocolate. They're my favorite, and I don't deserve them. "For extraordinary achievement in the act of...covering my ass?" he offers.

Okay, that's good. He's playful David after all. Maybe I was wrong when I sensed a strange vibe on the phone. His eyes look tired, so perhaps that's it. Understandable that he's exhausted.

My heart pounds warily. "You did not have to do that," I say, feeling like such a jerk as I take the gift.

He shakes his head adamantly. "I wanted to, and I did. And I appreciate everything you did last night. So I just wanted to say thank you as soon as I could."

Those words echo like a warning as I turn away

from him and set down the chocolates on the kitchen counter.

David is handling situations with grace, saying thanks as soon as he can. I didn't handle falling for his dad the same way. Or the right way. But I can't fix that with a confession now. Nick has to tell him. Nick's relationship with his son has to come first.

I have to tap dance my way out of more lies. Their talk will be soon. I'll get through this awkward moment, and then David can see Nick, and we'll deal.

I take a deep breath, then spin around, pasting on a smile. "How's Cynthia?"

"Really good," he says, affection in his tone. "Also, painkillers are, evidently, her new best friend. Direct quote."

I laugh, shifting into hostess mode. "Want a water? LaCroix? Want to grab a cup of coffee?" *Before your dad tells you in an hour that I sat on his face last night?*

"Nah. I just wanted to hear how last night went," he says.

"It was great," I chirp, but he's not listening.

His eyes stray to my window, overlooking Central Park West. He walks there slowly, stares out it a bit too long then scratches his jaw, turning back around. "Did you and my dad drive back together?"

Alarm bells ring.

I want to deny it, but if he's asking the question, he clearly saw something. I replay the walk from the parking garage to my place. Nick and I didn't hold hands. I don't think we acted like lovers.

"We did. We both wanted to get back to the city," I say evenly, then quickly I add, "I have a thing with Mia today. We're doing some collabs."

I hate myself a little bit more. I don't have a thing with Mia. But I'll definitely go to her store later on now that I've lied myself into a corner.

A corner for lying liars who lie.

He gestures to the window and the street beyond. "I thought I saw him at the end of your street," he says.

The hair on the back of my neck stands on end. I stay quiet. He didn't ask a question after all.

"When I turned onto your block a little while ago," he adds.

"Probably because I gave him a ride," I say evenly, and I should leave it at that. The more you say, the more obvious it is that you're lying. But I don't want David to figure out we're a thing before Nick talks to him in an hour. So I have to say more to explain why Nick was *here*. "And he insisted on dropping me off and said he'd make his own way home." I roll my eyes, like *how ridiculous is it that Nick brought me home rather than asked for a ride to his place.*

"That sounds like him. He doesn't like to impose," he says with an apologetic smile, but it burns off quickly and he's Detective David again. "I guess I didn't realize you were friends."

We're not friends at all. We're so much more. I just shrug. That way I don't technically have to answer.

David rubs his palms along his jeans, something he does when he's solving a problem. I remember it from when I tutored him. He's adding up details. "But hey, it's cool that you're friends. I just..." He shakes his head like he's shutting himself up.

My skin crawls. I want this conversation to end so much. "So tell me more about Cyn—"

"—I guess I didn't realize you'd met him in Miami," he says, his brow furrowed, both in confusion and clear frustration.

My heart explodes with fear. This is seriously bad if he knows about Miami. My own words from the night at the diner, when I bought the corset, when he *saw* the satin fabric in my bag, blare in my head. I said I had a date the next night with a "sexy, powerful man I met a few months ago at a conference."

David's connecting the dots. At Mach speed, I cycle through what he might possibly know for certain. "Oh?" I ask, vague and nonchalant as I try to buy some time.

"Raven sent me a text this morning, thanking me for letting her be a part of the auction. She landed some business already from it and then she said..." David stops to grab his phone and read a text. "P.S. Your dad was awesome. I missed his speech in Miami but heard it on a podcast and loved it. I'm sure you heard how great it was from Layla."

Forget bad. This is a disaster. He knows *something*.

I have no idea what he knows. No clue at all.

I think of my father. How he always told me to try to do my best.

Here goes, Dad.

This is my best.

"I did meet him in Miami. After his speech. It was great. And I'm sorry I didn't say anything sooner, but I had no idea he was your father," I say, taking a shaky breath. There. That's all completely true. Then I jump over the romantic details. Those aren't mine to tell. "And when we all met again at the diner, I should have told you I'd met him, but I was honestly surprised to see him and learn he was your dad."

David seems to accept that answer, nodding a few times. Trouble is, he's still rubbing his palms on his jeans. He's still working out the puzzle, and I feel like a twisted terrible person.

"Got it," he says. His tone is hollow.

My heart caves in. I've hurt my friend. I have to end this conversation before I hurt him more. "David. I have to go see Mia," I say.

He pops up in a heartbeat. "Yeah. Sounds like you have a lot going on."

In seconds, he's at the door and we're saying goodbye. It's more uncomfortable than when I broke up with him. The second the door snicks shut, I lean against the wall, and try to breathe past my skyrocketing pulse.

But there's no more time for self-care. I run to my phone and call Nick.

He doesn't answer. I text him to call me.

I pace. No reply.

I try again and again, pacing back and forth.

Till my phone buzzes.

"Thank god," I mutter, but it's my mother.

> Mom: My meetings in LA are going so well. I can't wait till you're part of this!

Great. Another thing I have to deal with. Another thing I have no clue how to handle.

38

A COUPLE OF BEERS

Nick

I'm in the shower, washing off the chlorine from a quick swim, counting down till David arrives in twenty minutes. I needed to clear my head of the weekend and get in the zone, so I hit the pool the second the Lyft dropped me off.

Now, tipping my hair back under the hot stream, I wash away last night and this morning, honing my focus to the present.

A podcast plays from the speaker as a futurist opines on the intersection between machine intelligence and philanthropy. It's like a brain cleanse, and it resets my attention.

When I'm out of the shower, I dry off, get dressed, and run a towel over my hair one more time as the episode ends on a hopeful but cautious note about respect for humanity as computers become even more powerful.

Hopeful but cautious.

That sounds like it ought to be my mantra this afternoon.

As I brush my teeth, I flash back on speeches I've given, pitches I've made. But I grumble out a *fuck that* after I spit out the toothpaste.

This isn't a speech for my kid.

It isn't a pitch for him to go with my funding.

I can't prep like it's a meeting.

I just have to speak from the heart.

And I also have to apologize.

As I set the toothbrush down on the counter, I peer in the mirror, nodding decisively. Yeah, that's the key. I have a lot to say I'm sorry for.

I hear my dad's gruff voice. *When you say you're sorry, don't make an excuse. Don't blame the other person. Don't "but" or "just" or "I only did it because." Just own it, like a man.*

He's right.

On that note, I grab my phone and head to the kitchen, checking messages along the way. David's due here any minute.

But my heart stutters when I see the barrage of texts and missed calls from Layla.

I barely read the first text.

> Layla: Nick, I think he knows. He stopped by. He was acting very strange. You have to call me.

My pulse sprints. But I try to slow down, get the facts. I scroll through the rest of the messages with gritted teeth.

But that's enough. I've got the picture.

I stab Layla's name in my contacts—she's no longer listed as **Friend**, she's in there under her name—and call her.

"What happened?" I ask the second she answers.

In no time, she tells me about a surprise visit from my son. With each successive sentence, the *oh shit* meter ticks higher.

When she's done, I blow out a frustrated breath. "Well, I really need to fix this, stat," I say.

"I did my best to say as little as possible. But I didn't want to lie any more than I had to."

Another reason my heart beats for this woman. "Thank you."

"Nick," she says, her voice stretched thin. "I'm sorry."

I shake my head adamantly. "No, *I'm* sorry. I should have said something to him that night at the diner. Thinking I could forget Miami ever happened was the real mistake."

I hang up and check the time. David should have arrived five minutes ago. He's not often late. I don't want to assume the worst though.

He's not a guy who usually shuts down. He's not someone who typically closes in on himself. He wears his big heart on his sleeve.

But he also stresses. And when he reaches a certain point, not only does he stress, sometimes he just...*stops*.

Shit.

This is the guy who freezes when he's overwhelmed. And what the fuck did I do to him? I piled on. His girlfriend is banged up with a broken leg, and he just discovered his dad leaving his ex's home the morning after he had to bail on his passion project.

I call David.

It rings and rings and goes to voicemail.

I pace around my home, tapping out a text. ***Want me to meet you somewhere? I'll come to you. Just let me know where you are.***

But five minutes later, there's no reply.

He doesn't answer when I call again. Or text again.

And again.

And...fuck this.

I know my kid.

I grab my wallet and go.

Thirty minutes later, I'm banging on the door to his building. He gave me a key code when he signed the lease, but I don't want to barrel in.

I'm just cautious. Hopefully he'll answer.

My instincts are right when his familiar voice comes over the intercom. "You have the code."

But his voice is distant, removed.

Of course it is, jackwad. Get the fuck in there and fix this mess you made.

"Thanks, David," I say, then punch in the code,

open the door, and rush up the steps to his third-floor sublet.

I'm lifting my fist to knock when the door swings open. He's behind it, so I can't see his face until I step inside. When he shuts it, I'm...devastated.

David's expression is cold.

That's not his style at all. He's funny, emotional, needy, happy, worried.

But never...unfeeling.

Now he is, though, and he retreats to the couch, slumps down, folds his arms across his chest. Then meets my gaze. And fires straight in my heart. "You didn't need to come all the way here to tell me you're fucking Layla. I figured it out. I'm not *that* clueless."

My heart plummets to the floor, crashing in a heap of missed opportunities and bad decisions. I handled this whole situation horribly. I cross to the couch and sit on the other end. "I'm sorry," I begin, but that barely covers it. I restart with, "I should have told you sooner."

With an eye roll, he shrugs. The *I don't give a shit about you* kind of shrug. "You told me. Thanks," he says, then carelessly flips a hand toward the door. "There's the door."

This is worse than I expected. "Can't we talk?"

As if in slow motion, he turns his face to me, then levels me with an *are you kidding me* stare. "If I wanted to talk, I would have gone to your place like we planned. But I didn't. So, no, I don't want to talk. I only answered the door to be polite. Like you taught me to be," he says, his brown eyes mean. "You also taught me to be honest, to help out, to work hard. How's all that working out for you?"

Oh, shit.

Talk about a low blow. But I deserve that, so I swallow the shock and stick to my plans. "David, I met her in Miami. I didn't know she was your friend."

"And my ex. Don't forget that," he adds, lifting a finger to make his point.

"I had no idea till I met her again at the diner."

"Dude. I get that. I'm literally not confused about a thing now. But my girlfriend is in the hospital with a broken leg, and you want to tell me about your love life. Cool, cool. Why don't you order another couple of meatball subs for us and some beers, and we'll have a man to man?"

Ouch.

I don't know what I expected from today, but it wasn't this. And for one of the first times in my life, I'm speechless.

David's not though. He points to the door. "You should go, Dad."

I don't fight it.

Sometimes, you don't get to fix your mistakes. You just have to live with them.

So with one last apology, I leave.

39

I, TOO, LOVE LEFTOVERS

Layla

I'm not a cook, so I don't offer to make dinner for Nick that night. I do, however, insist on picking up something, and I tell him as much over text.

You need to eat even when life is falling apart. I learned this from my mother.

She picked up dinner every night after my father's death. Yes, she stopped cooking. But she didn't stop taking care of me.

Fine, fine. We're not talking death here. But on Sunday night, I grab food from Thai Wisdom a few blocks away, then return to my building. At the concierge desk I tell Grady that he can put Nick Adams on the list.

"Along with Harlow Granger, Ethan Adair, and Anna Mayweather," he says, scanning the computer screen in front of him.

"Yes," I say, then I add Jules and Camden. I trust them too. I head upstairs, sadness still trailing me as I think about Nick's afternoon. He didn't give me details. He only said it didn't go well.

I wish there were something I could do. But at least I can feed him.

When I'm inside my home, I set the food on the counter. My phone rings.

"Hey. I'm here," he says, sounding a little hollow. "Heading into your building."

"You're on the list," I add, but I don't try to force too much cheer into my tone. He's going to feel what he's going to feel, and I can't change it with chipperness.

"Oh," he says, surprised. "But I'll probably still call you first anyway."

He doesn't say *the next time I come over*, but I hear it anyway, and I like it. "Fair enough."

A few minutes later, I unlock the door and let him in. His warm hazel eyes are so tired. His smile is half-hearted.

"Hey," I say gently.

"Hey, beautiful," he says, but it's like he's trying to stay upbeat.

He shuts the door behind him, and immediately I rope my arms around his neck and bring him in for a hug.

He murmurs against me, accepting my embrace, his big arms wrapping around my waist. I hold him like that for a while as the food grows colder, and the city turns darker.

When I let go, I point to the purple couch. "I don't have a table, but you need to sit and eat."

"Okay," he says, and he's thoroughly downbeat. This is not the Nick I'm used to. But this is what I signed up for. All of him.

He heads to the couch, flops onto it. David did that the day he was stressed and showed up at Nick's apartment in a flustered frenzy. Like father, like son.

This reassures me somewhat. They aren't that different, and I don't think Nick would hold a grudge forever against someone he loved. Probably not even for a night.

With that hope fueling me, I gather plates and forks, then cloth napkins. "Want wine? Whiskey? Or water?"

"You have whiskey?" he asks, like I just told him I scored first-base-line tickets to the World Series.

I poke my head out of the kitchen. "I picked some up today. For you. Whiskey, neat? Right?"

That earns me a smile—a thankful, real one. "Yes. Thank you."

I make his drink, then bring it to him. He takes it and knocks some back, then blows out a long breath. "I needed that."

"I know," I say and start toward the kitchen.

"Let me help you," he says and pushes up off the couch.

I shake my head, and spin around. "No way, mister." I push his shoulder, firmly shoving him back to the couch. "I got this."

A tiny smile comes my way. "Yes. You do."

I return to the kitchen and gather the rest of the meal, along with my glass of pinot gris. Then I join him on the couch. "I didn't know what you liked, so I got a bunch of things," I say, gesturing to the cartons. "Whatever you don't like, I'll eat for breakfast this week."

"You like leftovers for breakfast?" he asks as he spoons some royal noodles onto a plate.

"Of course I do. I am human after all," I say. "Why wouldn't I?"

"No reason. I just like learning these things about you."

Warmth rushes down my chest. In the midst of his bad day, he still wants to know me. "Well, if you must know, I like leftovers, and noodles, and curry, and sautéed veggies. Oh, and with Thai food, I love pumpkin curry most of all."

A sly smile lifts his lips as he takes a bite. When he finishes, he says, "I can make a killer pumpkin curry."

I laugh. "Of course you can, you cook."

"I'll make it for you sometime," he offers, truly upbeat for the first time tonight. That's Nick, loving to cook, loving to care.

"I'll eat it," I say.

As we dine, his mood doesn't entirely shift. He's still down, but I can tell he's trying to combat it by turning the spotlight on me. He asks me about The Makeover and Mia and what's next.

I don't want to talk about me right now, but I can read him. He doesn't want the attention on himself. And he doesn't want to talk yet about his son. That's understandable, and honestly, I don't need to weigh in.

I don't want to tell him how to parent. So I give him what he seems to need. A necessary distraction.

"We have some more collaborations coming up. Like how to use highlighter," I say.

He knits his brow. "Highlighter? Like pink and yellow markers?"

A laugh bursts from inside me. "No!" Setting down my fork, I run my finger along the inside of my eye, next to the bridge of my nose. "It can go here. Or your cheekbone. Or any place you want to contour. It's like the cherry on top of makeup."

"I like cherries," he says, a little seductive.

"I know you do," I say, teasing him back, then I take a drink of my wine and add, "and she also wants to integrate my app into her company. We're meeting about that next week."

"Wow. That's big, Layla," he says.

"I'm pretty excited." I cross my fingers then pick up my fork and dig in some more.

"Is that your goal?"

"A big payoff is our goal," I say.

"Sweetheart, you're hot," he says with a sexy rumble, then he adds, "If you ever want to run anything past me, let me know."

I appreciate that he doesn't suggest I ask him for advice, though I *would* ask. But he treats me like an equal, offering insight and a sounding board.

"I will," I say, and I'd be a fool not to use him as a resource. But I'm not going to use him tonight.

Instead, I tell him to stay put while I refill his whiskey, then clean up. When I'm done, I return to him.

"Turn around," I instruct, motioning for him to shift so I can sit behind him on the couch.

"Why?"

"Just do it," I command.

With a grumble he shifts so his back is to me. Settling in on the cushion, I curl my hands over his shoulders, then I knead his muscles.

"Oh, fuck," he moans.

"Good?"

"Great," he rasps out.

I rub his shoulders for several minutes, and the only sounds he makes are sighs and moans.

On a deeper sigh, he says, "I should have told him sooner."

But we're both to blame. "I should have as well."

"I just hope he…talks to me again," Nick says, worry and fear texturing his voice.

I kiss the back of his head, brushing my lips against his hair. "He will," I say, confidently.

"You think so?"

"I do," I say, believing it with my whole heart. "You're a good father. You raised a good man."

He grabs my hand, pulls it to his mouth and presses a thank you kiss there.

* * *

In the morning, we eat leftovers in my kitchen. "I, too, love leftovers," he says, then leaves for work.

40

A DECK OF CARDS

Nick

I don't normally swing by my son's cube when I reach the office. But normally, he's not icing me out.

On the way to work, I pick up an egg sandwich at the bodega around the corner, hoping he hasn't eaten. Usually, he hasn't. In the elevator, I'm that much closer to seeing him, and my nerves fray a little more. What will it take to make this right? A sandwich isn't enough. I know that. But what will it take? What if he cuts me out of his life? This is uncharted territory for me.

But wait...Is it?

My parents were livid when I told them I got a girl pregnant.

The night I told them, my father refused to talk to me the rest of the evening. My mother woke me in the morning with a knock on my door and an "I'm still mad at you. But get your butt out of bed."

They weren't happy with me for a while, but they didn't cut me out permanently. That gives me a small modicum of reassurance. Very small.

I step off the elevator and head straight for David's cubicle. He's not there, so I set the sandwich down on his desk, then grab a Post-It note and a pen. What do I say, though? I'm not going to explain myself again on a sticky pad.

Instead, I opt for a simple note.

I love you. Here's breakfast.

I turn to leave, but I stop short when I see him walking toward me.

He looks better than yesterday—less haggard, but more stoic, with his jaw set, and his gaze hard. When he nears me, I break the silence. "I got you breakfast," I say.

I brace myself for a caustic *thanks, but I already ate*. But he only grumbles, "Thanks."

And keeps on walking.

I don't know if that's better or worse than what I'd imagined.

* * *

Later that day, Finn ducks into my office with an expectant look. "Am I getting more tiramisu?"

I laugh humorlessly.

"I take it that's a yes," he says, then shuts the door and strides to the chair.

The Tryst

"I'll send some tonight. Since I finally told David the truth," I say.

Finn lifts a brow in question. "How did it go?"

"Well, he figured it out *before* I told him, so I'd say my brilliant plan to stop lying blew up in my face. And now, he's not speaking to me. Which is...fair," I admit.

"That sucks," he says.

I hold out my hands wide. "Honestly, I feel pretty hopeless right now."

"Why?" Finn asks, confused.

"Um, see above. My son isn't speaking to me. I'm an asshole dad. I broke his trust."

"I mean, yes," he says, shrugging like that's obvious and inevitable, "you did."

"Thanks, Finn," I say, and I don't bother to hide the sarcasm. This isn't helping.

"Well, you did break his trust. Did you expect him to suggest a double date tonight?"

"Shockingly, I didn't," I deadpan.

"Then, why are you acting like this?"

"Like what?" I ask, irritation rising in me.

"Like all is lost," he points out.

I breathe out hard, annoyed. But I say nothing as I turn over his comment in my head, considering it. Finally, I admit, "Fine. Maybe I expected too much."

"Then give it time. And don't give up," he says.

I scrub a hand across my chin, considering his advice. His wise advice. "Of course I won't give up."

"Good," he says. "So keep groveling."

"Is that what's required? Is that what Marilyn makes you do?"

He waves a dismissive hand. "Word to the wise—don't do what Marilyn and I do. Do the opposite. We are like..." He pauses to think. "A Taylor Swift tune."

"Shit, man. It's that bad?"

He sighs heavily. "It is that bad. I don't think we're going to last."

Even though I saw this coming, I don't say I told you so. I just tell him the truth. "I wish you weren't dealing with that, but I'm here anytime you need me."

With a faint smile, he taps the desk. "I know you are, Nick." He rises but looks hard at me one more time. "I mean it. Don't give up. Just keep trying."

"I will."

I won't give up at all. But trying again with David will have to wait a few hours, since there's something else I need to do tonight.

* * *

After work, I stop by a flower shop then head to the hospital during visiting hours. At the check-in desk, I ask the woman in scrubs if I can see Cynthia Sweeney. She makes a quick call to the room, then tells me, "She'd be happy to see you. Room 203."

I knew the number from sending flowers yesterday. I take the stairs to her floor. Carrying a get-well basket and another bouquet of flowers, I rap on the open door.

My son's girlfriend greets me with a bright smile. "Hi, Mr. Adams," she says and waves me in.

She lies in bed with her leg extended and supported by a pillow. Her dark hair is looped into a messy bun. A scratch cuts across her cheek, and a small blue bruise dots her chin. Poor kid.

"I'm guessing you've had better days," I say with sympathy, eyeing the bulky black brace on her leg.

"Well, you should see the other guy," she says dryly.

The man who hit her walked away with mere scratches, David told me. "Glad to see your sense of humor is uninjured." I'm glad to see, too, that she's not as shy as the first time I met her.

I hold up the flowers. "I got you a little something."

"Thank you. I don't have too many. Just from my parents and my brother, and the ones you sent yesterday morning," she says, gesturing to a handful of vases. "Oh, and Layla's too."

I note that Rose hasn't come by. Neither have the Bancrofts, David's maternal grandparents. Nor have they sent anything.

"David told me you liked flowers," I say, explaining the dahlias. "And I told Layla."

No point in hiding that detail when the cat's out of the bag.

"It was kind of you. And her," she says, then gestures to a plastic chair. "Want to sit? They're serving dinner soon."

Sounds like an invitation to keep her company, so I take it, since the room seems empty and she sounds eager. First though, I set the flowers down, then gesture to the basket. "There are some puzzles in there. Crossword puzzles and cards, and a few other little things."

"Cards," she says, brightening, like I brought candy to a kid.

"You like cards?"

"Card shark in the house," she says, tapping her chest. "Can you play gin rummy?"

I scoff. "Can I play gin rummy? What do you take me for?"

She stares at me. "Well? Can you?"

I open the deck and deal.

* * *

An hour later, I've been destroyed by the woman in the hospital bed. She's beaten me hand after hand, all while eating a sad-looking burger and sadder tater tots. The carrots, sagging in the middle of the plate, remain untouched.

The clock ticks closer to seven, and I don't want to overstay my welcome. "Well, I should get out of here."

She smiles and nods. "David is on his way."

Ah, so she knows that my son won't want to see me.

Another punch to the gut.

But I take the hint, grabbing my phone, and heading to the door. Before I go, she calls out, "Mr. Adams."

I pause in the doorway. "Yes?"

"Thank you. And, um, keep trying."

That lessens the blow, but only a little. "I will."

When I head down the hall, David's walking toward me, eyes narrowed. He stops a foot away. He's tall, like me, so we're eye to eye. "You gonna try and sleep with her too?"

What the hell? Anger rises in me, a thick, hot

plume. But I keep my voice low and controlled. "I didn't raise you to speak to people like that," I tell him, though I'm seething inside.

I don't fight with low blows. And he'd better not either. With me or anyone.

He huffs out hard, like a bull.

I'm not done, though. I go full dad and say, "Do better."

He swallows roughly, and there's a flicker of embarrassment in his eyes. Maybe even shame. Then, he disappears into Cynthia's room.

"Hey, babe," I hear him say, and he's clearly happy to see her.

"Hi," she says brightly.

He's happy now. That's what matters. Not whether or not he's happy with me.

That's what I tell myself the whole way home.

41

A DIFFERENT NOTE

Nick

In the morning, I wake to soft blonde hair fanned out on my pillow and a warm woman curled up in my arms. Layla rustles the sheets against me. I kiss the back of her neck.

"More," she whispers.

I push last night out of my mind. I can't please everyone, but I can make one person very happy this morning.

So I do that.

Later, I head to the office and Layla goes to see Mia. I stop by the bodega again, pick up an egg sandwich, and leave it on David's desk. This time, the note says:

Whenever you're ready, I'd really like to

talk to you. You know where to find me.
Love, your dad

Then, I leave for a meeting across town. As I'm walking, my father texts unexpectedly, telling me he has a doctor's appointment in the city, and he wants to know if I can grab a cup of coffee after.

If that isn't foreboding, I don't know what is. Immediately, I say yes, then hope he's not about to deliver more bad news.

"Is this where you tell me you have five months to live?" I ask my dad as I grab a table at Big Cup an hour later, handing him a steaming cup of Joe then setting mine down.

He waves a dismissive hand and then raps his knuckles on his ticker. "You're not getting rid of me. The doc says I'm in great health. It's possible I'm kept alive by salt and vinegar," he says.

Relieved, I lift my cup. "Sounds about right. And I'm glad all is well. I was bracing myself. Not gonna lie."

"Don't worry. I plan on haunting my sons for a long time," he says, then studies my face. "But you don't look like you're just worried about me. What's going on?"

Is he going to judge me for falling for a woman fifteen years younger? Falling for my son's ex? Hiding it from him? No idea, but I'm going to tell him anyway. "So I met this woman..."

When I'm done with the story, he nods and mutters a "huh."

Fuck. That's bad. I cross my arms and wait for him to tell me I messed up big time with my kid.

He lifts his cup, takes a drink, then asks, "What's she like?"

I laugh, incredulous. "You're not going to tell me to, I don't know, try harder with David?"

"Nah. You know what you did. And you're doing what you need to do to make it right. So, keep doing it till my grandson gets his head out of his ass and talks to you."

I break out in laughter, and it feels damn good. "Yeah, he was kind of being a little dick last night."

Dad arches a brow. "Wonder where he got that from. You were kind of a little dick when you'd get mad at me."

My eyes pop. "What? I was not. And you were mad at me, if I recall."

He snorts, shaking his head. "I'm not talking about the *big thing*. I mean, all the other things. You liked to huff and puff if you were pissed at me for not letting you go out with friends. For telling you to do your homework. For making you do more chores."

"Fine. I might remember that," I admit, begrudgingly. "But it's not the same."

"No, but I'm like that. And you're like that. And my grandson is like that," he points out then lifts his cup, adding, "Like father, like son."

I chew on that as I take a drink too. Maybe, if I keep doing things right, I can be having conversations like this with David down the road. Next week, next year, next decade.

"Now, tell me more about this love of your life," Dad says.

I blink, startled by his comment. Did I say she was the love of my life?

That feels...big.

But maybe not wrong.

I tell him about Layla, adding, "And she takes people on their own terms. Know what I mean?"

"I sure do."

"It's nice," I add, softly.

"It sure is," he says. "She sounds good for you."

"Yeah, she is. Really good for me," I say.

"If she's good for you, then you fight for that too. We fight for the good things in our lives."

After we finish our drinks, then say goodbye, his words echo in my mind. Layla is worth fighting for. Sometimes that means showing someone you're thinking of them.

As I walk back to work, I pass a makeup store. I stop, peer inside the window at a tube on the display shelf. Something called face primer, whatever the fuck that is. I take a picture and send her a text.

> Nick: This is what you use before you paint a house, right?

> Layla: Yes, just use this kind of brush.

She attaches a photo of a makeup brush. But it's strategically shot, since the makeup brush is resting on her vanity on top of something black and lacy that I want to strip off her. My temperature shoots higher.

> Nick: By the way, what are you doing Friday night?
>
> Layla: Wearing this sexy number somewhere :)
>
> Nick: Correct. I'm taking you out Friday night, and after, I want to see the rest of that.
>
> Layla: You're on my calendar.

* * *

When I return to my office, there's a sticky note on my desk.

I'm sorry for what I said yesterday at the hospital. Thank you for visiting Cynthia.

Sunlight floods my whole body. I take the note and tuck it away in my wallet. I'm not a sentimental guy. I don't hang onto things. But this? I'll keep it.

* * *

At the end of the day, I stop by his cube.

He's not here. He must have left. I'm disappointed, but not as much as I was yesterday. There will be time. When he's ready, I'll be here.

I take some comfort in the certainty that he knows that.

As I head home, listening to a podcast on cybersecurity, I run through my evening. I'll go for a swim, do some work, cook some honey mustard chicken since I found a new recipe.

But I throw those plans out the window when I find David waiting in the lobby.

42

GOOD TASTE

Nick

I take the temperature quickly. His hair's not a wild mess, like it is when he's stressed. His eyes aren't icy either.

I hold my breath as we head upstairs to my home, then go inside. He drops his messenger bag by the door, then says, "Sooooo."

I tuck that *sooooo* in my pocket as I sweep out an arm toward the kitchen counter. "Want a drink? Water? LaCroix?" That seems as safe a conversation starter as any.

"I'm good," he says, then beelines for a stool.

I join him. "Sooooo..."

He blows out a breath. "Sorry again about last night. What I said."

Dismissing it, I shake my head. "It's behind us."

"Good," he says, then drags a hand through his hair. "It just really sucks that you lied to me."

Damn, he doesn't hold back, and I admire the hell out of that. "I know it does," I say, owning it.

"And I know she did too, but I'm pissed at you," he says, pointing at me. Like I need the extra reminder.

"I get that," I say as evenly as I can, though inside I'm freaking out over the ominous sound of the word *pissed*.

"I mean, we spent all this time together, Dad," he says, full of intensity and hurt.

"We did." I don't try to argue with him. There is no argument.

"I was living here for a week. Were you—"

"—No."

That's all I'm going to say on that. He must sense it, because he drops that topic with a heavy, "Anyway." Then, he keeps going. "I just feel like, how could you encourage me with the fundraiser, and with work, and with Cynthia, and then you're seeing my friend?"

He stares at me, clearly waiting for an answer.

"I messed up. I should have said something. I thought I wouldn't see her again," I say, then hold up my hands in surrender. "In retrospect, that was foolish of me to think and to do. But I did it. And now I'm with her. And I'm sorry I lied about it."

Quizzically, David studies me, like he can find the answer to something in my expression. "You're not going to say you didn't think I could handle it? That's not why you didn't tell me?"

Seriously? "God, no. Well, I knew you had a lot on

your plate with the fundraiser and the new job. But I didn't think *that*. I think you're pretty good at handling most things. This included. I didn't tell you because I thought—wrongly—that I would stop seeing her."

"That didn't happen," he says.

"No. It didn't."

He's quiet again, eyes darting around the kitchen before he returns his gaze to me. "You really like her?"

That doesn't even begin to cut it. But I don't need or want to dive into the nuances of my emotions for Layla. That's not a conversation we should have. "I do," I say and leave it at that.

He leans his head back, like he's absorbing this new detail. "This is weird. You know this is weird, right?"

There's a hint of a laugh in his tone.

That gives me the okay to chuckle too. "I sure do."

"So this is real? You and Layla are a thing now?"

I nod decisively. "We are."

He goes quiet again, dipping his face, staring at the black marble as if he's lost in thought. "Thanks again for hosting the fundraiser. That meant a lot to me," he says to the counter, like he has to drag those words up from the depths of his soul. "And the flowers for Cynthia. And the breakfasts."

"Anytime," I say, grabbing onto some hope at last, clutching it in my hands.

When David raises his face, he no longer looks conflicted. He seems...resolved. "Cyn and I talked last night. She told me about your visit. That was super cool of you, to play cards with her."

It sounds like it costs him something to say that, but it also sounds like it's a cost he's willing to pay.

"I was happy to do it."

"It meant a lot to her…and it means a lot to me," he says, the hurt vanishing from his tone.

I'm tense, but it's a good tension, full of hope and possibility.

"It's still weird though," he says.

"I hear you."

"I mean…we dated the same girl, Dad," he says, then turns to me, his eyes saying *can you believe that*.

"Yeah," I say, then I just shrug like *what can you do?* "I guess good taste runs in the Adams men."

He snort-laughs. "Oh, god. Please. No dad jokes about Layla."

"That was *not* a dad joke."

"That *was* a dad joke," he insists.

I'll let him have this victory since I've won something better. His respect. "Fine. It was," I add, then I gesture to the kitchen. "Stay for dinner?"

He lifts one brow in the biggest question of all time. "She's not coming over for dinner, is she? Because I'm not ready for a family meal to meet your…*new girlfriend*."

I laugh. "No. She's not."

I picture Layla right now, maybe out with friends, or shooting a video, or practicing Krav Maga, but still concerned about David and his feelings. She's let me take the lead, but she wants to make things right with him as well. I set a hand on his shoulder. "She cares deeply about you. She thinks of you as a good friend and doesn't want to lose you."

David nods thoughtfully. "I'll see her soon. I promise. But it's going to take a while for me to get the image out of my head of her telling me at the diner that she was going to have a date with some *sexy, powerful man she met at a conference*." He mimes gagging.

I just laugh. What else can I do? Especially since that's a hell of a compliment.

But as I'm about to head to the kitchen, he grabs my arm, his face deadly serious. "Don't hurt her."

It's a cold, clear warning.

"I won't," I say, assuring him.

He squeezes harder. "I mean it. She's been through a lot. She's one of the strongest, toughest, brightest, most supportive people I know. And if you break her heart, I don't know that I can forgive you for that."

I fucking love him. I extend a hand. "That's fair. And I promise you, I won't break her heart."

He shakes. "Don't lie to me again either."

Chastened, I agree. "I won't."

On that note, our roles return to the way they were. I wave him into the kitchen. "Get in here. You need to learn to cook."

On a grumble, he follows me.

43

CLOSET ROMANTIC

Nick

I'm not a superstitious guy, but on Friday night, I do everything the same as I did when I had my first date with Layla.

After I shower, I play her videos as I trim my beard, brush my teeth, and get dressed.

"And for those of you just getting into makeup, no, a highlighter is not what you use in a book to underline your favorite parts," she says with the cheekiest of cheeky grins. "It's what you use to highlight your favorite parts of your face."

She blows a cherry-red kiss to the camera, and I growl in appreciation for my Layla, my Lola, and her private moment just for me.

I close out of her app, grab my wallet, head out of my building, and get into the town car waiting for me at the curb. After I tell the driver where to go, I raise the partition.

On the ride uptown, I catch up on work emails, but when the vehicle swings onto Central Park West, I tuck my phone away so I have a few minutes to get out of the work zone completely.

And get into the first-night-out zone.

I'm almost giddy at the prospect of taking her out with no secrets.

At Layla's building, I tell the driver I'll be right back. When I head into the lobby to pick her up at her apartment, the elevator doors whoosh open.

The breath is knocked out of my lungs at the sight of her.

The woman in blue.

A silky sapphire dress clings to her gorgeous frame, hugging her hips, showing off her legs, and proudly displaying her glorious ink.

Her signature.

Her presence.

Her life.

Gratitude washes over me, along with joy. I can't stop looking at her. And I don't have to. I don't have to hide a goddamn thing anymore.

Confidently, with a wonderful kind of certainty, I walk over to her, curl a hand over the daisy on her left shoulder, then brush a kiss to her soft cheek as I rub my thumb along the petals. "You are maddeningly gorgeous and all mine."

She leans into my hand, seeking me out. Like she

always has. She's been so bold all along, and I'm so damn grateful for who she is and *how* she is.

After a few seconds we separate, and she says, "I am yours, so take me out."

"Always," I say, then set a hand on her back and leave the building with her, like we did months ago in Miami, like we'll do now here in New York.

I can picture it perfectly. And I wonder if all my theories about coincidence are wrong.

* * *

I take her to a new restaurant in the Village. Finn told me about The Standards on Christopher Street, but there's nothing standard about the menu. The meal is sumptuous, a butternut squash ravioli with white wine sauce for her and Chilean sea bass for me.

Old standards play overhead. Yeah, I like them. Nobody has a thing on Frank and Ella, or Harry Connick Jr. for that matter.

As we dine and drink, our conversation meanders through friends and moments, then she tells me about her business partner, Geeta, how she met her in a thrift shop when they both reached for the same purple blouse.

"It's odd because we don't have the same taste. She's more punk rock," Layla explains, then runs a hand down her hair, her rings glinting in the soft candlelight as she goes. "She has this magenta streak in her hair, and a lip piercing."

"What's your style then?" I ask, eyeing her dress,

her skull rings, her ink. She's a lovely hodgepodge all her own.

Layla gives a coquettish shrug. "Sometimes I'm pinup, sometimes I'm nighttime, sometimes I'm super-casual girl. And sometimes I'm whatever I want."

"You know yourself well," I say.

"I guess I had to figure some things out," she says, and that makes all the sense in the world.

"So, who got the top? The purple one?" I ask.

"She did," Layla says with a smile. "I could tell she wanted it, so I told her to take it. I grabbed something else."

And I fall a little harder. "That's so you."

"You'd think we'd have met someplace else. Business school, or through a friend, or a mentor. Or Raven, even. But it was random."

I set my tumbler down. "Was it though?"

Her brow knits. "What do you mean?"

"Was it random? Or was it kismet? Do you believe in kismet?" I ask, though I doubt she does. Understandably.

"I don't think so," she says slowly, a little carefully, like she doesn't want to rain on my parade. "Do you?"

I shrug both wanting to admit it and not.

"You don't seem like a kismet kind of guy," she adds. "You're Mister Logic and Theories, and you study the world for patterns."

That is true. "I am that guy," I say, but as the music shifts to "It Had to Be You," that kismet feeling from earlier sharpens. As I picture the next few days and weeks and months, I'm pretty sure I'm *this guy* too. I offer her a hand. "Dance with me."

It's an order, but she likes orders, so she's up in no time, heading to the tiny corner of the restaurant with hardwood floors.

"Nick Adams, you dancer, you," she says with a sexy and sweet smile that I want to kiss off, that I *can* kiss off.

So I do, savoring the chance to touch her in public, in private, wherever and whenever we want at last.

No more hiding. No more need for secret trysts on dead-end streets.

As I brush my lips to hers, she shudders in my arms, pressing against me. I want her even more when she does that, so I break the kiss. "Don't want this to turn into an R-rated show," I say as we sway the slightest bit, slow dancing to the swoony song.

"That's for later."

"Absolutely. But for now," I say, running my fingers along her hair, returning to a thought that's got a hold of me in this moment, "I asked about kismet because I was thinking about fate and meeting you in the first place in Miami. Then about moving to New York. Then running into you."

"And you think meeting me in Miami was kismet?" she asks, her lips curving up in obvious delight as well as curiosity.

"At first I thought it was a coincidence, but I think maybe meeting you was meant to be after all."

"Yeah?" Her smile deepens, and that's a sign to keep going.

"I do," I say, and I feel uncorked. Completely free.

It's a fantastic feeling, so I give in to it completely.

"Why now?"

"Because here we are. Like this. First Miami, then New York," I say, even more caught up in her. "I don't mean I believe in kismet for everything. But I believe it now...for you."

Her smile is the most beautiful thing I've ever seen. Because it's all for me. "Are you a closet romantic?"

"Have I hidden it before?"

She lets go of my shoulder, holds up her hand to show a smidge of space between her thumb and forefinger. "You've never struck me that way."

I lift my face to the ceiling where the music and lyrics drift from the speakers. *I wandered around, and I finally found...the somebody who...could make me be true.* "I took you to a romantic restaurant. I'm slow dancing with you. I'm telling you I believe you and I aren't a coincidence, and you think I'm *not* romantic?"

"Okay, maybe a little romantic," she says, teasing me again.

"Good," I say, then I inch back, wanting to look her in the eyes. Wanting her to see all of me as I say the next thing. "Because I love you, Layla. I just do. Maybe it's soon, maybe it's madness, maybe that makes me a total romantic—"

She shuts me up with a kiss, and it's the most emotional kiss in the whole entire world. I can feel her love in the way she kisses, can hear it in her soft breath, can sense it in her hands on my face.

It's there whether she says it or not.

But when she breaks the kiss, she says, "It's not too

soon. I love you too."

I don't kiss her again. Instead, I say, "Let me show you how much."

In the backseat of the car, with the partition up, she's a goddess, arching against me, grabbing my shirt, and parting her lips as she shatters next to me.

Yes, fucking yes.

I slow the stroke of my fingers as she comes down from her high then turns to me, eyes starry, cheeks glowing.

I lick her off my fingers. Then, my greedy girl comes in for a naughty kiss.

"Mmm. I taste good on your mouth," she says when she pulls back.

"I should make sure though," I say darkly.

When we reach my home, I don't even bother to unzip her dress. I set her on the couch, kneel between her thighs, and push up the fabric.

A few minutes later, she's making my favorite sounds against my mouth. Then panting, gasping. "You're relentless, Nick," she murmurs.

I brush my beard against her thigh. "You demanded orgasms the night I met you. Did I misunderstand you?"

She laughs, then sits up and leans forward, sliding one hand down my chest and gripping my cock through the fabric of my pants.

I moan as she squeezes. "Play with my dick, sweetheart," I tell her then stand and help her along, unzipping my pants, pushing down my boxer briefs, and offering her my cock. Eagerly, she dips her face to my dick, rubbing the head against her lush red lips.

She reapplied her lipstick in the elevator of my building, and I intend to remove it very, very soon.

I nudge her lips open wider with my cock. Beautifully, she obeys. She licks the head reverently, like she's indulging in me. Hot sparks of pleasure shoot down my spine.

She swirls her tongue over me then lets go to lick a deliriously sexy stripe down my shaft.

I can't think anymore, it feels so good.

I breathe out hard, curling a hand around her head. "More," I urge.

She looks up at me, wicked and powerful as she says, "Patience, handsome."

I shake my head. "I can't be patient. God, I want you so much."

That seems to light her up since in no time, she's grabbed my hips and has dragged me deep into her throat. She's on my dick like it's her next meal, and I can barely stand how erotic this moment is.

My beautiful woman is devouring my cock in my penthouse, her red lips stretched and full of me, all of New York beyond us. But I don't think she's focused on the natural art views since she's so damn focused on my dick. She's sucking hard and purposefully, but it's too good. My thighs shake. My balls tingle.

I stop, ease out of her mouth.

She pouts. "But I like your dick."

"Then spend some time with it in my bed."

In my bedroom, I strip off my clothes the rest of the way as she tugs off her dress. But I stop and stare when the dress pools on the floor.

She's breathtaking in black lingerie. My throat goes dry as I point stupidly at the fabric hugging her breasts. "That's what was in your photo?"

"I bought it for our first New York date," she says, then runs her fingers down a black satin corset that nearly makes me lose my mind.

"Leave it on and get on my dick now," I tell her, then I grab a condom from the nightstand.

But once I'm in bed and she's climbing over me, she takes the condom and tosses it behind her.

That's interesting, and I hope it means everything I think it does. "Something you want to tell me?"

She leans closer, her hair swishing over her shoulders. "I started the pill recently. It's working now. And I'm safe."

I get to have her bare. My body is a furnace. "I'm safe too."

I offer her my cock, and she takes it.

My woman sinks down on my shaft, moaning as I fill her. A dirty smile spreads as she wriggles around on my dick, like she's never been happier.

Well, that makes two of us.

I am the luckiest man in the world as I fuck the woman I love.

Maybe it's kismet. Maybe it's coincidence. Or maybe it's making a choice and then doing everything in your power to own it.

44

A FIELD DAY

Layla

A frog valiantly tries to cross the street, hopscotching past trucks on the screen as festive retro arcade noises beep from the Frogger console.

I've arrived early at Cosmo's in the Village for the Saturday lunch I set up with David, so I'm at a booth, watching the door like a hawk as someone plays the retro arcade game nearby. But the frog pancakes, dying a pixelated death on the arcade screen.

I don't want to be the frog today with David. I twist the skulls on my fingers as I wait. I'm not usually fidgety. But waiting for David has nerves flying under my skin.

The last time I was here, he told me about the woman he fell for.

Now, we're going to *talk* about how I banged his pops.

Fun times.

I twist the rings some more, but the motion does nothing to settle my worries. I pop in my earbuds and turn to Ethan's newest tune. He sent "Blown Away" to Harlow and me, and I can't stop listening to it. But right when my friend's beautiful baritone threatens to break my heart, David steps into the doorway of the shop, scanning the room for me.

I hit stop so fast, then with an *I fucked up* smile, I wave to him.

I brace myself since I can't read his barometer. Especially when he gives me a chin nod, then strides over to me. A chin nod is not a smile.

"Hey, Mayweather," he says as he reaches me, and I'm not sure if I should hug him, so I don't pop up. I want to respect his need for space if he needs it.

"Hey, Bancroft," I say. Or maybe I squeak it.

He slides into the booth across from me. But before he can say a word, I dive headfirst into the most important thing. "How's Cynthia? She gets out tomorrow, right?"

"She does," he says, like he's proud of her. "And she got your self-care basket the other day and pretty much jumped out of bed."

"That's great. Not the jumping, but that she liked it," I say. I sent her a gift—some candles, face masks, makeup, and yummy lotion.

"She said she didn't know what half of the makeup brushes were for," he adds.

Shit. Does that mean I picked a stupid gift and she secretly hated it?

"Oh. I hope that wasn't a bad—"

"She really liked it. And I like that you sent it to her."

That's good, but I don't feel like we're making real progress.

He's quiet, and I can't tell where we stand or even where he *wants* to stand. Especially when he's studying the menu board on the wall like he's never been here before. I can barely tolerate the awkward and it's only been a minute.

"Are you hungry?" he asks, turning back to me at the same time I blurt out, "I'm sorry I wasn't honest with you. I'm sorry I didn't say anything sooner. I miss our friendship and our jokes and our teasing, and I really want to find a way to get it back. What can I do to make things right?"

He startles. "Oh."

"Oh?"

"I mean," he says, then scratches his jaw, furrows his brow. "Actually, I'm okay with everything."

I lean forward, my eyes popping. "You are?"

"I figure it'll be awkward, like the last few minutes were. But I think I get it, Layla."

"You do?" Color me shocked.

The corner of his mouth hooks into a grin. "Well, you clearly have a type."

Then he lets his grin widen like he caught me at something—liking Bancroft/Adams men.

I laugh, too. "Maybe I do."

He reaches across the table and ruffles my hair. "Listen, we don't have to rehash what happened. That shit was hard to do with my dad. I was a little exhausted and wrung out after I talked to him. And I decided I don't want to stay pissed at people. Especially people I love. There are too many other shitty things in the world. There are animals who need homes, and people who are starving, and a planet that needs saving. And *you*," he says, pointing at me. "You helped me plan a fundraiser for something that matters deeply to me. What kind of asshole would I be if I was annoyed at you for liking my dad?"

My heart balloons until it hardly fits in my chest. And I'm not sure there's much more to say, other than, "Thank you."

"No," he says, emphatic. "Thank you. You did all of that—you hosted it, you helped. There's no list of grievances." Then he sighs, long and pointed. "I mean, besides the fact that you cheated on me. But it's all in the family so I can accept it."

I laugh harder. "I'm so relieved."

He looks to the board with hunger in his eyes. "Want to eat and then come with me to see my girl?"

"I'd love to."

When we're done, he grabs a sandwich to go for Cynthia, just like Nick has done for him in the past. I hide my private smile. He's so much like his father in his love language.

On our way, he stops outside Cosmo's, his expression suddenly stern. "But let's just make one thing clear."

Solemnly, I nod, ready for whatever he wants from me. "Anything."

"When you marry him, I'm going to have a field day calling you stepmom."

There's too much to unpack there, so I zoom in on one thing. "Sure, *stepson*. Feel free."

At the hospital, I meet his girlfriend for the first time, and she's a total sweetie. In short, she's perfect for him.

She gestures to the makeup brushes. "Now, can you show me how all this stuff works?"

"I definitely can," I say, and spend the next hour doing her makeup.

45

I HAD A FEELING

Layla

On Sunday morning, I swing my tennis racket over my shoulder and head out the door to meet my mom at the club. Nick leaves with me, his hand on my ass the whole time we walk down the hallway to the elevator.

As we wait for the lift, he turns to me, a playful grin on his face. "Now remember, sweetheart. Just say these words to her. *Nick has a bigger, better cock than any man in the world, so stop setting me up.*"

"That's exactly what I was going to say."

"You can also tell her I give you multiple orgasms," he deadpans as the elevator arrives.

"I'll for sure let her know you love to eat my kitty," I say when we step inside the empty car.

He cups my chin. "Fair's fair. Tell her you love to suck my dick too."

Laughing, I say, "How about I just tell her my boyfriend has a filthy mouth and leave it at that?"

"You know who else has a filthy mouth?"

"Who?"

"Your boyfriend's girlfriend," he says in a low, sexy voice. He kisses my neck, first adoringly, then roughly like he's going to leave a mark. So very him.

But I push him away. "No hickeys. That will not impress Mama Mayweather."

He stops then takes my hand as we leave, his tone turning serious. "Someday, I'll impress her. *For you.*"

My chest flutters. Nick doesn't like to play the who's who game. He doesn't need to impress people for himself. He'd only want to make a good impression someday for my benefit. So Mom can breathe more easily, knowing I'm with someone who adores me.

I hold that sentiment close to my heart on the way to Randall's Island.

* * *

On the court, I bounce on my toes, waiting for Mom's serve. Like she was born to decimate people at this game, she lifts her racket and sends the ball screaming my way.

I lunge, but I don't stand a chance. The ball flies past me to the edge of the court.

Game. Set. Match.

Beads of sweat roll down my chest as I jog to the net and shake hands with her. "Good game."

She points her racquet at me. "Tell the truth. Did you let me win again?"

"No. You are just a beast."

With a closed-mouth smile, she walks to the bench at the side of the court and grabs her water bottle. After a long gulp, she nods to the club. "Shower and lunch?"

I glance around. The court is surprisingly empty. No one's waiting for it. I seize my chance. "Actually, there's something I wanted to talk to you about," I say, feeling ready and eager.

It's time. It's just finally time.

"Sure. What is it, darling?"

There's no way to dip a toe into this water. I jump. "I'm not going out with Kip next week. He reached out this morning to set up a time, and I told him I'm seeing someone."

"You are?"

"Yes. But even if I weren't seeing him, I don't want to be set up anymore, Mom. I don't like any of those guys. They're all self-centered, egotistical, pampered dude bros."

She winces, setting down her water bottle on the bench beside the court. "What even is that? A dude bro?"

"The opposite of Dad." That's the easiest way to put it.

"I see," she says calmly, fingering the wedding band she still wears. Maybe it's subconscious. Maybe it's intentional—a connection to her lost love. She's done it for years, touching it absently, when she's knocked off-kilter.

"But I met someone, and he's incredible," I continue, and I don't try to hide the hearts and flowers in my voice. I *can't* hide the way I feel.

"That's wonderful. Would I know him?"

As a matter of fact...

"Yes," I say, then square my shoulders. "I'm with Nick Adams."

She jerks her head, her mouth open like a fish. "Rose's ex?" she finally gasps.

"Yes. And he's David's father," I add so we don't have to go through everything one by one.

Her eyes widen. Her voice dips. "Darling. That's..."

"Scandalous?"

"Layla." It's a chide, like I've misbehaved.

"Well, is that what you mean?" I'm not holding back anymore. Her feelings matter, but mine do too.

"No," she says. "That's not what I meant."

But she doesn't elaborate. I didn't expect her to throw me a party for seeing her friend's ex-husband. I only want her to stop playing matchmaker and to start respecting my choices. "Look, you don't have to like him. You don't have to play tennis with him. But I'm in love with him, and he's in love with me. And that's that."

She grips her racket tighter. "Okay," she says, but it's harsh, like a bite, and it irritates me.

"Fine. You don't like him," I add. "I get it. That's your choice. But he's *my* choice. And you need to know that so you can stop setting me up."

She grabs my arm desperately, like she thinks I'll jet off. "I'm not upset with you. I'm upset with me. I feel foolish. I wish I'd known sooner. Why didn't you tell me you didn't want to be set up?"

Take care of Mom. Dad's last words echo daily in my head.

"Because I wanted you to be happy," I grit out past the inevitable swell of emotions. "That's what Dad would have wanted. For me to look out for you."

There. That's the truth. That's honoring him and her.

Letting go of me, she lifts her fingers to cover her mouth like she's holding back a deluge of tears.

I go on. "And I know you wanted me to be with a man from a family you know. With a pedigree. Who went to an Ivy League school and is a member of a country club."

Sharply, she says, "Stop."

I'm taken aback. She doesn't usually speak to me that way or stare at me with fierce fire in her gaze. This is boardroom Anna.

"That's not what I want. Do not conflate the two."

"But it seemed that way?"

"I want you with a man I trust because I want you to be safe," she says tightly, in a way that keeps her tears in check. "I don't care about a man's money. You don't need to marry a rich man. Like Cher said, *I am a rich man.* I make enough to take care of you if you ever need a thing. I want you with someone I trust because..." She takes a deep breath, perhaps for fuel. "I never trusted Joe. I had a feeling, and I *never* did a thing about it." Her voice wobbles, teetering on the edge of a sob. "I couldn't put a finger on it, so I never said anything, and that regret lives with me." She pokes her chest for emphasis. "It's not because of where he came from. It was a gut feeling, and I did nothing about it."

The guilt she must be carrying. The needless, misplaced guilt. It's heartbreaking.

I grab her arms, hold her tight. "Mom, it's not your fault," I say softly, full of emotion.

Tears run down her cheeks.

We're both sweaty from the game and messy from crying, but I don't care. I hug her, both of us needing the contact. "Don't carry that with you, Mom. No one could have known. Dad and Joe had a fight the week before, and Dad didn't know what Joe was capable of. *Joe* probably didn't know what he was capable of. I certainly didn't know when he walked past me into our building. It happened, Mom. It just happened, and only one person is to blame," I say, squeezing her hard, trying to give her some of my strength, my certainty.

She sniffles.

I let go but keep a grip on her shoulders as I look her in the eyes. "It's not your fault. It's not your fault. It's not your fault," I repeat.

Another thick tear rolls down her cheek. She shudders out a staggered breath, then lets go and swipes her face.

Then, she nods. Perhaps it's acceptance or the start of it.

"You can't change the past," I say. "You can only change how you live your present."

She manages the tiniest hint of a smile. "How did you get to be so wise?"

"I had to," I say, then I nod to the club. "Want to get a cobb salad?"

She rolls her eyes. "This place has the worst cobb salad. Can we go someplace else?"

"I know a good diner in the city."

"Let's go there."

* * *

At Neon Diner we don't talk about boys or men, or the past. We don't talk about the job she wants me to take on someday at her company.

Another time. Another time, too, I'll tell her I have a meeting with Mia later this week to talk about *next steps*.

Instead, we chat about the best and the worst restaurants in the city, about Ethan's band and Harlow's art gallery and Jules's work casting new TV shows, and Camden's burgeoning business.

Mom eats up every detail.

When we're done, we say goodbye on the street. We part ways without her mentioning Nick, or men, or Beautique.

Perhaps it's a new start for us.

And I hope it's one for her.

46

IT'S NOT MINE

Layla

Mia hardly seems like a person with a typical office in a skyscraper, so when she sent me her work address, a quick Google search confirmed my image of her in a cute little brownstone nestled in the Village, surrounded by flowers.

Now, on Wednesday morning, I'm here at the top of the stoop on this quaint-by-Manhattan-standards block, pressing the buzzer.

"Just a sec," she calls out from above. I look up. On the second floor, she's busily watering plants on a balcony. Okay, that tracks too. A giant floppy hat covers her hair. "Women of a certain age," she says, pointing to the hat.

That seems to be her mantra.

"A floppy hat is like Paris. It's always a good idea," I say cheerily.

"Let's market floppy hats too!"

If Mia did, indeed, launch a floppy hat line next I wouldn't be surprised.

A few seconds later, she buzzes me in, and I trot up the steps to her home. The door is peach—on brand too.

She swings it open. "Come in, love," she says, then ushers me down a hallway to a staid door and into her office.

An oak desk commands the center of the room with two navy-blue chairs opposite it. The walls are a cool white. It's a sleek and powerful contrast to her dancing-through-life style.

She pats the back of a chair for me, then takes the other. "I have a proposal for you, and I didn't want to talk in public," she says, firmly in business Mia mode. It's a little jarring since I'm used to the breezy side of her. But then, Mia's always had her public self and her private self. I suppose my mom's like this, too, and so am I.

People see what you let them see. But they also craft their own versions of you, whether you want them to or not. The key to survival is knowing when and with whom to share your different sides. That's all you can control.

"I want to buy The Makeover and make it part of Mia Jane," Mia says, and wow, that's cutting to the chase. I was not expecting an offer this quickly, if she made one at all.

She hands me a sheet of paper. A little stunned, I

take it then school my expression as I read the amount. It's a helluva return on our investment.

This can ease Geeta's burden. *A lot.*

But I'm still wary. Sometimes offers are too good to be true, so before I get ahead of myself, I nudge her with, "But I suspect that's not all?"

Mia smiles like I nailed the answer on a quiz show. "There *is* a condition. I want to integrate the app into my makeup brand, with the proviso"—yup, here comes the strings—"that you come on board as my second-in-command and run the company with me."

* * *

Mia's offer is amazing. I'm still reeling. But I'm not the only one who gets to decide. There are two of us. I hustle to Hoboken as fast as I can because this is an in-person conversation. When I reach Geeta at her favorite tea shop, she's buzzing, and I don't think it's from the chai half-finished in front of her.

"Can we get the money today?" she asks.

This is why we're a good team. She's full-speed ahead, and I'm more of a take-our-time gal. "Probably not. We should talk about it first," I say. "Do our due diligence and all."

She nods at supersonic speed. "Right. Of course. Especially since it has to work for you since they're buying *you* too," she says, her voice full of restrained hope that the deal will work for me.

That's the crux of the issue. I'm part of the deal.

Mia doesn't just want The Makeover. She wants me.

Am I even available? My mom wants me to join her at Beautique. She expects me to. She thinks my dad wanted me to join her.

I've been avoiding the decision. I've been dodging her comments about working together because I've enjoyed doing my own thing. I've put my head in the sand, refusing to make a real decision about the join-me-in-the-family-business expectation.

But I can't ignore it any longer. Now that someone's dangling an out-of-this-world chance to run a kick-ass, cruelty-free, forward-thinking makeup brand, I know exactly what I want.

To run Mia Jane with Mia.

But after the other day with my mom and finally making some progress, I don't want to hurt her again.

And I did make a promise to take care of her.

I meet Geeta's dark gaze. "I just need to think a little longer."

She tries to mask her disappointment with a smile, but it's unconvincing. "Of course."

When I leave, my smile is forced too. It masks the pang in my chest. The one that comes from not knowing what to do.

Even if I don't know what to do, I know where to go.

When I return to Manhattan, I grab a bagel sandwich from a bodega, then go straight to Central Park. My compass is pointing me to the bench. As I go, I cross my fingers that it's empty.

There have been times over the years when I came here to think and someone else was using it.

To eat, to read, to nap.

Today, I need it. I want it. I'll think and eat and listen to some music. It'll be all mine. My public secret.

I walk faster, my heart pounding a little too hard. I don't want to make a mistake. I don't want to hurt my mom. I don't want to hurt Geeta.

As I'm passing the lake, I start to jog. Like something's chasing me, I go faster, then I'm running past the water, around the bend, down the path and...

I stop short, panting.

A homeless man is sitting on the bench, picking through a takeout box that must have come from a garbage can.

I feel like I ran into a brick wall.

I do the only thing I can. I take the bagel sandwich from my purse and walk over to him. "Would you like this? I haven't touched it."

"Thank you."

I hand it to him, then turn around and leave.

The bench isn't truly mine after all. It belongs to others now. It belongs to whoever needs it, and so do the words on the plaque.

47

PLEASE OVERSTEP

Layla

My instinct is to find Harlow and Ethan. They've been my people for so long. They always will be.

But there's someone else who can help me more, someone who desperately loves to help.

As I leave the park, I write a text.

> Layla: Hi. I need to talk to you tonight. About a business thing. I'm kind of...lost.

I hit send before I can second guess myself.

Help isn't something I like asking for, unless it's from my two closest friends. But I suppose this is what having a relationship is all about.

A few minutes later, he replies.

> Nick: Of course. Anything you need.

I wince, a little embarrassed I need him for this question.

But I do. He's the only one who can help. After we make plans to meet at my place that evening, I head home, lock myself in, and shower without washing my hair. I change into fresh clothes, tossing on a tank top and pulling on jeans.

I loop my dry hair into a messy bun, then grab one of my makeup bags, ready to begin putting on my face.

I stare in the mirror, considering what kind of makeup to use. Maybe just some foundation and gloss? Add in a little mascara for a finishing touch? As I like to say, *you're never fully dressed without mascara.*

But when I grab the foundation brush, I have this sudden impulse to...*not* put on makeup.

It's weird, this feeling.

Great, just great. Another thing I don't know how to handle.

I put the brush back in the bag, set the bag on a shelf, and go to my living room, flopping down on my chaise longue and letting myself exist with this uncomfortable, naked feeling.

I click open a book, and I read until Nick texts:

> Nick: I'm on my way.

I pop up, feeling totally unsure of myself. But when he knocks and I yank open the door, my uncertainty vanishes.

At least I'm certain of this.

Him.

Us.

He looks like he did when I met him. Strong, powerful, wise. He wears charcoal slacks, and a burgundy button-down. His tie is unknotted. He's such a messy-tie guy after hours.

I tug on it, pulling him through the door and closer to me. "Hi. I need you."

"I'm here," he says.

A few minutes later, we're on my couch, and I've shared the digital copy of the deal memo Mia gave me earlier in the day.

That's not what I need Nick's advice on, though, that's where he starts. When he sets the phone down after reading, he asks, "Do you want to do this?"

Easiest answer ever. "Yes." I've been certain ever since I went to Mia's office. "It seems challenging and fun and meaningful and right up my alley."

"It does sound like you," he says, but he's not grinning. He watches me with concern, and before I can gather the nerve to ask my big question, he asks, "But you think you're breaking a promise?"

I'm so relieved he gets it, but I'm not surprised. Of course Nick would know why this weighs on me.

I swallow roughly. "It's just...the *take care of Mom* promise? I've always thought that meant I had to work for her, to look out for her, to make sure she's happy."

"I can see why you'd think that." He's careful when discussing my parents. I can tell he doesn't want to overstep.

"Nick, I need to know what *you* think it means...as a father," I implore. I never thought to ask him before. I didn't want to take advantage of his insight as a father. But I sure do now. "Tell me. It's been chasing me for years."

No, that's not true. The promise has done more than chase me. "It's defined me," I say, correcting myself.

Nick sighs deeply, shaking his head, but it's not a sad sigh. It's contemplative. "Layla," he begins quietly, importantly.

"Yes?"

He takes my hand. His gentle gaze stays on mine. "I believe it means he knew *you'd* be okay without him. He knew his strong, brave girl would be all right whatever she did, whatever she chose, whatever she decided."

Damn him. He's making me cry. Leaning close, he swipes a thumb across a tear on my cheek.

"He told you he loved you. That's what he wanted you to know. Then he told you to take care of her because he wanted someone to remember the woman he loved. But as a father, he'd never have wanted you to do something *just* for her. He'd have wanted you to be free to make the choices that are best for you. The choices you want to make."

My shoulders shake as relief and something almost like joy clobber me, but I swallow the next wave of tears. "You really think so?"

"I believe it completely," he says.

"You're not just saying that because you…"

He gives a tiny laugh. "Because I love you?"

"Yes."

He cups my cheek, runs his thumb down my bare face. "I'm saying that because it's what I believe to be true."

I feel lighter, freer. And I feel loved. "Nick," I whisper, a new kernel of hope pushing me on.

"Yes?"

"I think this is my dream job," I whisper reverently.

"I think it is too."

I climb onto his lap, straddle him, and kiss the hell out of him. "I love you more every day."

He wraps his arms around me then kisses my cheek. "Good. Your love is all I want."

Then I show him how much I love him. I take off my jeans and panties, then I undo his zipper, and sink down onto him.

"Yessss," he groans, leaning his head back against the couch cushion.

I don't rush. I just indulge in the feel of him and our intimacy. The way we grow closer in everything we do, in and out of bed.

For a while, I dodged any kind of connection. I was terrified of it.

I'm still scared of losing him. I'm sure I always will be. But I'd rather live with that worry than live without love.

48

THE COUNTER OFFER

Layla

I ask my mother to meet me at Neon Diner that weekend. I like it better than the club. I have a feeling she does too. No one whispers things about *that Layla Mayweather* or about *Anna*.

Only this isn't a typical mother-daughter outing. And I sincerely hope I'm not about to wallop my mother with a one-two punch. But a businesswoman has to do what a businesswoman has to do.

With the confidence of someone who finally knows what she wants, I yank open the door to my favorite diner. A Monkees tune blares overhead and servers scurry by in mint-green uniforms.

I smooth a hand down my shirt. It's new. I went shopping yesterday and Jules and Harlow helped me pick it out. "It'll be perfect for your first day on the job," Harlow had said.

That made me a little giddy, thinking about my first day at work. But today feels like my first day on the job, so I'm wearing it now. The top is a light blue peasant blouse from Champagne Taste, and I paired it with a short black skirt that Jules picked out for me.

It's not my mother's pink pantsuit, thank you very much.

When I find Mom at the table, she's dictating an email on her phone. She's like Jules.

Only Jules isn't always on. She turns it off. Maybe my mom needs someone to help her turn it off.

After we say hi and order, I begin. No deep breaths. No preamble. I'm direct and clear as I tell her about Mia's offer. "And it sounds like an incredible opportunity," I finish.

She's quiet and honestly a little terrifying as she sits so tall, so poised. So very Anna "Take No Prisoners" Mayweather.

"Interesting," she says at last, cool and professional. But then she's silent again.

I gulp, but I don't say anything. I don't try to fill the quiet by backpedaling or reassuring her.

"And are you going to take it?" she asks after a pause.

I hold my ground. "I am. It's what I want. And I want to thank you for offering me a job at Beautique. But this, it turns out, is my dream."

She purses her lips, and I brace myself for a retort like "*Is this what your father would have wanted?*"

But it doesn't come. Instead, she stares intensely at me with cool blue eyes. Hers are lighter than mine.

Some would say icier. But I've seen her other sides. I know she can be warm and loving, motherly, and kind.

"I can see this matters to you," she says, and my shoulders lose some of the tension I didn't realize I was holding.

She's understanding me more than I expected her to.

"Truly, I can," she adds with a resigned smile. That's a good sign. "But I'd be a terrible businesswoman if I didn't make a counteroffer."

I blink. "What?" Is this for real?

"I'll pay double to integrate The Makeover into Beautique. And to have you run it inside my company."

My jaw nearly drops from the shock, except...I don't let it. She's never offered to buy my app before. She's known all along we wanted to sell it. Why now? Why double it? Because someone else wants The Makeover?

No. It's because someone else wants me, I think.

"It could be a wonderful partnership," she says. "Getting to see each other at the office. Brainstorm ideas and new lines. Grab lunch while we discuss makeup and business."

And all at once, everything is illuminated. Why she wants me to work with her. Why she's clung to the idea of it.

She doesn't *need* me to work at her company. She needs to spend more time with me. She's lonely.

I fight back tears as the server arrives with our food. When she's gone, I say to my mom, "Let's eat and then I'll show you something."

Since I also know what to do next.

* * *

After lunch, I take her to Central Park. "We're almost there," I say as we near the bench.

Twenty feet away, she stops, so I do too. She turns to me, understanding in her eyes, shining along with her tears. "You got a bench."

"I did," I say.

"Your father loved these so," she says, her voice wistful and full of love.

"He did."

"You never told me." She doesn't sound upset. She sounds amazed.

"I needed it to be a secret for a long time," I say. But now I don't have to keep it to myself.

I take her hand. "I had a plaque made too," I add. I take her to the bench so she can read it. This is the real Herculean task—fighting off the waterworks. A whisper is all I can manage as I gesture to the plaque. "They're my last words to him."

She covers her mouth, tears streaking down her face as she gazes at the silver metal and the four words etched onto them.

I love you too.

* * *

We sit and talk and reminisce—about the places we liked to go with him, the way he'd laugh, and the things he'd said—as the afternoon wanes. It's time to leave, and I walk her across the park to Fifth Avenue, stopping when we reach the museum.

"Mom," I say, as cars and cabs and buses trudge down the avenue. "If you really mean your counteroffer, I have to take it to Geeta. But if you made it to spend more time with me, then I'd like to make you a counter-proposal."

That seems to surprise her. "Oh. Okay. Sure."

I've caught her off-guard, perhaps for the first time. I think she'll admire that about me. I hope she'll like my idea. "I could really use a mentor. Maybe a strong, passionate woman who's dealt with all sorts of challenges and opportunities in business." She smiles, unbidden, as I say more: "Do you happen to know anyone?"

She taps her chin, playful in a way she rarely is. "I believe I do."

"Then maybe this mentor and I could get together and talk shop every week. Say, at the Neon Diner?"

"Consider it scheduled," she says.

We say goodbye, and she heads to her side of the city, and I go to mine. But we're not so far apart anymore.

49

SPEAKING OF BOSSY

Layla

A few weeks and a signed deal later, I head to Gin Joint, feeling a little like a rock star.

Geeta's already found a live-in aide for her dad, so she feels like a rock star too. Storm sent me a "Welcome to Mia Jane" bouquet of daisies earlier this week, with a note saying, *I'm guessing they're your fave because of that gorgeous ink! Can't wait to work with you.*

I can't wait to work with him too. He nabbed a promotion, and he's now a director on the corporate side instead of a store manager.

But tonight is for friends.

I find my crew draped over velvet couches, looking frothy and fabulous. Or maybe everything feels that way tonight.

"My pets!" I call out, then I join Harlow, Ethan, and Camden. "Where's Jules?"

"In the ladies," Camden answers.

I hear the click of stilettos over the sound of the piano. "I take it mojitos are on you tonight?" Jules asks from behind me.

I turn to answer Jules, only, she's...blonde.

"Your hair," I say stupidly, pointing.

She smiles like a cat. "Oh this? It's a wig," she says, then waggles a brow as she sits next to me. "I think I'm into wigs now."

"Is this more of After-Dark Jules?" I ask, dying for details.

Camden jumps in with, "Take her to a club and you'll see what After-Dark Jules is like."

"I've been to dance clubs with you," I tell Jules, and I'm holy hell intrigued. The more I get to know her, the more layers I find.

Ethan stretches across the table and taps my knee. "I don't think she means dance clubs," he stage-whispers.

Jules just smiles and says, "Oh, hush."

I stare at my now-blonde friend, agape. "Mojitos are on me, but stories are on you, evidently. I want to hear more about your clubs."

She bobs a shoulder. "I'm not sure there's much to tell." She takes a beat, then adds, "Yet."

I laugh, surveying the faces of my friends, my found family. They're bright and sparkly, eyes twinkling, mouths lifting. I say to the group, "I feel like that *yet* is doing a lot of work in that sentence."

"It sure is," Harlow says.

Jules just gives another secretive smile.

Soon I suspect she'll share more of that *yet*. I'll be ready when she does. For now, we order drinks, and then toast.

"To Layla Mayweather," Ethan offers, holding up his cocktail. "AKA Lola Jones."

"May she continue to be fire," Harlow seconds, lifting her iced tea.

I chime in with, "And to new friends and old."

"And dirty little secrets," Camden adds, staring pointedly at Jules.

Who turns to me. "And to winning the heart of an Adams man," she says.

I clink, but that comment—*an Adams man*—plays a couple of times in my head.

But I put it out of my mind when I go to a gorgeous building in Gramercy Park to see my Adams man. Who's in bed. Listening to a podcast.

I strip out of my clothes and join him. He's wearing boxer briefs and a T-shirt, but that'll change soon if I have my way.

First, I turn his Future Think podcast all the way off. There's something I've wanted to ask him. "Do you still want to learn the tango?"

He laughs. "Are you offering me a refund on the tango refund?"

I nod. "It'd be fun. You and me. We could take dancing lessons."

He pulls me close. "I've always liked dancing with you, beautiful."

I snuggle next to him. "Good. Because I took the liberty of signing us up."

That earns me another laugh. "Well, aren't you bossy?"

Speaking of bossy...

"The whole evening kind of got me in the mood," I whisper, wriggling a little against him.

"That so?"

"Just a little."

The corner of his lips curves up. "Only a little?"

I rock my hips into his side. "Maybe more than a little."

His smile is dirty. His eyes flicker with filthy delight. "Let me get this right. While you were out with your friends, celebrating your brand-new job, enjoying mojitos and conversation, you were imagining seducing me?" He trails a hand down my neck, curving it over my shoulder.

"Yes," I answer on a tremble.

Pushing onto an elbow, he dips his face to my throat, presses a possessive kiss there. "Good. Because there's something I've wanted to do to you for a long time."

That excites me even more. "What is it?"

He pulls back then runs a hand down my chest, over one breast, traveling to my belly. "Do you have any idea how hard it was *not* to think about fucking you every time you came over before?"

Mmm. I like where this is going. "I don't have any idea," I say, innocently. "Why don't you tell me?"

He growls. "No. Why don't I show you what I was

thinking about all those times you were on my couch, in my living room, at my goddamn door?"

Oh, hello. Bossy Nick is in the house, and I am here for it.

"Show me."

50

NATURAL ART

Nick

I show her all right.

She's bent over the couch, and I'm balls deep in my woman. But I'm not pounding her. I'm taking it torturously, exquisitely slow.

I'm admiring the fuck out of all these views. The view of her long back. Her beautiful skin. Her silky hair.

"The day I moved in here," I tell her through tight teeth, "I fought off images of this."

A deep thrust from me. A shudder from her.

"Were you successful?" she asks, like she doesn't know the goddamn answer.

I lean closer, bring my face near her ear. "Not at all."

"Such a shame," she says, teasing me.

I curl my hands tighter around her hips, ease out, then play with her clit. "Then you came over and stared at the windows," I grit out, recounting that first day she walked into my home, when all I could think of was her, here, like this.

"I seem to remember a dirty look in your eyes," she says. "That must have been so hard."

I push deep into her. "Does it seem hard, sweetheart?"

She moans, then nods. "Yes. God yes." But then she recovers and teases me again. "But I feel so bad that you were struggling like that."

I grab her hair, curl it into my fist. "I wanted to bend you over my couch every single time. To show you exactly what I wanted most in New York."

She shudders. "What's that?"

"You," I whisper harshly, then ease out almost all the way.

"Nick," she whimpers.

Yes. Fucking yes. I love it when she begs for it. She gasps, then pushes back on my dick, seeking me out, hunting for me. "Nick, please," she says.

That's my woman.

Hot, hungry, and utterly horny for me. That's what I want. I stroke her clit, grip her hair, and fuck her hard. "Enjoy the view, sweetheart. Enjoy the fucking view."

I pull her head up as I rock into her with a deep, passionate rhythm till she's crying out and shuddering beneath me.

My control frays as I come hard, enjoying her, me, and the view of New York.

Just like I wanted. All of this. Every night.

* * *

A few mornings later, as I button up my shirt in the bedroom, I enjoy another view. I shamelessly watch my Layla as she applies some eye makeup in a new extra mirror in the bathroom. I installed a special one that pulls out from the wall and gives her a close-up view of her face.

Carefully, she concentrates as she draws on something, and I just enjoy the hell out of the moment.

This amazing woman in my home, doing what she loves.

When she's finished making her eyes a little silvery, I let out a low, appreciative whistle. "Damn, you look good."

"My makeup?"

"Your *you-ness*. Just you. Here," I say. "I never thought the sight of you doing makeup in my home would be one of my favorite things, but it is."

I come up behind her, press a kiss to her hair, and inhale her jasmine scent. She cranes her neck, arching against me like a cat. "I'm glad you like it."

"I sure do," I say, then I let her go so she can finish getting ready for work.

I head to the kitchen and keep myself busy. When she comes in all primped and stunning in a pink blouse with black polka dots and trim black slacks, I whistle again from the counter. "Executive Layla is in the house," I say.

She gives a little curtsy. "Why, thank you. What are you up to?" she asks, peering around me.

With a sly smile, I grab a brown paper bag from the counter and hand it to her. "In case you're too busy to go out to lunch. So, you can have it at work," I tell her.

"You made me lunch for my first day," she says with a smile that makes me feel like a king.

"I did," I say, then I take her hand and we leave together.

51

ANYTHING FOR YOU

Nick

Several Months Later

"What do you think?" David stands in my office holding out a blue velvet box, the top flipped open.

I shield my eyes from the shine of the diamond. "It's blinding me," I say. Then in all seriousness, I add, "It's gorgeous."

He closes the box, relieved. "Thanks. Layla helped me pick it out."

"Cynthia will love it." She'll be over the moon —those two are the real deal. After her recovery from the broken leg, she moved in with David in the city. She has a better boss and she's bartending at a new spot in Brooklyn. Bet it drives Rose and her parents batty that David fell for this *regular girl*, but I don't care what they think. I care that my kid is happy and thriving. "When are you asking her?"

"This weekend. We're going camping."

"Don't lose it in the woods," I warn him.

"I won't," he says, then tucks it in his pocket. "I should get back to work."

He's still at my firm, handling marketing and social media. But he's scaled back by a few hours so he can devote time to A Helping Paw. His charity's been growing both in funds and awareness. I'm so damn proud of this kid.

"Let me know when she says yes," I say.

David exits as Finn comes in. They exchange hellos, then Finn shuts the door. His expression shifts immediately to solemn and serious.

"She did it," he says as he slumps into a chair.

I don't have to ask who or what. I just move to the chair across from him and then listen as he tells me about the end of his marriage.

* * *

At a bowling alley in Brooklyn, a few weeks later, I nail all ten pins for a strike. *Sweet!*

I don't showboat—no one likes that—but I happily accept a kiss from my woman.

"You are such a bowling stud," Layla coos, then plants another kiss on my cheek.

"Are you leaving lipstick marks on me again?"

"I might be," she says coyly.

"Hmm. I might need to bend you over the bed and spank you for doing that," I whisper.

Her blue eyes sparkle. "Yes, please."

I growl, then shake off the dirty thoughts ravaging my brain. "Focus. Party. Stop distracting me like you did the day I met you."

"I can't help it," she says. When it's her turn with a bowling ball, I take a seat and enjoy watching her send the ten-pounder down the lane. She knocks down a handful of pins, then a few more, then stands aside to cheer on Cynthia as my son's fiancée takes her own turn.

We're here at Cynthia's new workplace for their engagement party. Spoiler alert: she said yes.

My dad and mom are here too, and no surprise, they love Layla. They've gotten to know her over the past several months. Layla moved in with me, so it's our home now, and it sure feels like one when we cook for friends and family. My parents sometimes, David and Cynthia at other times. Every now and then Layla's mom comes over. Anna even helps out in the kitchen, since she's started cooking again occasionally. Anna Mayweather and I aren't the best of friends, and we never will be. But she knows I make Layla happy, and she respects our relationship. That's all that matters. Also, Anna decided she's ready to start dating again. At the dinner table, Layla will go through her list of possible men and it's fucking hilarious to watch Layla try to set up her mom.

Right now though, I'm a proud dad and a happy

guy. My kid's getting married to the woman of his dreams. I'm living with the love of my life.

When Layla joins me on the yellow plastic seats, I thread my fingers through hers. Running my thumb across her skull rings, then along her ring finger, I picture another ring there someday.

Maybe someday soon.

For now, we're living our best life together.

Her friends are here tonight too. Harlow and Bridger are bowling with Ethan and a bandmate of his. Jules and Camden are on their team too.

My brother returns from grabbing a beer, parks himself by my side, and takes a drink. "You're up," I say, nodding to the lane.

But he doesn't answer. He's staring at Layla's friend Jules a lane away. She picks up a bowling ball, then laughs at something her redheaded friend says.

Jules glances toward him and dips her face to hide a smile.

What in the hell is going on?

"Yo, Uncle Finn! It's your turn," David calls out.

My brother blinks like he's clearing off a fog. "Right, thanks."

As he pops up and grabs his ball, I remember something he said months ago. *The other night, I met up with my friend Tate for dinner. His daughter was there. She's in her mid-twenties, I guess.*

Everything clicks. Jules is Jules Marley. Holy fuck. Her dad, Tate, is Finn's best friend.

Then, my brother nails a spare, and I swear he steals another glance at the woman a lane away.

* * *

In the morning, I zip up my carry-on, then head to the door. My driver waits at the curb to take me to the airport. I'm keynoting at a conference in San Francisco, and I expect Layla to give me a playfully stern send-off. Maybe something like *Imagine me in the audience uncrossing my legs*.

But when she emerges from the bedroom, her brow is knit.

Her lips are parted.

Her breath is coming fast in worry.

Something's wrong.

I drop the bag and cross to her. "What is it, sweetheart?"

Shakily, she shows me her phone. I read the text from Mia.

> Hey, hun! Can we chat this morning? There are some things I need to talk to you about.

That's ominous, but I stay upbeat for Layla. "It'll be fine. Whatever it is, we'll sort it out," I reassure her.

"Will we? What if I lose my job? I love this job."

"I know you do," I say, "and you've been great at it."

Facts are facts—the Mia Jane brand has grown tremendously since Layla joined. They've opened more stores, including one on the same block as Gin Joint, Layla's favorite hangout spot with her friends. Mia's also expanded her lines and become a bit of an online sensation with young people. The numbers are hot. The brand is vibing.

"But this doesn't sound good, Nick," she says, worry thick in her voice. "What if she's firing me?"

"She'd be a fool to fire you. I mean that completely."

She fidgets with her rings. "What if she's shutting down the company?"

"You'll find another job. You're in demand. You're Lola Jones. Do not ever let anyone forget that."

She exhales and nods. "I'm Lola Jones."

"Call me as soon as you know."

When I land in San Francisco, my phone rings. I answer as I'm walking along the jetway, and Layla wastes no time. "Mia's relocating the company to Los Angeles. She wants to be with her family, and they're in Santa Monica. She wants all the corporate staff to go and work with her in LA. Including me."

Layla doesn't have to say another word for me to know—she doesn't want to go.

But I make the offer anyway. "If you want to take it, I'll move with you."

She's quiet for several long seconds. "Nick," she says softly. "You'd do that?"

No questions asked. "I'd do anything for you."

52

MY HOME

Layla

I want to say yes to Nick's offer. But I can't. I just can't.

Two nights later, I'm wandering around our home, overlooking the New York skyline, talking to my guy. "I want to stay here," I tell him on the phone.

"Yeah?"

I gaze out the windows to the city that beckons me. This city is home to my greatest heartbreak, but also my greatest love.

It's the home of *all* my loves. "Everyone I love is here," I say, sad but resigned.

"Are you sure?"

"Positive. I'll find another job. These things happen, and I'll manage."

"I know you will," he says, warm and confident. "I'll be home soon."

Home. Yes, this is home. New York, here with him,

and Harlow and Ethan, and my mom, and David, and all my new friends too. Jules, Camden, and Storm.

But it's also *his* home. Nick's parents are here, and David and Cynthia. Nick loves working with his son every day. It'd be selfish of me to take the job in Los Angeles, and to take Nick away from his family.

"I can't wait to see you." I settle onto the couch and ask him about today's keynote. "Did you talk about opportunities?"

"I did. Because I know how to spot them."

He sure does.

* * *

"And that's how you *don't* overdraw your lips with a pencil," I say to the camera, winding up my *don'ts* video.

I'm in the studio at the Mia Jane offices a few days after formally resigning. I'm still unsure what's next or where to look for a new job.

But I have a job to finish before I say goodbye to the company I've come to love. Right now, I'm putting the final touches on my last few videos for The Makeover.

When I complete the shoot and leave the studio, Storm's waiting for me in the hallway of our offices. He wears a sad smile that matches mine. He isn't going to leave New York either. His partner lives here, directing Broadway shows.

"How's it going, girl?" he asks, and his heavy voice tells me everything about how he's managing.

"I'm...okay," I say, as cheery as I can be.

"Want to grab a drink and drown our work sorrows?"

Well, maybe I'm not *that* cheery. But I will be soon. "So much," I tell him.

I snag my purse from the office and we head out into the early evening of Manhattan, making our way toward Gin Joint. "Have you started looking for a new job around here?"

"Yes. And it irritated the hell out of me. I nearly tossed my sparkly eyeshadow at the wall," he says.

I squeeze his arm. "Don't hurt makeup. It's never makeup's fault."

He sighs. "True words. But at least there are martinis."

"And do not ever harm a martini either," I tell him.

"Never will I ever."

When we reach the block with Gin Joint, we make pouty faces at the Mia Jane store, closed for the night. "We'll miss you, MJ," I say, then pretend to paw at the glass in exaggerated longing.

"I love you so much I hate you," Storm says to the window, frowning.

Then we vow to let go of our sadness as we head into the speakeasy. At the bar over drinks, we trade ideas for each other about job hunting.

He lifts his martini and clinks it against my wine. "To new horizons."

"May we find them together. And may they be as fabulous as the ones we leave behind."

We down our drinks and stay a little longer, and when Storm leaves to see his guy, my friends join me.

With them, I brainstorm career plans too.

"You're going to do great," Harlow says, squeezing my shoulder.

I nod, resolute. "Thanks. I think so too. I'm sad about the Mia Jane job, but I'm strong enough to not let it get me down."

"There will be other chances," Ethan seconds.

"Life is all about seizing opportunities," I say. Then, I catch sight of the man walking through the door of Gin Joint.

My man.

Nick's not supposed to be home till tomorrow.

But he's here early, and I'm elated. I jump up as he reaches me, all intense and business-sexy in his crisp shirt and tie, even after a flight.

Actually, he doesn't look at all like he just stepped off a plane. That's odd.

"Hi, Harlow. Hi, Ethan. Can I steal Layla for a minute?"

"Sure," Harlow says, lips quirked in curiosity.

"She's yours," Ethan adds.

I'm damn curious what's gotten into Nick. He clasps my hand, whisks me outside and walks me to the Mia Jane store. There, he moves behind me and curls his hands around my shoulders.

"It's yours, Layla."

The hair on the back of my neck stands on end. "What did you say?" I whisper.

He presses a kiss on my cheek then spins me around. "I bought it for you."

He says it so easily, so casually.

But I'm floored. I can't speak for ages. When I finally form words, I say, "You bought the store for me?"

That doesn't quite make sense.

He shakes his head. "No. The company. Mia was happy to sell it. She wants to spend time with family in Los Angeles. And, as you said, you want to spend time with friends and family here. In New York. So I bought it for you."

I grab his shirt. "Are you serious?" I'm shaking inside with excitement.

He just grins. "Yes. I didn't tell you sooner, but I flew back this morning to finalize the offer."

I knew he didn't look like he traveled all day. "You've been here? In meetings all day?"

"I want you to have everything you want. This is your dream job. Stay in New York and run *your* company from here with Storm."

I throw my arms around his neck, and I kiss him fiercely and passionately.

When I let go, I whisper, "I can't believe you did this."

"Really? You really can't believe it?" he asks wryly.

Good point. This is so very him. "Actually, I can," I say, then I kiss him again on the streets of New York, the home of my great love and me.

EPILOGUE
A SULTRY SUMMER SKY

Layla

Many Months Later

I slide my skull rings on my fingers, then slick on some ruby red lipstick in the hotel room mirror in Miami.

There. I'm ready for today.

I press my lips together and blow a kiss to my reflection as my favorite person in the world comes up behind me, wrapping his strong arms around my waist.

"Beautiful," Nick says, meeting my gaze in the mirror as he brushes soft kisses to my hair.

He's always loved kissing my hair. I've always loved when he does it. He moves closer to my cheekbone, turning me on but also risking the time I've spent making my face look just so for today's big event.

"Don't mess up my lipstick though," I warn playfully.

"Who? Me?" There's a naughty rumble in his voice as he lays a kiss on my jawline.

"Yes, you. You're obsessed with wiping it off my lips."

He raises his face as he lifts a hand to swipe my hair off my neck, then brushes a tender, lingering kiss on my neck that makes my skin tingle.

"I like the way your lips taste," he says. "And I love the way your lipstick looks when you wrap those red lips around my cock."

I roll my eyes as I swat his forearm. "I do not have time to get on my knees right now."

He pouts. But he's relentless, tugging me closer, so I can feel his hard-on against my ass. "Later then. Or maybe I'll get on my knees and take care of you," he suggests, tempting me.

Absolutely tempting me.

But there's hardly time.

"We really need to go," I say, a little sad.

On a groan, he lets go of me. Then, like it's a superhuman feat, he pulls away completely and nods resolutely. It's like he's re-sorting all his thoughts to clean, business-like ones. "Let's do this. I can't wait to see the store," he says.

"Me either," I say, absolutely giddy about today.

* * *

Forget giddy.

I'm effervescent when I turn onto the block of the brand new makeup store in this trendy section of South Beach. It's as if bubbles are flowing through my bloodstream as I gaze at the sign at the end of the block.

Mia and Lola.

I kept Mia's name—well some of it—and combined it with mine. Now the stores and the brand are Mia and Lola. This shop I'm opening today in Miami will be my eighth location. I'm still kind of amazed every day that I have that many stores to run.

Well, I don't do it all by myself. Storm is my guy, and I depend on him as my chief operating officer to make all of this magic happen. He's overseen every aspect of this launch.

But all of this still sometimes feels like a dream.

"Is this real?" I ask Nick, quietly, a little reverently. I'm still in awe of what the man by my side did to make everything happen.

"So real, Layla," he says with obvious pride in his tone as we stare at the vibrant peach storefront at the end of the block, the store's name in a sapphire blue.

But what's truly amazing is the line snaking around the block—customers waiting for the doors to open in a little over twenty minutes. I'll let them in, then help them pick makeup to their heart's content.

"You did all this," he adds.

"You helped a little bit," I point out with a smile.

But Nick deflects my compliment with a shake of his head. "All the credit goes to you, my brilliant woman."

In a short time, Mia and Lola has become one of the most popular makeup brands.

Today for the opening, I'll do a how-to session, as I often do in my shops around the country. The one I have planned for today is fitting for Miami—how to do beach makeup.

Nick gives me another kiss on the cheek, then whispers, "Go get 'em."

I head over, waving and saying hello to the customers that are lined up. Then I go inside. I'm in my element and loving it.

* * *

Nick

That evening, she's glowing as we walk along the beach into the fading sun.

"And I met so many amazing people today," Layla says, practically bouncing as she talks.

No surprise there. My Layla has always been energized by business.

It's been such a thrill to watch her build and grow her brand. She's been telling me all about the session that spilled from the afternoon into the early evening since the lines were that long. I couldn't stay the whole time. I stepped out to meet with one of my portfolio companies here in Miami, then returned to meet her at the end of the day. That's how we usually are, heading off to our respective ventures by day, and coming back together at night.

"Tell me more about them," I say with my hand in hers and the sand under our feet.

But her smile disappears, a serious look in her bright blue eyes. "There was one woman here this afternoon who had a long, jagged scar on her arm," she says. "She'd been hurt by an ex."

I growl.

"He's in prison now," she says, reassuring.

"Good," I say.

"And she told me," she says, stopping for a beat as her voice chokes up, "how she learned to use makeup to conceal it. She watched one of my videos on how to artfully conceal scars. She said it changed her life."

My heart swells. "I'm so proud of you that you did that series."

She nods solemnly. "Me too. It's been one of the best things I've ever done at Mia and Lola."

I admire how she's used her past pain to help others. She's turned her trauma around with these videos and used her hurt for good. She says it helps heal her all over again.

So do some of her partnerships too.

Like the one she established a year ago when she partnered up with the tattoo artist who designed her daisy tattoo. They have a deal now where Layla funds tattoos for any woman who's been through trauma and wants art to cover up a scar or a wound. Layla covers all the costs for the tattoo. It's been a beautiful project to witness. I could not be prouder of my woman.

And I could not be more ready to take all the next steps with her. After we talk a little more about the day, we head toward the softly lapping waves as the sun dips toward the horizon. I draw a deep inhale of the ocean air, feeling more certain than I ever have about anything, more ready. And so I let her take a step or two ahead of me, our hands slipping apart.

That catches her attention and she turns around, quirking up a brow in question. But I'm faster. I'm down on one knee. "I have an idea for your next how-to video," I say, emotions welling up in my chest.

Her eyes widen. "You do?"

I reach into my pocket. "What if you do a video on… how to do wedding makeup?" I suggest, as I hold out a velvet box. "Because I would love nothing more in the entire world than to marry you. You are and always have been the absolute love of my life, and I would love if you'd do me the great honor of letting me be your husband."

She drops down to her knees, cups my cheek, and kisses me, her tears sealing the yes that comes from her lips.

"That sounds like a great idea," she says.

"The video?" I ask playfully.

She shakes her head. "Marrying you."

She holds out her hand, and I slide on a gorgeous sapphire stone set in platinum, perfect for my woman in blue.

"I love it. It matches my ink," she says quietly.

"And it's beautiful and as resilient as you," I say.

She offers me her mouth again. "You were so good resisting my lipstick all day. Kiss me all night, Nick."

"I will."

And for all the nights to come.

I kiss her in the city where we met once upon a time under a sultry summer sky.

Do you want more from these characters right now? Be sure to turn the pages for an extended epilogue about Nick's and Layla's life together! Want something to keep you captivated while you wait for Jules's and Finn's story next in The Tease to come to KU next? You'll love My So-Called Sex Life. It's a crossover, set in the same world in New York and it's also **FREE in KU**!

And you can grab Harlow's romance in The RSVP for FREE IN KU right now!

EXCERPT - MY SO-CALLED SEX LIFE

Hazel

Obviously, I believe in love.

If I didn't, I'd be the worst kind of romance writer—the kind who lies to her readers.

But there's something I believe in more fervently than love, and that's the meet-cute. You can't get to the happy ending without the unputdownable beginning.

The start of the story is my writing church, and I worship at the altar of those delicious moments when the hero and heroine meet for the first time.

Or meet again.

Tonight, I'll be researching a new here's-how-they-met possibility as I head to dinner in New York.

I'm one block away from the restaurant. My short, black ankle boots click against the sidewalk on Twenty-Fourth Street as I gaze up at the numbers on the buildings. I pass a tattoo parlor where a goth gal inks a burly man's arm, and then I acquire the target.

Menu.

"It's as trendy as it is annoying," my friend TJ said of the joint when he told me about it last week. "And I promise it'll inspire your next chapter one."

I was sold. I made a reservation right away.

Now, I'm here at the minimalist-style restaurant. Under the sign for Menu are the words *Meet, Eat, Mingle.*

Change your life.

Ambitious, but the way I see it, this place is going to be full of fodder. I can't wait. I draw a deep inhale of the May night air, then square my shoulders. "Cover me, I'm going in," I say to, well, no one.

Sometimes I talk to myself. It's a thing. Whatever.

I head inside, marching to the hostess stand. A woman wearing a black tunic and sporting a blonde undercut shoots me a bored look. Yeah, that's on point for a place called Menu.

"Hello. I have a reservation. Valentine. Party of one," I say.

"It's all parties of one," she says, monotone.

"Old habit," I say with a friendly shrug. "In any case, it's for seven-thirty."

With an aggrieved sigh, she scans the tablet screen, then meets my eyes. "The other party isn't here yet. If he or she is five minutes late, we'll have to ask you to leave."

Okaaaay.

It's a new world order. Restaurants have rigid rules.

But I knew what I'd signed up for. "Works for me," I say. You catch more flies with honey and all.

"Fine," she says, then she nods toward the dining room behind her. It's small and bare, in keeping with the theme, aka *we're cool, you're not*. The tables are black wood, the walls are steel gray, the tiles are white. Everything is ordinary, except the experience.

This restaurant is très chic because it seats strangers together.

As I follow her, I smile, giddy at the thought of an inspired meet-cute. Two sexy strangers happen to be seated together at a hipster restaurant just like this. They hit it off. Get it on that night. Then, oops! The next day he turns out to be her brand-new boss, perhaps?

But who is he? A mafia king? A sexy CEO?

The muses will let me know who the next hero is. Maybe he'll even reveal himself tonight.

Undercut brings me to a table at the back. She waves a limp hand in the direction of the framed QR code on the black wood surface. "We use QR codes. You scan them with your phone. Have you ever used one before?"

I'm thirty-one, missy. I can work a phone, a power drill, and a twenty-speed vibrator. Not all at once though. "I'm familiar with the concept of QR codes. Also, phones," I say.

"Cool," she says blandly, then walks away, her tunic swishing against her leggings.

Once I sit, I rub my palms on my jeans, a tiny bit

nervous. What if I'm seated with an over-sharer? An endless talker? A dullsville candidate?

But I'm excited too.

What if my companion is an enigmatic billionaire like in a romance novel? A broody rock musician? A hot tech nerd who's looking for a matchmaker?

Gah. The meet-cute possibilities are endless, and when I write this as the opening of my next book, it's going to be epic.

I just know it.

I'm making some notes on my phone about the vibe when a man's voice interrupts my thoughts.

"Four minutes and forty-five seconds." His tone is a little gravelly and a lot know-it-all-y.

Say it isn't so.

I was already dreading sharing a stage with Axel Huxley at the reader expo I'm doing this weekend. I can't believe fate would inflict him on me any sooner than necessary.

I turn my gaze toward the front of Menu, praying that's not my archnemesis. Maybe he has a vocal twin. Maybe that's a thing now.

But my prayers are unanswered. Standing tall at the hostess stand is the smart-mouthed, glasses-wearing, smirky-faced romantic-thriller writer.

Wearing black because of course he wears black.

And *of course* he's arguing with the hostess. He never met a statement he couldn't debate and dissect into a million julienned pieces, then pepper with disagreement.

He blah blah blahs a little more, finishing with, "So, you have to seat me. It's the policy of the restaurant."

I snort. *Get over yourself, Huxley. I hope they kick you out.*

I feel sorry for whichever sucker is getting seated with King Dick tonight.

Inspired, I make another note, chuckling fiendishly as I imagine my heroine running into her enemy before the clever, charming, hottie hero enters the scene. Then I check the menu options while waiting for my brilliant professor, my inscrutable tycoon, my good guy with a heart of gold in need of a makeover.

Until the sound of footsteps grows louder and closer. I look up.

At a face I want to punch.

Axel

A long time ago, in a decade far, far away, I'd been terrified to walk to the front of my eleventh grade English class and present a speech on the dangers of wealth in *The Great Gatsby*.

Speaking in front of a few dozen high schoolers who mostly didn't give a shit was horrifying.

My stepfather told me to picture everyone in the class naked. My brain did some extra credit. I didn't just undress everyone as I opined on Fitzgerald's depictions of the moneyed class. I imagined everyone in my class fucking.

A writer's habit was born.

Ever since then, I've mentally written character bios for almost everyone I've met, detailing traits all the way down to their bedroom preferences. Assigning habits—like if they talk during *The Godfather,* how many cardboard wrappers they could possibly need on a cup of coffee, and whether they like it doggie style or being tied up and taken—has become the way I keep everything in perspective.

The hostess? She only drinks soy chai lattes, and she brings her own cup to the artisan fair-trade coffee shop. She doesn't have a favorite position because sex is boring in the same way everything is boring to her.

Poor gal.

The bartender over there with the goatee? The ring says he's married but the way he stares at the hostess says he jerks it to her when the wife's asleep. That is, after he reads lit fic in hardback.

Then there's the redhead I'd recognize from several football fields away. Too bad I don't have the luxury of yards and yards. Instead, she's seated mere feet from me at the last table at the edge of the dining room. The woman with the long, lush hair, the dangerous green eyes, the pouty lips, and the sharpest mouth I've ever met.

Fuck her bio. I refuse to write one for Hazel Valentine.

Ever.

She'd better not be the other party at my dinner. I came here to research how to hire a hitman for my next book, not to share a meal with a woman who hates me.

But as the hostess walks me to the last table, the inevitable becomes my Friday night, and my brain concocts a bio in spite of my better judgment.

Hazel Valentine:

Emotional wounds—we're going to need a bigger boat for hers since someone clearly has daddy and boyfriend issues.

Coffee—ideally via an IV drip. At all times of the day.

Sex preferences—nope. Stop. Just stop. Don't go there.

As I near, Hazel looks up from her phone. For a moment she seems flustered but then she schools her expression. There's simply flint in her gaze.

The hostess waves to the table without speaking. I thank her and pull out a chair as she walks away, dismissing us already.

Hazel stares at me unflinchingly, as if challenging me to leave.

Won't happen, sweetheart.

I park myself, sliding into the chair across from the redhead, then smile without showing any teeth. I fold my hands and meet Hazel's steely gaze. "Let me guess. You're here to test oh-so-cute opening chapters for your next book," I say.

She tilts her head, smiling slyly. "And you must be researching how your next bad guy will off someone, hoping it will make your latest book more...scintillating."

Well, maybe she will give me some inspiration on how to hire a hitman after all.

Keep reading: My So-Called Sex Life!

And stay tuned for more romances featuring Jules, Camden, and Ethan! I'll share all the details on these books in my newsletter and my Facebook group!

BE A LOVELY

Want to be the first to know of sales, new releases, special deals and giveaways? Sign up for my newsletter today!

Want to be part of a fun, feel-good place to talk about books and romance, and get sneak peeks of covers and advance copies of my books? Be a Lovely!

MORE BOOKS BY LAUREN

I've written more than 100 books! **All of these titles below are FREE in Kindle Unlimited**!

The Virgin Society Series

Meet the Virgin Society – five great friends who'd do anything for each other. Indulge in five forbidden, emotionally-charged, and wildly sexy age-gap romances!

The RSVP

The Tryst

The Tease

The Chase

Front Man

The Dating Games Series

A fun, sexy romantic comedy series about friends in the city and their dating mishaps!

The Virgin Next Door

Two A Day

The Good Guy Challenge

How To Date Series (New and ongoing)

Four great friends. Four chances to learn how to date

again. Four standalone romantic comedies full of love, sex and meet-cute shenanigans.

My So-Called Sex Life

Plays Well With Others

The Anti-Romantic

Blown Away

Boyfriend Material

Four fabulous heroines. Four outrageous proposals. Four chances at love in this sexy rom-com series!

Asking For a Friend

Sex and Other Shiny Objects

One Night Stand-In

Overnight Service

Big Rock Series

My #1 New York Times Bestselling sexy as sin, irreverent, male-POV romantic comedy!

Big Rock

Mister O

Well Hung

Full Package

Joy Ride

Hard Wood

Happy Endings Series

Romance starts with a bang in this series of standalones

following a group of friends seeking and avoiding love!

Come Again

Shut Up and Kiss Me

Kismet

My Single-Versary

Ballers And Babes

Sexy sports romance standalones guaranteed to make you hot!

Most Valuable Playboy

Most Likely to Score

A Wild Card Kiss

Rules of Love Series

Athlete, virgins and weddings!

The Virgin Rule Book

The Virgin Game Plan

The Virgin Replay

The Virgin Scorecard

The Extravagant Series

Bodyguards, billionaires and hoteliers in this sexy, high-stakes series of standalones!

One Night Only

One Exquisite Touch

My One-Week Husband

The Guys Who Got Away Series

Friends in New York City and California fall in love in this fun and hot rom-com series!

Birthday Suit

Dear Sexy Ex-Boyfriend

The What If Guy

Thanks for Last Night

The Dream Guy Next Door

Sinful Men

A high-stakes, high-octane, sexy-as-sin romantic suspense series!

My Sinful Nights

My Sinful Desire

My Sinful Longing

My Sinful Love

My Sinful Temptation

From Paris With Love

Swoony, sweeping romances set in Paris!

Wanderlust

Part-Time Lover

One Love Series

A group of friends in New York falls in love one by one in this sexy rom-com series!

The Sexy One

The Hot One

The Knocked Up Plan

Come As You Are

Lucky In Love Series

A small town romance full of heat and blue collar heroes and sexy heroines!

Best Laid Plans

The Feel Good Factor

Nobody Does It Better

Unzipped

No Regrets

An angsty, sexy, emotional, new adult trilogy about one young couple fighting to break free of their pasts!

The Start of Us

The Thrill of It

Every Second With You

Unbreak My Heart

An standalone second chance emotional roller coaster of a romance

Joy Delivered Duet

A high-heat, wickedly sexy series of standalones that will set your sheets on fire!

Nights With Him

Forbidden Nights

I also write MM romance under the name L. Blakely!

Hopelessly Bromantic Duet (MM)

Roomies to lovers to enemies to fake boyfriends

Hopelessly Bromantic

Here Comes My Man

Men of Summer Series (MM)

Two baseball players on the same team fall in love in a forbidden romance spanning five epic years

Scoring With Him

Winning With Him

All In With Him

MM Standalone Novels

A Guy Walks Into My Bar

The Bromance Zone

One Time Only

The Best Men (Co-written with Sarina Bowen)

Winner Takes All Series (MM)

A series of emotionally-charged and irresistibly sexy standalone MM sports romances!

The Boyfriend Comeback

Turn Me On

A Very Filthy Game

Limited Edition Husband

Manhandled

You might also enjoy the following romances! Available on all retailers!

The Gift Series

An after dark series of standalones! Explore your fantasies!

The Engagement Gift

The Virgin Gift

The Decadent Gift

The Heartbreakers Series

Three brothers. Three rockers. Three standalone sexy romantic comedies.

Once Upon a Real Good Time

Once Upon a Sure Thing

Once Upon a Wild Fling

Always Satisfied Series

A group of friends in New York City find love and laughter in this series of sexy standalones!

Satisfaction Guaranteed

Instant Gratification

Never Have I Ever

PS It's Always Been You

Special Delivery

Good Love Series of sexy rom-coms co-written with Lili Valente!

The Caught Up in Love Series

A group of friends finds love!

The Pretending Plot

The Dating Proposal

The Second Chance Plan

The Private Rehearsal

Seductive Nights Series

A high heat series full of danger and spice!

Night After Night

After This Night

One More Night

A Wildly Seductive Night

If you want a personalized recommendation, email me at laurenblakelybooks@gmail.com!

AFTERWORD

The lyrics for It Had To Be You are in the public domain. Special thanks to Sawyer Bennett and Melissa Buyikian for legal insight.

CONTACT

I love hearing from readers! You can find me on Twitter at LaurenBlakely3, Instagram at LaurenBlakelyBooks, Facebook at LaurenBlakelyBooks, or online at LaurenBlakely.com. You can also email me at laurenblakelybooks@gmail.com

The Hot One

The Knocked Up Plan

Come As You Are

Lucky In Love Series

A small town romance full of heat and blue collar heroes and sexy heroines!

Best Laid Plans

The Feel Good Factor

Nobody Does It Better

Unzipped

No Regrets

An angsty, sexy, emotional, new adult trilogy about one young couple fighting to break free of their pasts!

The Start of Us

The Thrill of It

Every Second With You

Unbreak My Heart

An standalone second chance emotional roller coaster of a romance

Joy Delivered Duet

A high-heat, wickedly sexy series of standalones that will set your sheets on fire!

Nights With Him

Forbidden Nights

I also write MM romance under the name L. Blakely!

Hopelessly Bromantic Duet (MM)

Roomies to lovers to enemies to fake boyfriends

Hopelessly Bromantic

Here Comes My Man

Men of Summer Series (MM)

Two baseball players on the same team fall in love in a forbidden romance spanning five epic years

Scoring With Him

Winning With Him

All In With Him

MM Standalone Novels

A Guy Walks Into My Bar

The Bromance Zone

One Time Only

The Best Men (Co-written with Sarina Bowen)

Winner Takes All Series (MM)

A series of emotionally-charged and irresistibly sexy standalone MM sports romances!

The Boyfriend Comeback

Turn Me On

A Very Filthy Game

Limited Edition Husband

Manhandled

You might also enjoy the following romances! Available on all retailers!

The Gift Series

An after dark series of standalones! Explore your fantasies!

The Engagement Gift

The Virgin Gift

The Decadent Gift

The Heartbreakers Series

Three brothers. Three rockers. Three standalone sexy romantic comedies.

Once Upon a Real Good Time

Once Upon a Sure Thing

Once Upon a Wild Fling

Always Satisfied Series

A group of friends in New York City find love and laughter in this series of sexy standalones!

Satisfaction Guaranteed

Instant Gratification

Never Have I Ever

PS It's Always Been You

Special Delivery

Good Love Series of sexy rom-coms co-written with Lili Valente!

The Caught Up in Love Series

A group of friends finds love!

The Pretending Plot

The Dating Proposal

The Second Chance Plan

The Private Rehearsal

Seductive Nights Series

A high heat series full of danger and spice!

Night After Night

After This Night

One More Night

A Wildly Seductive Night

If you want a personalized recommendation, email me at laurenblakelybooks@gmail.com!